19X 3/00 √6/00

LJ

D1095254

Twenty-One Tales

Rudyard Kipling

TWENTY-ONE TALES

Selected and
with an introduction by
Tim Wilkinson
Drawings by Ian Ribbons

THE FOLIO SOCIETY

London 1972

*The text of this edition is used
by kind permission of Macmillan & Co Ltd*

Sixth impression 1985

PRINTED IN GREAT BRITAIN
*Printed and bound by The Bath Press, Bath
Set in Scotch Roman type 10 point leaded 1 point*

Contents

Illustrations

Introduction

THIS SELECTION of Kipling's stories is a personal one. I found myself with a preliminary list of some sixty stories which I thought together represented Kipling's best work. Somehow I had to reduce the number to fit a single volume. My first idea was to keep as many different subjects as possible to show the range of his work and while sorting the stories to do this I noticed that many of them seemed to reflect the circumstances of his own life. So I have kept to this idea of illuminating Kipling's life by the stories I have chosen while at the same time including only those I consider of the best.

Rudyard Kipling was born in India in December 1865. His father, Lockwood Kipling, was Professor of Architectural Sculpture, in Bombay, and his mother, Alice Macdonald, one of four lively and intelligent sisters the other three of whom married respectively Sir Edward Burne-Jones the pre-Raphaelite painter, Sir Edward Poynter, P.R.A. and Alfred Baldwin, M.P., father of Stanley Baldwin later to be Prime Minister. Lockwood Kipling was very much the poor relation who went to India to make his own way. At the age of six Rudyard was taken with his younger sister Trix to lodge with strangers at Southsea for seven long years. The story *Baa-Baa Black Sheep* is almost straight autobiography of this terrible time in his life. At the age of 13 he was discovered to have defective eyesight so that he arrived at his public school, United Services College, Westward Ho!, with the rare distinction for a boy of wearing glasses, hence his nickname 'Gig-lamps' or 'Gigger.' It meant that he found organized games difficult and he was presumably restricted in much of the boys' rough-and-tumble. In stature he was small though stocky and physically precocious being the first of the famous Stalky trio to start shaving. He left school at seventeen to take up a post as assistant editor—the only other Englishman on the staff—of the *Civil and Military Gazette*, a local newspaper at Lahore, where his father had become Principal of the Mayo School of Art and Curator of the Lahore Museum. Kipling describes this period and the two years he spent working for the sister paper *The Pioneer* at Allahabad as 'seven years hard.' As indeed they must have been as far as his work was concerned, but in another way they were probably among the happiest of his life. At home he had 'the family square' of his father, his mother and his sister, and the substantial luxury of unlimited servants, while at work he was not only storing up material for future stories but was perfecting his own craft, his highly individual brand of intense craftsmanship. So much so that on the strength of money received from the sale of those early stories he decided to quit *The Pioneer* and seek literary work—and fame—in London.

In 1889 at the age of 24 he arrived in London, more or less penniless, but with high hopes. Thanks to Andrew Lang who had read and admired his early work he was introduced into the literary circle centred upon the Savile Club and soon his work was so much in demand that he quickly learnt not to over-extend himself. This kind of quick learning or intuitive sophistication seems to have been a prominent characteristic of his. Not surprisingly his work was hailed as vigorous, vulgar, shocking, knowing, and generally heady stuff. Much of this time is thinly disguised as fiction in his novel *The Light that Failed*. He was charmed by Wolcott Balestier, an American literary entrepreneur, even to the extent of collaborating with him in a book *The Naulahka* which they literally wrote jointly. In 1891 Kipling set off on a world cruise—he could by now easily support himself by writing travel pieces and his books were bringing in a steady income. He was in Lahore, his last visit ever to India, when news of Balestier's death in Germany reached him. He returned immediately to London, a remarkable journey of only eight days, to find Wolcott's sister Caroline in charge of her mother and younger sister. Rudyard and Caroline were almost immediately married—very quietly they hoped; they were horrified to see outside the church afterwards newspaper placards announcing the fact. They set off westward round the world but turned back in Japan after a bank failure and settled, very modestly, on the land of Caroline's brother Beatty in Brattleboro', Vermont. Soon Kipling's wealth began to grow and he decided to build what was for the locality a grand house.

Unfortunately a quarrel occurred between Kipling and his brother-in-law; Beatty threatening violence and Kipling very foolishly having Beatty arrested. Largely because of the publicity the Kiplings virtually had to fly the country with their daughters Josephine born 1892 and Elsie born 1896. By this time Kipling had published the two *Jungle Books* in addition to five collections of stories, three novels and books of verse. His reputation and his wealth were by now well established. They settled first at Torquay, his story of *The House Surgeon* is based upon the house they took there, and then at Rottingdean with his Poynter, Baldwin and Burne-Jones cousins. During this time they spent each winter in South Africa where they became friends of Cecil Rhodes who gave them a life interest in a house 'The Woolsack.' The well-known verses 'If' are based upon the character of Dr Jameson, famous for his 'Raid.' Rudyard's son John was born in 1897 at Rottingdean, and in this Diamond Jubilee year his famous hymn 'Recessional' was published. By now Kipling had become the unofficial but wildly popular poet laureate.

In 1899 during a winter visit to New York, Kipling and his daughter Josephine became seriously ill of pneumonia; Kipling's condition was daily front page news and while he eventually recovered Josephine did not. This loss of their first-born was a crushing blow to Kipling and his wife.

Between 1900 and 1908 the family wintered each year in Cape Town at 'The Woolsack.' During the Boer War, Kipling was active in raising money for the comforts for the troops and in running a paper for the English general Lord Roberts, 'Bobs,' whom Kipling had known in India. In 1902 he bought a house 'Batemans' at Burwash and this was to be his home until his death. Much of the background of his imaginary histories *Puck of Pook's Hill* and *Rewards and Fairies* grew out of discoveries upon his land there. He continued, however, to winter abroad, from 1909 to 1913 in St Moritz, and after the war at various other places, mainly in France.

Throughout his life Kipling refused official honours preferring to remain a private citizen with the freedom of expression which that implies, but in 1907 began a series of honorary doctorates, Cambridge, Montreal, Durham, Oxford, and in 1908 that great distinction The Nobel Prize for Literature. In 1910 and 1911 his mother and father to whom he was much attached died.

Upon the outbreak of the First World War Kipling's son John joined the Irish Guards. He was posted missing, presumed dead after the battle of Loos in 1915; he was just 18 and his body was never found. In 1917 Kipling was appointed an Imperial War Graves Commissioner and a Rhodes Trustee, he also began writing the monumental history *The Irish Guards in the Great War*. After the war he found himself left alone in his imperialist views; he even resigned on principle from his Rhodes trusteeship because of the internationalist rather than imperialist direction the Trust was taking. He became increasingly a private citizen though he did issue the last of his famous warning poems 'The Storm Cone' in

1932 foreseeing the then unthinkable second world war. In the same
year he began the Sussex Edition of his works, the text of which is
used for this selection, which was not published until after his death.
He died in 1936 at the age of 70: practically all those at the funeral
were men of affairs and almost no great literary figures. His wife
died in 1939 at the age of 77.

There is little illuminating criticism of Kipling's work. Perhaps we
are still too near the stories which have remained remarkably
modern in spite of the fact that many of the best of them are now
over sixty years old. An amusing example of the difficulties which
critics almost seem to make for themselves is to be found in T. S.
Eliot's introduction to his own selection *A Choice of Kipling's
Verse* (1941). Eliot admits all the faults of the verse, admits that
Kipling was not really a poet, and invents a special category for
Kipling to be pre-eminent in! This is an unkind summary of
Eliot's essay which I personally find so obscure it is almost meaning-
less. The two most interesting collections of essays which both
contain approving and disapproving views are *Kipling and the
Critics* (1965) edited by Elliot L. Gilbert and *Kipling's Mind and
Art* (1964) edited by Andrew Rutherford. Curiously the recent
Kipling: The Critical Heritage (1971) edited by Roger Lancelyn
Green, one of a series which is restricted to pieces published during
a writer's lifetime, is somewhat disappointing. The most interesting
full scale studies, both by avowed disciples, are J. M. S. Tompkins:
The Art of Rudyard Kipling (1959) and Bonamy Dobrée: *Rudyard
Kipling* (1967). Perhaps the most balanced longer essay is to be
found in J. I. M. Stewart: *Eight Modern Writers* (1963); a simpler
version of this is the same writer's *Rudyard Kipling* (1966).

C. S. Lewis is perhaps the most perceptive of Kipling's critics. He
admits he loves the stories but that he becomes quickly sated with
them and repelled. He points out that they were never written to be
read together: they started life as diamonds among the mud of
local newspaper reporting and as such they were highly wrought
and densely concentrated. Hence the quickly constipating effect
when taken in excess. But Kipling gave glory to common things
and he was the first poet of work (H. G. Wells says this too: as a
young man while socialists were preaching the dignity of labour
Kipling was busily demonstrating it!). Lewis goes on to show that
though Kipling always stresses the basic brutality of learning and
of submitting to the discipline of work he nevertheless avoids questioning the reasons for the discipline, the ends for which the means

are fashioned—and that in the end this makes the reader uncom-
fortable. Finally he shows Kipling's recognition of the secret
society of fellow professionals, what Lewis calls the Inner Ring, and
the power of this group to get things done, and this leads on to
generous tolerance, for it is the group that matters and not what it
is formed for. It is worth quoting Lewis's conclusion in full.

'But he was a very great writer. This trade-passion, this business
of the Inner Ring, fills an immense area of human life. There, though
not in the conventional novel, it frequently proves itself stronger
than family affection, national loyalty, religion, and even vice.
Hence Kipling's deserved success with thousands of readers who
left the older fiction to be read by women and boys. He came home
to their bosoms by coming home to their business and showed them
life as they had found it to be. This is merit of a high order; it is
like the discovery of a new element or a new planet, it is, in its way
and as far as it goes, a "return to nature". The remedy for what is
partial and dangerous in his view of life is to go on from Kipling and
to add the necessary correctives—not to deny what he has shown.
After Kipling there is no excuse for the assumption that all the important things in a man's life happen between the end of one day's
work and the beginning of the next. There is no good putting on
airs about Kipling. The things he mistook for gods may have been
only "spirits of another sort" but they are real things and strong.'*

Those readers who know Kipling's work well will almost certainly
quarrel with my selection—not only for the inclusions but, I
expect, mostly for those favourites I have omitted. Kipling has
always had the power to raise strong feelings! Those who have
come new to his work and find that this selection has whetted
their appetites might go on to read the collections *A Diversity of
Creatures, Plain Tales from the Hills, Many Inventions* and *Life's
Handicap* which contain many of my favourite stories.

It is fitting to end with a quotation from Somerset Maugham—
no mean short story writer himself—from his introduction to *A
Choice of Kipling's Prose* (1952). 'The short story is not a form of
fiction in which the English have on the whole excelled. The English,
as their novels show, are inclined to diffuseness. They have never
been much interested in form. Succinctness goes against their grain.
But the short story demands form. It demands succinctness.
Diffuseness kills it. It depends on construction. It does not admit of
loose ends. It must be complete in itself. All these qualities you will

* 'Kipling's World': a lecture delivered 1948. Reprinted in *Kipling
and the Critics.*

find in Kipling's stories when he was at his magnificent best; and this, happily for us, he was in story after story. Rudyard Kipling is the only writer of short stories our country has produced who can stand comparison with Guy de Maupassant and Chekhov. He is our greatest story writer. I can't believe he will ever be equalled. I am sure he will never be excelled.'

                                        TIM WILKINSON

In the House of Suddhoo

A stone's throw out on either hand
From that well-ordered road we tread,
*   And all the world is wild and strange:*
Churel and ghoul and Djinn and sprite
Shall bear us company to-night,
For we have reached the Oldest Land
*   Wherein the Powers of Darkness range.*
FROM THE DUSK TO THE DAWN

THE HOUSE OF SUDDHOO, near the Taksali Gate, is two-storeyed, with four carved windows of old brown wood, and a flat roof. You may recognize it by five red hand-prints arranged like the Five of Diamonds on the whitewash between the upper windows. Bhagwan Dass the grocer and a man who says he gets his living by seal-cutting live in the lower storey with a troop of wives, servants, friends, and retainers. The two upper rooms used to be occupied by Janoo and Azizun, and a little black-and-tan terrier that was stolen from an Englishman's house and given to Janoo by a soldier. Today, only Janoo lives in the upper rooms. Suddhoo sleeps on the roof generally, except when he sleeps in the street. He used to go to Peshawur in the cold weather to visit his son who sells curiosities near the Edwardes' Gate, and then he slept under a real mud roof. Suddhoo is a great friend of mine, because his cousin had a son who secured, thanks to my recommendation, the post of head-messenger to a big firm in the station. Suddhoo says that God will make me a Lieutenant-Governor one of these days. I daresay his prophecy will come true. He is very, very old, with white hair and no teeth worth showing, and he has outlived his wits—outlived nearly everything except his fondness for his son at Peshawur. Janoo and Azizun are Kashmiris, Ladies of the City, and theirs was an ancient and more or less honourable profession; but Azizun has since married a medical student from the North-West and has settled down to a most respectable life somewhere near Bareilly. Bhagwan Dass is an extortioner and an adulterator. He is very rich. The man who is supposed to get his living by seal-cutting pretends to be very poor. This lets you know as much as is necessary of the four principal tenants in the House of Suddhoo. Then there is Me, of course; but I am only the chorus that comes in at the end to explain things. So I do not count.

Suddhoo was not clever. The man who pretended to cut seals was the cleverest of them all—Bhagwan Dass only knew how to lie —except Janoo. She was also beautiful, but that was her own affair.

Suddhoo's son at Peshawur was attacked by pleurisy, and old Suddhoo was troubled. The seal-cutter man heard of Suddhoo's anxiety and made capital out of it. He was abreast of the times. He got a friend in Peshawur to telegraph daily accounts of the son's health. And here the story begins.

Suddhoo's cousin's son told me, one evening, that Suddhoo wanted to see me; that he was too old and feeble to come personally, and that I should be conferring an everlasting honour on the House of Suddhoo if I went to him. I went; but I think, seeing how well off Suddhoo was then, that he might have sent something better than an *ekka*, which jolted fearfully, to haul out a future Lieutenant-Governor to the City on a muggy April evening. The *ekka* did not run quickly. It was full dark when we pulled up opposite the door of Ranjit Singh's Tomb near the main gate of the Fort. Here was Suddhoo, and he said that, by reason of my condescension, it was absolutely certain that I should become a Lieutenant-Governor while my hair was yet black. Then we talked about the weather and the state of my health, and the wheat crops, for fifteen minutes, in the Huzuri Bagh, under the stars.

Suddhoo came to the point at last. He said that Janoo had told him that there was an order of the Sirkar against magic, because it was feared that magic might one day kill the Empress of India. I didn't know anything about the state of the law; but I fancied that something interesting was going to happen. I said that so far from magic being discouraged by the Government, it was highly commended. The greatest officials of the State practised it themselves. (If the Financial Statement isn't magic, I don't know what is.) Then, to encourage him further, I said that, if there was any *jadoo* afoot, I had not the least objection to giving it my countenance and sanction, and to seeing that it was clean *jadoo*—white magic, as distinguished from the unclean *jadoo* which kills folk. It took a long time before Suddhoo admitted that this was just what he had asked me to come for. Then he told me, in jerks and quavers, that the man who said he cut seals was a sorcerer of the cleanest kind; that every day he gave Suddhoo news of the sick son in Peshawur more quickly than the lightning could fly, and that this news was always corroborated by the letters. Further, that he had told Suddhoo how a great danger was threatening his son, which could be removed by clean *jadoo*; and, of course, heavy payment. I began to see exactly

how the land lay, and told Suddhoo that I also understood a little
jadoo in the Western line, and would go to his house to see that
everything was done decently and in order. We set off together; and
on the way Suddhoo told me that he had paid the seal-cutter between one hundred and two hundred rupees already; and the *jadoo*
of that night would cost two hundred more. Which was cheap, he
said, considering the greatness of his son's danger; but I do not
think he meant it.

The lights were all cloaked in the front of the house when we
arrived. I could hear awful noises from behind the seal-cutter's
shop-front, as if someone were groaning his soul out. Suddhoo shook
all over, and while we groped our way upstairs told me that the
jadoo had begun. Janoo and Azizun met us at the stair-head, and
told us that the *jadoo*-work was coming off in their rooms, because
there was more space there. Janoo is a lady of a free-thinking turn
of mind. She whispered that the *jadoo* was an invention to get
money out of Suddhoo, and that the seal-cutter would go to a hot
place when he died. Suddhoo was nearly crying with fear and old
age. He kept walking up and down the room in the half-light, repeating his son's name over and over again, and asking Azizun if the
seal-cutter ought not to make a reduction in the case of his own
landlord. Janoo pulled me over to the shadow in the recess of the
carved bow-windows. The boards were up, and the rooms were only
lit by one tiny oil-lamp. There was no chance of my being seen if I
stayed still.

Presently, the groans below ceased, and we heard steps on the
staircase. That was the seal-cutter. He stopped outside the door as
the terrier barked and Azizun fumbled at the chain, and he told
Suddhoo to blow out the lamp. This left the place in jet darkness,
except for the red glow from the two hookahs that belonged to
Janoo and Azizun. The seal-cutter came in, and I heard Suddhoo
throw himself down on the floor and groan. Azizun caught her
breath, and Janoo backed on to one of the beds with a shudder.
There was a clink of something metallic, and then shot up a pale
blue-green flame near the ground. The light was just enough to show
Azizun, pressed against one corner of the room with the terrier between her knees; Janoo, with her hands clasped, leaning forward as
she sat on the bed; Suddhoo, face-down, quivering, and the seal-
cutter.

I hope I may never see another man like that seal-cutter. He was
stripped to the waist, with a wreath of white jasmine as thick as my
wrist round his forehead, a salmon-coloured loin-cloth round his

middle, and a steel bangle on each ankle. This was not awe-inspiring. It was the face of the man that turned me cold. It was blue-grey in the first place. In the second, the eyes were rolled back till you could see the whites of them; and, in the third, the face was the face of a demon—a ghoul—anything you please except of the sleek, oily old ruffian who sat in the daytime over his turning-lathe down-stairs. He was lying on his stomach with his arms turned and crossed behind him, as if he had been thrown down pinioned. His head and neck were the only parts of him off the floor. They were nearly at right angles to the body, like the head of a cobra at spring. It was ghastly. In the centre of the room, on the bare earth floor, stood a big, deep, brass basin, with a pale blue-green light floating in the centre like a night-light. Round that basin the man on the floor wriggled himself three times. How he did it I do not know. I could see the muscles ripple along his spine and fall smooth again; but I could not see any other motion. The head seemed the only thing alive about him, except that slow curl and uncurl of the labouring back-muscles. Janoo from the bed was breathing seventy to the minute; Azizun held her hands before her eyes; and old Suddhoo, fingering at the dirt that had got into his white beard, was crying to himself. The horror of it was that the creeping, crawly thing made no sound—only crawled! And, remember, this lasted for ten minutes, while the terrier whined, and Azizun shuddered, and Janoo gasped, and Suddhoo cried!

I felt the hair lift at the back of my head, and my heart thump like a thermantidote-paddle. Luckily, the seal-cutter betrayed himself by his most impressive trick and made me calm again. After he had finished that unspeakable triple crawl, he stretched his head away from the floor as high as he could, and sent out a jet of fire from his nostrils. Now, I knew how fire-spouting is done—I can do it myself—so I felt at ease. The business was a fraud. If he had only kept to that crawl without trying to raise the effect, goodness knows what I might not have thought. Both the girls shrieked at the jet of fire, and the head dropped, chin down on the floor, with a thud; the whole body lying there like a corpse with its arms trussed. There was a pause of five full minutes after this, and the blue-green flame died down. Janoo stooped to settle one of her anklets, while Azizun turned her face to the wall and took the terrier in her arms. Suddhoo put out an arm mechanically to Janoo's hookah, and she slid it across the floor with her foot. Directly above the body and on the wall were a couple of flaming portraits, in stamped-paper frames, of the Queen and the Prince of Wales. They looked down on the per-

formance, and, to my thinking, seemed to heighten the grotesqueness of it all.

Just when the silence was getting unendurable, the body turned over and rolled away from the basin to the side of the room, where it lay stomach-up. There was a faint 'plop' from the basin—exactly like the noise a fish makes when it takes a fly—and the green light in the centre revived.

I looked at the basin, and saw, bobbing in the water, the dried, shrivelled, black head of a native baby—open eyes, open mouth, and shaved scalp. It was worse, being so very sudden, than the crawling exhibition. We had no time to say anything before it began to speak.

Read Poe's account of the voice that came from the mesmerized dying man, and you will realize less than one-half of the horror of that head's voice.

There was an interval of a second or two between each word, and a sort of 'ring, ring, ring,' in the note of the voice, like the timbre of a bell. It pealed slowly, as if talking to itself, for several minutes before I got rid of my cold sweat. Then the blessed solution struck me. I looked at the body lying near the doorway, and saw, just where the hollow of the throat joins on the shoulders, a muscle that had nothing to do with any man's regular breathing twitching away steadily. The whole thing was a careful reproduction of the Egyptian teraphim that one reads about sometimes; and the voice was as clever and as appalling a piece of ventriloquism as one could wish to hear. All this time the head was 'lip-lip-lapping' against the side of the basin, and speaking. It told Suddhoo, on his face again whining, of his son's illness and of the state of the illness up to the evening of that very night. I always shall respect the seal-cutter for keeping so faithfully to the time of the Peshawur telegrams. It went on to say that skilled doctors were night and day watching over the man's life; and that he would eventually recover if the fee to the potent sorcerer, whose servant was the head in the basin, were doubled.

Here the mistake from the artistic point of view came in. To ask for twice your stipulated fee in a voice that Lazarus might have used when he rose from the dead, is absurd. Janoo, who is really a woman of masculine intellect, saw this as quickly as I did. I heard her say, '*Asli nahin! Fareib!*'* scornfully under her breath; and just as she said so, the light in the basin died out, the head stopped talking, and we heard the room door creak on its hinges. Then Janoo struck a match, lit the lamp, and we saw that head, basin,

* 'Not real. A trick.'

and seal-cutter were gone. Suddhoo was wringing his hands, and explaining to anyone who cared to listen that, if his chances of eternal salvation depended on it, he could not raise another two hundred rupees. Azizun was nearly in hysterics in the corner; while Janoo sat down composedly on one of the beds to discuss the probabilities of the whole thing being a *bunao*, or 'make-up.'

I explained as much as I knew of the seal-cutter's way of *jadoo*; but her argument was much more simple. 'The magic that is always demanding gifts is no true magic,' said she. 'My mother told me that the only potent love-spells are those which are told you for love. This seal-cutter man is a liar and a devil. I dare not tell, do anything, or get anything done, because I am in debt to Bhagwan Dass the *bunnia* for two gold rings and a heavy anklet. I must get my food from his shop. The seal-cutter is the friend of Bhagwan Dass, and he would poison my food. A fool's *jadoo* has been going on for ten days, and has cost Suddhoo many rupees each night. The seal-cutter used black hens and lemons and charms before. He never showed us anything like this till tonight. Azizun is a fool, and will be *purdahnashin** soon. Suddhoo has lost his strength and his wits. See now! I had hoped to get from Suddhoo many rupees while he lived, and many more after his death; and behold, he is spending everything on that offspring of a devil and a she-ass, the seal-cutter!'

Here I said, 'But what induced Suddhoo to drag *me* into the business? Of course I can speak to the seal-cutter, and he shall refund. The whole thing is child's talk—shame—and senseless.'

'Suddhoo *is* an old child,' said Janoo. 'He has lived on the roofs these seventy years and is as senseless as a milch-goat. He brought you here to assure himself that he was not breaking any law of the Sirkar, whose salt he ate many years ago. He worships the dust of the feet of the seal-cutter, and that cow-devourer has forbidden him to go and see his son. What does Suddhoo know of your laws or the lightning-post? I have to watch his money going day by day to the lying beast below.'

Janoo stamped her foot on the floor and nearly cried with vexation; while Suddhoo was whimpering under a blanket in the corner, and Azizun was trying to guide the pipe-stem to his foolish old mouth.

*

* Under coverture.

Now, the case stands thus. Unthinkingly, I have laid myself open to the charge of aiding and abetting the seal-cutter in obtaining money under false pretences, which is forbidden by Section 420 of the Indian Penal Code. I am helpless in the matter for these reasons. I cannot inform the Police. What witnesses would support my statements? Janoo refuses flatly, and Azizun is a married woman somewhere near Bareilly—lost in this big India of ours. I dare not again take the law into my own hands, and speak to the seal-cutter; for certain am I that, not only would Suddhoo disbelieve me, but this step would end in the poisoning of Janoo, who is bound hand and foot by her debt to the *bunnia*. Suddhoo is an old dotard; and whenever we meet mumbles my idiotic joke that the Sirkar rather patronizes the Black Art than otherwise. His son is well now; but Suddhoo is completely under the influence of the seal-cutter, by whose advice he regulates the affairs of his life. Janoo watches daily the money that she hoped to wheedle out of Suddhoo taken by the seal-cutter, and becomes daily more furious and sullen.

She will never tell, because she dare not; but, unless something happens to prevent her, I am afraid that the seal-cutter will die of cholera—the white arsenic kind—about the middle of May. And thus I shall be privy to a murder in the House of Suddhoo!

Plain Tales from the Hills, 1888*

* *Civil and Military Gazette*, 1886.

Tods' Amendment

The World hath set its heavy yoke
Upon the old white-bearded folk
  Who strive to please the King.
God's mercy is upon the young,
God's wisdom in the baby tongue
  That fears not anything.
      THE PARABLE OF CHAJJU BHAGAT

NOW TODS' MAMMA was a singularly charming woman, and everyone in Simla knew Tods. Most men had saved him from death on occasions. He was beyond his *ayah*'s control altogether, and perilled his life daily to find out what would happen if you pulled a Mountain Battery mule's tail. He was an utterly fearless young pagan, about six years old, and the only baby who ever broke the holy calm of the Supreme Legislative Council.

It happened this way: Tods' pet kid got loose, and fled up the hill, off the Boileaugunge road, Tods after it, until it burst in to the Viceregal Lodge lawn, then attached to Peterhof. The Council were sitting at the time, and the windows were open because it was warm. The Red Lancer in the porch told Tods to go away; but Tods knew the Red Lancer and most of the Members of Council personally. Moreover, he had firm hold of the kid's collar, and was being dragged all across the flower-beds. 'Give my *salaam* to the long Councillor Sahib, and ask him to help me take Moti back!' gasped Tods. The Council heard the noise through the open windows; and, after an interval, was seen the shocking spectacle of a Legal Member and a Lieutenant-Governor helping, under the direct patronage of a Commander-in-Chief and a Viceroy, one small and very dirty boy, in a sailor's suit and a tangle of brown hair, to coerce a lively and rebellious kid. They headed it off down the path to the Mall, and Tods went home in triumph and told his Mamma that *all* the Councillor Sahibs had been helping him to catch Moti. Whereat his Mamma smacked Tods for interfering with the administration of the Empire; but Tods met the Legal Member the next day, and told him in confidence that if the Legal Member ever wanted to catch a goat, he, Tods, would give him all the help in his power. 'Thank you, Tods,' said the Legal Member.

Tods was the idol of some eighty *jhampanis*, and half as many

saises. He saluted them all as 'O Brother.' It never entered his head
that any living human being could disobey his orders; and he was
the buffer between the servants and his Mamma's wrath. The working of that household turned on Tods, who was adored by everyone
from the *dhobi* to the dog-boy. Even Futteh Khan, the villainous
loafer *khit* from Mussoorie, shirked risking Tods' displeasure for fear
his co-mates should look down on him.

So Tods had honour in the land from Boileaugunge to Chota
Simla, and ruled justly according to his lights. Of course, he spoke
Urdu, but he had also mastered many queer side-speeches like the
chotee bolee of the women, and held grave converse with shop-
keepers and Hill-coolies alike. He was precocious for his age, and
his mixing with natives had taught him some of the more bitter
truths of life: the meanness and the sordidness of it. He used, over
his bread and milk, to deliver solemn and serious aphorisms, translated from the vernacular into the English, that made his Mamma
jump and vow that Tods *must* go Home next hot weather.

Just when Tods was in the bloom of his power, the Supreme
Legislature were hacking out a Bill for the Sub-Montane Tracts, a
revision of the then Act, smaller than the Punjab Land Bill, but
affecting a few hundred thousand people none the less. The Legal
Member had built, and bolstered, and embroidered, and amended
that Bill till it looked beautiful on paper. Then the Council began to
settle what they called the 'minor details.' As if any Englishman
legislating for natives knows enough to know which are the minor
and which are the major points, from the native point of view, of
any measure! That Bill was a triumph of 'safeguarding the interests
of the tenant.' One clause provided that land should not be leased
on longer terms than five years at a stretch; because, if the landlord had a tenant bound down for, say, twenty years, he would
squeeze the very life out of him. The notion was to keep up a stream
of independent cultivators in the Sub-Montane Tracts; and eth-
nologically and politically the notion was correct. The only drawback was that it was altogether wrong. A native's life in India
implies the life of his son. Wherefore, you cannot legislate for one
generation at a time. You must consider the next from the native
point of view. Curiously enough, the native now and then, and in
Northern India more particularly, hates being over-protected
against himself. There was a Naga village once, where they lived on
dead *and* buried Commissariat mules. . . . But that is another story.

For many reasons, to be explained later, the people concerned
objected to the Bill. The Native Member of Council knew as much

about Punjabis as he knew about Charing Cross. He had said in
Calcutta that 'the Bill was entirely in accord with the desires of that
large and important class, the cultivators'; and so on, and so on.
The Legal Member's knowledge of natives was limited to English-
speaking Durbaris, and his own red *chaprassis*; the Sub-Montane
Tracts concerned no one in particular; the Deputy-Commissioners
were a good deal too driven to make representations, and the
measure was one which dealt with small landholders only. Nevertheless, the Legal Member prayed that it might be correct, for he
was a nervously conscientious man. He did not know that no man
can tell what natives think unless he mixes with them with the
varnish off. And not always then. But he did the best he knew. So
the measure came up to the Supreme Council for the final touches,
while Tods patrolled the Burra Simla Bazar in his morning rides,
and played with the monkey belonging to Ditta Mull, the *bunnia*,
and listened, as a child listens, to all the stray talk about this new
freak of the Lat Sahib's.

One day there was a dinner-party at the house of Tods' Mamma,
and the Legal Member came. Tods was in bed, but he kept awake
till he heard the bursts of laughter from the men over the coffee.
Then he paddled out in his little red flannel dressing-gown and
his night-suit, and took refuge by the side of his father, knowing
that he would not be sent back. 'See the miseries of having a family!'
said Tods' father, giving Tods three prunes, some water in a glass
that had been used for claret, and telling him to sit still. Tods
sucked the prunes slowly, knowing that he would have to go when
they were finished, and sipped the pink water like a man of the
world, as he listened to the conversation. Presently, the Legal
Member, talking 'shop' to the Head of a Department, mentioned
his Bill by its full name—'The Sub-Montane Tracts *Ryotwari* Revised Enactment.' Tods caught the one native word, and lifting up
his small voice said:

'Oh, I know *all* about that! Has it been *murramutted* yet,
Councillor Sahib?'

'How much?' said the Legal Member.

'*Murramutted*—mended.—Put *theek*, you know—made nice to
please Ditta Mull!'

The Legal Member left his place and moved up next to Tods.

'What do you know about *ryotwari*, little man?' he said.

'I'm not a little man—I'm Tods—and I know *all* about it. Ditta
Mull, and Choga Lall, and Amir Nath, and—oh, *lakhs* of my friends
tell me about it in the bazars when I talk to them.'

'Oh, they do—do they? What do they say, Tods?'

Tods tucked his feet under his red flannel dressing-gown and said, 'I must *fink*.'

The Legal Member waited patiently. Then Tods, with infinite compassion:

'You don't speak my talk, do you, Councillor Sahib?'

'No; I am sorry to say I do not,' said the Legal Member.

'Very well,' said Tods, 'I must *fink* in English.'

He spent a minute putting his ideas in order, and began very slowly, translating in his mind from the vernacular to English, as many Anglo-Indian children do. You must remember that the Legal Member helped him on by questions when he halted, for Tods was not equal to the sustained flight of oratory that follows.

'Ditta Mull says, "This thing is the talk of a child, and was made up by fools." But *I* don't think you are a fool, Councillor Sahib,' said Tods hastily. 'You caught my goat. This is what Ditta Mull says: "I am not a fool, and why should the Sirkar say I am a child? *I* can see if the land is good and if the landlord is good. If I am a fool, the sin is upon my own head. For five years I take my ground for which I have saved money, and a wife I take too, and a little son is born." Ditta Mull has one daughter now, but he *says* he will have a son, soon. And he says, "At the end of five years, by this new *bundobust*, I must go. If I do not go, I must get fresh seals and *takkus*-stamps on the papers, perhaps in the middle of the harvest, and to go to the law-courts once is wisdom, but to go twice is *Jehannum*." That is *quite* true,' explained Tods gravely. 'All my friends say so. And Ditta Mull says, "Always fresh *takkus* and paying money to Vakils and *chaprassis* and law-courts every five years, or else the landlord makes me go. Why do I want to go? Am I a fool? If I am a fool and do not know, after forty years, good land when I see it, let me die! But if the new *bundobust* says for *fifteen* years, that is good and wise. My little son is a man, and I am burnt, and he takes the ground, or another ground, paying only once for the *takkus*-stamps on the papers, and his little son is born, and at the end of fifteen years is a man too. But what profit is there in five years and fresh papers? Nothing but *dikh*—trouble—*dikh*. We are not young men who take these lands, but old ones—not farmers, but tradesmen with a little money—and for fifteen years we shall have peace. Nor are we children that the Sirkar should treat us so." '

Here Tods stopped short, for the whole table were listening. The Legal Member said to Tods, 'Is that all?'

'All I can remember,' said Tods. 'But you should see Ditta Mull's big monkey. It's just like a Councillor Sahib.'

'Tods! Go to bed,' said his father.

Tods gathered up his dressing-gown tail and departed.

The Legal Member brought his hand down on the table with a crash. 'By Jove!' said the Legal Member, 'I believe the boy is right. The short tenure *is* the weak point.'

He left early, thinking over what Tods had said. Now, it was obviously impossible for the Legal Member to play with a *bunnia*'s monkey, by way of getting understanding; but he did better. He made inquiries, always bearing in mind the fact that the real native —not the hybrid, University-trained mule—is as timid as a colt, and, little by little, he coaxed some of the men whom the measure concerned most intimately to give in their views, which squared very closely with Tods' evidence.

So the Bill was amended in that clause; and the Legal Member was filled with an uneasy suspicion that Native Members represent very little except the Orders they carry on their bosoms. But he put the thought from him as illiberal. He was a most Liberal man.

After a time, the news spread through the bazars that Tods had got the Bill recast in the tenure-clause, and if Tods' Mamma had not interfered, Tods would have made himself sick on the baskets of fruit and pistachio nuts and Kabuli grapes and almonds that crowded the veranda. Till he went Home, Tods ranked some few degrees before the Viceroy in popular estimation. But for the little life of him Tods could not understand why.

In the Legal Member's private-paper-box still lies the rough draft of the Sub-Montane Tracts *Ryotwari* Revised Enactment; and, opposite the twenty-second clause, pencilled in blue chalk, and signed by the Legal Member, are the words *'Tods' Amendment.'*

Plain Tales from the Hills, 1888*

---

* *Civil and Military Gazette,* 1887.

Pig

Go, stalk the red deer o'er the heather,
  Ride, follow the fox if you can!
But, for pleasure and profit together,
  Allow me the hunting of Man—
The chase of the Human, the search for the Soul
  To its ruin—the hunting of Man.
THE OLD SHIKARRI

I BELIEVE THE DIFFERENCE began in the matter of a horse, with a twist in his temper, whom Pinecoffin sold to Nafferton, and by whom Nafferton was nearly slain. There may have been other causes of offence; the horse was the official stalking-horse. Nafferton was very angry; but Pinecoffin laughed, and said that he had never guaranteed the beast's manners. Nafferton laughed too, though he vowed that he would write off his fall against Pinecoffin if he waited five years. Now, a Dalesman from beyond Skipton will forgive an injury when the Strid lets a man live; but a South Devon man is as soft as a Dartmoor bog. You can see from their names that Nafferton had the race-advantage of Pinecoffin. He was a peculiar man, and his notions of humour were cruel. He taught me a new and fascinating form of *shikar*. He hounded Pinecoffin from Mithankot to Jagadri, and from Gurgaon to Abbottabad—up and across the Punjab, a large Province, and in places remarkably dry. He said that he had no intention of allowing Assistant Commissioners to 'sell him pups,' in the shape of ramping, screaming countrybreds, without making their lives a burden to them.

Most Assistant Commissioners develop a bent for some special work after their first hot weather in the country. The boys with digestions hope to write their names large on the Frontier, and struggle for dreary places like Bannu and Kohat. The bilious ones climb into the Secretariat; which is very bad for the liver. Others are bitten with a mania for District work, Ghaznevid coins or Persian poetry; while some, who come of farmers' stock, find that the smell of the earth after the Rains gets into their blood, and calls them to 'develop the resources of the Province.' These men are enthusiasts. Pinecoffin belonged to their class. He knew a great many facts bearing on the cost of bullocks, and temporary wells, and opium-scrapers, and what happens if you burn too much

rubbish on a field in the hope of enriching used-up soil. All the
Pinecoffins come of a landholding breed, and so the land only took
back her own again. Unfortunately—most unfortunately for Pinecoffin—he was a Civilian as well as a farmer. Nafferton watched
him, and thought about the horse. Nafferton said, 'See me chase
that boy till he drops!' I said, 'You can't get your knife into an
Assistant Commissioner.' Nafferton told me that I did not understand the administration of the Province.

Our Government is rather peculiar. It gushes on the agricultural
and general information side, and will supply a moderately respectable man with all sorts of 'economic statistics,' if he speaks to it
prettily. For instance, you are interested in gold-washing in
the sands of the Sutlej. You pull the string, and find that it wakes
up half-a-dozen Departments, and finally communicates, say, with
a friend of yours in the Telegraph, who once wrote some notes on
the customs of the gold-washers when he was on construction work
in their part of the Empire. He may or may not be pleased at being
ordered to write out everything he knows for your benefit. This
depends on his temperament. The bigger man you are, the more information and the greater trouble can you raise.

Nafferton was not a big man; but he had the reputation of being
very 'earnest.' An 'earnest' man can do much with a Government.
There was an earnest man once who nearly wrecked . . . But all
India knows *that* story. I am not sure what real 'earnestness' is. A
very fair imitation can be manufactured by neglecting to dress
decently, by mooning about in a dreamy, misty sort of way, by
taking office work home, after staying in the office till seven, and by
receiving crowds of native gentlemen on Sundays. That is one sort
of 'earnestness.'

Nafferton cast about for a peg whereon to hang his earnestness,
and for a string that would communicate with Pinecoffin. He found
both. They were Pig. Nafferton became an earnest inquirer after
Pig. He informed the Government that he had a scheme whereby a
very large percentage of the British Army in India could be fed, at
a very large saving, on Pig. Then he hinted that Pinecoffin might
supply him with the 'varied information necessary to the proper
inception of the scheme.' So the Government wrote on the back of
the letter, 'Instruct Mr Pinecoffin to furnish Mr Nafferton with any
information in his power.' Government is very prone to writing
things on the backs of letters which, later, lead to trouble and confusion.

Nafferton had not the faintest interest in Pig, but he knew that

Pinecoffin would flounce into the trap. Pinecoffin was delighted at being consulted about Pig. The Indian Pig is not exactly an important factor in agricultural life; but Nafferton explained to Pinecoffin that there was room for improvement, and corresponded direct with that young man.

You may think that there is not much to be evolved from Pig. It all depends how you set to work. Pinecoffin being a Civilian and wishing to do things thoroughly, began with an essay on the Primitive Pig, the Mythology of the Pig, and the Dravidian Pig. Nafferton filed that information—twenty-seven foolscap sheets—and wanted to know about the distribution of the Pig in the Punjab, and how it stood the Plains in the hot weather. From this point onwards remember that I am giving you only the barest outlines of the affair—the guy-ropes, as it were, of the web that Nafferton spun round Pinecoffin.

Pinecoffin made a coloured Pig-population map, and collected observations on the comparative longevity of Pig (*a*) in the submontane tracts of the Himalayas, and (*b*) in the Rechna Doab. Nafferton filed that, and asked what sort of people looked after Pig. This started an ethnological excursus on swine-herds, and drew from Pinecoffin long tables showing the proportion per thousand of the caste in the Derajat. Nafferton filed that bundle, and explained that the figures which he wanted referred to the Cis-Sutlej states, where he understood that Pigs were very fine and large, and where he proposed to start a Piggery. By this time Government had quite forgotten their instructions to Mr Pinecoffin. They were like the gentlemen in Keats' poem, who turned well-oiled wheels to skin other people. But Pinecoffin was just entering into the spirit of the Pig-hunt, as Nafferton well knew he would do. He had a fair amount of work of his own to clear away; but he sat up of nights reducing Pig to five places of decimals for the honour of his Service. He was not going to appear ignorant of so easy a subject as Pig.

Then Government sent him on special duty to Kohat, to 'inquire into' the big, seven-foot, iron-shod spades of that District. People had been killing each other with those peaceful tools; and Government wished to know 'whether a modified form of agricultural implement could not, tentatively and as a temporary measure, be introduced among the agricultural population without needlessly or unduly exacerbating the existing religious sentiments of the peasantry.'

Between those spades and Nafferton's Pig, Pinecoffin was rather heavily burdened.

Nafferton now began to take up '(*a*) The food-supply of the indigenous Pig, with a view to the improvement of its capacities as a flesh-former. (*b*) The acclimatization of the exotic Pig, maintaining its distinctive peculiarities.' Pinecoffin replied exhaustively that the exotic Pig would become merged in the indigenous type; and quoted horse-breeding statistics to prove this. The side-issue was debated at great length on Pinecoffin's side, till Nafferton owned that he had been in the wrong, and moved the previous question. When Pinecoffin had quite written himself out about flesh-formers, and fibrins, and glucose, and the nitrogenous constituents of maize and lucerne, Nafferton raised the question of expense. By this time Pinecoffin, who had been transferred from Kohat, had developed a Pig theory of his own, which he stated in thirty-three folio pages— all carefully filed by Nafferton; who asked for more.

These things took ten months, and Pinecoffin's interest in the potential Piggery seemed to die down after he had stated his own views. But Nafferton bombarded him with letters on 'the Imperial aspect of the scheme, as tending to officialize the sale of pork, and thereby calculated to give offence to the Mohammedan population of Upper India.' He guessed that Pinecoffin would want some broad, free-hand work after his niggling, stippling, decimal details. Pinecoffin handled the latest development of the case in masterly style, and proved that no 'popular ebullition of excitement was to be apprehended.' Nafferton said that there was nothing like Civilian insight in matters of this kind, and lured him up a by-path—'the possible profits to accrue to the Government from the sale of hog-bristles.' There is an extensive literature of hog-bristles, and the shoe, brush, and colourman's trades recognize more varieties of bristles than you would think possible. After Pinecoffin had wondered a little at Nafferton's rage for information, he sent back a monograph, fifty-one pages, on 'Products of the Pig.' This led him, under Nafferton's tender handling, straight to the Cawnpore factories, the trade in hog-skin for saddles—and thence to the tanners. Pinecoffin wrote that pomegranate-seed was the best cure for hog-skin, and suggested—the past fourteen months had wearied him— that Nafferton should 'raise his pigs before he tanned them.'

Nafferton went back to the second section of his fifth question. How could the exotic Pig be brought to give as much pork as it did in the West and yet 'assume the essentially hirsute characteristics of its Oriental congener'? Pinecoffin felt dazed, for he had forgotten what he had written sixteen months before, and fancied that he was about to reopen the entire question. He was too far involved in the hideous tangle to retreat, and, in a weak moment, he wrote, 'Consult my first letter'; which related to the Dravidian Pig. As a matter of fact, Pinecoffin had still to reach the acclimatization stage; having gone off on a side-issue on the merging of types.

Then Nafferton really unmasked his batteries! He complained to the Government, in stately language, of 'the paucity of help accorded to me in my earnest attempts to start a potentially remunerative industry, and the flippancy with which my requests for information are treated by a gentleman whose pseudo-scholarly attainments should at least have taught him the primary differences between the Dravidian and the Berkshire variety of the genus *Sus*. If I am to understand that the letter to which he refers me contains his serious views on the acclimatization of a valuable, though possibly uncleanly, animal, I am reluctantly compelled to believe,' etc. etc.

There was a new man at the head of the Department of Castigation. The wretched Pinecoffin was told that the Service was made for the Country, and not the Country for the Service, and that he had better begin to supply information about Pig.

Pinecoffin answered insanely that he had written everything that could be written about Pig, and that some furlough was due to him.

Nafferton got a copy of that letter, and sent it, with the essay on the Dravidian Pig, to a down-country paper which printed both in full. The essay was rather high-flown; but if the Editor had seen the stacks of paper, in Pinecoffin's handwriting, on Nafferton's table, he would not have been so sarcastic about the 'nebulous discursiveness and blatant self-sufficiency of the modern Competition-wallah, and his utter inability to grasp the practical issues of a practical question.' Many friends cut out these remarks and sent them to Pinecoffin.

I have already stated that Pinecoffin came of a soft stock. This last stroke frightened and shook him. He could not understand it; but he felt that he had been, somehow, shamelessly betrayed by Nafferton. He realized that he had wrapped himself up in the Pig-skin without need, and that he could not well set himself right with his Government. All his acquaintances asked after his 'nebulous discursiveness' or his 'blatant self-sufficiency,' and this made him miserable.

He took a train and went to Nafferton, whom he had not seen since the Pig business began. He also took the cutting from the paper, and blustered feebly and called Nafferton names, and then died down to a watery, weak protest of the 'I-say-it's-too-bad-you-know' order.

Nafferton was very sympathetic.

'I'm afraid I've given you a good deal of trouble, haven't I?' said he.

'Trouble!' whimpered Pinecoffin; 'I don't mind the trouble so much, though that was bad enough; but what I resent is this showing up in print. It will stick to me like a burr all through my service. And I *did* do my best for your interminable swine. It's too bad of you—on my soul it is!'

'I don't know,' said Nafferton. 'Have you ever been stuck with a horse? It isn't the money I mind, though that is bad enough; but what I resent is the chaff that follows, especially from the boy who stuck me. But I think we'll cry quits now.'

Pinecoffin found nothing to say save bad words; and Nafferton smiled ever so sweetly, and asked him to dinner.

Plain Tales from the Hills, 1888*

* *Civil and Military Gazette*, 1887.

The Story of Muhammad Din

*Who is the happy man? He that sees, in his own house at
home, little children crowned with dust, leaping and
falling and crying.*

MUNICHANDRA, translated by Professor Peterson

THE POLO-BALL was an old one, scarred, chipped, and dinted.
It stood on the mantelpiece among the pipe-stems which
Imam Din, *khitmutgar*, was cleaning for me.

'Does the Heaven-born want this ball?' said Imam Din deferentially.

The Heaven-born set no particular store by it; but of what use
was a polo-ball to a *khitmutgar*?

'By your Honour's favour, I have a little son. He has seen this
ball, and desires it to play with. I do not want it for myself.'

No one would for an instant accuse portly old Imam Din of
wanting to play with polo-balls. He carried out the battered thing
into the veranda; and there followed a hurricane of joyful squeaks, a
patter of small feet, and the *thud-thud-thud* of the ball rolling along
the ground. Evidently the little son had been waiting outside the
door to secure his treasure. But how had he managed to see that
polo-ball?

Next day, coming back from office half an hour earlier than usual,
I was aware of a small figure in the dining-room—a tiny, plump
figure in a ridiculously inadequate shirt which came, perhaps, half-
way down the tubby stomach. It wandered round the room, thumb
in mouth, crooning to itself as it took stock of the pictures. Un-
doubtedly this was the 'little son.'

He had no business in my room, of course; but was so deeply
absorbed in his discoveries that he never noticed me in the doorway. I stepped into the room and startled him nearly into a fit. He
sat down on the ground with a gasp. His eyes opened, and his
mouth followed suit. I knew what was coming, and fled, followed by
a long, dry howl which reached the servants' quarters far more
quickly than any command of mine had ever done. In ten seconds
Imam Din was in the dining-room. Then despairing sobs arose, and
I returned to find Imam Din admonishing the small sinner, who
was using most of his shirt as a handkerchief.

'This boy,' said Imam Din judicially, 'is a *budmash*—a big *bud-*

mash. He will, without doubt, go to the *jail-khana* for his behaviour.'
Renewed yells from the penitent, and an elaborate apology to myself from Imam Din.

'Tell the baby,' said I, 'that the Sahib is not angry, and take him
away.' Imam Din conveyed my forgiveness to the offender, who
had now gathered all his shirt round his neck, stringwise, and the
yell subsided into a sob. The two set off for the door. 'His name,'
said Imam Din, as though the name were part of the crime, 'is
Muhammad Din, and he is a *budmash.*' Freed from present danger,
Muhammad Din turned round in his father's arms, and said gravely,
'It is true that my name is Muhammad Din, Tahib, but I am not a
budmash. I am a *man!*'

From that day dated my acquaintance with Muhammad Din.
Never again did he come into my dining-room, but on the neutral
ground of the garden we greeted each other with much state,
though our conversation was confined to 'Talaam, Tahib' from his
side, and 'Salaam, Muhammad Din' from mine. Daily on my return
from office, the little white shirt and the fat little body used to rise
from the shade of the creeper-covered trellis where they had been
hid; and daily I checked my horse here, that my salutation might
not be slurred over or given unseemly.

Muhammad Din never had any companions. He used to trot
about the compound, in and out of the castor-oil bushes, on mysterious errands of his own. One day I stumbled upon some of his
handiwork far down the grounds. He had half buried the polo-ball
in dust, and stuck six shrivelled old marigold flowers in a circle
round it. Outside that circle again was a rude square, traced out in
bits of red brick alternating with fragments of broken china; the
whole bounded by a little bank of dust. The water-man from the
well-curb put in a plea for the small architect, saying that it was
only the play of a baby and did not much disfigure my garden.

Heaven knows that I had no intention of touching the child's
work then or later; but, that evening, a stroll through the garden
brought me unawares full on it; so that I trampled, before I knew,
marigold-heads, dust-bank, and fragments of broken soap-dish
into confusion past all hope of mending. Next morning, I came upon
Muhammad Din crying softly to himself over the ruin I had wrought.
Someone had cruelly told him that the Sahib was very angry with
him for spoiling the garden, and had scattered his rubbish, using
bad language the while. Muhammad Din laboured for an hour at
effacing every trace of the dust-bank and pottery fragments, and it
was with a tearful and apologetic face that he said, 'Talaam,

Tahib,' when I came home from office. A hasty inquiry resulted in Imam Din informing Muhammad Din that, by my singular favour, he was permitted to disport himself as he pleased. Whereat the child took heart and fell to tracing the ground-plan of an edifice which was to eclipse the marigold-polo-ball creation.

For some months the chubby little eccentricity revolved in his humble orbit among the castor-oil bushes and in the dust; always fashioning magnificent palaces from stale flowers thrown away by the bearer, smooth water-worn pebbles, bits of broken glass, and feathers pulled, I fancy, from my fowls—always alone, and always crooning to himself.

A gaily-spotted sea-shell was dropped one day close to the last of his little buildings; and I looked that Muhammad Din should build something more than ordinarily splendid on the strength of it. Nor was I disappointed. He meditated for the better part of an hour, and his crooning rose to a jubilant song. Then he began tracing in the dust. It would certainly be a wondrous palace, this one, for it was two yards long and a yard broad in ground-plan. But the palace was never completed.

Next day there was no Muhammad Din at the head of the carriage-drive, and no 'Talaam, Tahib' to welcome my return. I had grown accustomed to the greeting, and its omission troubled me. Next day Imam Din told me that the child was suffering slightly from fever and needed quinine. He got the medicine, and an English Doctor.

'They have no stamina, these brats,' said the Doctor, as he left Imam Din's quarters.

A week later, though I would have given much to have avoided it, I met on the road to the Mussulman burying-ground Imam Din, accompanied by one other friend, carrying in his arms, wrapped in a white cloth, all that was left of little Muhammad Din.

Plain Tales from the Hills, 1888*

* *Civil and Military Gazette*, 1886.

A Wayside Comedy

Because to every purpose there is time and judgement,
therefore the misery of man is great upon him.

ECCLESIASTES viii. 6

FATE AND THE GOVERNMENT of India have turned the Station of Kashima into a prison; and, because there is no help for the poor souls who are now lying there in torment, I write this story, praying that the Government of India may be moved to scatter the European population to the four winds.

Kashima is bounded on all sides by the rock-tipped circle of the Dosehri hills. In spring, it is ablaze with roses. In summer, the roses die and the hot winds blow from the hills. In autumn, the white mists from the *jhils* cover the place as with water, and in winter, the frosts nip everything young and tender to earth-level. There is but one view in Kashima—a stretch of perfectly flat pasture and plough-land, running up to the grey-blue scrub of the Dosehri hills.

There are no amusements, except snipe and tiger shooting; but the tigers have been long since hunted from their lairs in the rock-caves, and the snipe only come once a year. Narkarra—one hundred and forty-three miles by road—is the nearest Station to Kashima. But Kashima never goes to Narkarra, where there are at least twelve English people. It stays within the circle of the Dosehri hills.

All Kashima acquits Mrs Vansuythen of any intention to do harm; but all Kashima knows that she, and she alone, brought about their pain.

Boulte, the Engineer, Mrs Boulte, and Captain Kurrell know this. They are the English population of Kashima, if we except Major Vansuythen, who is of no importance whatever, and Mrs Vansuythen, who is the most important of all.

You must remember, though you will not understand, that all laws weaken in a small and hidden community where there is no public opinion. When a man is absolutely alone in a Station he runs a certain risk of falling into evil ways. This risk is multiplied by every addition to the population up to twelve—the Jury-number. After that, fear and consequent restraint begin, and human action becomes less grotesquely jerky.

There was deep peace in Kashima till Mrs Vansuythen arrived.

She was a charming woman, everyone said so everywhere; and she charmed everyone. In spite of this, or, perhaps, because of this, since Fate is so perverse, she cared only for one man, and he was Major Vansuythen. Had she been plain or stupid, this matter would have been intelligible to Kashima. But she was a fair woman, with very still grey eyes, the colour of a lake just before the light of the sun touches it. No man who had seen those eyes could, later on, explain what fashion of woman she was to look upon. The eyes dazzled him. Her own sex said that she was 'not bad-looking, but spoilt by pretending to be so grave.' And yet her gravity was natural. It was not her habit to smile. She merely went through life, looking at those who passed; and the women objected while the men fell down and worshipped.

She knows and is deeply sorry for the evil she has done to Kashima; but Major Vansuythen cannot understand why Mrs Boulte does not drop in to afternoon tea at least three times a week. 'When there are only two women in one Station, they ought to see a great deal of each other,' says Major Vansuythen.

Long and long before ever Mrs Vansuythen came out of those far-away places where there is society and amusement, Kurrell had discovered that Mrs Boulte was the one woman in the world for him and—you dare not blame them. Kashima was as out of the world as Heaven or the Other Place, and the Dosehri hills kept their secret well. Boulte had no concern in the matter. He was in camp for a fortnight at a time. He was a hard, heavy man, and neither Mrs Boulte nor Kurrell pitied him. They had all Kashima and each other for their very, very own; and Kashima was the Garden of Eden in those days. When Boulte returned from his wanderings he would slap Kurrell between the shoulders and call him 'old fellow,' and the three would dine together. Kashima was happy then when the Judgment of God seemed almost as distant as Narkarra or the railway that ran down to the sea. But the Government sent Major Vansuythen to Kashima, and with him came his wife.

The etiquette of Kashima is much the same as that of a desert island. When a stranger is cast away there, all hands go down to the shore to make him welcome. Kashima assembled at the masonry platform close to the Narkarra Road, and spread tea for the Vansuythens. That ceremony was reckoned a formal call, and made them free of the Station, its rights and privileges. When the Vansuythens settled down they gave a tiny house-warming to all Kashima; and that made Kashima free of their house, according to the immemorial usage of the Station.

Then the Rains came, when no one could go into camp, and the Narkarra Road was washed away by the Kasun River, and in the cup-like pastures of Kashima the cattle waded knee-deep. The clouds dropped down from the Dosehri hills and covered everything.

At the end of the Rains Boulte's manner towards his wife changed and became demonstratively affectionate. They had been married twelve years, and the change startled Mrs Boulte, who hated her husband with the hate of a woman who has met with nothing but kindness from her mate, and, in the teeth of this kindness, has done him a great wrong. Moreover, she had her own trouble to fight with—her watch to keep over her own property, Kurrell. For two months the Rains had hidden the Dosehri hills and many other things besides; but, when they lifted, they showed Mrs Boulte that her man among men, her Ted—for she called him Ted in the old days when Boulte was out of earshot—was slipping the links of the allegiance.

'The Vansuythen Woman has taken him,' Mrs Boulte said to herself; and when Boulte was away, wept over her belief, in the face of the over-vehement blandishments of Ted. Sorrow in Kashima is as fortunate as Love because there is nothing to weaken it save the flight of Time. Mrs Boulte had never breathed her suspicion to Kurrell because she was not certain; and her nature led her to be very certain before she took steps in any direction. That is why she behaved as she did.

Boulte came into the house one evening, and leaned against the door-post of the drawing-room, chewing his moustache. Mrs Boulte was putting some flowers into a vase. There is a pretence of civilization even in Kashima.

'Little woman,' said Boulte quietly, 'do you care for me?'

'Immensely,' said she, with a laugh. 'Can you ask it?'

'But I'm serious,' said Boulte. '*Do* you care for me?'

Mrs Boulte dropped the flowers, and turned round quickly. 'Do you want an honest answer?'

'Ye-es, I've asked for it.'

Mrs Boulte spoke in a low, even voice for five minutes, very distinctly, that there might be no misunderstanding her meaning. When Samson broke the pillars of Gaza, he did a little thing, and one not to be compared with the deliberate pulling down of a woman's homestead about her own ears. There was no wise female friend to advise Mrs. Boulte, the singularly cautious wife, to hold her hand. She struck at Boulte's heart, because her own was sick

with suspicion of Kurrell, and worn out with the long strain of watching alone through the Rains. There was no plan or purpose in her speaking. The sentences made themselves; and Boulte listened, leaning against the door-post with his hands in his pockets. When all was over, and Mrs Boulte began to breathe through her nose before breaking out into tears, he laughed and stared straight in front of him at the Dosehri hills.

'Is that all?' he said. 'Thanks, I only wanted to know, you know.'

'What are you going to do?' said the woman, between her sobs.

'Do! Nothing. What should I do? Kill Kurrell, or send you Home, or apply for leave to get a divorce? It's two days' *dâk* into Narkarra.' He laughed again and went on: 'I'll tell you what *you* can do. You can ask Kurrell to dinner tomorrow—no, on Thursday, that will allow you time to pack—and you can bolt with him. I give you my word I won't follow.'

He took up his helmet and went out of the room, and Mrs Boulte sat till the moonlight streaked the floor, thinking and thinking and thinking. She had done her best upon the spur of the moment to pull the house down; but it would not fall. Moreover, she could not understand her husband, and she was afraid. Then the folly of her useless truthfulness struck her, and she was ashamed to write to Kurrell, saying, 'I have gone mad and told everything. My husband says that I am free to elope with you. Get a *dâk* for Thursday, and we will fly after dinner.' There was a cold-bloodedness about that procedure which did not appeal to her. So she sat still in her own house and thought.

At dinner-time Boulte came back from his walk, white and worn and haggard, and the woman was touched at his distress. As the evening wore on she muttered some expression of sorrow, something approaching to contrition. Boulte came out of a brown study and said, 'Oh, *that*! I wasn't thinking about that. By the way, what does Kurrell say to the elopement?'

'I haven't seen him,' said Mrs Boulte. 'Good God, is that all?'

But Boulte was not listening, and her sentence ended in a gulp.

The next day brought no comfort to Mrs Boulte, for Kurrell did not appear, and the new life that she, in the five minutes' madness of the previous evening, had hoped to build out of the ruins of the old, seemed to be no nearer.

Boulte ate his breakfast, advised her to see her Arab pony fed in the veranda, and went out. The morning wore through, and at midday the tension became unendurable. Mrs Boulte could not cry. She had finished her crying in the night, and now she did not want to be left alone. Perhaps the Vansuythen Woman would talk to her; and, since talking opens the heart, perhaps there might be some comfort to be found in her company. She was the only other woman in the Station.

In Kashima there are no regular calling-hours. Every one can drop in upon every one else at pleasure. Mrs Boulte put on a big *terai* hat, and walked across to the Vansuythens' house to borrow last week's *Queen*. The two compounds touched, and instead of going up the drive, she crossed through the gap in the cactus-hedge, entering the house from the back. As she passed through the dining-room, she heard, behind the *purdah* that cloaked the drawing-room door, her husband's voice, saying:

'But on my Honour! On my Soul and Honour, I tell you she doesn't care for me. She told me so last night. I would have told you then if Vansuythen hadn't been with you. If it is for *her* sake that you'll have nothing to say to me, you can make your mind easy. It's Kurrell——'

'What?' said Mrs Vansuythen, with a hysterical little laugh. 'Kurrell! Oh, it can't be! You two must have made some horrible mistake. Perhaps you—you lost your temper, or misunderstood, or something. Things *can't* be as wrong as you say.'

Mrs Vansuythen had shifted her defence to avoid the man's pleading, and was desperately trying to keep him to a side-issue.

'There must be some mistake,' she insisted, 'and it can be all put right again.'

Boulte laughed grimly.

'It can't be Captain Kurrell! He told me that he had never taken the least—the least interest in your wife, Mr Boulte. Oh, *do* listen! He said he had not. He swore he had not,' said Mrs Vansuythen.

The *purdah* rustled, and the speech was cut short by the entry of a little thin woman, with big rings round her eyes. Mrs Vansuythen stood up with a gasp.

'What was that you said?' asked Mrs Boulte. 'Never mind that man. What did Ted say to you? What did he say to you? What did he say to you?'

Mrs Vansuythen sat down helplessly on the sofa, overborne by the trouble of her questioner.

'He said—I can't remember exactly what he said—but I understood him to say—that is—— But, really, Mrs Boulte, isn't it rather a strange question?'

'*Will* you tell me what he said?' repeated Mrs Boulte. Even a tiger will fly before a bear robbed of her whelps, and Mrs Vansuythen was only an ordinarily good woman. She began in a sort of desperation: 'Well, he said that he never cared for you at all, and, of course, there was not the least reason why he should have, and—and—that was all.'

'You said he *swore* he had not cared for me. Was that true?'

'Yes,' said Mrs Vansuythen very softly.

Mrs Boulte wavered for an instant where she stood, and then fell forward fainting.

'What did I tell you?' said Boulte, as though the conversation had been unbroken. 'You can see for yourself. She cares for *him*.' The light began to break into his dull mind, and he went on: 'And he—what was *he* saying to you?'

But Mrs Vansuythen, with no heart for explanations or impassioned protestations, was kneeling over Mrs Boulte.

'Oh, you brute!' she cried. 'Are *all* men like this? Help me to get her into my room—and her face is cut against the table. Oh, *will* you be quiet, and help me to carry her? I hate you, and I hate Captain Kurrell. Lift her up carefully, and now—go! Go away!'

Boulte carried his wife into Mrs Vansuythen's bedroom, and departed, impenitent and burning with jealousy. Kurrell had been making love to Mrs Vansuythen—would do Vansuythen as great a wrong as he had done Boulte, who caught himself considering whether Mrs Vansuythen would faint if she discovered that the man she loved had forsworn her.

In the middle of these meditations, Kurrell came cantering along the road and pulled up with a cheery 'Good mornin'. Been mashing Mrs Vansuythen as usual, eh? Bad thing for a sober, married man, that. What will Mrs Boulte say?'

Boulte raised his head and said slowly: 'Oh, you liar!' Kurrell's face changed. 'What's that?' he asked quickly.

'Nothing much,' said Boulte. 'Has my wife told you that you two are free to go off whenever you please? She has been good enough to explain the situation to me. You've been a true friend to me, Kurrell—old man—haven't you?'

Kurrell groaned, and tried to frame some sort of idiotic sentence about being willing to give 'satisfaction.' But his interest in the woman was dead, had died out in the Rains, and, mentally, he was abusing her for her amazing indiscretion. It would have been so easy to have broken off the thing gently and by degrees, and now he was saddled with—— Boulte's voice recalled him.

'I don't think I should get any satisfaction from killing you, and I'm pretty sure you'd get none from killing me.'

Then in a querulous tone, ludicrously disproportioned to his wrongs, Boulte added:

'Seems rather a pity that you haven't the decency to keep to the woman, now you've got her. You've been a true friend to *her* too, haven't you?'

Kurrell stared long and gravely. The situation was getting beyond him.

'What do you mean?' he said.

Boulte answered, more to himself than the questioner: 'My wife came over to Mrs Vansuythen's just now; and it seems you'd been telling Mrs Vansuythen that you'd never cared for Emma. I suppose you lied, as usual. What had Mrs Vansuythen to do with you, or you with her? Try to speak the truth for once in a way.'

Kurrell took the double insult without wincing, and replied by another question: 'Go on. What happened?'

'Emma fainted,' said Boulte simply. 'But, look here, what had you been saying to Mrs Vansuythen?'

Kurrell laughed. Mrs Boulte had, with unbridled tongue, made havoc of his plans; and he could at least retaliate by hurting the man in whose eyes he was humiliated and shown dishonourable.

'Saying to her? What *does* a man tell a lie like that for? I suppose I said pretty much what you've said, unless I'm a good deal mistaken.'

'I spoke the truth,' said Boulte, again more to himself than Kurrell. 'Emma told me she hated me. She has no right in me.'

'No! I suppose not. You're only her husband, y'know. And what did Mrs Vansuythen say after you had laid your disengaged heart at her feet?'

Kurrell felt almost virtuous as he put the question.

'I don't think that matters,' Boulte replied; 'and it doesn't concern you.'

'But it does! I tell you it does—' began Kurrell shamelessly.

The sentence was cut by a roar of laughter from Boulte's lips. Kurrell was silent for an instant, and then he, too, laughed—laughed long and loudly, rocking in his saddle. It was an unpleasant sound—the mirthless mirth of these men on the long white line of the Narkarra Road. There were no strangers in Kashima, or they might have thought that captivity within the Dosehri hills had driven half the European population mad. The laughter ended abruptly, and Kurrell was the first to speak.

'Well, what are you going to do?'

Boulte looked up the road, and at the hills. 'Nothing,' said he quietly. 'What's the use? It's too ghastly for anything. We must let the old life go on. I can only call you a hound and a liar, and I can't go on calling you names for ever. Besides which, I don't feel that I'm much better. We can't get out of this place. What *is* there to do?'

Kurrell looked round the rat-pit of Kashima and made no reply. The injured husband took up the wondrous tale.

'Ride on, and speak to Emma if you want to. God knows *I* don't care what you do.'

He walked forward, and left Kurrell gazing blankly after him. Kurrell did not ride on either to see Mrs Boulte or Mrs Vansuythen. He sat in his saddle and thought, while his pony grazed by the roadside.

The whir of approaching wheels roused him. Mrs Vansuythen was driving home Mrs Boulte, white and wan, with a cut on her forehead.

'Stop, please,' said Mrs Boulte. 'I want to speak to Ted.'

Mrs Vansuythen obeyed, but as Mrs Boulte leaned forward, putting her hand upon the splash-board of the dog-cart, Kurrell spoke.

'I've seen your husband, Mrs Boulte.'

There was no necessity for any further explanation. The man's eyes were fixed, not upon Mrs Boulte, but her companion. Mrs Boulte saw the look.

'Speak to him!' she pleaded, turning to the woman at her side. 'Oh, speak to him! Tell him what you told me just now. Tell him you hate him! Tell him you hate him!'

She bent forward and wept bitterly, while the *sais*, impassive, went forward to hold the horse. Mrs Vansuythen turned scarlet and dropped the reins. She wished to be no party to such unholy explanations.

'I've nothing to do with it,' she began coldly; but Mrs Boulte's sobs overcame her, and she addressed herself to the man. 'I don't know what I am to say, Captain Kurrell. I don't know what I can tell you. I think you've—you've behaved abominably, and she has cut her forehead terribly against the table.'

'It doesn't hurt. It isn't anything,' said Mrs Boulte feebly. '*That* doesn't matter. Tell him what you told me. Say you don't care for him. Oh, Ted, *won't* you believe her?'

'Mrs Boulte has made me understand that you were—that you were fond of her once upon a time,' went on Mrs Vansuythen.

'Well!' said Kurrell brutally. 'It seems to me that Mrs Boulte had better be fond of her own husband first.'

'Stop!' said Mrs Vansuythen. 'Hear me first. I don't care—I don't want to know anything about you and Mrs Boulte; but I want *you* to know that I hate you, that I think you are a cur, and that I'll never, *never* speak to you again. Oh, I don't dare to say what I think of you, you—man!'

'I want to speak to Ted,' moaned Mrs Boulte, but the dog-cart rattled on, and Kurrell was left on the road, shamed, and boiling with wrath against Mrs Boulte.

He waited till Mrs Vansuythen was driving back to her own house, and, she being freed from the embarrassment of Mrs Boulte's presence, learned for the second time her opinion of himself and his actions.

In the evenings it was the wont of all Kashima to meet at the platform on the Narkarra Road, to drink tea and discuss the trivialities of the day. Major Vansuythen and his wife found themselves alone at the gathering-place for almost the first time in their remembrance; and the cheery Major, in the teeth of his wife's remarkably reasonable suggestion that the rest of the Station might be sick, insisted upon driving round to the two bungalows and unearthing the population.

'Sitting in the twilight!' said he, with great indignation, to the Boultes. 'That'll never do! Hang it all, we're one family here! You *must* come out, and so must Kurrell. I'll make him bring his banjo.'

So great is the power of honest simplicity and a good digestion over guilty consciences that all Kashima did turn out, even down to the banjo; and the Major embraced the company in one expansive grin. As he grinned, Mrs Vansuythen raised her eyes for an instant and looked at all Kashima. Her meaning was clear. Major Vansuythen would never know anything. He was to be the outsider in that happy family whose cage was the Dosehri hills.

'You're singing villainously out of tune, Kurrell,' said the Major truthfully. 'Pass me that banjo.'

And he sang in excruciating wise till the stars came out and all Kashima went to dinner.

*

That was the beginning of the New Life of Kashima—the life that Mrs Boulte made when her tongue was loosened in the twilight.

Mrs Vansuythen has never told the Major; and since he insists upon keeping up a burdensome geniality, she has been compelled to break her vow of not speaking to Kurrell. This speech, which must of necessity preserve the semblance of politeness and interest, serves admirably to keep alight the flame of jealousy and dull hatred in Boulte's bosom, as it awakens the same passions in his wife's heart. Mrs Boulte hates Mrs Vansuythen because she has taken Ted from her, and, in some curious fashion, hates her because Mrs Vansuythen—and here the wife's eyes see far more clearly than the husband's—detests Ted. And Ted—that gallant captain and honourable man—knows now that it is possible to hate a woman once loved, to the verge of wishing to silence her for ever with blows. Above all is he shocked that Mrs Boulte cannot see the error of her ways.

Boulte and he go out tiger-shooting together in all friendship. Boulte has put their relationship on a most satisfactory footing.

'You're a blackguard,' he says to Kurrell, 'and I've lost any self-respect I may ever have had; but when you're with me, I can feel certain that you are not with Mrs Vansuythen, or making Emma miserable.'

Kurrell endures anything that Boulte may say to him. Sometimes they are away for three days together, and then the Major insists upon his wife going over to sit with Mrs Boulte; although Mrs Vansuythen has repeatedly declared that she prefers her husband's company to any in the world. From the way in which she clings to him, she would certainly seem to be speaking the truth.

But of course, as the Major says, 'in a little Station we must all be friendly.'

Wee Willie Winkie, 1888*

* *Week's News*, 1888.

The Man who would be King

'Brother to a Prince and fellow to a beggar if he be found worthy.'

THE LAW, AS QUOTED, lays down a fair conduct of life, and one not easy to follow. I have been fellow to a beggar again and again under circumstances which prevented either of us finding out whether the other was worthy. I have still to be brother to a Prince, though I once came near to kinship with what might have been a veritable King, and was promised the reversion of a Kingdom—army, law-courts, revenue, and policy all complete. But, today, I greatly fear that my King is dead, and if I want a crown I must go hunt it for myself.

The beginning of everything was in a railway train upon the road to Mhow from Ajmir. There had been a Deficit in the Budget, which necessitated travelling, not Second-class, which is only half as dear as First-class, but by Intermediate, which is very awful indeed. There are no cushions in the Intermediate class, and the population are either Intermediate, which is Eurasian, or Native, which for a long night journey is nasty, or Loafer, which is amusing though intoxicated. Intermediates do not buy from refreshment-rooms. They carry their food in bundles and pots, and buy sweets from the native sweetmeat-sellers, and drink the roadside water. That is why in the hot weather Intermediates are taken out of the carriages dead, and in all weathers are most properly looked down upon.

My particular Intermediate happened to be empty till I reached Nasirabad, when a big black-browed gentleman in shirt-sleeves entered, and, following the custom of Intermediates, passed the time of day. He was a wanderer and a vagabond like myself, but with an educated taste for whisky. He told tales of things he had seen and done, of out-of-the-way corners of the Empire into which he had penetrated, and of adventures in which he risked his life for a few days' food.

'If India was filled with men like you and me, not knowing more than the crows where they'd get their next day's rations, it isn't seventy millions of revenue the land would be paying—it's seven hundred millions,' said he; and as I looked at his mouth and chin I was disposed to agree with him.

We talked politics—the politics of Loaferdom, that sees things

from the underside where the lath and plaster is not smoothed off—
and we talked postal arrangements because my friend wanted to
send a telegram back from the next station to Ajmir, the turning-
off place from the Bombay to the Mhow line as you travel westward. My friend had no money beyond eight annas, which he
wanted for dinner, and I had no money at all, owing to the hitch in
the Budget before mentioned. Further, I was going into a wilderness where, though I should resume touch with the Treasury, there
were no telegraph offices. I was, therefore, unable to help him in
any way.

'We might threaten a Station-master, and make him send a wire
on tick,' said my friend, 'but that'd mean inquiries for you and for
me, and I've got my hands full these days. Did you say you are
travelling back along this line within any days?'

'Within ten,' I said.

'Can't you make it eight?' said he. 'Mine is rather urgent business.'

'I can send your telegram within ten days if that will serve you,'
I said.

'I couldn't trust the wire to fetch him, now I think of it. It's this
way. He leaves Delhi on the 23rd for Bombay. That means he'll be
running through Ajmir about the night of the 23rd.'

'But I'm going into the Indian Desert,' I explained.

'Well and good,' said he. 'You'll be changing at Marwar Junction
to get into Jodhpore territory—you must do that—and he'll be
coming through Marwar Junction in the early morning of the 24th
by the Bombay Mail. Can you be at Marwar Junction on that time?
'Twon't be inconveniencing you because I know that there's
precious few pickings to be got out of those Central India States—
even though you pretend to be correspondent of the *Backwoodsman*.'

'Have you ever tried that trick?' I asked.

'Again and again, but the Residents find you out, and then you
get escorted to the border before you've time to get your knife into
them. But about my friend here. I *must* give him a word o' mouth
to tell him what's come to me or else he won't know where to go.
I would take it more than kind of you if you was to come out of
Central India in time to catch him at Marwar Junction, and say to
him: "He has gone South for the week." He'll know what that
means. He's a big man with a red beard, and a great swell he is.
You'll find him sleeping like a gentleman with all his luggage
round him in a second-class compartment. But don't you be afraid.

Slip down the window, and say: "He has gone South for the week,"
and he'll tumble. It's only cutting your time of stay in those parts
by two days. I ask you as a stranger—going to the West,' he said
with emphasis.

'Where have *you* come from?' said I.

'From the East,' said he, 'and I am hoping that you will give him
the message on the Square—for the sake of my Mother as well as
your own.'

Englishmen are not usually softened by appeals to the memory
of their mothers, but for certain reasons, which will be fully
apparent, I saw fit to agree.

'It's more than a little matter,' said he, 'and that's why I asked
you to do it—and now I know that I can depend on you doing it.
A second-class carriage at Marwar Junction, and a red-haired man
asleep in it. You'll be sure to remember. I get out at the next station, and I must hold on there till he comes or sends me what I
want.'

'I'll give the message if I catch him,' I said, 'and for the sake of
your Mother as well as mine I'll give you a word of advice. Don't
try to run the Central India States just now as the correspondent of
the *Backwoodsman*. There's a real one knocking about there, and it
might lead to trouble.'

'Thank you,' said he simply, 'and when will the swine be gone?
I can't starve because he's ruining my work. I wanted to get hold of
the Degumber Rajah down here about his father's widow, and give
him a jump.'

'What did he do to his father's widow, then?'

'Filled her up with red pepper and slippered her to death as she
hung from a beam. I found that out myself, and I'm the only man
that would dare going into the State to get hush-money for it. They'll
try to poison me, same as they did in Chortumna when I went on
the loot there. But you'll give the man at Marwar Junction my
message?'

He got out at a little roadside station, and I reflected. I had
heard, more than once, of men personating correspondents of newspapers and bleeding small Native States with threats of exposure,
but I had never met any of the caste before. They lead a hard life,
and generally die with great suddenness. The Native States have a
wholesome horror of English newspapers which may throw light on
their peculiar methods of government, and do their best to choke
correspondents with champagne, or drive them out of their mind
with four-in-hand barouches. They do not understand that nobody

cares a straw for the internal administration of Native States so
long as oppression and crime are kept within decent limits, and the
ruler is not drugged, drunk, or diseased from one end of the year to
the other. They are the dark places of the earth, full of unimagin-
able cruelty, touching the Railway and the Telegraph on one side,
and, on the other, the days of Harun-al-Raschid. When I left the
train I did business with divers Kings, and in eight days passed
through many changes of life. Sometimes I wore dress-clothes and
consorted with Princes and Politicals, drinking from crystal and
eating from silver. Sometimes I lay out upon the ground and de-
voured what I could get, from a plate made of leaves, and drank the
running water, and slept under the same rug as my servant. It was
all in the day's work.

Then I headed for the Great Indian Desert upon the proper date,
as I had promised, and the night mail set me down at Marwar
Junction, where a funny, little, happy-go-lucky, native-managed
railway runs to Jodhpore. The Bombay Mail from Delhi makes a
short halt at Marwar. She arrived as I got in, and I had just time to
hurry to her platform and go down the carriages. There was only
one second-class on the train. I slipped the window and looked
down upon a flaming red beard, half covered by a railway rug. That
was my man, fast asleep, and I dug him gently in the ribs. He woke
with a grunt, and I saw his face in the light of the lamps. It was a
great and shining face.

'Tickets again?' said he.

'No,' said I. 'I am to tell you that he has gone South for the week.
He has gone South for the week!'

The train had begun to move out. The red man rubbed his eyes.
'He has gone South for the week,' he repeated. 'Now that's just like
his impidence. Did he say that I was to give you anything? Cause
I won't.'

'He didn't,' I said, and dropped away, and watched the red lights
die out in the dark. It was horribly cold because the wind was blowing off the sands. I climbed into my own train—not an Intermediate
carriage this time—and went to sleep.

If the man with the beard had given me a rupee I should have
kept it as a memento of a rather curious affair. But the conscious-
ness of having done my duty was my only reward.

Later on I reflected that two gentlemen like my friends could not
do any good if they forgathered and personated correspondents of
newspapers, and might, if they blackmailed one of the little rat-
trap states of Central India or Southern Rajputana, get themselves

into serious difficulties. I therefore took some trouble to describe them as accurately as I could remember to people who would be interested in deporting them; and succeeded, so I was later informed, in having them headed back from the Degumber borders.

Then I became respectable, and returned to an office where there were no Kings and no incidents outside the daily manufacture of a newspaper. A newspaper office seems to attract every conceivable sort of person, to the prejudice of discipline. Zenana-mission ladies arrive, and beg that the Editor will instantly abandon all his duties to describe a Christian prize-giving in a back-slum of a perfectly inaccessible village; Colonels who have been overpassed for command sit down and sketch the outline of a series of ten, twelve, or twenty-four leading articles on Seniority *versus* Selection; Missionaries wish to know why they have not been permitted to escape from their regular vehicles of abuse and swear at a brother-missionary under special patronage of the editorial We; stranded theatrical companies troop up to explain that they cannot pay for their advertisements, but on their return from New Zealand or Tahiti will do so with interest; inventors of patent punkah-pulling machines, carriage couplings, and unbreakable swords and axle-trees, call with specifications in their pockets and hours at their disposal; tea-companies enter and elaborate their prospectuses with the office pens; secretaries of ball-committees clamour to have the glories of their last dance more fully described; strange ladies rustle in and say, 'I want a hundred lady's cards printed *at once*, please,' which is manifestly part of an Editor's duty; and every dissolute ruffian that ever tramped the Grand Trunk Road makes it his business to ask for employment as a proof-reader. And, all the time, the telephone-bell is ringing madly, and Kings are being killed on the Continent, and Empires are saying, 'You're another,' and Mister Gladstone is calling down brimstone upon the British Dominions, and the little black copy-boys are whining, '*kaa-pi chay-ha-yeh*' [copy wanted] like tired bees, and most of the paper is as blank as Modred's shield.

But that is the amusing part of the year. There are six other months when none ever comes to call, and the thermometer walks inch by inch up to the top of the glass, and the office is darkened to just above reading-light, and the press-machines are red-hot of touch, and nobody writes anything but accounts of amusements in the Hill-stations or obituary notices. Then the telephone becomes a tinkling terror, because it tells you of the sudden deaths of men and women that you knew intimately, and the prickly-heat covers you with a garment, and you sit down and write: 'A slight increase of

sickness is reported from the Khuda Janta Khan District. The outbreak is purely sporadic in its nature, and, thanks to the energetic
efforts of the District authorities, is now almost at an end. It is,
however, with deep regret we record the death, etc.'

Then the sickness really breaks out, and the less recording and
reporting the better for the peace of the subscribers. But the
Empires and the Kings continue to divert themselves as selfishly as
before, and the Foreman thinks that a daily paper really ought to
come out once in twenty-four hours, and all the people at the Hill-
stations in the middle of their amusements say: 'Good gracious!
Why can't the paper be sparkling? I'm sure there's plenty going on
up here.'

That is the dark half of the moon, and, as the advertisements
say, 'must be experienced to be appreciated.'

It was in that season, and a remarkably evil season, that the
paper began running the last issue of the week on Saturday night,
which is to say Sunday morning, after the custom of a London
paper. This was a great convenience, for immediately after the
paper was put to bed, the dawn would lower the thermometer from
96° to almost 84° for half an hour, and in that chill—you have no
idea how cold is 84° on the grass until you begin to pray for it—a
very tired man could get off to sleep ere the heat roused him.

One Saturday night it was my pleasant duty to put the paper to
bed alone. A King or a courtier or courtesan or a Community was
going to die or get a new Constitution, or do something that was
important on the other side of the world, and the paper was to be
held open till the latest possible minute in order to catch the telegram.

It was a pitchy black night, as stifling as a June night can be, and
the *loo*, the red-hot wind from the westward, was booming among
the tinder-dry trees and pretending that the rain was on its heels.
Now and again a spot of almost boiling water would fall on the dust
with the flop of a frog, but all our weary world knew that was only
pretence. It was a shade cooler in the press-room than the office, so
I sat there, while the type ticked and clicked, and the night-jars
hooted at the windows, and the all but naked compositors wiped
the sweat from their foreheads, and called for water. The thing that
was keeping us back, whatever it was, would not come off, though
the *loo* dropped and the last type was set, and the whole round earth
stood still in the choking heat, with its finger on its lip, to wait the
event. I drowsed, and wondered whether the telegraph was a
blessing, and whether this dying man, or struggling people, might

be aware of the inconvenience the delay was causing. There was no special reason beyond the heat and worry to make tension, but, as the clock-hands crept up to three o'clock, and the machines spun their fly-wheels two or three times to see that all was in order before I said the word that would set them off, I could have shrieked aloud.

Then the roar and rattle of the wheels shivered the quiet into little bits. I rose to go away, but two men in white clothes stood in front of me. The first one said: 'It's him!' The second said: 'So it is!' And they both laughed almost as loudly as the machinery roared, and mopped their foreheads. 'We seed there was a light burning across the road, and we were sleeping in that ditch there for coolness, and I said to my friend here, "The Office is open. Let's come along and speak to him as turned us back from the Degumber State," ' said the smaller of the two. He was the man I had met in the Mhow train, and his fellow was the red-haired man of Marwar Junction. There was no mistaking the eyebrows of the one or the beard of the other.

I was not pleased, because I wished to go to sleep, not to squabble with loafers. 'What do you want?' I asked.

'Half an hour's talk with you, cool and comfortable, in the office,' said the red-bearded man. 'We'd *like* some drink—the Contrack doesn't begin yet, Peachey, so you needn't look—but what we really want is advice. We don't want money. We ask you as a favour, because we found out you did us a bad turn about Degumber State.'

I led from the press-room to the stifling office with the maps on the walls, and the red-haired man rubbed his hands. 'That's something like,' said he. 'This was the proper shop to come to. Now, sir, let me introduce to you Brother Peachey Carnehan, that's him, and Brother Daniel Dravot, that is *me*, and the less said about our professions the better, for we have been most things in our time. Soldier, sailor, compositor, photographer, proof-reader, street-preacher, *and* correspondent of the *Backwoodsman* when we thought the paper wanted one. Carnehan is sober, and so am I. Look at us first, and see that's sure. It will save you cutting into my talk. We'll take one of your cigars apiece, and you shall see us light up.'

I watched the test. The men were absolutely sober, so I gave them each a tepid whisky and soda.

'Well *and* good,' said Carnehan of the eyebrows, wiping the froth from his moustache. 'Let *me* talk now, Dan. We have been all over

India, mostly on foot. We have been boiler-fitters, engine-drivers, petty contractors, and all that, and we have decided that India isn't big enough for such as us.'

They certainly were too big for the office. Dravot's beard seemed to fill half the room and Carnehan's shoulders the other half, as they sat on the big table. Carnehan continued: 'The country isn't half worked out because they that governs it won't let you touch it. They spend all their blessed time in governing it and you can't lift a spade, nor chip a rock, nor look for oil, nor anything like that, without all the Government saying, "Leave it alone, and let us govern." Therefore, such *as* it is, we will let it alone, and go away to some other place where a man isn't crowded and can come to his own. We are not little men, and there is nothing that we are afraid of except Drink, and we have signed a Contrack on that. *Therefore*, we are going away to be Kings.'

'Kings in our own right,' muttered Dravot.

'Yes, of course,' I said. 'You've been tramping in the sun, and it's a very warm night, and hadn't you better sleep over the notion? Come tomorrow.'

'Neither drunk nor sunstruck,' said Dravot. 'We have slept over the notion half a year, and require to see Books and Atlases, and we have decided that there is only one place now in the world that two strong men can Sar-a-*whack*. They call it Kafiristan. By my reckoning it's the top right-hand corner of Afghanistan, not more than three hundred miles from Peshawur. They have two-and-thirty heathen idols there, and we'll be the thirty-third and fourth. It's a mountaineous country, and the women of those parts are very beautiful.'

'But that is provided against in the Contrack,' said Carnehan. 'Neither Woman nor Liqu-or, Daniel.'

'And that's all we know, except that no one has gone there, and they fight; and in any place where they fight, a man who knows how to drill men can always be a King. We shall go to those parts and say to any King we find—"D'you want to vanquish your foes?" and we will show him how to drill men; for that we know better than anything else. Then we will subvert that King and seize his Throne and establish a Dy-nasty.'

'You'll be cut to pieces before you're fifty miles across the Border,' I said. 'You have to travel through Afghanistan to get to that country. It's one mass of mountains and peaks and glaciers, and no Englishman has been through it. The people are utter brutes, and even if you reached them you couldn't do anything.'

'That's more like,' said Carnehan. 'If you could think us a little more mad we would be more pleased. We have come to you to know about this country, to read a book about it, and to be shown maps. We want you to tell us that we are fools and to show us your books.' He turned to the bookcases.

'Are you at all in earnest?' I said.

'A little,' said Dravot sweetly. 'As big a map as you have got, even if it's all blank where Kafiristan is, and any books you've got. We can read, though we aren't very educated.'

I uncased the big thirty-two-miles-to-the-inch map of India, and two smaller Frontier maps, hauled down volume INF-KAN of the *Encyclopaedia Britannica*, and the men consulted them.

'See here!' said Dravot, his thumb on the map. 'Up to Jagdallak, Peachey and me know the road. We was there with Roberts' Army. We'll have to turn off to the right at Jagdallak through Laghman territory. Then we get among the hills—fourteen thousand feet— fifteen thousand—it will be cold work there, but it don't look very far on the map.'

I handed him Wood on the *Sources of the Oxus*. Carnehan was deep in the *Encyclopœdia*.

'They're a mixed lot,' said Dravot reflectively; 'and it won't help us to know the names of their tribes. The more tribes the more they'll fight, and the better for us. From Jagdallak to Ashang— H'mm!'

'But all the information about the country is as sketchy and in- accurate as can be,' I protested. 'No one knows anything about it really. Here's the file of the *United Services' Institute*. Read what Bellew says.'

'Blow Bellew!' said Carnehan. 'Dan, they're a stinkin' lot of heathens, but this book here says they think they're related to us English.'

I smoked while the men pored over Raverty, Wood, the maps, and the *Encyclopaedia*.

'There is no use your waiting,' said Dravot politely. 'It's about four o'clock now. We'll go before six o'clock if you want to sleep, and we won't steal any of the papers. Don't you sit up. We're two harmless lunatics, and if you come tomorrow evening down to the Serai we'll say good-bye to you.'

'You *are* two fools,' I answered. 'You'll be turned back at the Frontier or cut up the minute you set foot in Afghanistan. Do you want any money or a recommendation down-country? I can help you to the chance of work next week.'

'Next week we shall be hard at work ourselves, thank you,' said Dravot. 'It isn't so easy being a King as it looks. When we've got our Kingdom in going order we'll let you know, and you can come up and help us to govern it.'

'Would two lunatics make a Contrack like that?' said Carnehan, with subdued pride, showing me a greasy half-sheet of notepaper on which was written the following. I copied it, then and there, as a curiosity:

This Contract between me and you persuing witnesseth in the name of God—Amen and so forth.
   (One)   That me and you will settle this matter together; i.e. to be Kings of Kafiristan.
   (Two)   That you and me will not, while this matter is being settled, look at any Liquor, nor any Woman black, white, or brown, so as to get mixed up with one or the other harmful.
   (Three) That we conduct ourselves with Dignity and Discretion, and if one of us gets into trouble the other will stay by him.
      Signed by you and me this day.
         Peachey Taliaferro Carnehan.
         Daniel Dravot.
         Both Gentlemen at Large.

'There was no need for the last article,' said Carnehan, blushing modestly; 'but it looks regular. Now you know the sort of men that loafers are—we *are* loafers, Dan, until we get out of India—and *do* you think that we would sign a Contrack like that unless we was in earnest? We have kept away from the two things that make life worth having.'

'You won't enjoy your lives much longer if you are going to try this idiotic adventure. Don't set the office on fire,' I said, 'and go away before nine o'clock.'

I left them still poring over the maps and making notes on the back of the 'Contrack.' 'Be sure to come down to the Serai to-morrow,' were their parting words.

The Kumharsen Serai is the great four-square sink of humanity where the strings of camels and horses from the North load and un-load. All the nationalities of Central Asia may be found there, and most of the folk of India proper. Balkh and Bokhara there meet Bengal and Bombay, and try to draw eye-teeth. You can buy ponies, turquoises, Persian pussy-cats, and saddle-bags, fat-tailed sheep, and musk in the Kumharsen Serai, and get many strange things for nothing. In the afternoon I went down to see whether my friends intended to keep their word or were lying there drunk.

A priest attired in fragments of ribbons and rags stalked up to me, gravely twisting a child's paper whirligig. Behind him was his servant bending under the load of a crate of mud toys. The two were loading up two camels, and the inhabitants of the Serai watched them with shrieks of laughter.

'The priest is mad,' said a horse-dealer to me. 'He is going up to Kabul to sell toys to the Amir. He will either be raised to honour or have his head cut off. He came in here this morning and has been behaving madly ever since.'

'The witless are under the protection of God,' stammered a flat-cheeked Uzbeg in broken Hindi. 'They foretell future events.'

'Would they could have foretold that my caravan would have been cut up by the Shinwaris almost within shadow of the Pass!' grunted the Yusufzai agent of a Rajputana trading-house whose goods had been diverted into the hands of other robbers just across the Border, and whose misfortunes were the laughing-stock of the bazar. 'Ohé, priest, whence come you and whither do you go?'

'From Roum have I come,' shouted the priest, waving his whirligig; 'from Roum, blown by the breath of a hundred devils across the sea! O thieves, robbers, liars, the blessing of Pir Khan on pigs, dogs, and perjurers! Who will take the Protected of God to the North to sell charms that are never still to the Amir? The camels shall not gall, the sons shall not fall sick, and the wives shall remain faithful while they are away, of the men who give me place in their caravan. Who will assist me to slipper the King of the Roos with a golden slipper with a silver heel? The protection of Pir Khan be upon his labours!' He spread out the skirts of his gaberdine and pirouetted between the lines of tethered horses.

'There starts a caravan from Peshawur to Kabul in twenty days, *Huzrut*,' said the Yusufzai trader. 'My camels go therewith. Do thou also go and bring us good luck.'

'I will go even now!' shouted the priest. 'I will depart upon my winged camels, and be at Peshawur in a day! Ho! Hazar Mir Khan,' he yelled to his servant, 'drive out the camels, but let me first mount my own.'

He leaped on the back of his beast as it knelt, and, turning round to me, cried: 'Come thou also, Sahib, a little along the road, and I will sell thee a charm—an amulet that shall make thee King of Kafiristan.'

Then the light broke upon me, and I followed the two camels out of the Serai till we reached open road and the priest halted.

'What d'you think o' that?' said he in English 'Carnehan can't talk their patter, so I've made him my servant. He makes a handsome servant. 'Tisn't for nothing that I've been knocking about the country for fourteen years. Didn't I do that talk neat? We'll hitch on to a caravan at Peshawur till we get to Jagdallak, and then we'll see if we can get donkeys for our camels, and strike into Kafiristan. Whirligigs for the Amir, oh, Lor! Put your hand under the camel-bags and tell me what you feel.'

I felt the butt of a Martini, and another and another.

'Twenty of 'em,' said Dravot placidly. 'Twenty of 'em and ammunition to correspond, under the whirligigs and the mud dolls.'

'Heaven help you if you are caught with those things!' I said. 'A Martini is worth her weight in silver among the Pathans.'

'Fifteen hundred rupees of capital—every rupee we could beg, borrow, or steal—are invested on these two camels,' said Dravot. 'We won't get caught. We're going through the Khyber with a regular caravan. Who'd touch a poor mad priest?'

'Have you got everything you want?' I asked, overcome with astonishment.

'Not yet, but we shall soon. Give us a memento of your kindness, *Brother*. You did me a service, yesterday, and that time in Marwar. Half my Kingdom shall you have, as the saying is.' I slipped a small charm compass from my watch-chain and handed it up to the priest.

'Good-bye,' said Dravot, giving me hand cautiously. 'It's the last time we'll shake hands with an Englishman these many days. Shake hands with him, Carnehan,' he cried, as the second camel passed me.

Carnehan leaned down and shook hands. Then the camels passed away along the dusty road, and I was left alone to wonder. My eye could detect no failure in the disguises. The scene in the Serai proved that they were complete to the native mind. There was just the chance, therefore, that Carnehan and Dravot would be able to wander through Afghanistan without detection. But, beyond, they would find death—certain and awful death.

Ten days later a native correspondent, giving me the news of the day from Peshawur, wound up his letter with: 'There has been much laughter here on account of a certain mad priest who is going in his estimation to sell petty gauds and insignificant trinkets which he ascribes as great charms to H.H. the Amir of Bokhara. He passed through Peshawur and associated himself to the Second Summer caravan that goes to Kabul. The merchants are pleased because through superstition they imagine that such mad fellows bring good fortune.'

The two, then, were beyond the Border. I would have prayed for them, but, that night, a real King died in Europe, and demanded an obituary notice.

*

The wheel of the world swings through the same phases again and again. Summer passed and winter thereafter, and came and passed again. The daily paper continued and I with it, and upon the third summer there fell a hot night, a night-issue, and a strained waiting for something to be telegraphed from the other side of the world, exactly as had happened before. A few great men had died in the past two years, the machines worked with more clatter, and some of the trees in the office garden were a few feet taller. But that was all the difference.

I passed over to the press-room, and went through just such a scene as I have already described. The nervous tension was stronger than it had been two years before, and I felt the heat more acutely. At three o'clock I cried, 'Print off,' and turned to go, when there crept to my chair what was left of a man. He was bent into a circle, his head was sunk between his shoulders, and he moved his feet one over the other like a bear. I could hardly see whether he walked or crawled—this rag-wrapped, whining cripple who addressed me by name, crying that he was come back. 'Can you give me a drink?' he whimpered. 'For the Lord's sake, give me a drink!'

I went back to the office, the man following with groans of pain, and I turned up the lamp.

'Don't you know me?' he gasped, dropping into a chair, and he turned his drawn face, surmounted by a shock of grey hair, to the light.

I looked at him intently. Once before had I seen eyebrows that met over the nose in an inch-broad black band, but for the life of me I could not recall where.

'I don't know you,' I said, handing him the whisky. 'What can I do for you?'

He took a gulp of the spirit raw, and shivered in spite of the suffocating heat.

'I've come back,' he repeated; 'and I was the King of Kafiristan —me and Dravot—crowned Kings we was! In this office we settled

it—you setting there and giving us the books. I am Peachey—
Peachey Taliaferro Carnehan, and you've been setting here ever
since—oh, Lord!'

I was more than a little astonished, and expressed my feelings
accordingly.

'It's true,' said Carnehan, with a dry cackle, nursing his feet,
which were wrapped in rags. 'True as gospel. Kings we were, with
crowns upon our heads—me and Dravot—poor Dan—oh, poor,
poor Dan, that would never take advice, not though I begged of
him!'

'Take the whisky,' I said, 'and take your own time. Tell me all
you can recollect of everything from beginning to end. You got
across the Border on your camels, Dravot dressed as a mad priest
and you his servant. Do you remember that?'

'I ain't mad—yet, but I shall be that way soon. Of course I
remember. Keep looking at me, or maybe my words will go all to
pieces. Keep looking at me in my eyes and don't say anything.'

I leaned forward and looked into his face as steadily as I could.
He dropped one hand upon the table and I grasped it by the wrist.
It was twisted like a bird's claw, and upon the back was a ragged
red diamond-shaped scar.

'No, don't look there. Look at *me*,' said Carnehan. 'That comes
afterwards, but for the Lord's sake don't distrack me. We left with
that caravan, me and Dravot playing all sorts of antics to amuse
the people we were with. Dravot used to make us laugh in the evenings when all the people was cooking their dinners—cooking their
dinners, and . . . what did they do then? They lit little fires with
sparks that went into Dravot's beard, and we all laughed—fit to die.
Little red fires they was, going into Dravot's big red beard—so
funny.' His eyes left mine and he smiled foolishly.

'You went as far as Jagdallak with that caravan,' I said at a
venture, 'after you had lit those fires. To Jagdallak where you
turned off to try to get into Kafiristan.'

'No, we didn't neither. What are you talking about? We turned
off before Jagdallak, because we heard the roads was good. But
they wasn't good enough for our two camels—mine and Dravot's.
When we left the caravan, Dravot took off all his clothes and mine
too, and said we would be heathen, because the Kafirs didn't allow
Mohammedans to talk to them. So we dressed betwixt and between,
and such a sight as Daniel Dravot I never saw yet nor expect to see
again. He burned half his beard, and slung a sheep-skin over his
shoulder, and shaved his head into patterns. He shaved mine, too,

and made me wear outrageous things to look like a heathen. That
was in a most mountaineous country, and our camels couldn't go
along any more because of the mountains. They were tall and black,
and coming home I saw them fight like wild goats—there are lots of
goats in Kafiristan. And these mountains, they never keep still, no
more than the goats. Always fighting they are, and don't let you
sleep at night.'

'Take some more whisky,' I said very slowly. 'What did you and
Daniel Dravot do when the camels could go no farther because of the
rough roads that led into Kafiristan?'

'What did which do? There was a party called Peachey Taliaferro
Carnehan that was with Dravot. Shall I tell you about him? He
died out there in the cold. Slap from the bridge fell old Peachey,
turning and twisting in the air like a penny whirligig that you can
sell to the Amir. No; they was two for three-ha'pence, those
whirligigs, or I am much mistaken and woeful sore. . . . And then
these camels were no use, and Peachey said to Dravot—"For the
Lord's sake let's get out of this before our heads are chopped off,"
and with that they killed the camels all among the mountains, not
having anything in particular to eat, but first they took off the
boxes with the guns and the ammunition, till two men came along
driving four mules. Dravot up and dances in front of them, singing:
"Sell me four mules." Says the first man: "If you are rich enough to
buy, you are rich enough to rob"; but before ever he could put his
hand to his knife, Dravot breaks his neck over his knee, and the
other party runs away. So Carnehan loaded the mules with the
rifles that was taken off the camels, and together we starts forward
into those bitter cold mountaineous parts, and never a road broader
than the back of your hand.'

He paused for a moment, while I asked him if he could remember
the nature of the country through which he had journeyed.

'I am telling you as straight as I can, but my head isn't as good
as it might be. They drove nails through it to make me hear better
how Dravot died. The country was mountaineous, and the mules
were most contrary, and the inhabitants was dispersed and solitary.
They went up and up, and down and down, and that other party,
Carnehan, was imploring of Dravot not to sing and whistle so loud,
for fear of bringing down the tremenjus avalanches. But Dravot
says that if a King couldn't sing it wasn't worth being King, and
whacked the mules over the rump, and never took no heed for ten
cold days. We came to a big level valley all among the mountains,
and the mules were near dead, so we killed them, not having any-

thing in special for them or us to eat. We sat upon the boxes, and played odd and even with the cartridges that was jolted out.

'Then ten men with bows and arrows ran down that valley, chasing twenty men with bows and arrows, and the row was tremenjus. They was fair men—fairer than you or me—with yellow hair and remarkable well built. Says Dravot, unpacking the guns: "This is the beginning of the business. We'll fight for the ten men," and with that he fires two rifles at the twenty men, and drops one of them at two hundred yards from the rock where he was sitting. The other men began to run, but Carnehan and Dravot sits on the boxes picking them off at all ranges, up and down the valley. Then we goes up to the ten men that had run across the snow too, and they fires a footy little arrow at us. Dravot he shoots above their heads and they all falls down flat. Then he walks over them and kicks them, and then he lifts them up and shakes hands all round to make them friendly like. He calls them and gives them the boxes to carry, and waves his hand for all the world as though he was King already. They takes the boxes and him across the valley and up the hill into a pine wood on the top, where there was half-a-dozen big stone idols. Dravot he goes to the biggest—a fellow they call Imbra—and lays a rifle and a cartridge at his feet, rubbing his nose respectful with his own nose, patting him on the head, and saluting in front of it. He turns round to the men and nods his head, and says: "That's all right. I'm in the know too, and all these old jim-jams are my friends." Then he opens his mouth and points down it, and when the first man brings him food, he says: "No"; and when the second man brings him food, he says: "No"; but when one of the old priests and the boss of the village brings him food, he says: "Yes," very haughty, and eats it slow. That was how we came to our first village, without any trouble, just as though we had tumbled from the skies. But we tumbled from one of those damned rope-bridges, you see, and—you couldn't expect a man to laugh much after that?'

'Take some more whisky and go on,' I said. 'That was the first village you came into. How did you get to be King?'

'I wasn't King,' said Carnehan. 'Dravot he was the King, and a handsome man he looked with the gold crown on his head and all. Him and the other party stayed in that village, and every morning Dravot sat by the side of old Imbra, and the people came and worshipped. That was Dravot's order. Then a lot of men came into the valley, and Carnehan and Dravot picks them off with the rifles before they knew where they was, and runs down into the valley and up again the other side and finds another village, same as the first one, and the people all falls down flat on their faces, and Dravot says: "Now what is the trouble between you two villages?" and the people points to a woman, as fair as you or me, that was carried off, and Dravot takes her back to the first village and counts up the dead—eight there was. For each dead man Dravot pours a little milk on the ground and waves his arms like a whirligig, and "That's all right," says he. Then he and Carnehan takes the big boss of each village by the arm and walks them down into the valley, and shows them how to scratch a line with a spear right down the valley, and gives each a sod of turf from both sides of the line. Then all the people comes down and shouts like the devil and all, and Dravot says: "Go and dig the land, and be fruitful and multiply," which they did, though they didn't understand. Then we asks the names of things in their lingo—bread and water and fire and idols and such, and Dravot leads the priest of each village up to the idol, and says he must sit there and judge the people, and if anything goes wrong he is to be shot.

'Next week they was all turning up the land in the valley as quiet as bees and much prettier, and the priests heard all the complaints and told Dravot in dumb show what it was about. "That's just the beginning," says Dravot. "They think we're Gods." He and Carnehan picks out twenty good men and shows them how to click off a rifle, and form fours, and advance in line, and they was very pleased to do so, and clever to see the hang of it. Then he takes out his pipe and his baccy-pouch and leaves one at one village, and one at the other, and off we two goes to see what was to be done in the next valley. That was all rock, and there was a little village there, and Carnehan says: "Send 'em to the old valley to plant," and takes 'em there, and gives 'em some land that wasn't took before. They were a poor lot, and we blooded 'em with a kid before letting 'em into the new Kingdom. That was to impress the people, and then they settled down quiet, and Carhehan went back to Dravot, who had got into another valley, all snow and ice and most mountaineous. There was no people there and the Army got afraid, so Dravot shoots one of them, and goes on till he finds some people in a village, and the Army explains that unless the people wants to be killed they had better not shoot their little matchlocks; for they had matchlocks. We makes friends with the priest, and I stays there alone with two of the Army, teaching the men how to drill, and a thundering big Chief comes across the snow with kettle-drums and horns twanging, because he heard there was a new God kicking

about. Carnehan sights for the brown of the men half a mile across
the snow and wings one of them. Then he sends a message to the
chief that, unless he wished to be killed, he must come and shake
hands with me and leave his arms behind. The Chief comes alone
first, and Carnehan shakes hands with him and whirls his arms
about, same as Dravot used, and very much surprised that Chief
was, and strokes my eyebrows. Then Carhehan goes along to the
Chief, and asks him in dumb show if he had an enemy he hated. "I
have," says the Chief. So Carnehan weeds out the pick of his men,
and sets the two of the Army to show them drill, and at the end of
two weeks the men can manoeuvre about as well as Volunteers. So
he marches with the Chief to a great big plain on the top of a mountain, and the Chief's men rushes into a village and takes it; we
three Martinis firing into the brown of the enemy. So we took that
village too, and I gives the Chief a rag from my coat and says,
"Occupy till I come"; which was scriptural. By way of a reminder,
when me and the Army was eighteen hundred yards away, I drops
a bullet near him standing on the snow, and all the people falls flat
on their faces. Then I sends a letter to Dravot wherever he be by
land or by sea.'

At the risk of throwing the creature out of train I interrupted:
'How could you write a letter up yonder?'

'The letter?—Oh!—The letter! Keep looking at me between the
eyes, please. It was a string-talk letter, that we'd learned the way of
it from a blind beggar in the Punjab.'

I remembered that there had once come to the office a blind man
with a knotted twig and a piece of string which he wound round the
twig according to some cipher of his own. He could, after the lapse
of days or weeks, repeat the sentence which he had reeled up. He
had reduced the alphabet to eleven primitive sounds, and tried to
teach me his method, but I could not understand.

'I sent that letter to Dravot,' said Carnehan; 'and told him to
come back because this Kingdom was growing too big for me to
handle, and then I struck for the first valley, to see how the priests
were working. They called the village we took along with the Chief,
Bashkai, and the first village we took, Er-Heb. The priests at Er-
Heb was doing all right, but they had a lot of pending cases about
land to show me, and some men from another village had been
firing arrows at night. I went out and looked for that village, and
fired four rounds at it from a thousand yards. That used all the
cartridges I cared to spend, and I waited for Dravot, who had been
away two or three months, and I kept my people quiet.

'One morning I heard the devil's own noise of drums and horns, and Dan Dravot marches down the hill with his Army and a tail of hundreds of men, and, which was the most amazing, a great gold crown on his head. "My Gord, Carnehan," says Daniel, "this is a tremenjus business, and we've got the whole country as far as it's worth having. I am the son of Alexander by Queen Semiramis, and you're my younger brother and a God too! It's the biggest thing we've ever seen. I've been marching and fighting for six weeks with the Army, and every footy little village for fifty miles has come in rejoiceful; and more than that, I've got the key of the whole show, as you'll see, and I've got a crown for you! I told 'em to make two of 'em at a place called Shu, where the gold lies in the rock like suet in mutton. Gold I've seen, and turquoise I've kicked out of the cliffs, and there's garnets in the sands of the river, and here's a chunk of amber that a man brought me. Call up all the priests and, here, take your crown."

'One of the men opens a black hair bag, and I slips the crown on. It was too small and too heavy, but I wore it for the glory. Hammered gold it was—five pound weight, like a hoop of a barrel.

' "Peachey," says Dravot, "we don't want to fight no more. The Craft's the trick, so help me!" and he brings forward that same Chief that I left at Bashkai—Billy Fish we called him afterwards, because he was so like Billy Fish that drove the big tank-engine at Mach on the Bolan in the old days. "Shake hands with him," says Dravot, and I shook hands and nearly dropped, for Billy Fish gave me the Grip. I said nothing, but tried him with the Fellow Craft Grip. He answers all right, and I tried the Master's Grip, but that was a slip. "A Fellow Craft he is!" I says to Dan. "Does he know the Word?" "He does," says Dan, "and all the priests know. It's a miracle! The Chiefs and the priests can work on a Fellow Craft Lodge in a way that's very like ours, and they've cut the mark on the rocks, but they don't know the Third Degree, and they've come to find out. It's Gord's Truth! I've known these long years that the Afghans knew up to the Fellow Craft Degree, but this is a miracle. A God and a Grand-Master of the Craft am I, and a Lodge in the Third Degree I will open, and we'll raise the head priests and the Chiefs of the villages."

' "It's against all the law," I says, "holding a Lodge without warrant from anyone; and you know we never held office in any Lodge."

' "It's a master-stroke o' policy," says Dravot. "It means running the country as easy as a four-wheeled bogie on a down grade.

We can't stop to inquire now, or they'll turn against us. I've forty Chiefs at my heel, and passed and raised according to their merit they shall be. Billet these men on the villages, and see that we run up a Lodge of some kind. The temple of Imbra will do for the Lodge-room. The women must make aprons as you show them. I'll hold a levee of Chiefs tonight and Lodge tomorrow."

'I was fair run off my legs, but I wasn't such a fool as not to see what a pull this Craft business gave us. I showed the priests' families how to make aprons of the degrees, but for Dravot's apron the blue border and marks was made of turquoise lumps on white hide, not cloth. We took a great square stone in the temple for the Master's chair, and little stones for the officers' chairs, and painted the black pavement with white squares, and did what we could to make things regular.

'At the levee which was held that night on the hillside with big bonfires, Dravot gives out that him and me were Gods and sons of Alexander, and Past Grand-Masters in the Craft, and was come to make Kafiristan a country where every man should eat in peace and drink in quiet, and 'specially obey us. Then the Chiefs come round to shake hands, and they were so hairy and white and fair it was just shaking hands with old friends. We gave them names according as they was like men we had known in India—Billy Fish, Holly Dilworth, Pikky Kergan, that was Bazar-master when I was at Mhow, and so on, and so on.

'*The* most amazing miracles was at Lodge next night. One of the old priests was watching us continuous, and I felt uneasy, for I knew we'd have to fudge the Ritual, and I didn't know what the men knew. The old priest was a stranger come in from beyond the village of Bashkai. The minute Dravot puts on the Master's apron that the girls had made for him, the priest fetches a whoop and a howl, and tries to overturn the stone that Dravot was sitting on. "It's all up now," I says. "That comes of meddling with the Craft without warrant!" Dravot never winked an eye, not when ten priests took and tilted over the Grand-Master's chair—which was to say the stone of Imbra. The priest begins rubbing the bottom end of it to clear away the black dirt, and presently he shows all the other priests the Master's Mark, same as was on Dravot's apron, cut into the stone. Not even the priests of the temple of Imbra knew it was there. The old chap falls flat on his face at Dravot's feet and kisses 'em. "Luck again," says Dravot, across the Lodge to me; "they say it's the missing Mark that no one could understand the why of. We're more than safe now." Then he bangs the butt of his

gun for a gavel and says: "By virtue of the authority vested in me
by my own right hand and the help of Peachey, I declare myself
Grand-Master of all Freemasonry in Kafiristan in this the Mother
Lodge o' the country, and King of Kafiristan equally with Peachey!"
At that he puts on his crown and I puts on mine—I was doing
Senior Warden—and we opens the Lodge in most ample form. It
was a amazing miracle! The priests moved in Lodge through the
first two degrees almost without telling, as if the memory was coming back to them. After that, Peachey and Dravot raised such as was
worthy—high priests and Chiefs of far-off villages. Billy Fish was
the first, and I can tell you we scared the soul out of him. It was not
in any way according to Ritual, but it served our turn. We didn't
raise more than ten of the biggest men, because we didn't want to
make the Degree common. And they was clamouring to be raised.

' "In another six months," says Dravot, "we'll hold another
Communication, and see how you are working." Then he asks them
about their villages, and learns that they was fighting one against
the other, and was sick and tired of it. And when they wasn't doing
that they was fighting with the Mohammedans. "You can fight
those when they come into our country," says Dravot. "Tell off
every tenth man of your tribes for a Frontier guard, and send two
hundred at a time to this valley to be drilled. Nobody is going to be
shot or speared any more so long as he does well, and I know that
you won't cheat me, because you're white people—sons of Alexander—and not like common, black Mohammedans. You are *my*
people, and by God," says he, running off into English at the end,
"I'll make a damned fine Nation of you, or I'll die in the making!"

'I can't tell all we did for the next six months, because Dravot
did a lot I couldn't see the hang of, and he learned their lingo in a
way I never could. My work was to help the people plough, and
now and again go out with some of the Army and see what the other
villages were doing, and make 'em throw rope-bridges across the
ravines which cut up the country horrid. Dravot was very kind to
me, but when he walked up and down in the pine-wood pulling that
bloody red beard of his with both fists I knew he was thinking plans
I could not advise about, and I just waited for orders.

'But Dravot never showed me disrespect before the people. They
were afraid of me and the Army, but they loved Dan. He was the
best of friends with the priests and the Chiefs; but anyone could
come across the hills with a complaint, and Dravot would hear him
out fair, and call four priests together and say what was to be done.
He used to call in Billy Fish from Bashkai, and Pikky Kergan from

Shu, and an old Chief we called Kafoozelum—it was like enough to
his real name—and hold councils with 'em when there was any
fighting to be done in small villages. That was his Council of War,
and the four priests of Bashkai, Shu, Khawak, and Madora was his
Privy Council. Between the lot of 'em they sent me, with forty men
and twenty rifles and sixty men carrying turquoises, into the Ghorband country to buy those hand-made Martini rifles, that come out
of the Amir's workshops at Kabul, from one of the Amir's Herati
regiments that would have sold the very teeth out of their mouths
for turquoises.

'I stayed in Ghorband a month, and gave the Governor there the
pick of my baskets for hush-money, and bribed the Colonel of the
regiment some more, and, between the two and the tribespeople,
we got more than a hundred hand-made Martinis, a hundred good
Kohat *jezails* that'll throw to six hundred yards, and forty man-
loads of very bad ammunition for the rifles. I came back with what
I had, and distributed 'em among the men that the Chiefs sent in to
me to drill. Dravot was too busy to attend to those things, but the
old Army that we first made helped me, and we turned out five
hundred men that could drill, and two hundred that knew how to
hold arms pretty straight. Even those corkscrewed, hand-made
guns was a miracle to them. Dravot talked big about powder-shops
and factories, walking up and down in the pine-wood when the
winter was coming on.

' "I won't make a Nation," says he. "I'll make an Empire! These
men aren't niggers; they're English! Look at their eyes—look at
their mouths. Look at the way they stand up. They sit on chairs in
their own houses. They're the Lost Tribes, or something like it, and
they've grown to be English. I'll take a census in the spring if the
priests don't get frightened. There must be a fair two million of 'em
in these hills. The villages are full o' little children. Two million
people—two hundred and fifty thousand fighting men—and all
English! They only want the rifles and a little drilling. Two hundred
and fifty thousand men, ready to cut in on Russia's right flank
when she tries for India! Peachey, man," he says, chewing his
beard in great hunks, "we shall be Emperors—Emperors of the
Earth! Rajah Brooke will be a suckling to us. I'll treat with the
Viceroy on equal terms. I'll ask him to send me twelve picked
English—twelve that I know of—to help us govern a bit. There's
Mackray, Sergeant-pensioner at Segowli—many's the good dinner
he's given me, and his wife a pair of trousers. There's Donkin, the
Warder of Tounghoo Jail. There's hundreds that I could lay my

hand on if I was in India. The Viceroy shall do it for me. I'll send a
man through in the spring for those men, and I'll write for a Dispen-
sation from the Grand Lodge for what I've done as Grand-Master.
That—and all the Sniders that'll be thrown out when the native
troops in India take up the Martini. They'll be worn smooth, but
they'll do for fighting in these hills. Twelve English, a hundred
thousand Sniders run through the Amir's country in driblets—I'd
be content with twenty thousand in one year—and we'd be an
Empire. When everything was shipshape, I'd hand over the crown
—this crown I'm wearing now—to Queen Victoria on my knees,
and she'd say: 'Rise up, Sir Daniel Dravot.' Oh, it's big! It's big, I
tell you! But there's so much to be done in every place—Bashkai,
Khawak, Shu, and everywhere else."

' "What is it?" I says. "There are no more men coming in to be
drilled this autumn. Look at those fat, black clouds. They're bringing the snow."

' "It isn't that," says Daniel, putting his hand very hard on my
shoulder; "and I don't wish to say anything that's against you, for
no other living man would have followed me and made me what I
am as you have done. You're a first-class Commander-in-Chief, and
the people know you; but—it's a big country, and somehow you
can't help me, Peachey, in the way I want to be helped."

' "Go to your blasted priests, then!" I said, and I was sorry when
I made that remark, but it did hurt me sore to find Daniel talking
so superior when I'd drilled all the men, and done all he told me.

' "Don't let's quarrel, Peachey," says Daniel without cursing.
"You're a King too, and the half of this Kingdom is yours; but
can't you see, Peachey, we want cleverer men than us now—three
or four of 'em, that we can scatter about for our Deputies. It's a
hugeous great State, and I can't always tell the right thing to do,
and I haven't time for all I want to do, and here's winter coming on
and all." He stuffed half his beard into his mouth, all red like the
gold of his crown.

' "I'm sorry, Daniel," says I. "I've done all I could. I've drilled
the men and shown the people how to stack their oats better; and
I've brought in those tinware rifles from Ghorband—but I know
what you're driving at. I take it Kings always feel oppressed that
way."

' "There's another thing too," says Dravot, walking up and down.
"The winter's coming and these people won't be giving much
trouble, and if they do we can't move about. I want a wife."

' "For Gord's sake, leave the women alone!" I says. "We've both

got all the work we can, though I *am* a fool. Remember the Contrack, and keep clear o' women.''

' ''The Contrack only lasted till such time as we was Kings; and
Kings we have been these months past,'' says Dravot, weighing his
crown in his hand. ''You go get a wife too, Peachey—a nice,
strappin', plump girl that'll keep you warm in the winter. They're
prettier than English girls, and we can take the pick of 'em. Boil
'em once or twice in hot water and they'll come out like chicken and
ham.''

' ''Don't tempt me!'' I says. ''I will not have any dealings with a
woman not till we are a dam' sight more settled than we are now.
I've been doing the work o' two men, and you've been doing the
work o' three. Let's lie off a bit, and see if we can get some better
tobacco from Afghan country and run in some good liquor; but no
women.''

' ''Who's talking o' *women*?'' says Dravot. ''I said *wife*—a Queen
to breed a King's son for the King. A Queen out of the strongest
tribe, that'll make them your blood-brothers, and that'll lie by your
side and tell you all the people thinks about you and their own
affairs. That's what I want.''

' ''Do you remember that Bengali woman I kept at Mogul Serai
when I was a platelayer?'' says I. ''A fat lot o' good she was to me.
She taught me the lingo and one or two other things; but what
happened? She ran away with the Station-master's servant and
half my month's pay. Then she turned up at Dadur Junction in tow
of a half-caste, and had the impidence to say I was her husband—
all among the drivers in the running-shed too!''

' ''We've done with that,'' says Dravot; ''these women are
whiter than you or me, and a Queen I will have for the winter
months.''

' ''For the last time o' asking, Dan, do *not*,'' I says. ''It'll only
bring us harm. The Bible says that Kings ain't to waste their
strength on women, 'specially when they've got a raw new Kingdom to work over.''

' ''For the last time of answering, I will,'' said Dravot, and he
went away through the pine-trees looking like a big red devil, the
sun being on his crown and beard and all.

'But getting a wife was not as easy as Dan thought. He put it
before the Council, and there was no answer till Billy Fish said that
he'd better ask the girls. Dravot damned them all round. ''What's
wrong with me?'' he shouts, standing by the idol Imbra. ''Am I a
dog or am I not enough of a man for your wenches? Haven't I put

the shadow of my hand over this country? Who stopped the last Afghan raid?" It was me really, but Dravot was too angry to remember. "Who bought your guns? Who repaired the bridges? Who's the Grand-Master of the Sign cut in the stone?" says he, and he thumped his hand on the block that he used to sit on in Lodge, and at Council, which opened like Lodge always. Billy Fish said nothing and no more did the others. "Keep your hair on, Dan," said I; "and ask the girls. That's how it's done at Home, and these people are quite English."

' "The marriage of the King is a matter of State," says Dan, in a red-hot rage, for he could feel, I hope, that he was going against his better mind. He walked out of the Council-room, and the others sat still, looking at the ground.

' "Billy Fish," says I to the Chief of Bashkai, "what's the difficulty here? A straight answer to a true friend."

' "You know," says Billy Fish. "How should a man tell you who knows everything? How can daughters of men marry Gods or Devils? It's not proper."

'I remembered something like that in the Bible; but if, after seeing us as long as they had, they still believed we were Gods, 'twasn't for me to undeceive them.

' "A God can do anything," says I. "If the King is fond of a girl he'll not let her die." "She'll have to," said Billy Fish. "There are all sorts of Gods and Devils in these mountains, and now and again a girl marries one of them and isn't seen any more. Besides, you two know the Mark cut in the stone. Only the Gods know that. We thought you were men till you showed the Sign of the Master."

'I wished then that we had explained about the loss of the genuine secrets of a Master-Mason at the first go-off; but I said nothing. All that night there was a blowing of horns in a little dark temple half-way down the hill, and I heard a girl crying fit to die. One of the priests told us that she was being prepared to marry the King.

' "I'll have no nonsense of that kind," says Dan. "I don't want to interfere with your customs, but I'll take my own wife." "The girl's a little bit afraid," says the priest. "She thinks she's going to die, and they are a-heartening of her up down in the temple."

' "Hearten her very tender, then," says Dravot, "or I'll hearten you with the butt of a gun so you'll never want to be heartened again." He licked his lips, did Dan, and stayed up walking about more than half the night, thinking of the wife that he was going to get in the morning. I wasn't any means comfortable, for I knew that dealings with a woman in foreign parts, though you was a crowned

King twenty times over, could not but be risky. I got up very early in the morning while Dravot was asleep, and I saw the priests talking together in whispers, and the Chiefs talking together too, and they looked at me out of the corners of their eyes.

' "What is up, Fish?" I says to the Bashkai man, who was wrapped up in his furs and looking splendid to behold.

' "I can't rightly say," says he; "but if you can make the King drop all this nonsense about marriage, you'll be doing him and me and yourself a great service."

' "That I do believe," says I. "But sure, you know, Billy, as well as me, having fought against and for us, that the King and me are nothing more than two of the finest men that God Almighty ever made. Nothing more, I do assure you."

' "That may be," says Billy Fish, "and yet I should be sorry if it was." He sinks his head upon his great fur cloak for a minute and thinks. "King," says he, "be you man or God or Devil, I'll stick by you today. I have twenty of my men with me, and they will follow me. We'll go to Bashkai until the storm blows over."

'A little snow had fallen in the night, and everything was white except them greasy fat clouds that blew down and down from the north. Dravot came out with his crown on his head, swinging his arms and stamping his feet, and looking more pleased than Punch.

' "For the last time, drop it, Dan," says I in a whisper. "Billy Fish here says that there will be a row."

' "A row among my people!" says Dravot. "Not much. Peachey, you're a fool not to get a wife too. Where's the girl?" says he with a voice as loud as the braying of a jackass. "Call up all the Chiefs and priests, and let the Emperor see if his wife suits him."

'There was no need to call anyone. They were all there leaning on their guns and spears round the clearing in the centre of the pine-wood. A lot of priests went down to the little temple to bring up the girl, and the horns blew fit to wake the dead. Billy Fish saunters round and gets as close to Daniel as he could, and behind him stood his twenty men with matchlocks. Not a man of them under six feet. I was next to Dravot, and behind me was twenty men of the regular Army. Up comes the girl, and a strapping wench she was, covered with silver and turquoises, but white as death, and looking back every minute at the priests.

' "She'll do," said Dan, looking her over. "What's to be afraid of, lass? Come and kiss me." He puts his arm round her. She shuts her eyes, gives a bit of a squeak, and down goes her face in the side of Dan's flaming red beard.

' "The slut's bitten me!" says he, clapping his hand to his neck, and, sure enough, his hand was red with blood. Billy Fish and two of his matchlock-men catches hold of Dan by the shoulders and drags him into the Bashkai lot, while the priests howls in their lingo: "Neither God nor Devil but a man!" I was all taken aback, for a priest cut at me in front, and the Army behind began firing into the Bashkai men.

' "God A'mighty!" says Dan. "What is the meaning o' this?"

' "Come back! Come away!" says Billy Fish. "Ruin and Mutiny's the matter. We'll break for Bashkai if we can."

'I tried to give some sort of orders to my men—the men o' the regular Army—but it was no use, so I fired into the brown of 'em with an English Martini and drilled three beggars in a line. The valley was full of shouting, howling people, and every soul was shrieking, "Not a God nor a Devil but only a man!" The Bashkai troops stuck to Billy Fish all they were worth, but their matchlocks wasn't half as good as the Kabul breech-loaders, and four of them dropped. Dan was bellowing like a bull, for he was very wrathy; and Billy Fish had a hard job to prevent him running out at the crowd.

' "We can't stand," says Billy Fish. "Make a run for it down the valley! The whole place is against us." The matchlock-men ran, and we went down the valley in spite of Dravot. He was swearing horrible and crying out he was a King. The priests rolled great stones on us, and the regular Army fired hard, and there wasn't more than six men, not counting Dan, Billy Fish, and me, that came down to the bottom of the valley alive.

'Then they stopped firing and the horns in the temple blew again. "Come away—for God's sake come away!" says Billy Fish. "They'll send runners out to all the villages before ever we get to Bashkai. I can protect you there, but I can't do anything now."

'My own notion is that Dan began to go mad in his head from that hour. He stared up and down like a stuck pig. Then he was all for walking back alone and killing the priests with his bare hands; which he could have done. "An Emperor am I," says Daniel, "and next year I shall be a Knight of the Queen."

' "All right, Dan," says I; "but come along now while there's time."

' "It's your fault," says he, "for not looking after your Army better. There was mutiny in the midst, and you didn't know—you damned engine-driving, plate-laying, missionary's-pass-hunting hound!" He sat upon a rock and called me every name he could lay tongue to. I was too heart-sick to care, though it was all his foolish-ness that brought the smash.

' "I'm sorry, Dan," says I, "but there's no accounting for natives. This business is our 'Fifty-Seven. Maybe we'll make some-thing out of it yet, when we've got to Bashkai."

' "Let's get to Bashkai, then," says Dan, "and, by God, when I come back here again I'll sweep the valley so there isn't a bug in a blanket left!"

'We walked all that day, and all that night Dan was stumping up and down on the snow, chewing his beard and muttering to him-self.

' "There's no hope o' getting clear," said Billy Fish. "The priests will have sent runners to the villages to say that you are only men. Why didn't you stick on as Gods till things was more settled? I'm a dead man," says Billy Fish, and he throws himself down on the snow and begins to pray to his Gods.

'Next morning we was in a cruel bad country—all up and down, no level ground at all, and no food either. The six Bashkai men looked at Billy Fish hungry-ways as if they wanted to ask some-thing, but they said never a word. At noon we came to the top of a flat mountain all covered with snow, and when we climbed up into it, behold, there was an Army in position waiting in the middle!

' "The runners have been very quick," says Billy Fish, with a little bit of a laugh. "They are waiting for us."

'Three or four men began to fire from the enemy's side, and a chance shot took Daniel in the calf of the leg. That brought him to his senses. He looks across the snow at the Army, and sees the rifles that we had brought into the country.

' "We're done for," says he. "They are Englishmen, these people —and it's my blasted nonsense that has brought you to this. Get back, Billy Fish, and take your men away. You've done what you could, and now cut for it. Carnehan," says he, "shake hands with me and go along with Billy. Maybe they won't kill you. I'll go and meet 'em alone. It's me that did it. Me, the King!"

' "Go!" says I. "Go to Hell, Dan! I'm with you here. Billy Fish, you clear out, and we two will meet those folk."

' "I'm a Chief," says Billy Fish, quite quiet. "I stay with you. My men can go."

'The Bashkai fellows didn't wait for a second word, but ran off, and Dan and me and Billy Fish walked across to where the drums were drumming and the horns were horning. It was cold—awful cold. I've got that cold in the back of my head now. There's a lump of it there.'

The punkah-coolies had gone to sleep. Two kerosene lamps were blazing in the office, and the perspiration poured down my face and splashed on the blotter as I leaned forward. Carnehan was shivering, and I feared that his mind might go. I wiped my face, took a fresh grip of the piteously mangled hands, and said: 'What happened after that?'

The momentary shift of my eyes had broken the clear current.

'What was you pleased to say?' whined Carnehan. 'They took them without any sound. Not a little whisper all along the snow, not though the King knocked down the first man that set hand on him—not though old Peachey fired his last cartridge into the brown of 'em. Not a single solitary sound did those swines make. They just closed up right, and I tell you their furs stunk. There was a man called Billy Fish, a good friend of us all, and they cut his throat, sir, then and there, like a pig; and the King kicks up the bloody snow and says: "We've had a dashed fine run for our money. What's coming next?" But Peachey, Peachey Taliaferro, I tell you, sir, in confidence as betwixt two friends, he lost his head, sir. No, he didn't neither. The King lost his head, so he did, all along o' one of those cunning rope-bridges. Kindly let me have the paper-cutter, sir. It tilted this way. They marched him a mile across that snow to a rope-bridge over a ravine with a river at the bottom. You may have seen such. They prodded him behind like an ox. "Damn your eyes!" says the King. "D'you suppose I can't die like a gentleman?" He turns to Peachey—Peachey that was crying like a child. "I've brought you to this, Peachey," says he. "Brought you out of your happy life to be killed in Kafiristan, where you was late Commander-in-Chief of the Emperor's forces. Say you forgive me, Peachey." "I do," says Peachey. "Fully and freely do I forgive you, Dan." "Shake hands, Peachey," says he. "I'm going now." Out he goes, looking neither right nor left, and when he was plumb in the middle of those dizzy dancing ropes—"Cut, you beggars," he shouts; and they cut, and old Dan fell, turning round and round and round, twenty thousand miles, for he took half an hour to fall till he struck the water, and I could see his body caught on a rock with the gold crown close beside.

'But do you know what they did to Peachey between two pine-trees? They crucified him, sir, as Peachey's hand will show. They used wooden pegs for his hands and his feet; and he didn't die. He hung there and screamed, and they took him down next day, and said it was a miracle that he wasn't dead. They took him down—poor old Peachey that hadn't done them any harm—that hadn't done them any——'

He rocked to and fro and wept bitterly, wiping his eyes with the back of his scarred hands and moaning like a child for some ten minutes.

'They was cruel enough to feed him up in the temple, because they said he was more of a God than old Daniel that was a man. Then they turned him out on the snow, and told him to go home, and Peachey came home in about a year, begging along the roads quite safe; for Daniel Dravot he walked before and said: "Come along, Peachey. It's a big thing we're doing." The mountains they danced at night, and the mountains they tried to fall on Peachey's head, but Dan he held up his hand, and Peachey came along bent double. He never let go of Dan's hand, and he never let go of Dan's head. They gave it to him as a present in the temple, to remind him not to come again, and though the crown was pure gold, and Peachey was starving, never would Peachey sell the same. You knew Dravot, sir! You knew Right Worshipful Brother Dravot! Look at him now!'

He fumbled in the mass of rags round his bent waist; brought out a black horsehair bag embroidered with silver thread, and shook therefrom on to my table—the dried, withered head of Daniel Dravot! The morning sun that had long been paling the lamps struck the red beard and blind sunken eyes; struck, too, a heavy circlet of gold studded with raw turquoises, that Carnehan placed tenderly on the battered temples.

'You behold now,' said Carnehan, 'the Emperor in his habit as he lived—the King of Kafiristan with his crown upon his head. Poor old Daniel that was a monarch once!'

I shuddered, for, in spite of defacements manifold, I recognized the head of the man of Marwar Junction. Carnehan rose to go. I attempted to stop him. He was not fit to walk abroad. 'Let me take away the whisky, and give me a little money,' he gasped. 'I was a King once. I'll go to the Deputy-Commissioner and ask to set in the Poorhouse till I get my health. No, thank you, I can't wait till you get a carriage for me. I've urgent private affairs—in the South—at Marwar.'

He shambled out of the office and departed in the direction of the Deputy-Commissioner's house. That day at noon I had occasion to go down the blinding hot Mall, and I saw a crooked man crawling along the white dust of the roadside, his hat in his hand, quavering dolorously after the fashion of street-singers at Home. There was not a soul in sight, and he was out of all possible earshot of the houses. And he sang through his nose, turning his head from right to left:

> *'The Son of God goes forth to war,*
> *A kingly crown to gain;*
> *His blood-red banner streams afar!*
> *Who follows in his train?'*

I waited to hear no more, but put the poor wretch into my carriage and drove him off to the nearest missionary for eventual transfer to the Asylum. He repeated the hymn twice while he was with me, whom he did not in the least recognize, and I left him singing it to the missionary.

Two days later I inquired after his welfare of the Superintendent of the Asylum.

'He was admitted suffering from sunstroke. He died early yesterday morning,' said the Superintendent. 'Is it true that he was half an hour bare-headed in the sun at mid-day?'

'Yes,' said I, 'but do you happen to know if he had anything upon him by any chance when he died?'

'Not to my knowledge,' said the Superintendent.

And there the matter rests.

Wee Willie Winkie, 1888

Baa Baa, Black Sheep

Baa Baa, Black Sheep,
Have you any wool?
Yes, Sir, yes, Sir, three bags full.
One for the Master, one for the Dame—
None for the Little Boy that cries down the lane.
NURSERY RHYME

THE FIRST BAG

'When I was in my father's house, I was in a better place.'

THEY WERE PUTTING Punch to bed—the *ayah* and the *hamal* and Meeta, the big *Surti* boy, with the red-and-gold turban. Judy, already tucked inside her mosquito-curtains, was nearly asleep. Punch had been allowed to stay up for dinner. Many privileges had been accorded to Punch within the last ten days, and a greater kindness from the people of his world had encompassed his ways and works, which were mostly obstreperous. He sat on the edge of his bed and swung his bare legs defiantly.

'Punch-*baba* going to bye-lo?' said the *ayah* suggestively.

'No,' said Punch. 'Punch-*baba* wants the story about the Ranee that was turned into a tiger. Meeta must tell it, and the *hamal* shall hide behind the door and make tiger-noises at the proper time.'

'But Judy-*baba* will wake up,' said the *ayah*.

'Judy-*baba* is waked,' piped a small voice from the mosquito-curtains. 'There was a Ranee that lived at Delhi. Go on, Meeta,' and she fell fast asleep again while Meeta began the story.

Never had Punch secured the telling of that tale with so little opposition. He reflected for a long time. The *hamal* made the tiger-noises in twenty different keys.

' 'Top!' said Punch authoritatively. 'Why doesn't Papa come in and say he is going to give me *put-put*?'

'Punch-*baba* is going away,' said the *ayah*. 'In another week there will be no Punch-*baba* to pull my hair any more.' She sighed softly, for the boy of the household was very dear to her heart.

'Up the Ghauts in a train?' said Punch, standing on his bed. 'All the way to Nassick where the Ranee-Tiger lives?'

'Not to Nassick this year, little Sahib,' said Meeta, lifting him on his shoulder. 'Down to the sea where the coconuts are thrown, and across the sea in a big ship. Will you take Meeta with you to *Belait*?'

'You shall all come,' said Punch, from the height of Meeta's strong arms. 'Meeta and the *ayah* and the *hamal* and Bhini-in-the-Garden, and the salaam-Captain-Sahib-snake-man.'

There was no mockery in Meeta's voice when he replied: 'Great is the Sahib's favour,' and laid the little man down in the bed, while the *ayah*, sitting in the moonlight at the doorway, lulled him to sleep with an interminable canticle such as they sing in the Roman Catholic Church at Parel. Punch curled himself into a ball and slept.

Next morning Judy shouted that there was a rat in the nursery, and thus he forgot to tell her the wonderful news. It did not much matter, for Judy was only three and she would not have understood. But Punch was five; and he knew that going to England would be much nicer than a trip to Nassick.

*

Papa and Mamma sold the brougham and the piano. and stripped the house, and curtailed the allowance of crockery for the daily meals, and took long counsel together over a bundle of letters bearing the Rocklington postmark.

'The worst of it is that one can't be certain of anything,' said Papa, pulling his moustache. 'The letters in themselves are excellent, and the terms are moderate enough.'

'The worst of it is that the children will grow up away from me,' thought Mamma; but she did not say it aloud.

'We are only one case among hundreds,' said Papa bitterly. 'You shall go Home again in five years, dear.'

'Punch will be ten then—and Judy eight. Oh, how long and long and long the time will be! And we have to leave them among strangers.'

'Punch is a cheery little chap. He's sure to make friends wherever he goes.'

'And who could help loving my Ju?'

They were standing over the cots in the nursery late at night, and I think that Mamma was crying softly. After Papa had gone away, she knelt down by the side of Judy's cot. The *ayah* saw her and put up a prayer that the Memsahib might never find the love of her children taken away from her and given to a stranger.

Mamma's own prayer was a slightly illogical one. Summarized it ran: 'Let strangers love my children and be as good to them as I should be, but let *me* preserve their love and their confidence for ever and ever. Amen.' Punch scratched himself in his sleep, and Judy moaned a little.

Next day they all went down to the sea, and there was a scene at the Apollo Bunder when Punch discovered that Meeta could not come too, and Judy learned that the *ayah* must be left behind. But Punch found a thousand fascinating things in the rope, block, and steam-pipe line on the big P. & O. steamer long before Meeta and the *ayah* had dried their tears.

'Come back, Punch-*baba*,' said the *ayah*.

'Come back,' said Meeta, 'and be a *Burra Sahib* [a big man].'

'Yes,' said Punch, lifted up in his father's arms to wave good-bye. 'Yes, I will come back, and I will be a *Burra Sahib Bahadur* [a very big man indeed]!'

At the end of the first day Punch demanded to be set down in England, which he was certain must be close at hand. Next day there was a merry breeze, and Punch was very sick. 'When I come back to Bombay,' said Punch on his recovery, 'I will come by the road—in a broom-*gharri*. This is a very naughty ship.'

The Swedish boatswain consoled him, and he modified his opinions as the voyage went on. There was so much to see and to handle and ask questions about that Punch nearly forgot the *ayah* and Meeta and the *hamal*, and with difficulty remembered a few words of the Hindustani once his second speech.

But Judy was much worse. The day before the steamer reached Southampton, Mamma asked her if she would not like to see the *ayah* again. Judy's blue eyes turned to the stretch of sea that had swallowed all her tiny past, and she said: '*Ayah!* What *ayah?*'

Mamma cried over her and Punch marvelled. It was then that he heard for the first time Mamma's passionate appeal to him never to let Judy forget Mamma. Seeing that Judy was young, ridiculously young, and that Mamma, every evening for four weeks past, had come into the cabin to sing her and Punch to sleep with a mysterious rune that he called 'Sonny, my soul,' Punch could not understand what Mamma meant. But he strove to do his duty; for, the moment Mamma left the cabin, he said to Judy: 'Ju, you bemember Mamma?'

' 'Torse I do,' said Judy.

'Then *always* bemember Mamma, 'r else I won't give you the paper ducks that the red-haired Captain Sahib cut out for me.'

So Judy promised always to 'bemember Mamma.'

Many and many a time was Mamma's command laid upon Punch,

and Papa would say the same thing with an insistence that awed the child.

'You must make haste and learn to write, Punch,' said Papa, 'and then you'll be able to write letters to us in Bombay.'

'I'll come into your room,' said Punch, and Papa choked.

Papa and Mamma were always choking in those days. If Punch took Judy to task for not 'bemembering,' they choked. If Punch sprawled on the sofa in the Southampton lodging-house and sketched his future in purple and gold, they choked; and so they did if Judy put up her mouth for a kiss.

Through many days all four were vagabonds on the face of the earth—Punch with no one to give orders to, Judy too young for anything, and Papa and Mamma grave, distracted, and choking.

'Where,' demanded Punch, wearied of a loathsome contrivance on four wheels with a mound of luggage atop—'*where* is our broom-*gharri*? This thing talks so much that *I* can't talk. Where is our *own* broom-*gharri*? When I was at Bandstand before we comed away, I asked Inverarity Sahib why he was sitting in it, and he said it was his own. And I said, "I will *give* it you"—I like Inverarity Sahib—and I said, "Can you put your legs through the pully-wag loops by the windows?" And Inverarity Sahib said No, and laughed. *I* can put my legs through the pully-wag loops. I can put my legs through *these* pully-wag loops. Look! Oh, Mamma's crying again! I didn't know I wasn't not to do *so*.'

Punch drew his legs out of the loops of the four-wheeler: the door opened and he slid to the earth, in a cascade of parcels, at the door of an austere little villa whose gates bore the legend 'Downe Lodge.' Punch gathered himself together and eyed the house with disfavour. It stood on a sandy road, and a cold wind tickled his knickerbockered legs.

'Let us go away,' said Punch. 'This is not a pretty place.'

But Mamma and Papa and Judy had left the cab, and all the luggage was being taken into the house. At the doorstep stood a woman in black, and she smiled largely, with dry chapped lips. Behind her was a man, big, bony, grey, and lame as to one leg—behind him a boy of twelve, black-haired and oily in appearance. Punch surveyed the trio, and advanced without fear, as he had been accustomed to do in Bombay when callers came and he happened to be playing in the veranda.

'How do you do?' said he. 'I am Punch.' But they were all looking at the luggage—all except the grey man, who shook hands with Punch, and said he was 'a smart little fellow.' There was much run-

ning about and banging of boxes, and Punch curled himself up on
the sofa in the dining-room and considered things.

'I don't like these people,' said Punch. 'But never mind. We'll go
away soon. We have always went away soon from everywhere. I
wish we was gone back to Bombay *soon*.'

The wish bore no fruit. For six days Mamma wept at intervals,
and showed the woman in black all Punch's clothes—a liberty which
Punch resented. 'But p'raps she's a new white *ayah*,' he thought.
'I'm to call her Antirosa, but she doesn't call *me* Sahib. She says
just Punch,' he confided to Judy. 'What is Antirosa?'

Judy didn't know. Neither she nor Punch had heard anything of
an animal called an aunt. Their world had been Papa and Mamma,
who knew everything, permitted everything, and loved everybody—even Punch when he used to go into the garden at Bombay
and fill his nails with mould after the weekly nail-cutting, because,
as he explained between two strokes of the slipper to his sorely-tried
father, his fingers 'felt so new at the ends.'

In an undefined way Punch judged it advisable to keep both
parents between himself and the woman in black and the boy with
black hair. He did not approve of them. He liked the grey man, who
had expressed a wish to be called 'Uncleharri.' They nodded at each
other when they met, and the grey man showed him a little ship
with rigging that took up and down.

'She is a model of the *Brisk*—the little *Brisk* that was sore exposed
that day at Navarino.' The grey man hummed the last words and
fell into a reverie. 'I'll tell you about Navarino, Punch, when we go
for walks together; and you mustn't touch the ship, because she's
the *Brisk*.'

Long before that walk, the first of many, was taken, they roused
Punch and Judy in the chill dawn of a February morning to say
Good-bye; and of all people in the wide earth to Papa and Mamma
—both crying this time. Punch was very sleepy and Judy was cross.

'Don't forget us,' pleaded Mamma. 'Oh, my little son, don't forget us, and see that Judy remembers too.'

'I've told Judy to bemember,' said Punch, wriggling, for his
father's beard tickled his neck, 'I've told Judy—ten—forty—'leven
thousand times. But Ju's so young—quite a baby—isn't she?'

'Yes,' said Papa, 'quite a baby, and you must be good to Judy,
and make haste to learn to write and—and—and——'

Punch was back in his bed again. Judy was fast asleep, and there
was the rattle of a cab below. Papa and Mamma had gone away. Not
to Nassick; that was across the sea. To some place much nearer, of

course, and equally of course they would return. They came back after dinner-parties, and Papa had come back after he had been to a place called 'The Snows,' and Mamma with him, to Punch and Judy at Mrs Inverarity's house in Marine Lines. Assuredly they would come back again. So Punch fell asleep till the true morning, when the black-haired boy met him with the information that Papa and Mamma had gone to Bombay, and that he and Judy were to stay at Downe Lodge 'for ever.' Antirosa, tearfully appealed to for a contradiction, said that Harry had spoken the truth, and that it behoved Punch to fold up his clothes neatly on going to bed. Punch went out and wept bitterly with Judy, into whose fair head he had driven some ideas of the meaning of separation.

When a matured man discovers that he has been deserted by Providence, deprived of his God, and cast without help, comfort, or sympathy, upon a world which is new and strange to him, his despair, which may find expression in evil living, the writing of his experiences, or the more satisfactory diversion of suicide, is generally supposed to be impressive. A child, under exactly similar circumstances as far as its knowledge goes, cannot very well curse God and die. It howls till its nose is red, its eyes are sore, and its head aches. Punch and Judy, through no fault of their own, had lost all their world. They sat in the hall and cried; the black-haired boy looking on from afar.

The model of the ship availed nothing, though the grey man assured Punch that he might pull the rigging up and down as much as he pleased; and Judy was promised free entry into the kitchen. They wanted Papa and Mamma, gone to Bombay beyond the seas, and their grief while it lasted was without remedy.

When the tears ceased the house was very still. Antirosa had decided that it was better to let the children 'have their cry out,' and the boy had gone to school. Punch raised his head from the floor and sniffed mournfully. Judy was nearly asleep. Three short years had not taught her how to bear sorrow with full knowledge. There was a distant, dull boom in the air—a repeated heavy thud. Punch knew that sound in Bombay in the monsoon. It was the sea—the sea that must be traversed before anyone could get to Bombay.

'Quick, Ju!' he cried. 'We're close to the sea. I can hear it! Listen! That's where they've went. P'raps we can catch them if we was in time. They didn't mean to go without us. They've only forgot.'

'Iss,' said Judy. 'They've only forgotted. Less go to the sea.'

The hall-door was open and so was the garden-gate.

'It's very, very big, this place,' he said, looking cautiously down

the road, 'and we will get lost. But *I* will find a man and order him to take me back to my house—like I did in Bombay.'

He took Judy by the hand, and the two ran hatless in the direction of the sound of the sea. Downe Lodge was almost the last of a range of newly-built houses running out, through a field of brick-mounds, to a heath where gipsies occasionally camped and where the Garrison Artillery of Rocklington practised. There were few people to be seen, and the children might have been taken for those of the soldiery who ranged far. Half an hour the wearied little legs tramped across heath, potato-patch, and sand-dune.

'I'se so tired,' said Judy, 'and Mamma will be angry.'

'Mamma's *never* angry. I suppose she is waiting at the sea now while Papa gets tickets. We'll find them and go along with them. Ju, you mustn't sit down. Only a little more and we'll come to the sea. Ju, if you sit down I'll *thmack* you!' said Punch.

They climbed another dune, and came upon the great grey sea at low tide. Hundreds of crabs were scuttling about the beach, but there was no trace of Papa and Mamma, not even of a ship upon the waters—nothing but sand and mud for miles and miles.

And 'Uncleharri' found them by chance—very muddy and very forlorn—Punch dissolved in tears, but trying to divert Judy with an 'ickle trab,' and Judy wailing to the pitiless horizon for 'Mamma, Mamma!'—and again 'Mamma!'

THE SECOND BAG

Ah, well-a-day, for we are souls bereaved!
Of all the creatures under Heaven's wide scope
We are most helpless, who had once most hope,
And most beliefless, who had most believed.
THE CITY OF DREADFUL NIGHT

ALL THIS TIME not a word about Black Sheep. He came later, and Harry, the black-haired boy, was mainly responsible for his coming.

Judy—who could help loving little Judy?—passed, by special permit, into the kitchen and thence straight to Aunty Rosa's heart. Harry was Aunty Rosa's one child, and Punch was the extra boy about the house. There was no special place for him or his little affairs, and he was forbidden to sprawl on sofas and explain his ideas about the manufacture of this world and his hopes for his future. Sprawling was lazy and wore out sofas, and little boys were not expected to talk. They were talked to, and the talking-to was intended for the benefit of their morals. As the unquestioned despot of the house at Bombay, Punch could not quite understand how he came to be of no account in this his new life.

Harry might reach across the table and take what he wanted; Judy might point and get what she wanted. Punch was forbidden to do either. The grey man was his great hope and stand-by for many months after Mamma and Papa left, and he had forgotten to tell Judy to 'bemember Mamma.'

This lapse was excusable, because in the interval he had been introduced by Aunty Rosa to two very impressive things—an abstraction called God, the intimate friend and ally of Aunty Rosa, generally believed to live behind the kitchen-range because it was hot there—and a dirty brown book filled with unintelligible dots and marks. Punch was always anxious to oblige everybody. He therefore welded the story of the Creation on to what he could recollect of his Indian fairy tales, and scandalized Aunty Rosa by repeating the result to Judy. It was a sin, a grievous sin, and Punch was talked to for a quarter of an hour. He could not understand where the iniquity came in, but was careful not to repeat the offence, because Aunty Rosa told him that God had heard every word he had said and was very angry. If this were true why didn't God come and say so, thought Punch, and dismissed the matter from his mind. Afterwards he learned to know the Lord as the only thing in the world more awful than Aunty Rosa—as a Creature that stood in the background and counted the strokes of the cane.

But the reading was, just then, a much more serious matter than any creed. Aunty Rosa sat him upon a table and told him that A B meant ab.

'Why?' said Punch. 'A is a and B is bee. *Why* does A B mean ab?'

'Because I tell you it does,' said Aunty Rosa, ' and you've got to say it.'

Punch said it accordingly, and for a month, hugely against his will, stumbled through the brown book, not in the least comprehending what it meant. But Uncle Harry, who walked much and generally alone, was wont to come into the nursery and suggest to Aunty Rosa that Punch should walk with him. He seldom spoke, but he showed Punch all Rocklington, from the mud-banks and the sand of the back-bay to the great harbours where ships lay at anchor, and the dockyards where the hammers were never still, and the marine-store shops, and the shiny brass counters in the Offices where Uncle Harry went once every three months with a slip of blue paper and received sovereigns in exchange; for he held a wound-pension. Punch heard, too, from his lips the story of the battle of Navarino, where the sailors of the Fleet, for three days afterwards, were deaf as posts and could only sign to each other. 'That was because of the noise of the guns,' said Uncle Harry, 'and I have got the wadding of a bullet somewhere inside me now.'

Punch regarded him with curiosity. He had not the least idea what wadding was, and his notion of a bullet was a dockyard cannon-ball bigger than his own head. How could Uncle Harry keep a cannon-ball inside him? He was afraid to ask, for fear Uncle Harry might be angry.

Punch had never known what anger—real anger—meant until one terrible day when Harry had taken his paint-box to paint a boat with, and Punch had protested. Then Uncle Harry had appeared on the scene and, muttering something about 'strangers' children,' had with a stick smitten the black-haired boy across the shoulders till he wept and yelled, and Aunty Rosa came in and abused Uncle Harry for cruelty to his own flesh and blood, and Punch shuddered to the tips of his shoes. 'It wasn't my fault,' he explained to the boy, but both Harry and Aunty Rosa said that it was, and that Punch had told tales, and for a week there were no more walks with Uncle Harry.

But that week brought a great joy to Punch.

He had repeated till he was thrice weary the statement that 'The Cat lay on the Mat and the Rat came in.'

'Now I can truly read,' said Punch, 'and now I will never read anything in the world.'

He put the brown book in the cupboard where his school-books lived and accidentally tumbled out a venerable volume, without covers, labelled *Sharpe's Magazine*. There was the most portentous picture of a Griffin on the first page, with verses below. The Griffin carried off one sheep a day from a German village, till a man came with a 'falchion' and split the Griffin open. Goodness only knew what a falchion was, but there was the Griffin, and his history was an improvement upon the eternal Cat.

'This,' said Punch, 'means things, and now I will know all about everything in all the world.' He read till the light failed, not understanding a tithe of the meaning, but tantalized by glimpses of new worlds hereafter to be revealed.

'What is a "falchion"? What is a "e-wee lamb"? What is a "base *uss*urper"? What is a "verdant me-ad"?' he demanded, with flushed cheeks, at bedtime, of the astonished Aunty Rosa.

'Say your prayers and go to sleep,' she replied, and that was all

the help Punch then or afterwards found at her hands in the new
and delightful exercise of reading.

'Aunty Rosa only knows about God and things like that,' argued
Punch. 'Uncle Harry will tell me.'

The next walk proved that Uncle Harry could not help either; but
he allowed Punch to talk, and even sat down on a bench to hear
about the Griffin. Other walks brought other stories as Punch ranged
farther afield, for the house held large store of old books that no one
ever opened—from *Frank Fairlegh* in serial numbers, and the earlier poems of Tennyson, contributed anonymously to *Sharpe's
Magazine*, to '62 Exhibition Catalogues, gay with colours and
delightfully incomprehensible, and odd leaves of *Gulliver's Travels*.

As soon as Punch could string a few pot-hooks together he wrote
to Bombay, demanding by return of post 'all the books in all the
world.' Papa could not comply with this modest indent, but sent
Grimm's Fairy Tales and a *Hans Andersen*. That was enough. If he
were only left alone Punch could pass, at any hour he chose, into a
land of his own, beyond reach of Aunty Rosa and her God, Harry
and his teasements, and Judy's claims to be played with.

'Don't disturve me, I'm reading. Go and play in the kitchen,'
grunted Punch. 'Aunty Rosa lets *you* go there.' Judy was cutting her
second teeth and was fretful. She appealed to Aunty Rosa, who descended on Punch.

'I was reading,' he explained, 'reading a book. I *want* to read.'

'You're only doing that to show off,' said Aunty Rosa. 'But
we'll see. Play with Judy now, and don't open a book for a
week.'

Judy did not pass a very enjoyable playtime with Punch, who
was consumed with indignation. There was a pettiness at the bottom of the prohibition which puzzled him.

'It's what I like to do,' he said, 'and she's found out that and
stopped me. Don't cry, Ju—it wasn't your fault—*please* don't cry,
or she'll say I made you.'

Ju loyally mopped up her tears, and the two played in their nursery, a room in the basement and half underground, to which they
were regularly sent after the mid-day dinner while Aunty Rosa
slept. She drank wine—that is to say, something from a bottle in
the cellaret—for her stomach's sake, but if she did not fall asleep
she would sometimes come into the nursery to see that the children
were really playing. Now bricks, wooden hoops, ninepins, and china-
ware cannot amuse for ever, especially when all Fairyland is to be
won by the mere opening of a book, and, as often as not, Punch

would be discovered reading to Judy or telling her interminable tales. That was an offence in the eyes of the law, and Judy would be whisked off by Aunty Rosa, while Punch was left to play alone, 'and be sure that I hear you doing it.'

It was not a cheering employ, for he had to make a playful noise. At last, with infinite craft, he devised an arrangement whereby the table could be supported as to three legs on toy bricks, leaving the fourth clear to bring down on the floor. He could work the table with one hand and hold a book with the other. This he did till an evil day when Aunty Rosa pounced upon him unawares and told him that he was 'acting a lie.'

'If you're old enough to do that,' she said—her temper was always worst after dinner—'you're old enough to be beaten.'

'But—I'm—I'm not a animal!' said Punch aghast. He remembered Uncle Harry and the stick, and turned white. Aunty Rosa had hidden a light cane behind her, and Punch was beaten then and there over the shoulders. It was a revelation to him. The room-door was shut, and he was left to weep himself into repentance and work out his own gospel of life.

Aunty Rosa, he argued, had the power to beat him with many stripes. It was unjust and cruel, and Mamma and Papa would never have allowed it. Unless perhaps, as Aunty Rosa seemed to imply, they had sent secret orders. In which case he was abandoned indeed. It would be discreet in the future to propitiate Aunty Rosa, but then again, even in matters in which he was innocent, he had been accused of wishing to 'show off.' He had 'shown off' before visitors when he had attacked a strange gentleman—Harry's uncle, not his own—with requests for information about the Griffin and the falchion, and the precise nature of the Tilbury in which Frank Fairlegh rode—all points of paramount interest which he was bursting to understand. Clearly it would not do to pretend to care for Aunty Rosa.

At this point Harry entered and stood afar off, eyeing Punch, a dishevelled heap in the corner of the room, with disgust.

'You're a liar—a young liar,' said Harry, with great unction, 'and you're to have tea down here because you're not fit to speak to us. And you're not to speak to Judy again till Mother gives you leave. You'll corrupt her. You're only fit to associate with the servant. Mother says so.'

Having reduced Punch to a second agony of tears, Harry departed upstairs with the news that Punch was still rebellious.

Uncle Harry sat uneasily in the dining-room. 'Damn it all, Rosa,' said he at last, 'can't you leave the child alone? He's a good enough little chap when I meet him.'

'He puts on his best manners with you, Henry,' said Aunty Rosa, 'but I'm afraid, I'm very much afraid, that he is the Black Sheep of the family.'

Harry heard and stored up the name for future use. Judy cried till she was bidden to stop, her brother not being worth tears; and the evening concluded with the return of Punch to the upper regions and a private sitting at which all the blinding horrors of Hell were revealed to Punch with such store of imagery as Aunty Rosa's narrow mind possessed.

Most grievous of all was Judy's round-eyed reproach, and Punch went to bed in the depths of the Valley of Humiliation. He shared his room with Harry and knew the torture in store. For an hour and a half he had to answer that young gentleman's questions as to his motives for telling a lie, and a grievous lie, the precise quantity of punishment inflicted by Aunty Rosa, and had also to profess his deep gratitude for such religious instruction as Harry thought fit to impart.

From that day began the downfall of Punch, now Black Sheep.

'Untrustworthy in one thing, untrustworthy in all,' said Aunty Rosa, and Harry felt that Black Sheep was delivered into his hands. He would wake him up in the night to ask him why he was such a liar.

'I don't know,' Punch would reply.

'Then don't you think you ought to get up and pray to God for a new heart?'

'Y-yess.'

'Get out and pray, then!' And Punch would get out of bed with raging hate in his heart against all the world, seen and unseen. He was always tumbling into trouble. Harry had a knack of cross-examining him as to his day's doings, which seldom failed to lead him, sleepy and savage, into half-a-dozen contradictions—all duly reported to Aunty Rosa next morning.

'But it *wasn't* a lie,' Punch would begin, charging into a laboured explanation that landed him more hopelessly in the mire. 'I said that I didn't say my prayers *twice* over in the day, and *that* was on Tuesday. *Once* I did. I *know* I did, but Harry said I didn't,' and so forth, till the tension brought tears, and he was dismissed from the table in disgrace.

'You usen't to be as bad as this,' said Judy, awe-stricken at the catalogue of Black Sheep's crimes. 'Why are you so bad now?'

'I don't know,' Black Sheep would reply. 'I'm not, if I only wasn't bothered upside-down. I knew what I *did*, and I want to say so; but Harry always makes it out different somehow, and Aunty Rosa doesn't believe a word I say. Oh, Ju! Don't *you* say I'm bad too.'

'Aunty Rosa says you are,' said Judy. 'She told the Vicar so when he came yesterday.'

'Why does she tell all the people outside the house about me? It isn't fair,' said Black Sheep. 'When I was in Bombay, and was bad —*doing* bad, not made-up bad like this—Mamma told Papa, and Papa told me he knew, and that was all. *Outside* people didn't know too—even Meeta didn't know.'

'I don't remember,' said Judy wistfully. 'I was all little then. Mamma was just as fond of you as she was of me, wasn't she?'

' 'Course she was. So was Papa. So was everybody.'

'Aunty Rosa likes me more than she does you. She says that you are a Trial and a Black Sheep, and I'm not to speak to you more than I can help.'

'Always? Not outside of the times when you mustn't speak to me at all?'

Judy nodded her head mournfully. Black Sheep turned away in despair, but Judy's arms were round his neck.

'Never mind, Punch,' she whispered. 'I *will* speak to you just the same as ever and ever. You're my own own brother though you are —though Aunty Rosa says you're bad, and Harry says you are a little coward. He says that if I pulled your hair hard, you'd cry.'

'Pull, then,' said Punch.

Judy pulled gingerly.

'Pull harder—as hard as you can! There! I don't mind how much you pull it *now*. If you'll speak to me same as ever I'll let you pull it as much as you like—pull it out if you like. But I know if Harry came and stood by and made you do it I'd cry.'

So the two children sealed the compact with a kiss, and Black Sheep's heart was cheered within him, and by extreme caution and careful avoidance of Harry he acquired virtue, and was allowed to read undisturbed for a week. Uncle Harry took him for walks, and consoled him with rough tenderness, never calling him Black Sheep. 'It's good for you, I suppose, Punch,' he used to say. 'Let us sit down. I'm getting tired.' His steps led him now not to the beach, but to the Cemetery of Rocklington, amid the potato-fields. For hours the grey man would sit on a tombstone, while Black Sheep would read epitaphs, and then with a sigh would stump home again.

'I shall lie there soon,' said he to Black Sheep, one winter evening, when his face showed white as a worn silver coin under the light of the lych-gate. 'You needn't tell Aunty Rosa.'

A month later he turned sharp round, ere half a morning walk was completed, and stumped back to the house. 'Put me to bed, Rosa,' he muttered. 'I've walked my last. The wadding has found me out.'

They put him to bed, and for a fortnight the shadow of his sickness lay upon the house, and Black Sheep went to and fro unobserved. Papa had sent him some new books, and he was told to keep quiet. He retired into his own world, and was perfectly happy. Even at night his felicity was unbroken. He could lie in bed and string himself tales of travel and adventure while Harry was downstairs.

'Uncle Harry's going to die,' said Judy, who now lived almost entirely with Aunty Rosa.

'I'm very sorry,' said Black Sheep soberly. 'He told me that a long time ago.'

Aunty Rosa heard the conversation. 'Will nothing check your wicked tongue?' she said angrily. There were blue circles round her eyes.

Black Sheep retreated to the nursery and read *Cometh up as a Flower* with deep and uncomprehending interest. He had been forbidden to open it on account of its 'sinfulness,' but the bonds of the Universe were crumbling, and Aunty Rosa was in great grief.

'I'm glad,' said Black Sheep. 'She's unhappy now. It wasn't a lie, though. *I* knew. He told me not to tell.'

That night Black Sheep woke with a start. Harry was not in the room, and there was a sound of sobbing on the next floor. Then the voice of Uncle Harry, singing the song of the Battle of Navarino, came through the darkness:

> '*Our vanship was the* Asia—
> *The* Albion *and* Genoa!'

'He's getting well,' thought Black Sheep, who knew the song through all its seventeen verses. But the blood froze at his little heart as he thought. The voice leapt an octave, and rang shrill as a boatswain's pipe:

> '*And next came on the lovely* Rose,
> *The* Philomel, *her fire-ship, closed,*
> *And the little* Brisk *was sore exposed*
> *That day at Navarino.*'

'That day at Navarino, Uncle Harry!' shouted Black Sheep, half wild with excitement and fear of he knew not what.

A door opened, and Aunty Rosa screamed up the staircase: 'Hush! For God's sake hush, you little devil! Uncle Harry is *dead*!'

THE THIRD BAG

Journeys end in lovers' meeting,
Every wise man's son doth know.

'I WONDER WHAT will happen to me now,' thought Black Sheep, when semi-pagan rites peculiar to the burial of the Dead in middle-class houses had been accomplished, and Aunty Rosa, awful in black crape, had returned to this life. 'I don't think I've done anything bad that she knows of. I suppose I will soon. She will be very cross after Uncle Harry's dying, and Harry will be cross too. I'll keep in the nursery.'

Unfortunately for Punch's plans, it was decided that he should be sent to a day-school which Harry attended. This meant a morning walk with Harry, and perhaps an evening one; but the prospect of freedom in the interval was refreshing. 'Harry'll tell everything I do, but I won't do anything,' said Black Sheep. Fortified with this virtuous resolution, he went to school only to find that Harry's version of his character had preceded him, and that life was a burden in consequence. He took stock of his associates. Some of them were unclean, some of them talked in dialect, many dropped their h's, and there were two Jews and a negro, or someone quite as dark, in the assembly. 'That's a *hubshi*,' said Black Sheep to himself. 'Even Meeta used to laugh at a *hubshi*. I don't think this is a proper place.' He was indignant for at least an hour, till he reflected that any expostulation on his part would be by Aunty Rosa construed into 'showing off,' and that Harry would tell the boys.

'How do you like school?' said Aunty Rosa at the end of the day.

'I think it is a very nice place,' said Punch quietly.

'I suppose you warned the boys of Black Sheep's character?' said Aunty Rosa to Harry.

'Oh yes,' said the censor of Black Sheep's morals. 'They know all about him.'

'If I was with my father,' said Black Sheep, stung to the quick, 'I shouldn't *speak* to those boys. He wouldn't let me. They live in shops. I saw them go into shops—where their fathers live and sell things.'

'You're too good for that school, are you?' said Aunty Rosa, with a bitter smile. 'You ought to be grateful, Black Sheep, that those boys speak to you at all. It isn't every school that takes little liars.'

Harry did not fail to make much capital out of Black Sheep's ill-considered remark; with the result that several boys, including the *hubshi*, demonstrated to Black Sheep the eternal equality of the human race by smacking his head, and his consolation from Aunty Rosa was that it 'served him right for being vain.' He learned, however, to keep his opinions to himself, and by propitiating Harry in carrying books and the like to get a little peace. His existence was not too joyful. From nine till twelve he was at school, and from two to four, except on Saturdays. In the evenings he was sent down into the nursery to prepare his lessons for the next day, and every night came the dreaded cross-questionings at Harry's hand. Of Judy he saw but little. She was deeply religious—at six years of age Religion is easy to come by—and sorely divided between her natural love for Black Sheep and her love for Aunty Rosa, who could do no wrong.

The lean woman returned that love with interest, and Judy, when she dared, took advantage of this for the remission of Black Sheep's penalties. Failures in lessons at school were punished at home by a week without reading other than school-books, and Harry brought the news of such a failure with glee. Further, Black Sheep was then bound to repeat his lessons at bedtime to Harry, who generally succeeded in making him break down, and consoled him by gloomiest forebodings for the morrow. Harry was at once spy, practical joker, inquisitor, and Aunty Rosa's deputy executioner. He filled his many posts to admiration. From his actions, now that Uncle Harry was dead, there was no appeal. Black Sheep had not been permitted to keep any self-respect at school: at home he was, of course, utterly discredited, and grateful for any pity that the servant-girls—they changed frequently at Downe Lodge because they, too, were liars—might show. 'You're just fit to row in the same boat with Black Sheep,' was a sentiment that each new Jane or Eliza might expect to hear, before a month was over, from Aunty Rosa's lips; and Black Sheep was used to ask new girls whether they had yet been compared to him. Harry was 'Master Harry' in their mouths; Judy was officially 'Miss Judy'; but Black Sheep was never anything more than Black Sheep *tout court*.

As time went on and the memory of Papa and Mamma became wholly overlaid by the unpleasant task of writing them letters, under Aunty Rosa's eye, each Sunday, Black Sheep forgot what manner of life he had led in the beginning of things. Even Judy's appeals to 'try and remember about Bombay' failed to quicken him.

'I can't remember,' he said. 'I know I used to give orders and Mamma kissed me.'

'Aunty Rosa will kiss you if you are good,' pleaded Judy.

'Ugh! I don't want to be kissed by Aunty Rosa. She'd say I was doing it to get something more to eat.'

The weeks lengthened into months, and the holidays came; but just before the holidays Black Sheep fell into deadly sin.

Among the many boys whom Harry had incited to 'punch Black Sheep's head because he daren't hit back,' was one more aggravating than the rest, who, in an unlucky moment, fell upon Black Sheep when Harry was not near. The blows stung, and Black Sheep struck back at random with all the power at his command. The boy dropped and whimpered. Black Sheep was astounded at his own act, but, feeling the unresisting body under him, shook it with both his hands in blind fury and then began to throttle his enemy; meaning honestly to slay him. There was a scuffle, and Black Sheep was torn off the body by Harry and some colleagues, and cuffed home tingling but exultant. Aunty Rosa was out. Pending her arrival, Harry set himself to lecture Black Sheep on the sin of murder—which he described as the offence of Cain.

'Why didn't you fight him fair? What did you hit him when he was down for, you little cur?'

Black Sheep looked up at Harry's throat and then at a knife on the dinner-table.

'I don't understand,' he said wearily. 'You always set him on me and told me I was a coward when I blubbed. Will you leave me alone until Aunty Rosa comes in? She'll beat me if you tell her I ought to be beaten; so it's all right.'

'It's all wrong,' said Harry magisterially. 'You nearly killed him, and I shouldn't wonder if he dies.'

'Will he die?' said Black Sheep.

'I daresay,' said Harry, 'and then you'll be hanged, and go to Hell.'

'All right,' said Black Sheep, picking up the table-knife. 'Then I'll kill *you* now. You say things and do things and—and *I* don't know how things happen, and you never leave me alone—and I don't care *what* happens!'

He ran at the boy with the knife, and Harry fled upstairs to his room, promising Black Sheep the finest thrashing in the world when Aunty Rosa returned. Black Sheep sat at the bottom of the stairs, the table-knife in his hand, and wept for that he had not killed Harry. The servant-girl came up from the kitchen, took the knife away, and consoled him. But Black Sheep was beyond consolation. He would be badly beaten by Aunty Rosa; then there would be another beating at Harry's hands; then Judy would not be allowed to speak to him; then the tale would be told at school, and then—

There was no one to help and no one to care, and the best way out of the business was by death. A knife would hurt, but Aunty Rosa had told him, a year ago, that if he sucked paint he would die. He went into the nursery, unearthed the now disused Noah's Ark, and sucked the paint off as many animals as remained. It tasted abominably, but he had licked Noah's Dove clean by the time Aunty Rosa and Judy returned. He went upstairs and greeted them with: 'Please, Aunty Rosa, I believe I've nearly killed a boy at school, and I've tried to kill Harry, and when you've done all about God and Hell, will you beat me and get it over?'

The tale of the assault as told by Harry could only be explained on the ground of possession by the Devil. Wherefore Black Sheep was not only most excellently beaten, once by Aunty Rosa, and once, when thoroughly cowed down, by Harry, but he was further prayed for at family prayers, together with Jane, who had stolen a cold rissole from the pantry, and snuffled audibly as her sin was brought before the Throne of Grace. Black Sheep was sore and stiff but triumphant. He would die that very night and be rid of them all. No, he would ask for no forgiveness from Harry, and at bedtime would stand no questioning at Harry's hands, even though addressed as 'Young Cain.'

'I've been beaten,' said he, 'and I've done other things. I don't care what I do. If you speak to me tonight, Harry, I'll get out and try to kill you. Now you can kill me if you like.'

Harry took his bed into the spare room, and Black Sheep lay down to die.

It may be that the makers of Noah's Arks know that their animals are likely to find their way into young mouths, and paint them accordingly. Certain it is that the common, weary next morning broke through the windows and found Black Sheep quite well and a good deal ashamed of himself, but richer by the knowledge that he could, in extremity, secure himself against Harry for the future.

When he descended to breakfast on the first day of the holidays, he was greeted with the news that Harry, Aunty Rosa, and Judy were going away to Brighton, while Black Sheep was to stay in the house with the servant. His latest outbreak suited Aunty Rosa's plans admirably. It gave her good excuse for leaving the extra boy behind. Papa in Bombay, who really seemed to know a young sinner's wants to the hour, sent, that week, a package of new books. And with these, and the society of Jane on board-wages, Black Sheep was left alone for a month.

The books lasted for ten days. They were eaten too quickly in long gulps of twelve hours at a time. Then came days of doing absolutely nothing, of dreaming dreams and marching imaginary armies up and down stairs, of counting the number of banisters, and of measuring the length and breadth of every room in handspans— fifty down the side, thirty across, and fifty back again. Jane made many friends, and, after receiving Black Sheep's assurance that he would not tell of her absences, went out daily for long hours. Black Sheep would follow the rays of the sinking sun from the kitchen to the dining-room and thence upward to his own bedroom until all was grey dark, and he ran down to the kitchen fire and read by its light. He was happy in that he was left alone and could read as much as he pleased. But, later, he grew afraid of the shadows of window-curtains and the flapping of doors and the creaking of shutters. He went out into the garden, and the rustling of the laurel-bushes frightened him.

He was glad when they all returned—Aunty Rosa, Harry, and Judy—full of news, and Judy laden with gifts. Who could help loving loyal little Judy? In return for all her merry babblement, Black Sheep confided to her that the distance from the hall-door to the top of the first landing was exactly one hundred and eighty-four handspans. He had found it out himself!

Then the old life recommenced; but with a difference, and a new sin. To his other iniquities Black Sheep had now added a phenomenal clumsiness—was as unfit to trust in action as he was in word. He himself could not account for spilling everything he touched, upsetting glasses as he put his hand out, and bumping his head against doors that were manifestly shut. There was a grey haze upon all his world, and it narrowed month by month, until at last it left Black Sheep almost alone with the flapping curtains that were so like ghosts, and the nameless terrors of broad daylight that were only coats on pegs after all.

Holidays came and holidays went, and Black Sheep was taken to see many people whose faces were all exactly alike; was beaten when occasion demanded, and tortured by Harry on all possible occasions; but defended by Judy through good and evil report, though she hereby drew upon herself the wrath of Aunty Rosa.

The weeks were interminable and Papa and Mamma were clean forgotten. Harry had left school and was a clerk in a Banking-Office. Freed from his presence, Black Sheep resolved that he should no longer be deprived of his allowance of pleasure-reading. Consequently when he failed at school he reported that all was well, and conceived a large contempt for Aunty Rosa as he saw how easy it was to deceive her. 'She says I'm a little liar when I don't tell lies, and now I do, she doesn't know,' thought Black Sheep. Aunty Rosa had credited him in the past with petty cunning and stratagem that had never entered into his head. By the light of the sordid knowledge that she had revealed to him he paid her back full tale. In a household where the most innocent of his motives, his natural yearning for a little affection, had been interpreted into a desire for more bread and jam, or to ingratiate himself with strangers and so put Harry into the background, his work was easy. Aunty Rosa could penetrate certain kinds of hypocrisy, but not all. He set his child's wits against hers and was no more beaten. It grew monthly more and more of a trouble to read the school-books, and even the pages of the open-print story-books danced and were dim. So Black Sheep brooded in the shadows that fell about him and cut him off from the world, inventing horrible punishments for 'dear Harry,' or plotting another line of the tangled web of deception that he wrapped round Aunty Rosa.

Then the crash came and the cobwebs were broken. It was impossible to foresee everything. Aunty Rosa made personal inquiries as to Black Sheep's progress and received information that startled her. Step by step, with a delight as keen as when she convicted an underfed housemaid of the theft of cold meats, she followed the trail of Black Sheep's delinquencies. For weeks and weeks, in order to escape banishment from the book-shelves, he had made a fool of Aunty Rosa, of Harry, of God, of all the world! Horrible, most horrible, and evidence of an utterly depraved mind.

Black Sheep counted the cost. 'It will only be one big beating and then she'll put a card with "Liar" on my back, same as she did before. Harry will whack me and pray for me, and she will pray for me at prayers and tell me I'm a Child of the Devil and give me hymns to learn. But I've done all my reading and she never knew. She'll say she knew all along. She's an old liar too,' said he.

For three days Black Sheep was shut in his own bedroom—to prepare his heart. 'That means two beatings. One at school and one here. *That* one will hurt most.' And it fell even as he thought. He was thrashed at school before the Jews and the *hubshi* for the heinous crime of carrying home false reports of progress. He was thrashed at home by Aunty Rosa on the same count, and then the placard was produced. Aunty Rosa stitched it between his shoulders and bade him go for a walk with it upon him.

'If you make me do that,' said Black Sheep very quietly, 'I shall burn this house down, and perhaps I'll kill you. I don't know whether I *can* kill you—you're so bony—but I'll try.'

No punishment followed this blasphemy, though Black Sheep held himself ready to work his way to Aunty Rosa's withered throat and grip there till he was beaten off. Perhaps Aunty Rosa was afraid, for Black Sheep, having reached the Nadir of Sin, bore himself with a new recklessness.

In the midst of all the trouble there came a visitor from over the seas to Downe Lodge, who knew Papa and Mamma, and was commissioned to see Punch and Judy. Black Sheep was sent to the drawing-room and charged into a solid tea-table laden with china.

'Gently, gently, little man,' said the visitor, turning Black Sheep's face to the light slowly. 'What's that big bird on the palings?'

'What bird?' asked Black Sheep.

The visitor looked deep down into Black Sheep's eyes for half a minute, and then said suddenly: 'Good God, the little chap's nearly blind!'

It was a most businesslike visitor. He gave orders, on his own responsibility, that Black Sheep was not to go to school or open a book until Mamma came home. 'She'll be here in three weeks, as you know, of course,' said he, 'and I'm Inverarity Sahib. I ushered you into this wicked world, young man, and a nice use you seem to have made of your time. You must do nothing whatever. Can you do that?'

'Yes,' said Punch in a dazed way. He had known that Mamma was coming. There was a chance, then, of another beating. Thank Heaven, Papa wasn't coming too. Aunty Rosa had said of late that he ought to be beaten by a man.

For the next three weeks Black Sheep was strictly allowed to do nothing. He spent his time in the old nursery looking at the broken toys, for all of which account must be rendered to Mamma. Aunty Rosa hit him over the hands if even a wooden boat were broken. But that sin was of small importance compared to the other revelations, so darkly hinted at by Aunty Rosa. 'When your Mother comes, and hears what I have to tell her, she may appreciate you properly,' she said grimly, and mounted guard over Judy lest that small maiden should attempt to comfort her brother, to the peril of her soul.

And Mamma came—in a four-wheeler—fluttered with tender excitement. Such a Mamma! She was young, frivolously young, and beautiful, with delicately flushed cheeks, eyes that shone like stars, and a voice that needed no appeal of outstretched arms to draw little ones to her heart. Judy ran straight to her, but Black Sheep hesitated. Could this wonder be 'showing off'? She would not put out her arms when she knew of his crimes. Meantime was it possible that by fondling she wanted to get anything out of Black Sheep? Only all his love and all his confidence; but that Black Sheep did not know. Aunty Rosa withdrew and left Mamma, kneeling between her children, half laughing, half crying, in the very hall where Punch and Judy had wept five years before.

'Well, chicks, do you remember me?'

'No,' said Judy frankly, 'but I said, "God bless Papa and Mamma" ev'vy night.'

'A little,' said Black Sheep. 'Remember I wrote to you every week, anyhow. That isn't to show off, but 'cause of what comes afterwards.'

'What comes after? What should come after, my darling boy?' And she drew him to her again. He came awkwardly, with many angles. 'Not used to petting,' said the quick Mother-soul. 'The girl is.'

'She's too little to hurt anyone,' thought Black Sheep, 'and if I said I'd kill her, she'd be afraid. I wonder what Aunty Rosa will tell.'

There was a constrained late dinner, at the end of which Mamma picked up Judy and put her to bed with endearments manifold. Faithless little Judy had shown her defection from Aunty Rosa already. And that lady resented it bitterly. Black Sheep rose to leave the room.

'Come and say good night,' said Aunty Rosa, offering a withered cheek.

'Huh!' said Black Sheep. 'I never kiss you, and I'm not going to show off. Tell that woman what I've done, and see what she says.'

Black Sheep climbed into bed feeling that he had lost Heaven after a glimpse through the gates. In half an hour 'that woman' was bending over him. Black Sheep flung up his right arm. It wasn't fair to come and hit him in the dark. Even Aunty Rosa never tried that. But no blow followed.

'Are you showing off? I won't tell you anything more than Aunty

Rosa has, and *she* doesn't know everything,' said Black Sheep as clearly as he could for the arms round his neck.

'Oh, my son—my little, little son! It was my fault—*my* fault, darling—and yet how could we help it? Forgive me, Punch.' The voice died out in a broken whisper, and two hot tears fell on Black Sheep's forehead.

'Has she been making you cry too?' he asked. 'You should see Jane cry. But you're nice, and Jane is a Born Liar—Aunty Rosa says so.'

'Hush, Punch, hush! My boy, don't talk like that. Try to love me a little bit—a little bit. You don't know how I want it. Punch-*baba*, come back to me! I am your Mother—your own Mother—and never mind the rest. I know—yes, I know, dear. It doesn't matter now. Punch, won't you care for me a little?'

It is astonishing how much petting a big boy of ten can endure when he is quite sure that there is no one to laugh at him. Black Sheep had never been made much of before, and here was this beautiful woman treating him—Black Sheep, the Child of the Devil and the inheritor of undying flame—as though he were a small God.

'I care for you a great deal, Mother dear,' he whispered at last, 'and I'm glad you've come back; but are you sure Aunty Rosa told you everything?'

'Everything. What *does* it matter? But——' the voice broke with a sob that was also laughter—'Punch, my poor, dear, half-blind darling, don't you think it was a little foolish of you?'

'*No.* It saved a lickin'.'

Mamma shuddered and slipped away in the darkness to write a long letter to Papa. Here is an extract:

'. . . Judy is a dear, plump little prig who adores the woman, and wears with as much gravity as her religious opinions—only eight, Jack!—a venerable horse-hair atrocity which she calls her Bustle! I have just burnt it, and the child is asleep in my bed as I write. She will come to me at once. Punch I cannot quite understand. He is well nourished, but seems to have been worried into a system of small deceptions which the woman magnifies into deadly sins. Don't you recollect our own upbringing, dear, when the Fear of the Lord was so often the beginning of falsehood? I shall win Punch to me before long. I am taking the children away into the country to get them to know me, and, on the whole, I am content, or shall be when you come home, dear boy, and then, thank God, we shall be all under one roof again at last!'

Three months later, Punch, no longer Black Sheep, has discovered that he is the veritable owner of a real, live, lovely Mamma, who is also a sister, comforter, and friend, and that he must protect her till the Father comes home. Deception does not suit the part of a protector, and, when one can do anything without question, where is the use of deception?

'Mother would be awfully cross if you walked through that ditch,' says Judy, continuing a conversation.

'Mother's never angry,' says Punch. 'She'd just say, "You're a little *pagal* [idiot]"; and that's not nice, but I'll show.'

Punch walks through the ditch and mires himself to the knees. 'Mother dear,' he shouts, 'I'm just as dirty as I can pos-*sib*-ly be!'

'Then change your clothes as quickly as you pos-*sib*-ly can!' Mother's clear voice rings out from the house. 'And don't be a little *pagal!*'

'There! Told you so,' says Punch. 'It's all different now, and we are just as much Mother's as if she had never gone.'

Not altogether, O Punch, for when young lips have drunk deep of the bitter waters of Hate, Suspicion, and Despair, all the Love in the world will not wholly take away that knowledge; though it may turn darkened eyes for a while to the light, and teach Faith where no Faith was.

Wee Willie Winkie, 1888*

* *Week's News*, 1888.

Without Benefit of Clergy

Before my Spring I garnered Autumn's gain,
Out of her time my field was white with grain,
  The year gave up her secrets to my woe.
Forced and deflowered each sick season lay,
In mystery of increase and decay;
I saw the sunset ere men saw the day,
  Who am too wise in that I should not know.
BITTER WATERS

ONE

BUT IF IT BE A GIRL?'
  'Lord of my life, it cannot be. I have prayed for so many
nights, and sent gifts to Sheikh Badl's shrine so often, that I know
God will give us a son—a man-child that shall grow into a man.
Think of this and be glad. My mother shall be his mother till I can
take him again, and the mullah of the Pattan mosque shall cast his
nativity—God send he be born in an auspicious hour!—and then,
and then thou wilt never weary of me, thy slave.'
  'Since when hast thou been a slave, my queen?'
  'Since the beginning—till this mercy came to me. How could I
be sure of thy love when I knew that I had been bought with silver?'
  'Nay, that was the dowry. I paid it to thy mother.'
  'And she has buried it, and sits upon it all day long like a hen.
What talk is yours of dower! I was bought as though I had been a
Lucknow dancing-girl instead of a child.'
  'Art thou sorry for the sale?'
  'I have sorrowed; but today I am glad. Thou wilt never cease
to love me now?—answer, my king.'
  'Never—never. No.'
  'Not even though the *mem-log*—the white women of thine own
blood—love thee? And remember, I have watched them driving in
the evening; they are very fair.'
  'I have seen fire-balloons by the hundred. I have seen the moon,
and—then I saw no more fire-balloons.'
  Ameera clapped her hands and laughed. 'Very good talk,' she
said. Then with an assumption of great stateliness, 'It is enough.
Thou hast my permission to depart—if thou wilt.'
  The man did not move. He was sitting on a low red-lacquered

couch in a room furnished only with a blue-and-white floor-cloth, some rugs, and a very complete collection of native cushions. At his feet sat a woman of sixteen, and she was all but all the world in his eyes. By every rule and law she should have been otherwise, for he was an Englishman, and she a Mussulman's daughter bought two years before from her mother, who, being left without money, would have sold Ameera shrieking to the Prince of Darkness if the price had been sufficient.

It was a contract entered into with a light heart; but even before the girl had reached her bloom she came to fill the greater portion of John Holden's life. For her, and the withered hag her mother, he had taken a little house overlooking the great red-walled city, and found—when the marigolds had sprung up by the well in the court-yard, and Ameera had established herself according to her own ideas of comfort, and her mother had ceased grumbling at the inadequacy of the cooking-places, the distance from the daily market, and at matters of house-keeping in general—that the house was to him his home. Anyone could enter his bachelor's bungalow by day or night, and the life that he led there was an unlovely one. In the house in the city his feet only could pass beyond the outer courtyard to the women's rooms; and when the big wooden gate was bolted behind him he was king in his own territory, with Ameera for queen. And there was going to be added to this kingdom a third person whose arrival Holden felt inclined to resent. It interfered with his perfect happiness. It disarranged the orderly peace of the house that was his own. But Ameera was wild with delight at the thought of it, and her mother not less so. The love of a man, and particularly a white man, was at the best an inconstant affair, but it might, both women argued, be held fast by a baby's hands. 'And then,' Ameera would always say, 'then he will never care for the white *mem-log*. I hate them all—I hate them all.'

'He will go back to his own people in time,' said the mother; 'but by the blessing of God that time is yet afar off.'

Holden sat silent on the couch thinking of the future, and his thoughts were not pleasant. The drawbacks of a double life are manifold. The Government, with singular care, had ordered him out of the station for a fortnight on special duty in the place of a man who was watching by the bedside of a sick wife. The verbal notification of the transfer had been edged by a cheerful remark that Holden ought to think himself lucky in being a bachelor and a free man. He came to break the news to Ameera.

'It is not good,' she said slowly, 'but it is not all bad. There is my mother here, and no harm will come to me—unless indeed I die of pure joy. Go thou to thy work and think no troublesome thoughts. When the days are done I believe . . . nay, I am sure. And—and then I shall lay *him* in thy arms, and thou wilt love me for ever. The train goes tonight, at midnight, is it not? Go now, and do not let thy heart be heavy by cause of me. But thou wilt not delay in returning? Thou wilt not stay on the road to talk to the bold white *mem-log*? Come back to me swiftly, my life.'

As he left the courtyard to reach his horse that was tethered to the gate-post, Holden spoke to the white-haired old watchman who guarded the house, and bade him under certain contingencies dispatch the filled-up telegraph-form that Holden gave him. It was all that could be done, and with the sensations of a man who has attended his own funeral Holden went away by the night mail to his exile. Every hour of the day he dreaded the arrival of the telegram, and every hour of the night he pictured to himself the death of Ameera. In consequence his work for the State was not of first-rate quality, nor was his temper towards his colleagues of the most amiable. The fortnight ended without a sign from his home, and, torn to pieces by his anxieties, Holden returned to be swallowed up for two precious hours by a dinner at the Club, wherein he heard, as a man hears in a swoon, voices telling him how execrably he had performed the other man's duties, and how he had endeared himself to all his associates. Then he fled on horseback through the night with his heart in his mouth. There was no answer at first to his blows on the gate, and he had just wheeled his horse round to kick it in when Pir Khan appeared with a lantern and held his stirrup.

'Has aught occurred?' said Holden.

'The news does not come from my mouth, Protector of the Poor, but——' He held out his shaking hand as befitted the bearer of good news who is entitled to a reward.

Holden hurried through the courtyard. A light burned in the upper room. His horse neighed in the gateway, and he heard a shrill little wail that sent all the blood into the apple of his throat. It was a new voice, but it did not prove that Ameera was alive.

'Who is there?' he called up the narrow brick staircase.

There was a cry of delight from Ameera, and then the voice of the mother, tremulous with old age and pride: 'We be two women and—the—man—thy—son.'

On the threshold of the room Holden stepped on a naked dagger, that was laid there to avert ill-luck, and it broke at the hilt under his impatient heel.

'God is great!' cooed Ameera in the half-light. 'Thou hast taken his misfortunes on thy head.'

'Ay, but how is it with thee, life of my life? Old woman, how is it with her?'

'She has forgotten her sufferings for joy that the child is born. There is no harm; but speak softly,' said the mother.

'It only needed thy presence to make me all well,' said Ameera. 'My king, thou hast been very long away. What gifts hast thou for me? Ah, ah! It is I that bring gifts this time. Look, my life, look. Was there ever such a babe? Nay, I am too weak even to clear my arm from him.'

'Rest then, and do not talk. I am here, *bachari* [little woman].'

'Well said, for there is a bond and a heel-rope [*peecharee*] between us now that nothing can break. Look—canst thou see in this light? He is without spot or blemish. Never was such a man-child. *Ya illah!* he shall be a pundit—no, a trooper of the Queen. And, my life, dost thou love me as well as ever, though I am faint and sick and worn? Answer truly.'

'Yea. I love as I have loved, with all my soul. Lie still, pearl, and rest.'

'Then do not go. Sit by my side here—so. Mother, the lord of this house needs a cushion. Bring it.' There was an almost imperceptible movement on the part of the new life that lay in the hollow of Ameera's arm. 'Aho!' she said, her voice breaking with love. 'The babe is a champion from his birth. He is kicking me in the side with mighty kicks. Was there ever such a babe! And he is ours to us— thine and mine. Put thy hand on his head, but carefully, for he is very young, and men are unskilled in such matters.'

Very cautiously Holden touched with the tips of his fingers the downy head.

'He is of the Faith,' said Ameera; 'for lying here in the night-watches I whispered the call to prayer and the profession of faith into his ears. And it is most marvellous that he was born upon a Friday, as I was born. Be careful of him, my life; but he can almost grip with his hands.'

Holden found one helpless little hand that closed feebly on his finger. And the clutch ran through his body till it settled about his heart. Till then his sole thought had been for Ameera. He began to realize that there was someone else in the world, but he could not feel that it was a veritable son with a soul. He sat down to think, and Ameera dozed lightly.

'Get hence, Sahib,' said her mother under her breath. 'It is not good that she should find you here on waking. She must be still.'

'I go,' said Holden submissively. 'Here be rupees. See that my *baba* gets fat and finds all that he needs.'

The chink of the silver roused Ameera. 'I am his mother, and no hireling,' she said weakly. 'Shall I look to him more or less for the sake of money? Mother, give it back. I have borne my lord a son.'

The deep sleep of weakness came upon her almost before the sentence was completed. Holden went down to the courtyard very softly with his heart at ease. Pir Khan, the old watchman, was chuckling with delight. 'This house is now complete,' he said, and without further comment thrust into Holden's hands the hilt of a sabre worn many years ago when he, Pir Khan, served the Queen in the Police. The bleat of a tethered goat came from the well-kerb.

'There be two,' said Pir Khan, 'two goats of the best. I bought them, and they cost much money; and since there is no birth-party assembled their flesh will be all mine. Strike craftily, Sahib! 'Tis an ill-balanced sabre at the best. Wait till they raise their heads from cropping the marigolds.'

'And why?' said Holden, bewildered.

'For the birth-sacrifice. What else? Otherwise the child being unguarded from fate may die. The Protector of the Poor knows the fitting words to be said.'

Holden had learned them once with little thought that he would ever speak them in earnest. The touch of the cold sabre-hilt in his palm turned suddenly to the clinging grip of the child upstairs— the child that was his own son—and a dread of loss filled him.

'Strike!' said Pir Khan. 'Never life came into the world but life was paid for it. See, the goats have raised their heads. Now! With a drawing cut!'

Hardly knowing what he did, Holden cut twice as he muttered the Mohammedan prayer that runs: 'Almighty! In place of this my son I offer life for life, blood for blood, head for head, bone for bone, hair for hair, skin for skin.' The waiting horse snorted and bounded in his pickets at the smell of the raw blood that spirted over Holden's riding-boots.

'Well smitten!' said Pir Khan, wiping the sabre. 'A swordsman was lost in thee. Go with a light heart, Heaven-born. I am thy servant, and the servant of thy son. May the Presence live a thousand years and . . . the flesh of the goats is all mine?' Pir Khan drew back richer by a month's pay. Holden swung himself into the saddle and rode off through the low-hanging wood-smoke of the

evening. He was full of riotous exultation, alternating with a vast
vague tenderness directed towards no particular object, that
made him choke as he bent over the neck of his uneasy horse. 'I
never felt like this in my life,' he thought. 'I'll go to the Club and
pull myself together.'

A game of pool was beginning, and the room was full of men.
Holden entered, eager to get to the light and the company of his
fellows, singing at the top of his voice:

> '*In Baltimore a-walking, a lady I did meet!*'

'Did you?' said the Club Secretary from his corner. 'Did she
happen to tell you that your boots were wringing wet? Great
goodness, man, it's blood!'

'Bosh!' said Holden, picking his cue from the rack. 'May I cut
in? It's dew. I've been riding through high crops. My faith! my
boots are in a mess though!

> '*And if it be a girl she shall wear a wedding-ring,*
> *And if it be a boy he shall fight for his King,*
> *With his dirk, and his cap, and his little jacket blue,*
> *He shall walk the quarter-deck—*'

'Yellow on blue—green next player,' said the marker monoton-
ously.

'*He shall walk the quarter-deck*—Am I green, marker? *He shall
walk the quarter-deck*—eh! that's a bad shot—*as his daddy used
to do!*'

'I don't see that you have anything to crow about,' said a zealous
junior Civilian acidly. 'The Government is not exactly pleased with
your work when you relieved Sanders.'

'Does that mean a wigging from headquarters?' said Holden with
an abstracted smile. 'I think I can stand it.'

The talk beat up round the ever-fresh subject of each man's
work, and steadied Holden till it was time to go to his dark empty
bungalow, where his butler received him as one who knew all his
affairs. Holden remained awake for the greater part of the night,
and his dreams were pleasant ones.

TWO

'HOW OLD IS HE NOW?'

'*Ya illah!* What a man's question! He is all but six weeks old;
and on this night I go up to the house-top with thee, my life, to
count the stars. For that is auspicious. And he was born on a Friday

under the sign of the Sun, and it has been told to me that he will outlive us both and get wealth. Can we wish for aught better, beloved?'

'There is nothing better. Let us go up to the roof, and thou shalt count the stars—but a few only, for the sky is heavy with cloud.'

'The winter rains are late, and maybe they come out of season. Come, before all the stars are hid. I have put on my richest jewels.'

'Thou hast forgotten the best of all.'

'*Ai!* Ours. He comes also. He has never yet seen the skies.'

Ameera climbed the narrow staircase that led to the flat roof. The child, placid and unwinking, lay in the hollow of her right arm, gorgeous in silver-fringed muslin with a small skull-cap on his head. Ameera wore all that she valued most. The diamond nose-stud that takes the place of the Western patch in drawing attention to the curve of the nostril, the gold ornament in the centre of the forehead studded with tallow-drop emeralds and flawed rubies, the heavy circlet of beaten gold that was fastened round her neck by the softness of the pure metal, and the chinking curb-patterned silver anklets hanging low over the rosy ankle-bone. She was dressed in jade-green muslin as befitted a daughter of the Faith, and from shoulder to elbow and elbow to wrist ran bracelets of silver tied with floss silk, frail glass bangles slipped over the wrist in proof of the slenderness of the hand, and certain heavy gold bracelets that had no part in her country's ornaments, but, since they were Holden's gift and fastened with a cunning European snap, delighted her immensely.

They sat down by the low white parapet of the roof, overlooking the city and its lights.

'They are happy down there,' said Ameera. 'But I do not think that they are as happy as we. Nor do I think the white *mem-log* are as happy. And thou?'

'I know they are not.'

'How dost thou know?'

'They give their children over to the nurses.'

'I have never seen that,' said Ameera with a sigh, 'nor do I wish to see. *Ahi!*'—she dropped her head on Holden's shoulder—'I have counted forty stars, and I am tired. Look at the child, love of my life, he is counting too.'

The baby was staring with round eyes at the dark of the heavens. Ameera placed him in Holden's arms, and he lay there without a cry.

'What shall we call him among ourselves?' she said. 'Look! Art thou ever tired of looking? He carries thy very eyes. But the mouth——'

'Is thine, most dear. Who should know better than I?'

' 'Tis such a feeble mouth. Oh, so small! And yet it holds my heart between its lips. Give him to me now. He has been too long away.'

'Nay, let him lie; he has not yet begun to cry.'

'When he cries thou wilt give him back—eh? What a man of mankind thou art! If he cried he were only the dearer to me. But, my life, what little name shall we give him?'

The small body lay close to Holden's heart. It was utterly helpless and very soft. He scarcely dared to breathe for fear of crushing it. The caged green parrot that is regarded as a sort of guardian-spirit in most native households moved on its perch and fluttered a drowsy wing.

'There is the answer,' said Holden. 'Mian Mittu has spoken. He shall be The Parrot. When he is ready he will talk mightily and run about. Mian Mittu is The Parrot in thy—in the Mussulman tongue, is it not?'

'Why put me so far off?' said Ameera fretfully. 'Let it be like unto some English name—but not wholly. For he is mine.'

'Then call him Tota, for that is likest English.'

'Ay, Tota, and that is still The Parrot. Forgive me, my lord, for a minute ago, but in truth he is too little to wear all the weight of Mian Mittu for name. He shall be Tota—our Tota to us. Hearest thou, O small one? Littlest, thou art Tota.' She touched the child's cheek, and he waking wailed, and it was necessary to return him to his mother, who soothed him with the wonderful rhyme of *Aré koko, Jaré koko!* which says:

'Oh, crow! Go, crow! Baby's sleeping sound,
And the wild plums grow in the jungle, only a penny a pound.
Only a penny a pound, baba, only a penny a pound.'

Reassured many times as to the price of those plums, Tota cuddled himself down to sleep. The two sleek, white well-bullocks in the courtyard were steadily chewing the cud of their evening meal; old Pir Khan squatted at the head of Holden's horse, his Police sabre across his knees, pulling drowsily at a big water-pipe that croaked like a bull-frog in a pond. Ameera's mother sat spinning in the lower veranda, and the wooden gate was shut and barred. The music of a marriage-procession came to the roof above the gentle hum of the city, and a string of flying-foxes crossed the face of the low moon.

'I have prayed,' said Ameera after a long pause, 'I have prayed for two things. First, that I may die in thy stead if thy death is demanded, and in the second, that I may die in the place of the child. I have prayed to the Prophet and to Bibi Miriam [the Virgin Mary]. Thinkest thou either will hear?'

'From thy lips who would not hear the lightest word?'

'I asked for straight talk, and thou hast given me sweet talk. Will my prayers be heard?'

'How can I say? God is very good.'

'Of that I am not sure. Listen now. When I die, or the child dies, what is thy fate? Living, thou wilt return to the bold white *mem-log*, for kind calls to kind.'

'Not always.'

'With a woman, no; with a man it is otherwise. Thou wilt in this life, later on, go back to thine own folk. That I could almost endure, for I should be dead. But in thy very death thou wilt be taken away to a strange place and a Paradise that I do not know.'

'Will it be Paradise?'

'Surely, for who would harm thee? But we two—I and the child —shall be elsewhere, and we cannot come to thee, nor canst thou come to us. In the old days, before the child was born, I did not think of these things; but now I think of them always. It is very hard talk.'

'It will fall as it will fall. Tomorrow we do not know, but today and love we know well. Surely we are happy now.'

'So happy that it were well to make our happiness assured. And thy Bibi Miriam should listen to me: for she is also a woman. But then she would envy me! It is not seemly for men to worship a woman.'

Holden laughed aloud at Ameera's little spasm of jealousy.

'Is it not seemly? Why didst thou not turn me from worship of thee, then?'

'Thou a worshipper! And of me? My king, for all thy sweet words, well I know that I am thy servant and thy slave, and the dust under thy feet. And I would not have it otherwise. See!'

Before Holden could prevent her she stooped forward and touched his feet; recovering herself with a little laugh she hugged Tota closer to her bosom. Then, almost savagely:

'Is it true that the bold white *mem-log* live for three times the length of my life? Is it true that they make their marriages not before they are old women?'

'They marry as do others—when they are women.'

'That I know, but they wed when they are twenty-five. Is that true?'

'That is true.'

'*Ya illah!* At twenty-five! Who would of his own will take a wife even of eighteen? She is a woman—ageing every hour. Twenty-five! I shall be an old woman at that age, and—— Those *mem-log* remain young for ever. How I hate them!'

'What have they to do with us?'

'I cannot tell. I know only that there may now be alive on this earth a woman ten years older than I who may come to thee and take thy love ten years after I am an old woman, grey-headed, and the nurse of Tota's son. That is unjust and evil. They should die too.'

'Now, for all thy years thou art a child, and shalt be picked up and carried down the staircase.'

'Tota! Have a care for Tota, my lord! Thou at least art as foolish as any babe!' Ameera tucked Tota out of harm's way in the hollow of her neck, and was carried downstairs laughing in Holden's arms, while Tota opened his eyes and smiled after the manner of the lesser angels.

He was a silent infant, and, almost before Holden could realize that he was in the world, developed into a small gold-coloured little god and unquestioned despot of the house overlooking the city. Those were months of absolute happiness to Holden and Ameera —happiness withdrawn from the world, shut in behind the wooden gate that Pir Khan guarded. By day Holden did his work with an immense pity for such as were not so fortunate as himself and a sympathy for small children that amazed and amused many mothers at the little station-gatherings. At nightfall he returned to Ameera—Ameera, full of the wondrous doings of Tota; how he had been seen to clap his hands together and move his fingers with intention and purpose—which was manifestly a miracle—how, later, he had of his own initiative crawled out of his low bedstead on to the floor and swayed on both feet for the space of three breaths.

'And they were long breaths, for my heart stood still with delight,' said Ameera.

Then Tota took the beasts into his councils—the well-bullocks, the little grey squirrels, the mongoose that lived in a hole near the well, and especially Mian Mittu, the parrot, whose tail he grievously pulled, and Mian Mittu screamed till Ameera and Holden arrived.

'Oh, villain! Child of strength! This to thy brother on the

house-top! *Tobah, tobah!* Fie! Fie! But I know a charm to make him wise as Suleiman and Aflatoun [Solomon and Plato]. Now look,' said Ameera. She drew from an embroidered bag a handful of almonds. 'See! we count seven. In the name of God!'

She placed Mian Mittu, very angry and rumpled, on the top of his cage, and seating herself between the babe and the bird she cracked and peeled an almond less white than her teeth. 'This is a true charm, my life, and do not laugh. See! I give the parrot one-half and Tota the other.' Mian Mittu with careful beak took his share from between Ameera's lips, and she kissed the other half into the mouth of the child, who ate it slowly with wondering eyes. 'This I will do each day of seven, and without doubt he who is ours will be a bold speaker and wise. Eh, Tota, what wilt thou be when thou art a man and I am grey-headed?' Tota tucked his fat legs into adorable creases. He could crawl, but he was not going to waste the spring of his youth in idle speech. He wanted Mian Mittu's tail to tweak.

When he was advanced to the dignity of a silver belt—which, with a magic square engraved on silver and hung round his neck, made up the greater part of his clothing—he staggered on a perilous journey down the garden to Pir Khan, and proffered him all his jewels in exchange for one little ride on Holden's horse, having seen his mother's mother chaffering with pedlars in the veranda. Pir Khan wept and set the untried feet on his own grey head in sign of fealty, and brought the bold adventurer to his mother's arms, vowing that Tota would be a leader of men ere his beard was grown.

One hot evening, while he sat on the roof between his father and mother watching the never-ending warfare of the kites that the city boys flew, he demanded a kite of his own with Pir Khan to fly it, because he had a fear of dealing with anything larger than himself, and when Holden called him a 'spark,' he rose to his feet and answered slowly in defence of his new-found individuality, '*Hum 'park nahin hai. Hum admi hai.* [I am no spark, but a man.]'

The protest made Holden choke and devote himself very seriously to a consideration of Tota's future. He need hardly have taken the trouble. The delight of that life was too perfect to endure. Therefore it was taken away as many things are taken away in India—suddenly and without warning. The little lord of the house, as Pir Khan called him, grew sorrowful and complained of pains who had never known the meaning of pain. Ameera, wild with terror, watched him through the night, and in the dawning of the second day the life was shaken out of him by fever—the seasonal autumn fever. It seemed altogether impossible that he could die, and neither Ameera nor Holden at first believed the evidence of the little body on the bedstead. Then Ameera beat her head against the wall and would have flung herself down the well in the garden had Holden not restrained her by main force.

One mercy only was granted to Holden. He rode to his office in broad daylight and found waiting him an unusually heavy mail that demanded concentrated attention and hard work. He was not, however, alive to this kindness of the Gods.

THREE

THE FIRST SHOCK of a bullet is no more than a brisk pinch. The wrecked body does not send in its protest to the soul till ten or fifteen seconds later. Holden realized his pain slowly, exactly as he had realized his happiness, and with the same imperious necessity for hiding all trace of it. In the beginning he only felt that there had been a loss, and that Ameera needed comforting, where she sat with her head on her knees shivering as Mian Mittu from the house-top called, *Tota! Tota! Tota!* Later all his world and the daily life of it rose up to hurt him. It was an outrage that any one of the children at the band-stand in the evening should be alive and clamorous, when his own child lay dead. It was more than mere pain when one of them touched him, and stories told by over-fond fathers of their children's latest performances cut him to the quick. He could not declare his pain. He had neither help, comfort, nor sympathy; and Ameera at the end of each weary day would lead him through the hell of self-questioning reproach which is reserved for those who have lost a child, and believe that with a little—just a little more care—it might have been saved.

'Perhaps,' Ameera would say, 'I did not take sufficient heed. Did I, or did I not? The sun on the roof that day when he played so long alone and I was—*ahi!* braiding my hair—it may be that the sun then bred the fever. If I had warned him from the sun he might have lived. But, oh, my life, say that I am guiltless! Thou knowest that I loved him as I love thee. Say that there is no blame on me, or I shall die—I shall die!'

'There is no blame—before God, none. It was written, and how could we do aught to save? What has been, has been. Let it go, beloved.'

'He was all my heart to me. How can I let the thought go when my arm tells me every night that he is not here? *Ahi! Ahi!* Oh, Tota, come back to me—come back again, and let us be all together as it was before!'

'Peace, peace! For thine own sake, and for mine also, if thou lovest me—rest.'

'By this I know thou dost not care; and how shouldst thou? The white men have hearts of stone and souls of iron. Oh, that I had married a man of mine own people—though he beat me—and had never eaten the bread of an alien!'

'Am I an alien—mother of my son?'

'What else—Sahib? . . . Oh, forgive me—forgive! The death has driven me mad. Thou art the life of my heart, and the light of my eyes, and the breath of my life, and—and I have put thee from me, though it was but for a moment. If thou goest away, to whom shall I look for help? Do not be angry. Indeed, it was the pain that spoke and not thy slave.'

'I know, I know. We be two who were three. The greater need therefore that we should be one.'

They were sitting on the roof as of custom. The night was a warm one in early spring, and sheet-lightning was dancing on the horizon to a broken tune played by far-off thunder. Ameera settled herself in Holden's arms.

'The dry earth is lowing like a cow for the rain, and I—I am afraid. It was not like this when we counted the stars. But thou lovest me as much as before, though a bond is taken away? Answer!'

'I love more because a new bond has come out of the sorrow that we have eaten together, and that thou knowest.'

'Yea, I knew,' said Ameera in a very small whisper. 'But it is good to hear thee say so, my life, who art so strong to help. I will be a child no more, but a woman and an aid to thee. Listen! Give me my *sitar* and I will sing bravely.'

She took the light silver-studded *sitar* and began a song of the great hero Rajah Rasalu. The hand failed on the strings, the tune halted, checked, and at a low note turned off to the poor little nursery-rhyme about the wicked crow:

'*And the wild plums grow in the jungle, only a penny a pound.*
Only a penny a pound, baba—*only . . .*'

Then came the tears, and the piteous rebellion against fate till she slept, moaning a little in her sleep, with the right arm thrown clear of the body as though it protected something that was not

there. It was after this night that life became a little easier for
Holden. The ever-present pain of loss drove him into his work, and
the work repaid him by filling up his mind for nine or ten hours a
day. Ameera sat alone in the house and brooded, but grew happier
when she understood that Holden was more at ease, according to
the custom of women. They touched happiness again, but this time
with caution.

'It was because we loved Tota that he died. The jealousy of God
was upon us,' said Ameera. 'I have hung up a large black jar before
our window to turn the evil eye from us, and we must make no
protestations of delight, but go softly underneath the stars, lest
God finds us out. Is that not good talk, worthless one?'

She had shifted the accent on the word that means 'beloved,' in
proof of the sincerity of her purpose. But the kiss that followed the
new christening was a thing that any deity might have envied.
They went about henceforward saying, 'It is naught, it is naught;'
and hoping that all the Powers heard.

The Powers were busy on other things. They had allowed thirty
million people four years of plenty, wherein men fed well and the
crops were certain, and the birth-rate rose year by year; the
Districts reported a purely agricultural population varying from
nine hundred to two thousand to the square mile of the over-
burdened earth; and the Member for Lower Tooting, wandering
about India in top-hat and frock-coat, talked largely of the benefits
of British rule, and suggested as the one thing needful the establishment of a duly qualified electoral system and a general bestowal
of the franchise. His long-suffering hosts smiled and made him
welcome, and when he paused to admire, with pretty wicked words,
the blossom of the blood-red *dhak*-tree that had flowered untimely
for a sign of what was coming, they smiled more than ever.

It was the Deputy-Commissioner of Kot-Kumharsen, staying at
the Club for a day, who lightly told a tale that made Holden's
blood run cold as he overheard the end.

'He won't bother anyone any more. Never saw a man so astonished in my life. By Jove, I thought he meant to ask a question in
the House about it. Fellow-passenger in his ship—dined next him—
bowled over by cholera and died in eighteen hours. You needn't
laugh, you fellows. The Member for Lower Tooting is awfully angry
about it; but he's more scared. I think he's going to take his en-
lightened self out of India.'

'I'd give a good deal if he were knocked over. It might keep a
few vestrymen of his kidney to their own parish. But what's this

about cholera? It's full early for anything of that kind,' said the warden of an unprofitable salt-lick.

'Don't know,' said the Deputy Commissioner reflectively. 'We've got locusts with us. There's sporadic cholera all along the north —at least we're calling it sporadic for decency's sake. The spring crops are short in five districts, and nobody seems to know where the rains are. It's nearly March now. I don't want to scare anybody, but it seems to me that Nature's going to audit her accounts with a big red pencil this summer.'

'Just when I wanted to take leave, too!' said a voice across the room.

'There won't be much leave this year, but there ought to be a great deal of promotion. I've come in to persuade the Government to put my pet canal on the list of famine-relief works. It's an ill-wind that blows no good. I shall get that canal finished at last.'

'Is it the old programme then,' said Holden; 'famine, fever, and cholera?'

'Oh no. Only local scarcity and an unusual prevalence of seasonal sickness. You'll find it all in the reports if you live till next near. You're a lucky chap. *You* haven't got a wife to send out of harm's way. The hill-stations ought to be full of women this year.'

'I think you're inclined to exaggerate the talk in the bazars,' said a young Civilian in the Secretariat. 'Now I have observed——'

'I daresay you have,' said the Deputy-Commissioner, 'but you've a great deal more to observe, my son. In the meantime, I wish to observe to you——' and he drew him aside to discuss the construction of the canal that was so dear to his heart. Holden went to his bungalow and began to understand that he was not alone in the world, and also that he was afraid for the sake of another— which is the most soul-satisfying fear known to man.

Two months later, as the Deputy had foretold, Nature began to audit her accounts with a red pencil. On the heels of the spring reapings came a cry for bread, and the Government, which had decreed that no man should die of want, sent wheat. Then came the cholera from all four quarters of the compass. It struck a pilgrim-gathering of half a million at a sacred shrine. Many died at the feet of their god; the others broke and ran over the face of the land carrying the pestilence with them. It smote a walled city and killed two hundred a day. The people crowded the trains, hanging on to the footboards and squatting on the roofs of the carriages, and the cholera followed them, for at each station they dragged out the dead and the dying. They died by the roadside, and the horses of the Englishmen shied at the corpses in the grass. The Rains did not come, and the earth turned to iron lest man should escape death by hiding in her. The English sent their wives away to the Hills and went about their work, coming forward as they were bidden to fill the gaps in the fighting-line. Holden, sick with fear of losing his chiefest treasure on earth, had done his best to persuade Ameera to go away with her mother to the Himalayas.

'Why should I go?' said she, one evening on the roof.

'There is sickness, and people are dying, and all the white *mem-log* have gone.'

'All of them?'

'All—unless perhaps there remain some old scald-head who vexes her husband's heart by running risk of death.'

'Nay; who stays is my sister, and thou must not abuse her, for I will be a scald-head too. I am glad all the bold *mem-log* are gone.'

'Do I speak to a woman or a babe? Go to the Hills, and I will see to it that thou goest like a queen's daughter. Think, child. In a red-lacquered bullock-cart, veiled and curtained, with brass peacocks upon the pole and red cloth hangings. I will send two orderlies for guard and——'

'Peace! Thou art the babe in speaking thus. What use are those toys to me? *He* would have patted the bullocks and played with the housings. For his sake, perhaps—thou hast made me very English—I might have gone. Now, I will not. Let the *mem-log* run.'

'Their husbands are sending them, beloved.'

'Very good talk. Since when hast thou been my husband to tell me what to do? I have but borne thee a son. Thou art only all the desire of my soul to me. How shall I depart when I know that if evil befall thee by the breadth of so much as my littlest finger-nail—is that not small?—I should be aware of it though I were in Paradise. And here, this summer, thou mayest die—*ai, janee*, die! and in dying they might call to tend thee a white woman, and she would rob me in the last of thy love!'

'But love is not born in a moment or on a death-bed!'

'What dost thou know of love, stoneheart? She would take thy thanks at least and, by God and the Prophet and Bibi Miriam the mother of thy Prophet, that I will never endure. My lord and my love, let there be no more foolish talk of going away. Where thou art, I am. It is enough.' She put an arm round his neck and a hand on his mouth.

There are not many happinesses so complete as those that are snatched under the shadow of the sword. They sat together and laughed, calling each other openly by every pet name that could move the wrath of the Gods. The city below them was locked up in its own torments. Sulphur fires blazed in the streets; the conches in the Hindu temples screamed and bellowed, for the Gods were inattentive in those days. There was a service in the great Mohammedan shrine, and the call to prayer from the minarets was almost unceasing. They heard the wailing in the houses of the dead, and once the shriek of a mother who had lost a child and was calling for its return. In the grey dawn they saw the dead borne out through the city gates, each litter with its own little knot of mourners. Wherefore they kissed each other and shivered.

It was a red and heavy audit, for the land was very sick and needed a little breathing-space ere the torrent of cheap life should flood it anew. The children of immature fathers and undeveloped mothers made no resistance. They were cowed and sat still, waiting till the sword should be sheathed in November if it were so willed. There were gaps among the English, but the gaps were filled. The work of superintending famine-relief, cholera-sheds, medicine-distribution, and what little sanitation was possible, went forward because it was so ordered.

Holden had been told to keep himself in readiness to move to replace the next man who should fall. There were twelve hours in each day when he could not see Ameera, and she might die in three. He was considering what his pain would be if he could not see her for three months, or if she died out of his sight. He was absolutely certain that her death would be demanded—so certain, that when he looked up from the telegram and saw Pir Khan breathless in the doorway, he laughed aloud. 'And?' said he——

'When there is a cry in the night and the spirit flutters into the throat, who has a charm that will restore? Come swiftly, Heaven-born! It is the black cholera.'

Holden galloped to his home. The sky was heavy with clouds, for the long-deferred Rains were near and the heat was stifling. Ameera's mother met him in the courtyard, whimpering, 'She is dying. She is nursing herself into death. She is all but dead. What shall I do, Sahib?'

Ameera was lying in the room in which Tota had been born. She made no sign when Holden entered, because the human soul is a very lonely thing and, when it is getting ready to go away, hides itself in a misty borderland where the living may not follow. The black cholera does its work quietly and without explanation. Ameera was being thrust out of life as though the Angel of Death had himself put his hand upon her. The quick breathing seemed to show that she was either afraid or in pain, but neither eyes nor mouth gave any answer to Holden's kisses. There was nothing to be said or done. Holden could only wait and suffer. The first drops of the rain began to fall on the roof and he could hear shouts of joy in the parched city.

The soul came back a little and the lips moved. Holden bent down to listen. 'Keep nothing of mine,' said Ameera. 'Take no hair from my head. *She* would make thee burn it later on. That flame I should feel. Lower! Stoop lower! Remember only that I was thine and bore thee a son. Though thou wed a white woman to-morrow, the pleasure of receiving in thine arms thy first son is taken from thee for ever. Remember me when thy son is born— the one that shall carry thy name before all men. His misfortunes be on my head. I bear witness—I bear witness'—the lips were forming the words on his ear—'that there is no God but—thee, beloved!'

Then she died. Holden sat still, and all thought was taken from him—till he heard Ameera's mother lift the curtain.

'Is she dead, Sahib?'

'She is dead.'

'Then I will mourn, and afterwards take an inventory of the furniture in this house. For that will be mine. The Sahib does not mean to resume it? It is so little, so very little, Sahib, and I am an old woman. I would like to lie softly.'

'For the mercy of God be silent a while. Go out and mourn where I cannot hear.'

'Sahib, she will be buried in four hours.'

'I know the custom. I shall go ere she is taken away. That matter is in thy hands. Look to it that the bed on which—on which she lies——'

'Aha! That beautiful red-lacquered bed. I have long desired——'

'That the bed is left here untouched for my disposal. All else in the house is thine. Hire a cart, take everything, go hence, and before sunrise let there be nothing in this house but that which I have ordered thee to respect.'

'I am an old woman. I would stay at least for the days of mourning, and the Rains have just broken. Whither shall I go?'

'What is that to me? My order is that there is a going. The house-gear is worth a thousand rupees and my orderly shall bring thee a hundred rupees tonight.'

'That is very little. Think of the cart-hire.'

'It shall be nothing unless thou goest, and with speed. O woman, get hence and leave me with my dead!'

The mother shuffled down the staircase, and in her anxiety to take stock of the house-fittings forgot to mourn. Holden stayed by Ameera's side, and the rain roared on the roof. He could not think connectedly by reason of the noise, though he made many attempts to do so. Then four sheeted ghosts glided dripping into the room and stared at him through their veils. They were the washers of the dead. Holden left the room and went out to his horse. He had come in a dead, stifling calm through ankle-deep dust. He found the courtyard a rain-lashed pond alive with frogs; a torrent of yellow water ran under the gate, and a roaring wind drove the bolts of the rain like buckshot against the mud walls. Pir Khan was shivering in his little hut by the gate, and the horse was stamping uneasily in the water.

'I have been told the Sahib's order,' said Pir Khan. 'It is well. This house is now desolate. I go also, for my monkey-face would be a reminder of that which has been. Concerning the bed, I will bring that to thy house yonder in the morning; but remember, Sahib, it will be to thee a knife turning in a green wound. I go upon a pilgrimage, and I will take no money. I have grown fat in the protection of the Presence whose sorrow is my sorrow. For the last time I hold his stirrup.'

He touched Holden's foot with both hands and the horse sprang out into the road, where the creaking bamboos were whipping the sky and all the frogs were chuckling. Holden could not see for the rain in his face. He put his hands before his eyes and muttered:

'Oh, you brute! You utter brute!'

The news of his trouble was already in his bungalow. He read the knowledge in his butler's eyes when Ahmed Khan brought in food, and for the first and last time in his life laid a hand upon his master's shoulder, saying, 'Eat, Sahib, eat. Meat is good against sorrow. I also have known. Moreover the shadows come and go, Sahib; the shadows come and go. These be curried eggs.'

Holden could neither eat nor sleep. The heavens sent down eight inches of rain in that night and washed the earth clean. The waters tore down walls, broke roads, and scoured open the shallow graves on the Mohammedan burying-ground. All next day it rained, and Holden sat still in his house considering his sorrow. On the morning of the third day he received a telegram which said only, 'Ricketts, Myndonie. Dying. Holden relieve. Immediate.' Then he thought that before he departed he would look at the house wherein he had been master and lord. There was a break in the weather, and the rank earth steamed with vapour.

He found that the rains had torn down the mud pillars of the gateway, and the heavy wooden gate that had guarded his life hung lazily from one hinge. There was grass three inches high in the courtyard; Pir Khan's lodge was empty, and the sodden thatch sagged between the beams. A grey squirrel was in possession of the veranda as if the house had been untenanted for thirty years instead of three days. Ameera's mother had removed everything except some mildewed matting. The *tick-tick* of the little scorpions as they hurried across the floor was the only sound in the house. Ameera's room and the other one where Tota had lived were heavy with mildew; and the narrow staircase leading to the roof was streaked and stained with rain-borne mud. Holden saw all these things, and came out again to meet in the road Durga Dass, his landlord— portly, affable, clothed in white muslin, and driving a Cee-spring buggy. He was overlooking his property to see how the roofs stood the stress of the first rains.

'I have heard,' said he, 'you will not take this place any more, Sahib?'

'What are you going to do with it?'

'Perhaps I shall let it again.'

'Then I will keep it on while I am away.'

Durga Dass was silent for some time. 'You shall not take it on, Sahib,' he said. 'When I was a young man I also——, but today I am a member of the Municipality. Ho! Ho! No. When the birds have gone what need to keep the nest? I will have it pulled down —the timber will sell for something always. It shall be pulled down, and the Municipality shall make a road across, as they desire, from the burning-ghat to the city wall, so that no man may say where the house stood.'

Life's Handicap, 1891*

* *Macmillan's Magazine*, 1890.

Moti Guj—Mutineer

ONCE UPON A TIME there was a coffee-planter in India who wished to clear some forest land for coffee-planting. When he had cut down all the trees and burned the under-wood the stumps still remained. Dynamite is expensive and slow-fire slow. The happy medium for stump-clearing is the lord of all beasts, who is the elephant. He will either push the stump out of the ground with his tusks, if he has any, or drag it out with ropes. The planter, therefore, hired elephants by ones and twos and threes, and fell to work. The very best of all the elephants belonged to the very worst of all the drivers or mahouts; and the superior beast's name was Moti Guj. He was the absolute property of his mahout, which would never have been the case under native rule, for Moti Guj was a creature to be desired by kings; and his name, being translated, meant the Pearl Elephant. Because the British Government was in the land, Deesa, the mahout, enjoyed his property undisturbed. He was dissipated. When he had made much money through the strength of his elephant, he would get extremely drunk and give Moti Guj a beating with a tent-peg over the tender nails of the forefeet. Moti Guj never trampled the life out of Deesa on these occasions, for he knew that after the beating was over Deesa would embrace his trunk, and weep and call him his love and his life and the liver of his soul, and give him some liquor. Moti Guj was very fond of liquor—arrack for choice, though he would drink palm-tree toddy if nothing better offered. Then Deesa would go to sleep between Moti Guj's forefeet, and as Deesa generally chose the middle of the public road, and as Moti Guj mounted guard over him and would not permit horse, foot, or cart to pass by, traffic was congested till Deesa saw fit to wake up.

There was no sleeping in the daytime on the planter's clearing: the wages were too high to risk. Deesa sat on Moti Guj's neck and gave him orders, while Moti Guj rooted up the stumps—for he owned a magnificent pair of tusks, or pulled at the end of a rope— for he had a magnificent pair of shoulders, while Deesa kicked him behind the ears and said he was the king of elephants. At evening time Moti Guj would wash down his three hundred pounds' weight of green food with a quart of arrack, and Deesa would take his share and sing songs between Moti Guj's legs till it was time to go to bed. Once a week Deesa led Moti Guj down to the river, and Moti Guj lay on his side luxuriously in the shallows, while Deesa went over him with a coir-swab and a brick. Moti Guj never mistook the pounding blow of the latter for the smack of the former that warned him to get up and turn over on the other side. Then Deesa would look at his feet, and examine his eyes, and turn up the fringes of his mighty ears in case of sores or budding ophthalmia. After inspection, the two would 'come up with a song from the sea,' Moti Guj all black and shining, waving a torn tree-branch twelve feet long in his trunk, and Deesa knotting up his own long wet hair.

It was a peaceful, well-paid life till Deesa felt the return of the desire to drink deep. He wished for an orgy. The little draughts that led nowhere were taking the manhood out of him.

He went to the planter, and 'My mother's dead,' said he, weeping.

'She died on the last plantation two months ago; and she died once before that when you were working for me last year,' said the planter, who knew something of the ways of nativedom.

'Then it's my aunt, and she was just the same as a mother to me,' said Deesa, weeping more than ever. 'She has left eighteen small children entirely without bread, and it is I who must fill their little stomachs,' said Deesa, beating his head on the floor.

'Who brought you the news?' said the planter.

'The post,' said Deesa.

'There hasn't been a post here for the past week. Get back to your lines!'

'A devastating sickness has fallen on my village, and all my wives are dying,' yelled Deesa, really in tears this time.

'Call Chihun, who comes from Deesa's village,' said the planter. 'Chihun, has this man a wife?'

'He!' said Chihun. 'No. Not a woman of our village would look at him. They'd sooner marry the elephant.' Chihun snorted. Deesa wept and bellowed.

'You will get into a difficulty in a minute,' said the planter. 'Go back to your work!'

'Now I will speak Heaven's truth,' gulped Deesa, with an inspiration. 'I haven't been drunk for two months. I desire to depart in order to get properly drunk afar off and distant from this heavenly plantation. Thus I shall cause no trouble.'

A flickering smile crossed the planter's face. 'Deesa,' said he, 'you've spoken the truth, and I'd give you leave on the spot if

anything could be done with Moti Guj while you're away. You
know that he will only obey your orders.'

'May the Light of the Heavens live forty thousand years! I shall
be absent but ten little days. After that, upon my faith and honour
and soul, I return. As to the inconsiderable interval, have I the
gracious permission of the Heaven-born to call up Moti Guj?'

Permission was granted, and, in answer to Deesa's shrill yell, the
lordly tusker swung out of the shade of a clump of trees where he
had been squirting dust over himself till his master should return.

'Light of my heart, Protector of the Drunken, Mountain of
Might, give ear,' said Deesa, standing in front of him.

Moti Guj gave ear, and saluted with his trunk. 'I am going away,'
said Deesa.

Moti Guj's eyes twinkled. He liked jaunts as well as his master.
One could snatch all manner of nice things from the roadside then.

'But you, you fubsy old pig, must stay behind and work.'

The twinkle died out as Moti Guj tried to look delighted. He
hated stump-hauling on the plantation. It hurt his teeth.

'I shall be gone for ten days, O Delectable One. Hold up your
near forefoot and I'll impress the fact upon it, warty toad of a dried
mud-puddle.' Deesa took a tent-peg and banged Moti Guj ten
times on the nails. Moti Guj grunted and shuffled from foot to foot.

'Ten days,' said Deesa, 'you must work and haul and root trees
as Chihun here shall order you. Take up Chihun and set him on
your neck!' Moti Guj curled the tip of his trunk. Chihun put his foot
there and was swung on to the neck. Deesa handed Chihun the
heavy *ankus,* the iron elephant-goad.

Chihun thumped Moti Guj's bald head as a paviour thumps a
kerbstone.

Moti Guj trumpeted.

'Be still, hog of the backwoods! Chihun's your mahout for ten
days. And now bid me good-bye, beast after mine own heart. Oh,
my lord, my king! Jewel of all created elephants, lily of the herd,
preserve your honoured health; be virtuous. Adieu!'

Moti Guj lapped his trunk round Deesa and swung him into the
air twice. That was his way of bidding the man good-bye.

'He'll work now,' said Deesa to the planter. 'Have I leave to go?'

The planter nodded, and Deesa dived into the woods. Moti Guj
went back to haul stumps.

Chihun was very kind to him, but he felt unhappy and forlorn
notwithstanding. Chihun gave him balls of spices, and tickled him
under the chin, and Chihun's little baby cooed to him after work

was over, and Chihun's wife called him a darling; but Moti Guj was a bachelor by instinct, as Deesa was. He did not understand the domestic emotions. He wanted the light of his universe back again—the drink and the drunken slumber, the savage beatings and the savage caresses.

None the less he worked well, and the planter wondered. Deesa had vagabonded along the road: till he met a marriage procession of his own caste and, drinking, dancing, and tippling, had drifted past all knowledge of the lapse of time.

The morning of the eleventh day dawned, and there returned no Deesa. Moti Guj was loosed from his ropes for the daily stint. He swung clear, looked round, shrugged his shoulders, and began to walk away, as one having business elsewhere.

'Hi! ho! Come back, you,' shouted Chihun. 'Come back, and put me on your neck, Misborn Mountain. Return, Splendour of the Hillsides. Adornment of all India, heave to, or I'll bang every toe off your fat forefoot!'

Moti Guj gurgled gently, but did not obey. Chihun ran after him with a rope and caught him up. Moti Guj put his ears forward, and Chihun knew what that meant, though he tried to carry it off with high words.

'None of your nonsense with me,' said he. 'To your pickets, Devil-son.'

'Hrrump!' said Moti Guj, and that was all—that and the forebent ears.

Moti Guj put his hands in his pockets, chewed a branch for a toothpick, and strolled about the clearing, making jest of the other elephants, who had just set to work.

Chihun reported the state of affairs to the planter, who came out with a dog-whip and cracked it furiously. Moti Guj paid the white man the compliment of charging him nearly a quarter of a mile across the clearing and 'Hrrumphing' him into the veranda. Then he stood outside the house chuckling to himself, and shaking all over with the fun of it, as an elephant will.

'We'll thrash him,' said the planter. 'He shall have the finest thrashing that ever elephant received. Give Kala Nag and Nazim twelve foot of chain apiece, and tell them to lay on twenty blows.'

Kala Nag—which means Black Snake—and Nazim were two of the biggest elephants in the lines, and one of their duties was to administer the graver punishments, since no man can beat an elephant properly.

They took the whipping-chains and rattled them in their trunks as they sidled up to Moti Guj, meaning to hustle him between them. Moti Guj had never, in all his life of thirty-nine years, been whipped and he did not intend to open new experiences. So he waited, weaving his head from right to left, and measuring the precise spot in Kala Nag's fat side where a blunt tusk would sink deepest. Kala Nag had no tusks; the chain was his badge of authority; but he judged it good to swing wide of Moti Guj at the last minute, and to appear as if he had brought out the chain for amusement. Nazim turned round and went home early. He did not feel fighting-fit that morning, and so Moti Guj was left standing alone with his ears cocked.

That decided the planter to argue no more, and Moti Guj rolled back to his inspection of the clearing. An elephant who will not work, and is not tied up, is not quite so manageable as an eighty-one-ton gun loose in a heavy sea-way. He slapped old friends on the back and asked them if the stumps were coming away easily; he talked nonsense concerning labour and the inalienable rights of elephants to a long nooning; and, wandering to and fro, thoroughly demoralized the garden till sundown, when he returned to his pickets for food.

'If you won't work you shan't eat,' said Chihun angrily. 'You're a wild elephant, and no educated animal at all. Go back to your jungle.'

Chihun's little brown baby, rolling on the floor of the hut, stretched its fat arms to the huge shadow in the doorway. Moti Guj knew well that it was the dearest thing on earth to Chihun. He swung out his trunk with a fascinating crook at the end, and the brown baby threw itself shouting upon it. Moti Guj made fast and pulled up till the brown baby was crowing in the air twelve feet above his father's head.

'Great Chief!' said Chihun. 'Flour-cakes of the best, twelve in number, two feet across, and soaked in rum shall be yours on the instant, and two hundred pounds' weight of fresh-cut young sugar-cane therewith. Deign only to put down safely that insignificant brat who is my heart and my life to me.'

Moti Guj tucked the brown baby comfortably between his forefeet, that could have knocked into toothpicks all Chihun's hut, and waited for his food. He ate it, and the brown baby crawled away. Moti Guj dozed, and thought of Deesa. One of many mysteries connected with the elephant is that his huge body needs less sleep than anything else that lives. Four or five hours in the night suffice—two just before midnight, lying down on one side;

two just after one o'clock, lying down on the other. The rest of the
silent hours are filled with eating and fidgeting and long grumbling
soliloquies.

At midnight, therefore, Moti Guj strode out of his pickets, for a
thought had come to him that Deesa might be lying drunk somewhere in the dark forest with none to look after him. So all that
night he chased through the undergrowth, blowing and trumpeting
and shaking his ears. He went down to the river and blared across
the shallows where Deesa used to wash him, but there was no
answer. He could not find Deesa, but he disturbed all the elephants
in the lines, and nearly frightened to death some gipsies in the
woods.

At dawn Deesa returned to the plantation. He had been very
drunk indeed, and he expected to fall into trouble for outstaying
his leave. He drew a long breath when he saw that the bungalow
and the plantation were still uninjured; for he knew something
of Moti Guj's temper; and reported himself with many lies and
salaams. Moti Guj had gone to his pickets for breakfast. His
night exercise had made him hungry.

'Call up your beast,' said the planter, and Deesa shouted in the
mysterious elephant-language, that some mahouts believe came
from China at the birth of the world, when elephants and not men
were masters. Moti Guj heard and came. Elephants do not gallop.
They move from spots at varying rates of speed. If an elephant
wished to catch an express train he could not gallop, but he could
catch the train. Thus Moti Guj was at the planter's door almost
before Chihun noticed that he had left his pickets. He fell into
Deesa's arms trumpeting with joy, and the man and beast wept
and slobbered over each other, and handled each other from head
to heel to see that no harm had befallen.

'Now we will get to work,' said Deesa. 'Lift me up, my son and
my joy.'

Moti Guj swung him up and the two went to the coffee-clearing
to look for irksome stumps.

The planter was too astonished to be very angry.

Life's Handicap, 1891

In the Rukh

The Only Son lay down again and dreamed that he dreamed a dream.
The last ash dropped from the dying fire with the click of a falling spark,
And the Only Son woke up again and called across the dark:
'Now, was I born of womankind and laid in a mother's breast?
For I have dreamed of a shaggy hide whereon I went to rest.
And was I born of womankind and laid on a father's arm?
For I have dreamed of long white teeth that guarded me from harm.
Oh, was I born of womankind and did I play alone?
For I have dreamed of playmates twain that bit me to the bone.
And did I break the barley bread and steep it in the tyre?
For I have dreamed of a youngling kid new riven from the byre.
An hour it lacks and an hour it lacks to the rising of the moon,
But I can see the black roof-beams as plain as it were noon!
'Tis a league and a league to the Lena Falls where the trooping sambhur go,
But I can hear the little fawn that bleats behind the doe!
'Tis a league and a league to the Lena Falls where the crop and the upland
   meet,
But I can smell the warm wet wind that whispers through the wheat!'

THE ONLY SON

O F THE WHEELS of public service which turn under the Indian
Government, there is none more important than the Department of Woods and Forests. The reboisement of all India is in its
hands; or will be when Government has the money to spend. Its
servants wrestle with wandering sand-torrents and shifting dunes:
wattling them at the sides, damming them in front, and pegging
them down atop with coarse grass and spindling pine after the rules
of Nancy. They are responsible for all the timber in the State forests
of the Himalayas, as well as for the denuded hillsides that the
monsoons wash into dry gullies and aching ravines; each cut a
mouth crying aloud what carelessness can do. They experiment
with battalions of foreign trees, and coax the blue gum to take root
and, perhaps, dry up the Canal fever. In the Plains the chief part
of their duty is to see that the belt fire-lines in the forest reserves
are kept clean, so that when drought comes and the cattle starve,
they may throw the reserve open to the villager's herds and allow
the man himself to gather sticks. They poll and lop for the stacked
railway-fuel along the lines that burn no coal; they calculate the
profit of their plantations to five points of decimals; they are the

doctors and midwives of the huge teak forests of Upper Burma, the rubber of the Eastern Jungles, and the gall-nuts of the South; and they are always hampered by lack of funds. But since a Forest Officer's business takes him far from the beaten roads and the regular Stations, he learns to grow wise in more than wood-lore alone; to know the people and the polity of the jungle; meeting tiger, bear, leopard, wild-dog, and all the deer, not once or twice after days of beating, but again and again in the execution of his duty. He spends much time in saddle or under canvas—the friend of newly-planted trees, the associate of uncouth rangers and hairy trackers—till the woods, that show his care, in turn set their mark upon him, and he ceases to sing the naughty French songs he learned at Nancy, and grows silent with the silent things of the underbrush.

Gisborne of the Woods and Forests had spent four years in the Service. At first he loved it without comprehension, because it led him into the open on horseback and gave him authority. Then he hated it furiously, and would have given a year's pay for one month of such society as India affords. That crisis over, the forests took him back again, and he was content to serve them, to deepen and widen his fire-lines, to watch the green mist of his new plantation against the older foliage, to dredge out the choked stream, and to follow and strengthen the last struggle of the forest where it broke down and died among the long pig-grass. On some still day that grass would be burned off, and a hundred beasts that had their homes there would rush out before the pale flames at high noon. Later, the forest would creep forward over the blackened ground in orderly lines of saplings, and Gisborne, watching, would be well pleased. His bungalow, a thatched white-walled cottage of two rooms, was set at one end of the great *rukh* and overlooking it. He made no pretence at keeping a garden, for the *rukh* swept up to his door, curled over in a thicket of bamboo, and he rode from his veranda into its heart without the need of any carriage-drive.

Abdul Gafur, his fat Mohammedan butler, fed him when he was at home, and spent the rest of the time gossiping with the little band of native servants whose huts lay behind the bungalow. There were two grooms, a cook, a water-carrier, and a sweeper, and that was all. Gisborne cleaned his own guns and kept no dog. Dogs scared the game, and it pleased the man to be able to say where the subjects of his kingdom would drink at moonrise, eat before dawn, and lie up in the day's heat. The rangers and Forest-guards lived in little huts far away in the *rukh*, only appearing when one of them had been injured by a falling tree or a wild beast. Thus Gisborne was alone.

In spring the *rukh* put out few new leaves, but lay dry and still untouched by the finger of the year, waiting for rain. Only there was then more calling and roaring in the dark on a quiet night; the tumult of a battle-royal among the tigers, the bellowing of arrogant buck, or the steady wood-chopping of an old boar sharpening his tushes against a bole. Then Gisborne laid aside his little-used gun altogether, for it was to him a sin to kill. In summer, through the furious May heats, the *rukh* reeled in the haze, and Gisborne watched for the first sign of curling smoke that should betray a forest fire. Then came the Rains with a roar, and the *rukh* was blotted out in fetch after fetch of warm mist, and the broad leaves drummed the night through under the big drops; and there was a noise of running water, and of juicy green stuff crackling where the wind struck it, and the lightning wove patterns behind the dense matting of the foliage, till the sun broke loose again and the *rukh* stood with hot flanks smoking to the newly-washed sky. Then the heat and the dry cold subdued everything to tiger-colour again. So Gisborne learned to know his *rukh* and was very happy. His pay came month by month, but he had very little need for money. The currency notes accumulated in the drawer where he kept his home-letters and the recapping-machine. If he drew anything, it was to make a purchase from the Calcutta Botanical Gardens, or to pay a ranger's widow a sum that the Government of India would never have sanctioned for her man's death.

Payment was good, but vengeance was also necessary, and he took that when he could. One night of many nights a runner, breathless and gasping, came to him with the news that a Forest-guard lay dead by the Kanye stream, the side of his head smashed in as though it had been an egg-shell. Gisborne went out at dawn to look for the murderer. It is only travellers, and now and then young soldiers, who are known to the world as great hunters. The Forest Officers take their *shikar* as part of the day's work, and no one hears of it. Gisborne went on foot to the place of the kill: the widow was wailing over the corpse as it lay on a bedstead, while two or three men were looking at footprints on the moist ground. 'That is the Red One,' said a man. 'I knew he would turn to man in time, but surely there is game enough even for him. This must have been done for devilry.'

'The Red One lies up in the rocks at the back of the *sal* trees,' said Gisborne. He knew the tiger under suspicion.

'Not now, Sahib, not now. He will be raging and ranging to and fro. Remember that the first kill is a triple kill always. Our blood makes them mad. He may be behind us even as we speak.'

'He may have gone to the next hut,' said another. 'It is only four *koss*. Wallah, who is this?'

Gisborne turned with the others. A man was walking down the dried bed of the stream, naked except for the loin-cloth, but crowned with a wreath of the tasselled blossoms of the white convolvulus-creeper. So noiselessly did he move over the little pebbles that even Gisborne, used to the soft-footedness of trackers, started.

'The tiger that killed,' he began, without any salute, 'has gone to drink, and now he is asleep under a rock beyond that hill.' His voice was clear and bell-like, utterly different from the usual whine of the native, and his face as he lifted it in the sunshine might have been that of an angel strayed among the woods. The widow ceased wailing above the corpse and looked round-eyed at the stranger, returning to her duty with double strength.

'Shall I show the Sahib?' he said simply.

'If thou art sure——' Gisborne began.

'Sure indeed. I saw him only an hour ago—the dog. It is before his time to eat man's flesh. He has yet a dozen sound teeth in his evil head.'

The men kneeling above the footprints slunk off quietly, for fear that Gisborne should ask them to go with him, and the young man laughed a little to himself.

'Come, Sahib,' he cried, and turned on his heel, walking before his companion.

'Not so fast. I cannot keep that pace,' said the white man. 'Halt there. Thy face is new to me.'

'That may be. I am but newly come into this forest.'

'From what village?'

'I am without a village. I came from over there.' He flung out his arm towards the north.

'A gipsy then?'

'No, Sahib. I am a man without caste, and for matter of that without a father.'

'What do men call thee?'

'Mowgli, Sahib. And what is the Sahib's name?'

'I am the warden of this *rukh*—Gisborne is my name.'

'How? Do they number the trees and the blades of grass here?'

'Even so; lest such gipsy fellows as thou set them afire.'

'I! I would not hurt the Jungle for any gift. That is my home.'

He turned to Gisborne with a smile that was irresistible, and held up a warning hand.

'Now, Sahib, we must go a little quietly. There is no need to wake the dog, though he sleeps heavily enough. Perhaps it were better if I went forward alone and drove him down wind to the Sahib.'

'Allah! Since when have tigers been driven to and fro like cattle by naked men?' said Gisborne, aghast at the man's audacity.

He laughed again softly. 'Nay, then, come along with me and shoot him in thine own way with the big English rifle.'

Gisborne stepped in his guide's track, twisted, crawled, and clomb and stooped and suffered through all the many agonies of a jungle-stalk. He was purple and dripping with sweat when Mowgli at the last bade him raise his head and peer over a blue baked rock near a tiny hill pool. By the waterside lay the tiger extended and at ease, lazily licking clean again an enormous elbow and fore-paw. He was old, yellow-toothed, and not a little mangy, but in that setting and sunshine, imposing enough.

Gisborne had no false ideas of sport where the man-eater was concerned. This thing was vermin, to be killed as speedily as possible. He waited to recover his breath, rested the rifle on the rock, and whistled. The brute's head turned slowly not twenty feet from the rifle-mouth, and Gisborne planted his shots, businesslike, one behind the shoulder and the other a little below the eye. At that range the heavy bones were no guard against the rending bullets.

'Well, the skin was not worth keeping at any rate,' said he, as the smoke cleared away and the beast lay kicking and gasping in the last agony.

'A dog's death for a dog,' said Mowgli quietly. 'Indeed there is nothing in that carrion worth taking away.'

'The whiskers. Dost thou not take the whiskers?' said Gisborne, who knew how the Forest rangers valued such things.

'I? Am I a lousy *shikari* of the jungle to paddle with a tiger's muzzle? Let him lie. Here come his friends already.'

A dropping kite whistled shrilly overhead, as Gisborne snapped out the empty shells and wiped his face.

'And if thou art not a *shikari*, where didst thou learn thy knowledge of the tiger-folk?' said he. 'No tracker could have done better.'

'I hate all tigers,' said Mowgli curtly. 'Let the Sahib give me his

gun to carry. It is a very fine one. And where does the Sahib go
now?'

'To my house.'

'May I come? I have never yet looked withinsides a white man's
house.'

Gisborne returned to his bungalow, Mowgli striding noiselessly
before him, his brown skin glistening in the sunlight.

He stared curiously at the veranda and the two chairs there,
fingered the split bamboo shade curtains with suspicion, and
entered, looking always behind him. Gisborne loosed a curtain to
keep out the sun. It dropped with a clatter, but almost before it
touched the flagging of the veranda Mowgli had leaped clear, and
was standing with heaving chest in the open.

'It is a trap!' he said quickly.

Gisborne laughed. 'White men do not trap men. Indeed thou art
altogether of the jungle.'

'I see,' said Mowgli, 'it has neither catch nor fall. I—I never
beheld these things till today.'

He came in on tiptoe and stared with large eyes at the furniture
of the two rooms. Abdul Gafur, who was laying lunch, looked at
him with deep disgust.

'So much trouble to eat, and so much trouble to lie down after
you have eaten!' said Mowgli with a grin. 'We do better in the
jungle. It is very wonderful. There are very many rich things here.
Is the Sahib not afraid that he may be robbed? I have never seen
such wonderful things.' He was staring at a dusty Benares brass
plate on a rickety bracket.

'Only a thief from the jungle would rob here,' said Abdul Gafur,
setting down a plate with a clatter. Mowgli opened his eyes wide
and stared at the white-bearded Mohammedan.

'In my country when goats bleat very loud we cut their throats,'
he returned cheerfully. 'But have no fear, thou. I am going.'

He turned and disappeared into the *rukh*. Gisborne looked after
him with a laugh that ended in a little sigh. There was not much
outside his regular work to interest the Forest Officer, and this son
of the forest, who seemed to know tigers as other people know dogs,
would have been a diversion.

'He's a most wonderful chap,' thought Gisborne, 'he's like the
illustrations in the Classical Dictionary. I wish I could have made
him a gun-boy. There's no fun in *shikaring* alone, and this fellow
would have been a perfect *shikari*. I wonder what in the world he
is.'

That evening he sat on the veranda under the stars, smoking as
he wondered. A puff of smoke curled from the pipe-bowl. As it
cleared he was aware of Mowgli sitting with arms crossed on the
veranda edge. A ghost could not have drifted up more noiselessly.
Gisborne started and let the pipe drop.

'There is no man to talk to out there in the *rukh*,' said Mowgli.
'I came here, therefore.' He picked up the pipe and returned it to
Gisborne.

'Oh,' said Gisborne, and after a long pause, 'What news is there
in the *rukh*? Hast thou found another tiger?'

'The nilghai are changing their feeding-ground against the new
moon, as is their custom. The pig are feeding near the Kanye river
now, because they will not feed with the nilghai; and one of their
sows has been killed by a leopard in the long grass at the water-
head. I do not know any more.'

'And how didst thou know all these things?' said Gisborne, leaning forward and looking at the eyes that glittered in the starlight.

'How should I not know? The nilghai has his custom and his
use, and a child knows that pig will not feed with him.'

'I do not know this,' said Gisborne.

'Tck! Tck! And thou art in charge—so the men of the huts tell
me—in charge of all this *rukh*?' He laughed to himself.

'It is well enough to talk and to tell child's tales,' Gisborne
retorted, nettled at the chuckle. 'To say that this and that goes on
in the *rukh*. No man can deny thee.'

'As for the sow's carcass, I will show thee her bones tomorrow,'
Mowgli returned, absolutely unmoved. 'Touching the matter of the
nilghai, if the Sahib will sit here very still I will drive one nilghai
up to this place, and by listening to the sounds carefully, the Sahib
can tell whence that nilghai has been driven.'

'Mowgli, the jungle has made thee mad,' said Gisborne. 'Who
can drive nilghai?'

'Still!—Sit still, then. I go.'

'Gad, the man's a ghost!' said Gisborne; for Mowgli had faded
out into the darkness and there was no sound of feet. The *rukh* lay
out in great velvety folds in the uncertain shimmer of the star-
dust—so still that the least little wandering wind among the tree-
tops came up as the sigh of a child sleeping equably. Abdul Gafur
in the cook-house was clicking plates together.

'Be still there!' shouted Gisborne, and composed himself to
listen as a man can who is used to the stillness of the *rukh*. It had
been his custom, to preserve his self-respect in his isolation, to

dress for dinner each night, and the stiff white shirt-front creaked with his regular breathing till he shifted a little sideways. Then the tobacco of a somewhat foul pipe began to purr, and he threw the pipe from him. Now, except for the night-breath in the *rukh*, everything was dumb.

From an inconceivable distance, and drawled through immeasurable darkness, came the faint, faint echo of a wolf's howl. Then silence again for, it seemed, long hours. At last, when his legs below the knees had lost all feeling, Gisborne heard something that might have been a crash far off through the undergrowth. He doubted till it was repeated again and yet again.

'That's from the west,' he muttered; 'there's something on foot there.' The noise increased—crash on crash, plunge on plunge— with the thick grunting of a hotly pressed nilghai, flying in panic terror and taking no heed to his course.

A shadow blundered out from between the tree-trunks, wheeled back, turned again grunting, and with a clatter on the bare ground dashed up almost within reach of his hand. It was a bull nilghai dripping with dew—his withers hung with a torn trail of creeper, his eyes shining in the light from the house. The creature checked at sight of the man, and fled along the edge of the *rukh* till he melted in the darkness. The first idea in Gisborne's bewildered mind was the indecency of thus dragging out for inspection the big Blue Bull of the *rukh*—the putting him through his paces in the night which should have been his own.

Then said a smooth voice at his ear as he stood staring:

'He came from the water-head where he was leading the herd. From the west he came. Does the Sahib believe now, or shall I bring up the herd to be counted? The Sahib is in charge of this *rukh*.'

Mowgli had reseated himself on the veranda, breathing a little quickly. Gisborne looked at him with open mouth. 'How was that accomplished?' he said.

'The Sahib saw. The bull was driven—driven as a buffalo is. Ho! ho! he will have a fine tale to tell when he returns to the herd.'

'That is a new trick to me. Canst thou run as swiftly as the nilghai, then?'

'The Sahib has seen. If the Sahib needs more knowledge at any time of the movings of the game, I, Mowgli, am here. This is a good *rukh*. I shall stay in it.'

'Stay, then, and if thou hast need of a meal at any time my servants shall give thee one.'

'Yes, indeed. I am fond of cooked food,' Mowgli answered quickly. 'No man may say that I do not eat boiled and roast as much as any other man. I will come for that meal. Now, on my part, I promise that the Sahib shall sleep safely in his house by night, and no thief shall break in to carry away his so rich treasures.'

The conversation ended itself on Mowgli's abrupt departure. Gisborne sat long smoking, and the upshot of his thoughts was that in Mowgli he had found at last that ideal ranger and Forest-guard for whom he and the Department were always looking.

'I must get him into Government service somehow. A man who can drive nilghai would know more about the *rukh* than fifty men. He's a miracle—a *lusus naturae*—and a Forest-guard he must be if he'll only settle down in one place,' said Gisborne.

Abdul Gafur's opinion was less favourable. He confided to Gisborne at bedtime that strangers from God-knew-where were more than likely to be professional thieves, and that he personally did not approve of naked outcastes who had not the proper manner of addressing white people. Gisborne laughed and bade him go to his quarters, and Abdul Gafur retreated growling. Later in the night he found occasion to rise up and beat his thirteen-year-old daughter. Nobody knew the cause of dispute, but Gisborne heard the cry.

Through the days that followed, Mowgli came and went like a shadow. He had established himself and his wild house-keeping close to the bungalow, but on the edge of the *rukh*, where Gisborne, going out on to the veranda for a breath of cool air, would see him sometimes sitting in the moonlight, his forehead on his knees, or lying out along the fling of a branch, closely pressed to it as some beast of the night. Thence Mowgli would throw him a salutation and bid him sleep at ease, or descending would weave prodigious stories of the manners of the beasts in the *rukh*. Once he wandered into the stables and was found looking at the horses with deep interest.

'That,' said Abdul Gafur pointedly, 'is sure sign that some day he will steal one. Why, if he lives about this house, does he not take an honest employment? But no, he must wander up and down like a loose camel, turning the heads of fools and opening the jaws of the unwise to folly.' So Abdul Gafur would give harsh orders to Mowgli when they met, would bid him fetch water and pluck fowls, and Mowgli, laughing unconcernedly, would obey.

'He has no caste,' said Abdul Gafur. 'He will do anything. Look to it, Sahib, that he does not do too much. A snake is a snake, and a jungle-gipsy is a thief till the death.'

'Be silent, then,' said Gisborne. 'I allow thee to correct thine own household if there is not too much noise, because I know thy customs and use. *My* custom thou dost not know. The man is without doubt a little mad.'

'Very little mad indeed,' said Abdul Gafur. 'But we shall see what comes thereof.'

A few days later on, his business took Gisborne into the *rukh* for three days. Abdul Gafur being old and fat was left at home. He did not approve of lying up in rangers' huts, and was inclined to levy contributions in his master's name of grain and oil and milk from those who could ill afford such benevolences. Gisborne rode off early one dawn a little vexed that his man of the woods was not at the veranda to accompany him. He liked him—liked his strength, fleetness, and silence of foot, and his ever-ready open smile; his ignorance of all forms of ceremony and salutations, and the child-like tales that he would tell (and Gisborne would credit now) of what the game was doing in the *rukh*. After an hour's riding through the greenery, he heard a rustle behind him, and Mowgli trotted at his stirrup.

'We have a three days' work toward,' said Gisborne, 'among the new trees.'

'Good,' said Mowgli. 'It is always good to cherish young trees. They make cover if the beasts leave them alone. We must shift the pig again.'

'Again? How?' Gisborne smiled.

'Oh, they were rooting and tusking among the young *sal* last night, and I drove them off. Therefore I did not come to the veranda this morning. The pig should not be on this side of the *rukh* at all. We must keep them below the head of the Kanye river.'

'If a man could herd clouds he might do that thing; but, Mowgli, if as thou sayest, thou art herder in the *rukh* for no gain and for no pay——'

'It is the Sahib's *rukh*,' said Mowgli, quickly looking up. Gisborne nodded thanks and went on: 'Would it not be better to work for pay from the Government? There is a pension at the end of long service.'

'Of that I have thought,' said Mowgli, 'but the rangers live in huts with shut doors, and all that is all too much a trap to me. Yet I think——' *

'Think well, then, and tell me later. Here we will stay for breakfast.'

Gisborne dismounted, took his morning meal from his home-made saddle-bags, and saw the day open hot above the *rukh*. Mowgli lay in the grass at his side staring up to the sky.

Presently he said in a lazy whisper: 'Sahib, is there any order at the bungalow to take out the white mare today?'

'No, she is fat and old and a little lame besides. Why?'

'She is being ridden now and *not* slowly on the road that runs to the railway line.'

'Bah, that is two *koss* away. It is a woodpecker.'

Mowgli put up his forearm to keep the sun out of his eyes.

'The road curves in with a big curve from the bungalow. It is not more than a *koss*, at the farthest, as the kite goes; and sound flies with the birds. Shall we see?'

'What folly! To run a *koss* in this sun to see a noise in the forest.'

'Nay, the pony is the Sahib's pony. I meant only to bring her here. If she is not the Sahib's pony, no matter. If she is, the Sahib can do what he wills. She is certainly being ridden hard.'

'And how wilt thou bring her here, madman?'

'Has the Sahib forgotten? By the road of the nilghai and no other.'

'Up, then, and run if thou art so full of zeal.'

'Oh, I do not run!' He put out his hand to sign for silence, and still lying on his back called aloud thrice—with a deep gurgling cry that was new to Gisborne.

'She will come,' he said at the end. 'Let us wait in the shade.' The long eyelashes drooped over the wild eyes as Mowgli began to doze in the morning hush. Gisborne waited patiently: Mowgli was surely mad, but as entertaining a companion as a lonely Forest Officer could desire.

'Ho! ho!' said Mowgli lazily, with shut eyes. 'He has dropped off. Well, first the mare will come and then the man.' Then he yawned as Gisborne's pony stallion neighed. Three minutes later Gisborne's white mare, saddled, bridled, but riderless, tore into the glade where they were sitting, and hurried to her companion.

'She is not very warm,' said Mowgli, 'but in this heat the sweat comes easily. Presently we shall see her rider, for a man goes more slowly than a horse—especially if he chance to be a fat man and old.'

'Allah! This is devils' work,' cried Gisborne, leaping to his feet, for he heard a yell in the jungle.

'Have no care, Sahib. He will not be hurt. He also will say that it is devils' work. Ah! Listen! Who is that?'

It was the voice of Abdul Gafur in an agony of terror, crying out upon unknown things to spare him and his grey hairs.

'Nay, I cannot move another step,' he howled. 'I am old and my turban is lost. *Arré! Arré!* But I will move. Indeed I will hasten. I will run! O Devils of the Pit, I am a Mussulman!'

The undergrowth parted and gave up Abdul Gafur, turbanless, shoeless, with his waist-cloth unbound, mud and grass in his clutched hands, and his face purple. He saw Gisborne, yelled anew, and pitched forward, exhausted and quivering, at his feet. Mowgli watched him with a sweet smile.

'This is no joke,' said Gisborne sternly. 'The man is like to die, Mowgli.'

'He will not die. He is only afraid. There was no need that he should have come out of a walk.'

Abdul Gafur groaned and rose up, shaking in every limb.

'It was witchcraft—witchcraft and devildom!' he sobbed, fumbling with his hand in his breast. 'Because of my sin I have been whipped through the woods by devils. It is all finished. I repent. Take them, Sahib!' He held out a roll of dirty paper.

'What is the meaning of this, Abdul Gafur?' said Gisborne, already knowing what would come.

'Put me in the jail-*khana*—the notes are all here—but lock me up safely that no devils may follow. I have sinned against the Sahib and his salt which I have eaten; and but for those accursed wood-demons, I might have bought land afar off and lived in peace all my days.' He beat his head upon the ground in an agony of despair and mortification. Gisborne turned the roll of notes over and over. It was his accumulated back-pay for the last nine months—the roll that lay in the drawer with the home-letters and the recapping-machine. Mowgli watched Abdul Gafur, laughing noiselessly to himself. 'There is no need to put me on the horse again. I will walk home slowly with the Sahib, and then he can send me under guard to the jail-*khana*. The Government deals out many years for this offence,' said the butler sullenly.

Loneliness in the *rukh* affects very many ideas about very many things. Gisborne stared at Abdul Gafur, remembering that he was a very good servant, and that a new butler must be broken into the ways of the house from the beginning, and at the best would be a new face and a new tongue.

'Listen, Abdul Gafur,' he said. 'Thou hast done great wrong, and altogether lost thy *izzat* and thy reputation. But I think that this came upon thee suddenly.'

'Allah! I had never desired the notes before. The Evil took me by the throat while I looked.'

'That also I can believe. Go, then, back to my house, and when I return I will send the notes by a runner to the Bank, and there shall be no more said. Thou art too old for the jail-*khana*. Also thy household is guiltless.'

For answer Abdul Gafur sobbed between Gisborne's cowhide riding-boots.

'Is there no dismissal then?' he gulped.

'That we shall see. It hangs upon thy conduct when we return. Get upon the mare and ride slowly back.'

'But the devils! The *rukh* is full of devils.'

'No matter, my father. They will do thee no more harm unless, indeed, the Sahib's orders be not obeyed,' said Mowgli. 'Then, perchance, they may drive thee home—by the road of the nilghai.'

Abdul Gafur's lower jaw dropped as he twisted up his waist-cloth, staring at Mowgli.

'Are they *his* devils? His devils! And I had thought to return and lay the blame upon this warlock!'

'That was well thought of, Huzrut; but before we make a trap we see first how big the game is that may fall into it. Now, *I* thought no more than that a man had taken one of the Sahib's horses. I did not know that the design was to make me a thief before the Sahib, or my devils had haled thee here by the legs. It is not too late now.'

Mowgli looked inquiringly at Gisborne; but Abdul Gafur waddled hastily to the white mare, scrambled on her back, and fled, the woodways crashing and echoing behind him.

'That was well done,' said Mowgli. 'But he will fall again unless he holds by the mane.'

'Now it is time to tell me what these things mean,' said Gisborne a little sternly. 'What is this talk of thy devils? How can men be driven up and down the *rukh* like cattle? Give answer.'

'Is the Sahib angry because I have saved him his money?'

'No, but there is trick-work in this that does not please me.'

'Very good. Now if I rose and stepped three paces into the *rukh* there is no one, not even the Sahib, could find me till I chose. As I would not willingly do this, so I would not willingly tell. Have patience a little, Sahib, and some day I will show thee everything, for, if thou wilt, some day we will drive the buck together. There is no devil-work in the matter at all. Only . . . I know the *rukh* as a man knows the cooking-place in his house.'

Mowgli was speaking as he would speak to an impatient child. Gisborne, puzzled, baffled, and a great deal annoyed, said nothing, but stared on the ground and thought. When he looked up, the man of the woods had gone.

'It is not good,' said a level voice from the thicket, 'for friends to be angry. Wait till the evening, Sahib, when the air cools.'

Left to himself thus, dropped as it were in the heart of the *rukh*, Gisborne swore, then laughed, remounted his pony, and rode on. He visited a ranger's hut, overlooked a couple of new plantations, left some orders as to the burning of a patch of dry grass, and set out for a camping-ground of his own choice, a pile of splintered rocks roughly roofed over with branches and leaves, not far from the banks of the Kanye stream. It was twilight when he came in sight of his resting-place, and the *rukh* was waking to the hushed ravenous life of the night.

A camp-fire flickered on the knoll, and there was the smell of a very good dinner in the wind.

'Um,' said Gisborne, 'that's better than cold meat at any rate. Now the only man who'd be likely to be here'd be Muller, and, officially, he ought to be looking over the Changamanga *rukh*. I suppose that's why he's on my ground.'

The gigantic German who was the head of the Woods and Forests of all India, Head Ranger from Burma to Bombay, had a habit of flitting bat-like without warning from one place to another, and turning up exactly where he was least looked for. His theory was that sudden visitations, the discovery of shortcomings, and a word-of-mouth upbraiding of a subordinate were infinitely better than the slow processes of correspondence, which might end in a written and official reprimand—a thing in after years to be counted against a Forest Officer's record. As he explained it: 'If I only talk to my boys like a Dutch uncle, dey say, "It was only dot damned old Muller," and dey do better next time. But if my fat-head glerk he write und say dot Muller der Inspecdor-General fail to onderstand und is much annoyed—first dot does no goot because I am not dere, und, second, der fool dot comes after me he may say to my best boys: "Look here, you haf been wigged by my bredecessor." I tell you der big brass-hat pizness does not make der trees grow.'

Muller's deep voice was coming out of the darkness behind the firelight as he bent over the shoulders of his pet cook. 'Not so much sauce, you son of Belial! Worcester sauce he is a gondiment und not a fluid. Ah, Gisborne, you haf come to a very bad dinner. Where is your camp?' and he walked up to shake hands.

'I'm the camp, sir,' said Gisborne. 'I didn't know you were about here.'

Muller looked at the young man's trim figure. 'Goot! That is very goot! One horse und some cold dings to eat. When I was young I did my camp so. Now you shall dine with me. I went into Headquarters to make up my rebort last month. I haf written half —ho! ho!—und der rest I haf leaved to my glerks und come out for a walk. Der Government is mad about dose reborts. I dold der Viceroy so at Simla.'

Gisborne chuckled, remembering the many tales that were told of Muller's conflicts with the Supreme Government. He was the chartered libertine of all the offices, for as a Forest Officer he had no equal.

'If I find you, Gisborne, sitting in your bungalow und hatching reborts to me about der blantations instead of riding der blantations, I will dransfer you to der middle of der Bikanir Desert to reforest *him*. I am sick of reborts und chewing paper when we should do our work.'

'There's not much danger of my wasting time over my annuals. I hate them as much as you do, sir.'

The talk went over at this point to professional matters. Muller had some questions to ask, and Gisborne orders and hints to receive, till dinner was ready. It was the most civilized meal Gisborne had eaten for months. No distance from the base of supplies was allowed to interfere with the work of Muller's cook; and that table spread in the wilderness began with devilled small fresh-water fish, and ended with coffee and cognac.

'Ah!' said Muller at the end, with a sigh of satisfaction as he lighted a cheroot and dropped into his much-worn camp-chair. 'When I am making reborts I am Freethinker und Atheist, but here in der *rukh* I am more than Christian. I am Bagan also.' He rolled the cheroot-butt luxuriously under his tongue, dropped his hands on his knees, and stared before him into the dim shifting heart of the *rukh*, full of stealthy noises; the snapping of twigs like the snapping of the fire behind him; the sigh and rustle of a heat-bended branch recovering her straightness in the cool night; the incessant mutter of the Kanye stream, and the undernote of the many-peopled grass uplands out of sight beyond a swell of hill. He blew out a thick puff of smoke, and began to quote Heine to himself.

'Yes, it is very goot. Very goot. "Yes, I work miracles, und, by Gott, dey come off too." I remember when dere was no *rukh* more big than your knee, from here to der plough-lands, und in drought-time der cattle ate bones of dead cattle up und down. Now der trees haf come back. Dey were planted by a Freethinker, because he know shust der cause dot made der effect. But der trees dey had der cult of der old Gods—"und der Christian Gods howl loudly." Dey could not live in der *rukh*, Gisborne.'

A shadow moved in one of the bridle-paths—moved and stepped out into the starlight.

'I haf said true. Hush! Here is Faunus himself come to see der Insbector-General. Himmel, he is der god! Look!'

It was Mowgli, crowned with his wreath of white flowers and walking with a half-peeled branch—Mowgli, very mistrustful of the firelight and ready to fly back to the thicket on the least alarm.

'That's a friend of mine,' said Gisborne. 'He's looking for me. Ohé, Mowgli!'

Muller had barely time to gasp before the man was at Gisborne's side, crying: 'I was wrong to go. I was wrong, but I did not know then that the mate of him that was killed by this river was awake looking for thee. Else I should not have gone away. She tracked thee from the back-ranges, Sahib.'

'He is a little mad,' said Gisborne, 'and he speaks of all the beasts about here as if he was a friend of theirs.'

'Of course—of course. If Faunus does not know, who should know?' said Muller gravely. 'What does he say about tigers—dis god who knows you so well?'

Gisborne relighted his cheroot, and before he had finished the story of Mowgli and his exploits it was burned down to moustache-edge. Muller listened without interruption. 'Dot is madness,' he said at last when Gisborne had described the driving of Abdul Gafur. 'Dot is not madness at all.'

'What is it, then? He left me in a temper this morning because I asked him to tell how he did it. I fancy the chap's possessed in some way.'

'No, dere is no bossession, but it is most wonderful. Normally they die young—dese beople. Und you say now dot your thief servant did not say what drove der pony, und of course der nilghai he could not speak.'

'No, but, confound it, there wasn't anything. I listened, and I can hear most things. The bull and the man simply came headlong —mad with fright.'

For answer Muller looked Mowgli up and down from head to foot, then beckoned him nearer. He came as a buck treads a tainted trail.

'There is no harm,' said Muller in the vernacular. 'Hold out an arm.'

He ran his hand down to the elbow, felt that, and nodded. 'So I thought. Now the knee.' Gisborne saw him feel the knee-cap and smile. Two or three white scars just above the ankle caught his eye.

'Those came when thou wast very young?' he said.

'Ay,' Mowgli answered with a smile. 'They were love-tokens from the little ones.' Then to Gisborne over his shoulder: 'This Sahib knows everything. Who is he?'

'That comes after, my friend. Now, where are *they*?' said Muller.

Mowgli swept his hand round his head in a circle.

'So! And thou canst drive nilghai? See! There is my mare in her pickets. Canst thou bring her to me without frightening her?'

'Can I bring the mare to the Sahib without frightening her!' Mowgli repeated, raising his voice a little above its normal pitch. 'What is more easy if the heel-ropes are loose?'

'Loosen the head and heel-pegs,' shouted Muller to the groom. They were hardly out of the ground before the mare, a huge black Australian, flung up her head and cocked her ears.

'Careful! I do not wish her driven into the *rukh*,' said Muller.

Mowgli stood still fronting the blaze of the fire—in the very form and likeness of that Greek god who is so lavishly described in the novels. The mare whickered, drew up one hind leg, found that the heel-ropes were free, and moved swiftly to her master, on whose bosom she dropped her head, sweating lightly.

'She came of her own accord. My horses will do that,' cried Gisborne.

'Feel if she sweats,' said Mowgli.

Gisborne laid a hand on the damp flank.

'It is enough,' said Muller.

'It is enough,' Mowgli repeated, and a rock behind him threw back the word.

'That's uncanny, isn't it?' said Gisborne.

'No, only wonderful—most wonderful. Still you do not know, Gisborne?'

'I confess I don't.'

'Well, then, I shall not tell. He says dot some day he will show you what it is. It would be gruel if I told. But why he is not dead I do not understand. Now listen thou.' Muller faced Mowgli, and returned to the vernacular. 'I am the head of all the *rukhs* in the country of India and others across the Black Water. I do not know how many men be under me—perhaps five thousand, perhaps ten. Thy business is this—to wander no more up and down the *rukh* and drive beasts for sport or for show, but to take service under me, who am the Government in the matter of Woods and Forests, and to live in this *rukh* as a Forest-guard; to drive the villagers' goats away when there is no order to feed them in the *rukh*; to admit them when there is an order; to keep down, as thou canst keep down, the boar and the nilghai when they become too many; to tell Gisborne Sahib how and where tigers move, and what game there is in the forests; and to give sure warning of all the fires in the *rukh*; for thou canst give warning more quickly than any other. For that work there is a payment each month in silver, and at the end, when thou hast gathered a wife and cattle and, maybe, children, a pension. What answer?'

'That's just what I——' Gisborne began.

'My Sahib spoke this morning of such a service. I walked all day alone considering the matter, and my answer is ready here. I serve, *if* I serve in this *rukh* and no other: *with* Gisborne Sahib and with no other.'

'It shall be so. In a week comes the written order that pledges the honour of the Government for the pension. After that thou wilt take up thy hut where Gisborne Sahib shall appoint.'

'I was going to speak to you about it,' said Gisborne.

'I did not want to be told when I saw dot man. Dere will never be a Forest-guard like him. He is a miracle. I tell you, Gisborne, some day you will find it so. Listen, he is blood-brother to every beast in der *rukh*!'

'I should be easier in my mind if I could understand him.'

'Dot will come. Now I tell you dot only once in my service, und dot is thirty years, haf I met a boy dot began as this man began. Und he died. Sometimes you hear of dem in der census reports, but dey all die. Dis man haf lived, und he is an anachronism, for he is before der Iron Age, und der Stone Age. Look here, he is at der beginnings of der history of man—Adam in der Garden, und now

we want only an Eva! No! He is older dan dot child-tale, shust as
der *rukh* is older dan der Gods. Gisborne, I am a Bagan now, once
for all.'

Through the rest of the long evening Muller sat smoking and
smoking, and staring and staring into the darkness, his lips moving
in multiplied quotations, and great wonder upon his face. He went
to his tent, but presently came out again in his majestic pink
sleeping-suit, and the last words that Gisborne heard him address
to the *rukh* through the deep hush of midnight were these, delivered
with immense emphasis:

> '*Dough we shivt und bedeck und bedrape us,*
>   *Dou art noble und nude und andeek;*
> *Libidina dy moder, Briapus*
>   *Dy fader, a God und a Greek.*

Now I know dot, Bagan *or* Christian, I shall nefer know der
inwardness of der *rukh*!'

                              *

It was midnight in the bungalow a week later when Abdul
Gafur, ashy-grey with rage, stood at the foot of Gisborne's bed and
whispering bade him awake.

'Up, Sahib,' he stammered. 'Up and bring thy gun. Mine honour
is gone. Up and kill before any see.'

The old man's face had changed, so that Gisborne stared
stupidly.

'It was for this, then, that that jungle outcaste helped me to
polish the Sahib's table, and drew water and plucked fowls. They
have gone off together for all my beatings, and now he sits among
his devils dragging her soul to the Pit. Up, Sahib, and come with
me!'

He thrust a rifle into Gisborne's half-wakened hand and almost
dragged him from the room on to the veranda.

'They are there in the *rukh*; even within gunshot of the house.
Come softly with me.'

'But what is it? What is the trouble, Abdul?'

'Mowgli, and his devils. Also my own daughter,' said Abdul
Gafur. Gisborne whistled and followed his guide. Not for nothing,
he knew, had Abdul Gafur beaten his daughter of nights, and not
for nothing had Mowgli helped in the housework a man whom his
own powers, whatever those were, had convicted of theft. Also, a
forest wooing goes quickly.

There was the breathing of a flute in the *rukh*, as it might have been the song of some wandering wood-god, and, as they came nearer, a murmur of voices. The path ended in a little semicircular glade walled partly by high grass and partly by trees. In the centre, upon a fallen trunk, his back to the watchers and his arm round the neck of Abdul Gafur's daughter, sat Mowgli, newly crowned with flowers, playing upon a rude bamboo flute, to whose music four huge wolves danced solemnly on their hind legs.

'Those are his devils,' Abdul Gafur whispered. He held a bunch of cartridges in his hand. The beasts dropped to a long-drawn quavering note and lay still with steady green eyes, glaring at the girl.

'Behold,' said Mowgli, laying aside the flute. 'Is there anything of fear in that? I told thee, little Stoutheart, that there was not, and thou didst believe. Thy father said—and oh, if thou couldst have seen thy father being driven by the road of the nilghai!—thy father said that they were devils; and by Allah, who is thy God, I do not wonder that he so believed.'

The girl laughed a little rippling laugh, and Gisborne heard Abdul grind his few remaining teeth. This was not at all the girl that Gisborne had seen with a half-eye slinking about the compound veiled and silent, but another—a woman full blown in a night as the orchid puts out in one hour's moist heat.

'But they are my playmates and my brothers, children of that mother that gave me suck, as I told thee behind the cook-house,' Mowgli went on. 'Children of the father that lay between me and the cold at the mouth of the cave when I was a little naked child. Look'—a wolf raised his grey jowl, slavering at Mowgli's knee—'my brother knows that I speak of them. Yes, when I was a little child he was a cub rolling with me on the clay.'

'But thou hast said that thou art human-born,' cooed the girl, nestling closer to the shoulder. 'Thou *art* human-born?'

'Said! Nay, I know that I am human-born, because my heart is in thy hold, little one.' Her head dropped under Mowgli's chin. Gisborne put up a warning hand to restrain Abdul Gafur, who was not in the least impressed by the wonder of the sight.

'But I was a wolf among wolves none the less till a time came when Those of the jungle bade me go because I was a man.'

'Who bade thee go? That is not like a true man's talk.'

'The very beasts themselves. Little one, thou wouldst never believe that telling, but so it was. The beasts of the jungle bade me go, but these four followed me because I was their brother.

Then was I a herder of cattle among men, having learned their language. Ho! ho! The herds paid toll to my brothers, till a woman, an old woman, beloved, saw me playing by night with my brethren in the crops. They said that I was possessed of devils, and drove me from that village with sticks and stones, and the four came with me by stealth and not openly. That was when I had learned to eat cooked meat and to talk boldly. From village to village I went, heart of my heart, a herder of cattle, a tender of buffaloes, a tracker of game, but there was no man that dared lift a finger against me twice.' He stooped down and patted one of the heads. 'Do thou also like this. There is neither hurt nor magic in them. See, they know thee.'

'The woods are full of all manner of devils,' said the girl with a shudder.

'A lie. A child's lie,' Mowgli returned confidently. 'I have lain out in the dew under the stars and in the dark night, and I know. The jungle is my house. Shall a man fear his own roof-beams or a woman her man's hearth? Stoop down and pat them.'

'They are dogs and unclean,' she murmured, bending forward with averted head.

'Having eaten the fruit, now we remember the Law!' said Abdul Gafur bitterly. 'What is the need of this waiting, Sahib? Kill!'

'H'sh, thou. Let us learn what has happened,' said Gisborne.

'That is well done,' said Mowgli, slipping his arm round the girl again. 'Dogs or no dogs, they were with me through a thousand villages.'

'*Ahi*, and where was thy heart then? Through a thousand villages. Thou hast seen a thousand maids. I—that am—that am a maid no more, have I thy heart?'

'What shall I swear by? By Allah, of whom thou speakest?'

'Nay, by the life that is in thee, and I am well content. Where was thy heart in those days?'

Mowgli laughed a little. 'In my belly, because I was young and always hungry. So I learned to track and to hunt, sending and calling my brothers back and forth as a king calls his armies. Therefore I drove the nilghai for the foolish young Sahib, and the big fat mare for the big fat Sahib, when they questioned my power. It were as easy to have driven the men themselves. Even now,'— his voice lifted a little—'even now I know that behind me stand thy father and Gisborne Sahib. Nay, do not run, for no ten men dare move a pace forward. Remembering that thy father beat thee more than once, shall I give the word and drive him again in rings through the *rukh*?' A wolf stood up with bared teeth.

Gisborne felt Abdul Gafur tremble at his side. Next, his place was empty, and the fat man was skimming down the glade.

'Remains only Gisborne Sahib,' said Mowgli, still without turning; 'but I have eaten Gisborne Sahib's bread, and presently I shall be in his service, and my brothers will be his servants to drive game and carry the news. Hide thou in the grass.'

The girl fled, the tall grass closed behind her and a guardian wolf that followed, and Mowgli turning with his three retainers faced Gisborne as the Forest Officer came forward.

'That is all the magic,' he said, pointing to the three. 'The fat Sahib knew that we who are bred among wolves run on our elbows and our knees for a season. Feeling my arms and legs, he felt the truth which thou didst not know. Is it so wonderful, Sahib?'

'Indeed, it is all more wonderful than magic. These wolves drove the nilghai?'

'Ay, as they would drive Eblis if I gave the order. They are my eyes and feet to me.'

'Look to it, then, that Eblis does not carry a double rifle. They have yet something to learn, thy devils, for they stand one behind the other, so that two shots would kill the three.'

'Ah, but they know they will be thy servants as soon as I am a Forest-guard.'

'Guard or no guard, Mowgli, thou hast done great shame to Abdul Gafur. Thou hast dishonoured his house and blackened his face.'

'For that, it was blackened when he took thy money, and made blacker still when he whispered in thy ear a little while since to kill a naked man. I myself will talk to Abdul Gafur, for I am a man of the Government service, with a pension. He shall make the marriage by whatsoever rite he will, or he shall run once more. I will speak to him in the dawn. For the rest, the Sahib has his house and this is mine. It is time to sleep again, Sahib.'

Mowgli turned on his heel and disappeared into the grass, leaving Gisborne alone. The hint of the wood-god was not to be mistaken; and Gisborne went back to the bungalow, where Abdul Gafur, torn by rage and fear, was raving in the veranda.

'Peace, peace,' said Gisborne, shaking him, for he looked as though he were going to have a fit. 'Muller Sahib has made the man a Forest-guard, and as thou knowest, there is a pension at the end of that business, and it is Government service.'

'He is an outcaste—a *Mlech*—a dog among dogs; an eater of carrion! What pension can pay for that?'

'Allah knows; and thou hast heard that the mischief is done. Wouldst thou blaze it to all the other servants? Make the *shadi* swiftly, and the girl will make him a Mussulman. He is very comely. Canst thou wonder that after thy beatings she went to him?'

'Did he say that he would chase me with his beasts?'

'So it seemed to me. If he be a wizard, he is at least a very strong one.'

Abdul Gafur thought awhile, and then broke down and howled, forgetting that he was a Mussulman:

'Thou art a Brahmin! I am thy cow! Make thou the matter plain, and save my honour if it can be saved!'

A second time then Gisborne plunged into the *rukh* and called Mowgli. The answer came from high overhead, and in no submissive tones.

'Speak softly,' said Gisborne, looking up. 'There is yet time to strip thee of thy place and hunt thee with thy wolves. The girl must go back to her father's house tonight. Tomorrow there will be the *shadi*, by the Mussulman law, and then thou canst take her away. Bring her to Abdul Gafur.'

'I hear.' There was a murmur of two voices conferring among the leaves. 'Also, we will obey—for the last time.'

*

A year later Muller and Gisborne were riding through the *rukh* together, talking of their business. They came out among the rocks near the Kanye stream; Muller riding a little in advance. Under the shade of a thorn thicket sprawled a naked brown baby, and from the brake immediately behind him peered the head of a grey wolf. Gisborne had just time to strike up Muller's rifle, and the bullet tore spattering through the branches above.

'Are you mad?' thundered Muller. 'Look!'

'I see,' said Gisborne quietly. 'The mother's somewhere near. You'll wake the whole pack, by jove!'

The bushes parted once more, and a woman unveiled snatched up the child.

'Who fired, Sahib?' she cried to Gisborne.

'This Sahib. He had not remembered thy man's people.'

'Not remembered? But indeed it may be so, for we who live with them forget that they are strangers at all. Mowgli is down the stream catching fish. Does the Sahib wish to see him? Come out, ye lacking manners. Come out of the bushes, and make your service to the Sahibs.'

Muller's eyes grew rounder and rounder. He swung himself off the plunging mare and dismounted, while the jungle gave up four wolves that fawned round Gisborne. The mother stood nursing her child and spurning them aside as they brushed against her bare feet.

'You were quite right about Mowgli,' said Gisborne. 'I meant to have told you, but I've got so used to these fellows in the last twelve months that it slipped my mind.'

'Oh, don't apologize,' said Muller. 'It's nothing. Gott in Himmel! "Und I work miracles—und dey come off too!"'

Many Inventions, 1893

'Brugglesmith'

'This day the ship went down, and all hands was drowned but me.'

THE FIRST OFFICER of the *Breslau* asked me to dinner on board, before the ship went round to Southampton to pick up her passengers. The *Breslau* was lying below London Bridge, her fore-hatches opened for cargo, and her deck littered with nuts and bolts, and screws and chains. The Black McPhee had been putting some finishing touches to his adored engines, and McPhee is the most tidy of chief engineers. If the leg of a cockroach gets into one of his slide-valves the whole ship knows it, and half the ship has to clean up the mess.

After dinner, which the first officer, McPhee, and I ate in one little corner of the empty saloon, McPhee returned to the engine-room to attend to some brass-fitters. The first officer and I smoked on the bridge and watched the lights of the crowded shipping till it was time for me to go home. It seemed, in the pauses of our conversation, that I could catch an echo of fearful bellowings from the engine-room, and the voice of McPhee singing of home and the domestic affections.

'McPhee has a friend aboard tonight—a man who was a boiler-maker at Greenock when McPhee was a 'prentice,' said the first officer. 'I didn't ask him to dine with us because——'

'I see—I mean, I hear,' I answered. We talked for a few minutes longer, and McPhee came up from the engine-room with his friend on his arm.

'Let me present ye to this gentleman,' said McPhee. 'He's a great admirer o' your wor-rks. He has just hearrd o' them.'

McPhee could never pay a compliment prettily. The friend sat down suddenly on a bollard, saying that McPhee had understated the truth. Personally, he on the bollard considered that Shakespeare was trembling in the balance solely on my account, and if the first officer wished to dispute this he was prepared to fight the first officer then or later, 'as per invoice.' 'Man, if ye only knew,' said he, wagging his head, 'the times I've lain in my lonely bunk readin' *Vanity Fair* an' sobbin'—ay, weepin' bitterly at the pure fascination of it.'

He shed a few tears for guarantee of good faith, and the first officer laughed. McPhee resettled the man's hat, that had tilted over one eyebrow.

'That'll wear off in a little. It's just the smell o' the engine-room,' said McPhee.

'I think I'll wear off myself,' I whispered to the first officer. 'Is the dinghy ready?'

The dinghy was at the gangway, which was down, and the first officer went forward to find a man to row me to the bank. He returned with a very sleepy Lascar, who knew the river.

'Are ye going?' said the man on the bollard. 'Well, I'll just see ye home. McPhee, help me down the gangway. It has as many ends as a cat-o'-nine-tails, and—losh!—how innumerable are the dinghies!'

'You'd better let him come with you,' said the first officer. 'Muhammad Jan, put the drunk Sahib ashore first. Take the sober Sahib to the next stairs.'

I had my foot in the bow of the dinghy, the tide was making upstream, when the man cannoned against me, pushed the Lascar back on the gangway, cast loose the painter, and the dinghy began to saw, stern-first, along the side of the *Breslau*.

'We'll have no exter-r-raneous races here,' said the man. 'I've known the Thames for thirty years——'

There was no time for argument. We were drifting under the *Breslau*'s stern, and I knew that her propeller was half out of water, in the middle of an inky tangle of buoys, low-lying hawsers, and moored ships, with the tide ripping through them.

'What shall I do?' I shouted to the first officer.

'Find the Police Boat as soon as you can, and for God's sake get way on the dinghy. Steer with the oar. The rudder's unshipped and——'

I could hear no more. The dinghy slid away, bumped on a mooring-buoy, swung round and jigged off irresponsibly as I hunted for the oar. The man sat in the bow, his chin on his hands, smiling.

'Row, you ruffian,' I said. 'Get her out into the middle of the river——'

'It's a preevilege to gaze on the face o' genius. Let me go on thinkin'. There was *Little Barrnaby Dorrit* and *The Mystery o' the Bleak Druid*. I sailed in a ship called the *Druid* once—badly found, she was. It all comes back to me so sweet. It all comes back to me. Man, ye steer like a genius.'

We bumped round another mooring-buoy and drifted on to the bows of a Norwegian timber-ship—I could see the great square holes on either side of the cutwater. Then we dived into a string

of barges and scraped through them by the paint on our planks. It was a consolation to think that the dinghy was being reduced in value at every bump, but the question before me was when she would begin to leak. The man looked ahead into the pitchy darkness and whistled.

'Yon's a Castle liner; her ties are black. She's swinging across stream. Keep her port light on our starboard bow, and go large,' he said.

'How can I keep anything anywhere? You're sitting on the oars. Row, man, if you don't want to drown.'

He took the sculls, saying sweetly: 'No harm comes to a drunken man. That's why I wished to come wi' *you*. Man, ye're not fit to be alone in a boat.'

He flirted the dinghy round the big ship, and for the next ten minutes I enjoyed—positively enjoyed—an exhibition of first-class steering. We threaded in and out of the Mercantile Marine of Great Britain as a ferret threads a rabbit-hole, and we, he that is to say, sang joyously to each ship till men looked over bulwarks and cursed us. When we came to some moderately clear water he gave the sculls to me, and said:

'If ye could row as ye write, I'd respect you for all your vices. Yon's London Bridge. Take her through.'

We shot under the dark ringing arch, and came out the other side, going up swiftly with the tide, chanting songs of victory. Except that I wished to get home before morning, I was growing reconciled to the jaunt. There were one or two stars visible, and by keeping into the centre of the stream, we could not come to any very serious danger.

The man began to sing loudly:

> *The smartest clipper that you could find,*
> *Yo ho! Oho!*
> *Was the* Marg'ret Evans *of the Black X Line,*
> *A hundred years ago!*

Incorporate that in your next book—which is marvellous.' Here he stood up in the bows and declaimed:

> '*Ye Towers o' Julia, London's lasting wrong,*
> *By mony a foul an' midnight murder fed—*
> *Sweet Thames, run softly till I end my song—*
> *And yon's the grave as little as my bed.*

I'm a poet mysel', an' I can feel for others.'

'Sit down,' said I. 'You'll have the boat over.'

'Ay, I'm settin'—settin' like a hen.' He plumped down heavily, and added, shaking his forefinger at me:

Lear-rn, prudent, cautious self-control
Is wisdom's root.

How did a man o' your parts come to be so drunk? Oh, it's a sinfu' thing, an' ye may thank God on all fours that I'm with ye. What's yon boat?'

We had drifted far up the river, and a boat manned by four men, who rowed with a soothingly regular stroke, was overhauling us.

'It's the River Police,' I said, at the top of my voice.

'Oh ay! If your sin do not find you out on dry land, it will find you out in the deep waters. Is it like they'll give us drink?'

'Exceedingly likely. I'll hail them.' I hailed.

'What are you doing?' was the answer from the boat.

'It's the *Breslau*'s dinghy broken loose,' I began.

'It's a vara drunken man broke loose,' roared my companion, 'an' I'm takin' him home by watter, for he cannot stand on dry land.' Here he shouted my name twenty times running, and I could feel the blushes racing over my body three deep.

'You'll be locked up in ten minutes, my friend,' I said, 'and I don't think you'll be bailed either.'

'H'sh, man, h'sh. They think I'm your uncle.' He caught up a scull and began splashing the boat as it ranged alongside.

'You're a nice pair,' said the Sergeant at last.

'I am anything you please so long as you take that fiend away. Tow us in to the nearest station, and I'll make it worth your while,' I said.

'Corruption—corruption!' roared the man, throwing himself flat in the bottom of the boat. 'Like unto the worms that perish, so is man! And all for the sake of a filthy half-crown to be arrested by the River Police at my time o' life!'

'For pity's sake, row,' I shouted. 'The man's drunk.'

They rowed us to a flat—a fire- or a police-station; it was too dark to see which. I could feel that they regarded me in no better light than the other man. I could not explain, for I was holding the far end of the painter, and feeling cut off from all respectability.

We got out of the boat, my companion falling flat on his wicked face, and the Sergeant asked us rude questions about the dinghy. My companion washed his hands of all responsibility. He was an

old man; he had been lured into a stolen boat by a young man—
probably a thief—he had saved the boat from wreck (this was
absolutely true), and now he expected salvage in the shape of hot
whisky and water. The Sergeant turned to me. Fortunately I was
in evening dress, and had a card to show. More fortunately still,
the Sergeant happened to know the *Breslau* and McPhee. He
promised to send the dinghy down next tide, and was not beyond
accepting my thanks, in silver.

As this was satisfactorily arranged, I heard my companion say
angrily to a constable, 'If ye willna give it to a dry man, ye maun
to a drookit.' Then he walked deliberately off the edge of the flat
into the water. Somebody stuck a boat-hook into his clothes and
hauled him out.

'Now,' said he triumphantly, 'under the rules o' the R-royal
Humane Society, ye must give me hot whisky an' watter. Do not
put temptation before the laddie. He's my nephew an' a good boy
i' the main. Tho' why he should masquerade as Mister Thackeray
on the high seas is beyond my comprehension. Oh, the vanity o'
youth! McPhee told me ye were as vain as a peacock. I mind that
now.'

'You had better give him something to drink and wrap him up
for the night. I don't know who he is,' I said desperately, and when
the man had settled down to a drink supplied on my representations, I escaped and found that I was near a bridge.

I went towards Fleet Street, intending to take a hansom and go
home. After the first feeling of indignation died out, the absurdity
of the experience struck me fully and I began to laugh aloud in the
empty streets, to the scandal of a policeman. The more I reflected
the more heartily I laughed, till my mirth was quenched by a
hand on my shoulder, and turning I saw him who should have
been in bed at the River Police-station. He was damp all over;
his wet silk hat rode far at the back of his head, and round his
shoulders hung a striped yellow blanket, evidently the property of
the State.

'The cracklin' o' thorns under a pot,' said he solemnly. 'Laddie,
have ye not thought o' the sin of idle laughter? My heart misgave
me that ever ye'd get home, an' I've just come to convoy you a
piece. They're sore uneducate down there by the river. They
wouldna listen to me when I talked o' your worrks, so I e'en left
them. Cast the blanket about you, laddie. It's fine an' cold.'

I groaned inwardly. Providence evidently intended that I should
frolic through eternity with McPhee's infamous acquaintance.

'Go away,' I said. 'Go home, or I'll give you in charge!'

He leaned against a lamp-post and laid his finger to his nose—his dishonourable, carnelian neb.

'I mind now that McPhee told me ye were vainer than a peacock, an' your castin' me adrift in a boat shows ye were drunker than an owl. A good name is as a savoury bakemeat. I ha' nane.' He smacked his lips joyously.

'Well, I know that,' I said.

'Ay, but *ye* have. I mind now that McPhee spoke o' your reputation that ye're so proud of. Laddie, if ye gie me in charge —I'm old enough to be your father—I'll bla-ast your reputation as far as my voice can carry; for I'll call you by name till the cows come hame. It's no jestin' matter to be a friend to me. If ye discard my friendship, ye must come to Vine Street wi' me for stealin' the *Breslau*'s dinghy.'

Then he sang at the top of his voice:

> '*In the morrnin*',
> *I' the morrnin' by the black van*—
> *We'll toodle up to Vine Street i' the morrnin*'!

Yon's my own composeetion, but *I*'m not vain. We'll go home together, laddie. We'll go home together.' And he sang 'Auld Lang Syne' to show that he meant it.

A policeman suggested that we had better move on, and we moved on to the Law Courts near St Clement Danes. My companion was quieter now, and his speech, which up till that time had been distinct—it was a marvel to hear how in his condition he could talk dialect—began to slur and slide and slummock. He bade me observe the architecture of the Law Courts and linked himself lovingly to my arm. Then he saw a policeman, and before I could shake him off, whirled me up to the man, singing:

> ' *Every member of the Force*
> *Has a watch and chain of course*—'

and threw his dripping blanket over the helmet of the Law. In any other country in the world we should have run an exceedingly good chance of being shot, or dirked, or clubbed—and clubbing is worse than being shot. But I reflected in that wet-cloth tangle that this was England, where the police are made to be banged and battered and bruised, that they may the better endure a police-court reprimand next morning. We three fell in a festoon, he calling on me by name—that was the tingling horror of it!—to sit on the policeman's head and cut the traces. I wriggled clear first and shouted to the policeman to kill the blanket-man.

Naturally the policeman answered: 'You're as bad as 'im,' and chased me, as the smaller man, round St Clement Danes into Holywell Street, where I ran into the arms of another policeman. That flight could not have lasted more than a minute and a half, but it seemed to me as long and as wearisome as the foot-bound flight of a nightmare. I had leisure to think of a thousand things as I ran; but most I thought of the great and godlike man who held a sitting in the north gallery of St Clement Danes a hundred odd years ago. I know that he at least would have felt for me. So occupied was I with these considerations, that when the other policeman hugged me to his bosom and said: 'What are you tryin' to do?' I answered with exquisite politeness: 'Sir, let us take a walk down Fleet Street.' 'Bow Street'll do *your* business, I think,' was the answer, and for a moment I thought so too, till it seemed I might scuffle out of it. Then there was a hideous scene, and it was complicated by my companion hurrying up with the blanket and telling me—always by name—that he would rescue me or perish in the attempt.

'Knock him down,' I pleaded. 'Club his head open first and I'll explain afterwards.'

The first policeman, the one who had been outraged, drew his truncheon and cut at my companion's head. The high silk hat crackled and the owner dropped like a log.

'Now you've done it,' I said. 'You've probably killed him.'

Holywell Street never goes to bed. A small crowd gathered on the spot, and some one of German extraction shrieked: 'You haf killed the man.'

Another cried: 'Take his bloomin' number! I saw him strook cruel 'ard. Yah!'

Now the street was empty when the trouble began, and, saving the two policemen and myself, no one had seen the blow. I said, therefore, in a loud and cheerful voice:

'The man's a friend of mine. He's fallen down in a fit. Bobby, will you bring the ambulance?' Under my breath I added: 'It's five shillings apiece, and the man didn't hit you.'

'No, but 'im and you tried to scrob me,' said the policeman.

This was not a thing to argue about.

'Is Dempsey on duty at Charing Cross?' I said.

'Wot d'you know of Dempsey, you bloomin' garrotter?' said the policeman.

'If Dempsey's there, he knows me. Get the ambulance quick, and I'll take him to Charing Cross.'

'You're coming to Bow Street, *you* are,' said the policeman crisply.

'The man's dying'—he lay groaning on the pavement. 'Get the ambulance,' said I.

There is an ambulance at the back of St Clement Danes, whereof I know more than most people. The policeman seemed to possess the keys of the box in which it lived. We trundled it out—it was a three-wheeled affair with a hood—and we bundled the body of the man upon it.

A body in an ambulance looks very extremely dead. The policeman softened at the sight of the stiff boot-heels.

'Now then,' said they, and I fancied that they still meant Bow Street.

'Let me see Dempsey for three minutes if he's on duty,' I answered.

'Very good. He is.'

Then I knew that all would be well, but before we started I put my head under the ambulance-hood to see if the man were alive. A guarded whisper came to my ear.

'Laddie, you maun pay me for a new hat. They've broken it. Dinna desert me now, laddie. I'm o'er old to go to Bow Street in my grey hairs for a fault of yours. Laddie, dinna desert me.'

'You'll be lucky if you get off under seven years.' I said to the policeman.

Moved by a very lively fear of having exceeded their duty, the two policemen left their beats, and the mournful procession wound down the empty Strand. Once west of the Adelphi, I knew I should be in my own country; and the policemen had reason to know that too, for as I was pacing proudly a little ahead of the catafalque, another policeman said 'Good night, sir,' to me as he passed.

'Now you see,' I said, with condescension. 'I wouldn't be in your shoes for something. On my word, I've a great mind to march you two down to Scotland Yard.'

'If the gentleman's a friend o' yours, per'aps——' said the policeman who had given the blow, and was reflecting on the consequences.

'Perhaps you'd like me to go away and say nothing about it,' I said. Then there hove into view the figure of Constable Dempsey, glittering in his oilskins, and an angel of light to me. I had known him for months; he was an esteemed friend of mine, and we used to talk together in the early mornings. The fool seeks to ingratiate himself with Princes and Ministers; and Courts and Cabinets leave him to perish miserably. The wise man makes allies among the police and the hansoms, so that his friends spring up from the police-station and the cab-rank, and even his offences become triumphal processions.

'Dempsey,' said I, 'have the police been on strike again? They've put some things on duty at St Clement Danes that want to take me to Bow Street for garrotting.'

'Lor', sir!' said Dempsey indignantly.

'Tell them I'm not a garrotter, nor a thief. It's simply disgraceful that a gentleman can't walk down the Strand without being man-handled by these roughs. One of them has done his best to kill my friend here; and I'm taking the body home. Speak for me, Demp-sey.'

There was no time for the much misrepresented policemen to say a word. Dempsey spoke to them in language calculated to frighten. They tried to explain, but Dempsey launched into a glowing catalogue of my virtues, as noted by gas in the early hours. 'And,' he concluded vehemently, ' 'e writes for the papers, too. How'd *you* like to be written about in the papers—in verse, too, which is 'is 'abit? You leave 'im alone. 'Im an' me have been friends for months.'

'What about the dead man?' said the policeman who had not given the blow.

'I'll tell you,' I said, relenting, and to the three policemen under the lights of Charing Cross assembled, I recounted faithfully and at length the adventures of the night, beginning with the *Breslau* and ending at St Clement Danes. I described the sinful old ruffian in the ambulance in words that made him wriggle where he lay, and never since the Metropolitan Police was founded did three police-men laugh as those three laughed. The Strand echoed to it, and the unclean birds of the night stood and wondered.

'Oh lor'!' said Dempsey, wiping his eyes, 'I'd ha' given anything to see that old man runnin' about with a wet blanket an' all! Excuse me, sir, but you ought to get took up every night for to make us 'appy.' He dissolved into fresh guffaws.

There was a clinking of silver and the two policemen of St Clement Danes hurried back to their beats, laughing as they ran.

'Take 'im to Charing Cross,' said Dempsey between shouts. 'They'll send the ambulance back in the morning.'

'Laddie, ye've misca'ed me shameful names, but I'm o'er old to go to a hospital. Dinna desert me, laddie. Tak' me hame to my wife,' said the voice in the ambulance.

'He's none so bad. 'Is wife'll comb 'is hair for 'im proper,' said Dempsey, who was a married man.

'Where d'you live?' I demanded.

'Brugglesmith,' was the answer.

'What's that?' I said to Dempsey, more skilled than I in portmanteau-words.

'Brook Green, 'Ammersmith,' Dempsey translated promptly.

'Of course,' I said. 'That's just the sort of place he would choose to live in. I only wonder that it wasn't Kew.'

'Are you going to wheel him 'ome, sir,' said Dempsey.

'I'd wheel him home if he lived in —— Paradise. He's not going to get out of this ambulance while I'm here. He'd drag me into a murder for tuppence.'

'Then strap 'im up an' make sure,' said Dempsey, and he deftly buckled two straps that hung by the side of the ambulance over the man's body. Brugglesmith—I know not his other name—was sleeping deeply. He even smiled in his sleep.

'That's all right,' said Dempsey, and I moved off, wheeling my devil's perambulator before me. Trafalgar Square was empty except for the few that slept in the open. One of these wretches ranged alongside and begged for money, asserting that he had been a gentleman once.

'So have I,' I said. 'That was long ago. I'll give you a shilling if you'll help me to push this thing.'

'Is it a murder?' said the vagabond, shrinking back. 'I've not got to *that* yet.'

'No, it's going to be one,' I answered. 'I have.'

The man slunk back into the darkness and I pressed on, through Cockspur Street, and up to Piccadilly, wondering what I should do with my treasure. All London was asleep, and I had only this drunken carcass to bear me company. It was silent—silent as chaste Piccadilly. A young man of my acquaintance came out of a pink brick club as I passed. A faded carnation drooped from his button-hole. He had been playing cards, and was walking home before the dawn, when he overtook me.

'What are you doing?' he said.

I was far beyond any feeling of shame. 'It's for a bet,' said I. 'Come and help.'

'Laddie, who's yon?' said the voice beneath the hood.

'Good Lord!' said the young man, leaping across the pavement. Perhaps card-losses had told on his nerves. Mine were steel that night.

'The Lord, The Lord?' the passionless, incurious voice went on. 'Dinna be profane, laddie. He'll come in His ain good time.'

The young man looked at me with horror.

'It's all part of the bet,' I answered. 'Do come and push!'

'W—where are you going to?' said he.

'Brugglesmith,' said the voice within. 'Laddie, d'ye ken my wife?'

'No,' said I.

'Well, she's just a tremenjus wumman. Laddie, I want a drink. Knock at one o' those braw houses, laddie, an'—an'—ye may kiss the girrl for your pains.'

'Lie still, or I'll gag you,' I said savagely.

The young man with the carnation crossed to the other side of Piccadilly, and hailed the only hansom visible for miles. What he thought I cannot tell.

I pressed on—wheeling, eternally wheeling—to Brook Green, Hammersmith. There I would abandon Brugglesmith to the gods of that desolate land. We had been through so much together that I could not leave him bound in the street. Besides, he would call after me, and oh! it is a shameful thing to hear one's name ringing down the emptiness of London in the dawn.

So I went on, past Apsley House, even to the coffee-stall, but there was no coffee for Brugglesmith. And into Knightsbridge—respectable Knightsbridge—I wheeled my burden, the body of Brugglesmith.

'Laddie, what are ye going to do wi' me?' he said when opposite the barracks.

'Kill you,' I said briefly, 'or hand you over to your wife. Be quiet.'

He would not obey. He talked incessantly—sliding in one sentence from clear-cut dialect to wild and drunken jumble. At the Albert Hall he said that I was the 'Hattle Gardle buggle,' which I apprehend is the Hatton Garden burglar. At Kensington High Street he loved me as a son, but when my weary legs came to the Addison Road Bridge he implored me with tears to unloose the straps and to fight against the sin of vanity. No man molested us. It was as though a bar had been set between myself and all humanity till I had cleared my account with Brugglesmith. The glimmering of light grew in the sky; the cloudy brown of the wood pavement turned to heather-purple; I made no doubt that I should be allowed vengeance on Brugglesmith ere the evening.

At Hammersmith the heavens were steel-grey, and the day came weeping. All the tides of the sadness of an unprofitable dawning poured into the soul of Brugglesmith. He wept bitterly, because the puddles looked cold and houseless. I entered a half-waked public-house—in evening dress and an ulster. I marched to the bar —and got him whisky on condition that he should cease kicking at the canvas of the ambulance. Then he wept more bitterly, for that he had ever been associated with me, and so seduced into stealing the *Breslau*'s dinghy.

The day was white and wan when I reached my long journey's end, and, putting back the hood, bade Brugglesmith declare where he lived. His eyes wandered disconsolately round the red-and-grey houses till they fell on a villa in whose garden stood a staggering board with the legend 'To Let.' It needed only this to break him down utterly, and with the breakage fled his fine fluency in his guttural northern tongue, for liquor levels all.

'Olely lil while,' he sobbed. 'Olely lil while. Home—falmy— besht of falmies—wife too—*you* dole know my wife! Left them all a lil while ago. Now everything's sold—all sold. Wife—falmy—all sold! Lemmegellup!'

I unbuckled the straps cautiously. Brugglesmith rolled off his resting-place and staggered to the house.

'Wattle I do?' he said.

Then I understood the baser depths in the mind of Mephistopheles.

'Ring,' I said. 'Perhaps they are in the attic or the cellar.'

'You dole know my wife. She shleeps on soful in the dorlin' room, waiting meculhome. *You* dole know my wife.'

He took off his boots, covered them with his tall hat, and craftily as a Red Indian picked his way up the garden path and smote the bell marked 'Visitors' a severe blow with the clenched fist.

'Bell sole too. Sole electick bell! Wassor bell this? *I* can't riggle bell,' he moaned despairingly.

'You pull it—pull it hard,' I repeated, keeping a wary eye down the road. Vengeance was coming and I desired no witnesses.

'Yes, I'll pull it hard.' He slapped his forehead with inspiration. 'I'll pull it out.'

Leaning back he grasped the knob with both hands and pulled. A wild ringing in the kitchen was his answer. Spitting on his hands he pulled with renewed strength, and shouted for his wife. Then he bent his ear to the knob, shook his head, drew out an enormous yellow-and-red handkerchief, tied it round the knob, turned his back to the door, and pulled over his shoulder.

Either the handkerchief or the wire, it seemed to me, was bound to give way. But I had forgotten the bell. Something cracked in the kitchen, and Brugglesmith moved slowly down the doorsteps, pulling valiantly. Three feet of wire followed him.

'Pull, oh, pull!' I cried. 'It's coming now.'

'Qui' ri',' he said. '*I*'ll riggle bell.'

He bowed forward, the wire creaking and straining behind him, the bell-knob clasped to his bosom, and from the noises within I fancied the bell was taking away with it half the woodwork of the kitchen and all the basement banisters.

'Get a purchase on her,' I shouted, and he spun round, lapping that good copper wire about him. I opened the garden gate politely, and he passed out, spinning his own cocoon. Still the bell came up, hand over hand, and still the wire held fast. He was in the middle of the road now, whirling like an impaled cockchafer, and shouting madly for his wife and family. There he met with the ambulance, the bell within the house gave one last peal, and bounded from the far end of the hall to the inner side of the hall-door, where it stayed fast. So did not my friend Brugglesmith. He fell upon his face, embracing the ambulance as he did so, and the two turned over together in the toils of the never-sufficiently-to-be advertised copper wire.

'Laddie,' he gasped, his speech returning, 'have I a legal remedy?'

'I will go and look for one,' I said, and, departing, found two policemen. These I told that daylight had surprised a burglar in Brook Green while he was engaged in stealing lead from an empty house. Perhaps they had better take care of that bootless thief. He seemed to be in difficulties.

I led the way to the spot, and behold! in the splendour of the dawning, the ambulance, wheels uppermost, was walking down the muddy road on two stockinged feet—was shuffling to and fro in a quarter-circle whose radius was copper wire, and whose centre was the bell-plate of the empty house.

Next to the amazing ingenuity with which Brugglesmith had contrived to lash himself under the ambulance, the thing that appeared to impress the constables most was the fact of the St Clement Danes ambulance being at Brook Green, Hammersmith.

They even asked me, of all people in the world, whether I knew anything about it!

*

They extricated him; not without pain and dirt. He explained that he was repelling boarding-attacks by a 'Hattle Gardle buggle' who had sold his house, wife, and family. As to the bell-wire, he offered no explanation, and was borne off shoulder-high between the two policemen. Though his feet were not within six inches of the ground, they paddled swiftly, and I saw that in his magnificent mind he was running—furiously running.

Sometimes I have wondered whether he wished to find me.

Many Inventions, 1893*

* *Harper's Weekly*, 1891

'Love-o'-Women'

'A lamentable tale of things
Done long ago, and ill done.'
John Ford

T HE HORROR, the confusion, and the separation of the murderer
from his comrades were all over before I came. There remained
only on the barrack-square the blood of man calling from the
ground. The hot sun had dried it to a dusky goldbeater's-skin film,
cracked lozenge-wise by the heat; and as the wind rose, each lozenge,
rising a little, curled up at the edges as if it were a dumb tongue.
Then a heavier gust blew all away down wind in grains of dark-
coloured dust. It was too hot to stand in the sunshine before breakfast. The men were in barracks talking the matter over. A knot of
soldiers' wives stood by one of the entrances to the married quarters,
while inside a woman shrieked and raved with wicked filthy words.

A quiet and well-conducted sergeant had shot down, in broad
daylight just after early parade, one of his own corporals, had then
returned to barracks and sat on a cot till the guard came for him.
He would, therefore, in due time be handed over to the High Court
for trial. Further, but this he could hardly have considered in his
scheme of revenge, he would horribly upset my work; for the
reporting of that trial would fall on me without a relief. What that
trial would be like I knew even to weariness. There would be the
rifle carefully uncleaned, with the fouling-marks about breech and
muzzle, to be sworn to by half-a-dozen superfluous privates; there
would be heat, reeking heat, till the wet pencil slipped sideways
between the fingers; and the punkah would swish and the pleaders
would jabber in the verandas, and his Commanding Officer would
put in certificates to the prisoner's moral character, while the jury
would pant and the summer uniforms of the witnesses would smell
of dye and soaps; and some abject barrack-sweeper would lose his
head in cross-examination, and the young barrister who always
defended soldiers' cases for the credit that they never brought him
would say and do wonderful things, and would then quarrel with
me because I had not reported him correctly. At the last, for he
surely would not be hanged, I might meet the prisoner again,
ruling blank account-forms in the Central Jail, and cheer him with
the hope of his being made a warder in the Andamans.

The Indian Penal Code and its interpreters do not treat murder, under any provocation whatever, in a spirit of jest. Sergeant Raines would be very lucky indeed if he got off with seven years, I thought. He had slept the night upon his wrongs, and killed his man at twenty yards before any talk was possible. That much I knew. Unless, therefore, the case was doctored a little, seven years would be his least; and I fancied it was exceedingly well for Sergeant Raines that he had been popular with his Company.

That same evening—no day is so long as the day of a murder— I met Ortheris with the dogs, and he plunged defiantly into the middle of the matter. 'I'll be one o' the witnesses,' said he. 'I was in the veranda when Mackie come along. 'E come from Mrs Raines's quarters. Quigley, Parsons, an' Trot, they was in the inside veranda, so *they* couldn't 'ave 'eard nothing. Sergeant Raines was in the veranda talkin' to me, an' Mackie 'e come along acrost the square an' 'e sez, "Well," sez 'e, " 'ave they pushed your 'elmet off yet, Sergeant?" 'e sez. An' at that Raines 'e catches 'is breath an' 'e sez, "My Gawd, I can't stand this!" sez 'e, an' 'e picks up my rifle an' shoots Mackie. See?'

'But what were you doing with your rifle in the outer veranda an hour after parade?'

'Cleanin' 'er,' said Ortheris, with the sullen brassy stare that always went with his choicer lies.

He might as well have said that he was dancing naked, for at no time did his rifle need hand or rag on her twenty minutes after parade. Still, the High Court would not know the routine.

'Are you going to stick to that—on the Book?' I asked.

'Yes. Like a bloomin' leech.'

'All right, I don't want to know any more. Only remember that Quigley, Parsons, and Trot couldn't have been where you say without hearing something; and there's nearly certain to be a barrack-sweeper who was knocking about the square at the time. There always is.'

' 'Twasn't the sweeper. It was the beastie. 'E's all right.'

Then I knew that there was going to be some spirited doctoring, and I felt sorry for the Government Advocate who would conduct the prosecution.

When the trial came on I pitied him more, for he was always quick to lose his temper and made a personal matter of each lost cause. Raines's young barrister had for once put aside his unslaked and welling passion for alibis and insanity, had forsworn gymnastics and fireworks, and worked soberly for his client. Mercifully the hot

weather was yet young, and there had been no flagrant cases of
barrack-shootings up to the time; and the jury was a good one,
even for an Indian jury, where nine men out of every twelve are
accustomed to weighing evidence. Ortheris stood firm and was not
shaken by any cross-examination. The one weak point in his tale
—the presence of his rifle in the outer veranda—went unchallenged
by civilian wisdom, though some of the witnesses could not help
smiling. The Government Advocate called for the rope, contending
throughout that the murder had been a deliberate one. Time had
passed, he argued, for that reflection which comes so naturally to
a man whose honour is lost. There was also the Law, ever ready
and anxious to right the wrongs of the common soldier, if, indeed,
wrong had been done. But he doubted much whether there had
been any sufficient wrong. Causeless suspicion over-long brooded
upon had led, by his theory, to deliberate crime. But his attempts
to minimise the motive failed. The most disconnected witness knew
— had known for weeks—the causes of offence; and the prisoner,
who naturally was the last of all to know, groaned in the dock
while he listened. The one question that the trial circled round was
whether Raines had fired under sudden and blinding provocation
given that very morning; and in the summing-up it was clear that
Ortheris's evidence told. He had contrived most artistically to
suggest that he personally hated the Sergeant, who had come into
the veranda to give him a talking-to for insubordination. In a
weak moment the Government Advocate asked one question too
many. 'Beggin' *your* pardon, sir,' Ortheris replied, ' 'e was callin'
me a dam' impudent little lawyer.' The Court shook. The jury
brought it in a killing, but with every provocation and extenuation
known to God or man, and the Judge put his hand to his brow
before giving sentence, and the Adam's apple in the prisoner's
throat went up and down like mercury pumping before a cyclone.

In consideration of all considerations, from his Commanding
Officer's certificate of good conduct to the sure loss of pension,
service, and honour, the prisoner would get two years, to be served
in India, and—there need be no demonstration in Court. The
Government Advocate scowled and picked up his papers; the guard
wheeled with a clash, and the prisoner was relaxed to the Secular
Arm, and driven to the jail in a broken-down *ticca-gharri*.

His guard and some ten or twelve military witnesses, being less
important, were ordered to wait till what was officially called the
cool of the evening before marching back to cantonments. They
gathered together in one of the deep red-brick verandas of a

disused lock-up and congratulated Ortheris, who bore his honours modestly. I sent my work in to the office and joined them. Ortheris watched the Government Advocate driving off to lunch.

'That's a nasty little bald-'eaded little butcher, that is,' he said. ' 'E don't please me. 'E's got a collie dorg wot do, though. I'm goin' up to Murree in a week. That dorg'll bring fifteen rupees anywheres.'

'You had better spend ut in Masses,' said Terence, unbuckling his belt; for he had been on prisoner's guard, standing helmeted and bolt upright for three long hours.

'Not me,' said Ortheris cheerfully. 'Gawd'll put it down to B Comp'ny's barrick-damages one o' these days. You look strapped, Terence.'

'Faith, I'm not so young as I was. That guard-mountin' wears on the sole av the fut, and this'—he sniffed contemptuously at the brick veranda—'is as hard settin' as standin'!'

'Wait a minute. I'll get the cushions out of my cart,' I said.

''Strewth—sofies. We're goin' it gay,' said Ortheris, as Terence dropped himself section by section on the leather cushions, saying prettily, 'May ye never want a soft place wheriver you go, an' power to share ut wid a frind. Another for yoursilf? That's good. Ut lets me sit longways. Stanley, pass me a poipe. Augrrh! An' that's another man gone all to pieces bekaze av a woman. I must ha' been on forty or fifty prisoners' gyards, first an' last; an' I hate ut more ivry time.'

'Let's see. You were on Losson's, Lancey's, Dugard's, and Stebbins's, that I can remember,' I said.

'Ay, an' before that an' before that—scores av thim,' he answered with a worn smile. ''Tis better to die than to live for thim, though. Whin Raines comes out—he'll be changin' his kit at the jail now— he'll think that too. He shud ha' shot himself an' the woman by rights an' made a clane wipe av all. Now he's left the woman—she tuk tay wid Dinah Sunday gone last—an' he's left himsilf. Mackie's the lucky man.'

'He's probably getting it hot where he is,' I ventured, for I knew something of the dead Corporal's record.

'Be sure av that,' said Terence, spitting over the edge of the veranda. 'But fwhat he'll get there is light marchin'-ordher to fwhat he'd ha' got here if he'd lived.'

'Surely not. He'd have gone on and forgotten—like the others.'

'Did ye know Mackie well, sorr?' said Terence.

'He was on the Patiala guard of honour last winter, and I went

out shooting with him in an *ekka* for the day, and I found him
rather an amusing man.'

'Well, he'll ha' got shut av amusemints, excipt turnin' from wan
side to the other, these few years to come. I knew Mackie, an' I've
seen too many to be mistuk in the muster av wan man. He might
ha' gone on an' forgot as you say, sorr, but he was a man wid an
educashin, an' he used ut for his schemes; an' the same educashin,
an' talkin', an' all that made him able to do fwhat he had
a mind to wid a woman, that same wud turn back agin in the
long run an' tear him alive. I can't say fwhat that I mane tu say
bekaze I don't know how, but Mackie was the spit an' livin' image
av a man that I saw march the same march *all but*; an' 'twas
worse for him that he did not come by Mackie's ind. Wait while I
remimber now. 'Twas whin I was in the Black Tyrone, an' he was
drafted us from Portsmouth; an' fwhat was his misbegotten name?
Larry—Larry Tighe ut was; an' wan of the draf' said he was a
gentleman-ranker, an' Larry tuk an' three-parts killed him for
sayin' so. An' he was a big man, an' a strong man, an' a handsome
man, an' that tells heavy in practice wid some women, but, takin'
thim by an' large, not wid all. Yet 'twas wid all that Larry dealt—
all—for he cud put the comether on any woman that trod the
green earth av God, an he knew ut. Like Mackie that's roastin'
now, he knew ut, an' niver did he put the comether on any woman
save an' excipt for the black shame. 'Tis not me that shud be
talkin', dear knows, dear knows, but the most av my mis—
misallyances was for pure devilry, an' mighty sorry I have been
whin harm came; an' time an' agin wid a gurl, ay, an' a woman
too, for the matther av that, whin I have seen by the eyes av her
that I was makin' more throuble than I talked, I have hild off an'
let be for the sake av the mother that bore me. But Larry, I'm
thinkin', he was suckled by a she-divil, for he niver let wan go that
came nigh to listen to him. 'Twas his business, as it might ha' been
sinthry-go. He was a good soldier too. Now there was the Colonel's
governess—an' he a privit too!—that was never known in barricks;
an' wan av the Major's maids, and she was promust to a man; an'
some more outside; an' fwhat ut was amongst us we'll never know
till Judgmint Day. 'Twas the natur' av the baste to put the
comether on the best av thim—not the prettiest by any manner
av manes—but the like av such women as you cud lay your hand
on the Book an' swear there was niver thought av foolishness in.
An' for that very reason, mark you, he was niver caught. He came
close to ut wanst or twice, but caught he niver was, an' that cost

him more at the ind than the beginnin'. He talked to me more
than most, bekaze he tould me, barrin' the accident av my educashin, I'd ha' been the same kind av divil he was. "An' is ut like,"
he wud say, houldin' his head high—"is ut like that I'd iver be
thrapped? For fwhat am I whin all's said an' done?" he sez. "A
damned privit," sez he. "An' is ut like, think you, that thim I know
wud be connect wid a privit like me? Number tin thousand four
hundher' an' sivin," he sez, grinnin'. I knew by the turn av his
spache whin he was not takin' care to talk rough-shod that he was a
gentleman-ranker.

'"I do not undherstan' ut at all," I sez; "but I know," sez I,
"that the Divil looks out av your eyes, an' I'll have no share wid
you. A little fun by way av amusemint where 'twill do no harm,
Larry, is right an' fair, but I am mistook if 'tis any amusemint to
you," I sez.

'"You are much mistook," he sez. "An' I counsel you not to
judge your betthers."

'"My betthers!" I sez. "God help you, Larry. There's no betther
in this. 'Tis all bad, as ye will find for yoursilf."

'"You're not like me," he says, tossin' his head.

'"Praise the Saints, I am not," I sez. "Fwhat I have done I have
done an' been crool sorry for. Whin your time comes," sez I, "ye'll
remimber fwhat I say."

'"An' whin that time comes," sez he, "I'll come to you for
ghostly consolation, Father Terence," an' at that he wint off afther
some more divil's business—for to get expayrience, he tould me.
He was wickud—rank wickud—wickud as all Hell! I'm not con-
struct by natur' to go in fear av *anny* man, but, begad, I was afraid
av Larry. He'd come into barricks wid his cap on three hairs, an'
lie on his cot an' stare at the ceilin', an' now an' agin he'd fetch a
little laugh, the like av a splash in the bottom av a well, an' by
that I knew he was schamin' new wickudness, an' I'd be afraid.
All this was long an' long ago, but ut hild me straight—for a
while.

'I tould you, did I not, sorr, that I was caressed an' pershuaded
to lave the Tyrone on account av a throuble?'

'Something to do with a belt and a man's head, wasn't it?'
Terence had never given me the tale in full.

'Ut was. Faith, ivry time I go on prisoner's gyard in coort I
wondher fwhy I was not where the pris'ner is. But the man I
strook tuk it in fair fight, an' he had the good sinse not to die.
Considher now, fwhat wud ha' come to the Arrmy if he had! I was

enthreated to exchange, an' my Commandin' Orf'cer pled wid me.
I wint, not to be disobligin', an' Larry tould me he was powerful
sorry to lose me, though fwhat I'd done to make him sorry I do
not know. So to the Ould Rig'mint I came, lavin' Larry to go to the
divil his own way, an' niver expectin' to see him agin excipt as a
shootin'-case in barricks. . . . Who's that quittin' the compound?'
Terence's quick eye had caught sight of a white uniform skulking
behind the hedge.

'The Sergeant's gone visiting,' said a voice.

'Thin I take on here, an' I will have no snakin' away to the
bazar, an' huntin' for you wid a pathrol at midnight. Nalson, for I
know ut's you, come back to the veranda.'

Nalson, detected, slunk back to his fellows. There was a grumble
that died away in a minute or two, and Terence, turning on the
other side, went on:

'That was the last I saw av Larry for a while. Exchange is the
same as death for not thinkin', an' by token I married Dinah, an'
that kept me from remimberin' ould times. Thin we wint up to the
Front, an' ut tore my heart in tu to lave Dinah at the Depôt in
Pindi. Consequint, whin I was at the Front I fought circumspectuous till I warrmed up, an' thin I fought double tides. You remimber
fwhat I tould you in the gyard-gate av the fight at Silver's
Theatre?' *

'Wot's that about Silver's Theayter?' said Ortheris quickly, over
his shoulder.

'Nothin', little man. A tale that ye know. As I was sayin', afther
that fight, us av the Ould Rig'mint an' the Tyrone was all mixed
together takin' shtock av the dead, an' av coorse I wint about to
find if there was any man that remimbered me. The second man I
came acrost—an' how I'd missed him in the fight I do not know—
was Larry, an' a fine man he looked, but oulder, by reason that he
had fair call to be. "Larry," sez I, "how is ut wid you?"

' "Ye're callin' the wrong man," he sez, wid his gentleman's
smile. "Larry has been dead these three years. They call him
'Love-o'-Women' now," he sez. By that I knew the ould divil was
in him yet, but the ind av a fight is no time for the beginnin' av
confession, so we sat down an' talked av times.

' "They tell me you're a married man," he sez, puffin' slow at his
poipe. "Are ye happy?"

' "I will be whin I get back to Depôt," I sez. " 'Tis a reconnais-
sance-honeymoon now."

*'With the Main Guard.' *Soldiers Three.*

' "I'm married too," he sez, puffin' slow an' more slow, an' stopperin' wid his forefinger.

' "Send you happiness," I sez. "That's the best hearin' for a long time."

' "Are ye av that opinion?" he sez; an' thin he began talkin' av the campaign. The sweat av Silver's Theatre was not dhry upon him an' he was prayin' for more work. I was well contint to lie and listen to the cook-pot lids.

'Whin he got up off the ground he shtaggered a little, an' laned over all twisted.

' "Ye've got more than ye bargained for," I sez. "Take an inventory, Larry. 'Tis like you're hurt."

'He turned round stiff as a ramrod an' damned the eyes av me up an' down for an impartinent Irish-faced ape. If that had been in barricks, I'd ha' stretched him an' no more said; but 'twas at the Front, an' afther such a fight as Silver's Theatre I knew there was no callin' a man to account for his timpers. He might as well ha' kissed me. Afthewards I was well pleased I kept my fistes home. Thin our Captain Crook—Cruik-na-bulleen—came up. He'd been talkin' to the little orf'cer bhoy av the Tyrone. "We're all cut to windystraws," he sez, "but the Tyrone are damned short for non-coms. Go you over there, Mulvaney, an' be Deputy-Sargint, Corp'ril, Lance, an' ivrything else ye can lay hands on till I bid you stop."

'I wint over an' tuk hoult. There was wan sargint left standin', an' they'd pay no heed to him. The remnint was me, an' 'twas full time I came. Some I talked to, an' some I did not, but before night the bhoys av the Tyrone stud to attention, begad, if I sucked on my poipe above a whishper. Betune you an' me an' Bobs I was commandin' the comp'ny, an' that was fwhat Crook had thransferred me for; an' the little orf'cer bhoy knew ut, and I knew ut, but the comp'ny did not. And *there*, mark you, is the vartue that no money an' no dhrill can buy—the vartue av the ould soldier that knows his orf'cer's work an' does ut for him at the salute!

'Thin the Tyrone, wid the Ould Rig'mint in touch, was sint maraudhin' an' prowlin' acrost the hills promishcuous an' onsatisfactory. 'Tis my privit opinion that a gin'ral does not know half his time fwhat to do wid three-quarthers his command. So he shquats on his hunkers an' bids thim run round an' round forninst him while he considhers on ut. Whin by the process av natur' they get sejuced into a big fight that was none av their seekin', he sez: "Obsarve my shuperior janius. I meant ut to come so." We ran round an' about, an' all we got was shootin' into the camp at night, an' rushin' empty *sungars* wid the long bradawl, an' bein' hit from behind rocks till we was wore out—all excipt Love-o'-Women. That puppy-dog business was mate an' dhrink to him. Begad, he cud niver get enough av ut. Me well knowin' that ut is just this desultorial campaignin' that kills the best men, an' suspicionin' that if I was cut, the little orf'cer bhoy wud expind all his men in thryin' to get me out, I wud lie most powerful doggo whin I heard a shot, an' curl my long legs behind a bowlder, an' run like blazes whin the ground was clear. Faith, if I led the Tyrone in rethreat wanst I led thim forty times! Love-o'-Women wud stay pottin' an' pottin' from behind a rock, an' wait till the fire was heaviest, an' thin stand up an' fire man-height clear. He wud lie out in camp too at night, snipin' at the shadows, for he niver tuk a mouthful av slape. My Commandin' Orf'cer—save his little sowl!—cud not see the beauty av my strategims, an' whin the Ould Rig-mint crossed us, an' that was wanst a week, he'd throt off to Crook, wid his big blue eyes as round as saucers, an' lay an information agin' me. I heard thim wanst talkin' through the tent-wall, an' I nearly laughed.

' "He runs—runs like a hare," sez the little orf'cer bhoy. " 'Tis demoralizin' my men."

' "Ye damned little fool," sez Crook, laughin', "he's larnin' you your business. Have ye been rushed at night yet?"

' "No," sez that child; wishful he had been.

' "Have you any wounded?" sez Crook.

' "No," he sez, "There was no chanst for that. They follow Mulvaney too quick," he sez.

' "Fwhat more do you want, thin?" sez Crook. "Terence is bloodin' you neat an' handy," he sez. "He knows fwhat you do not, an' that's that there's a time for ivrything. He'll not lead you wrong," he sez, "but I'd give a month's pay to larn fwhat he thinks av you."

'That kept the babe quiet, but Love-o'-Women was pokin' at me for ivrything I did, an' specially my manoeuvres.

' "Mr Mulvaney," he sez wan evenin', very contempshus, "you're growin' very *jeldy* on your feet. Among gentlemen," he sez, "among gentlemen that's called no pretty name."

' "Among privits 'tis different," I sez. "Get back to your tint. I'm Sargint here," I sez.

'There was just enough in the voice av me to tell him he was playin' wid his life betune his teeth. He wint off, an' I noticed that this man that was contempshus set off from the halt wid a shunt as tho' he was bein' kicked behind. That same night there was a Paythan picnic in the hills about, an' firin' into our tints fit to wake the livin' dead. "Lie down all," I sez. "Lie down an' kape still. They'll no more than waste ammunition."

'I heard a man's feet on the ground, an' thin a 'Tini joinin' in the chorus. I'd been lyin' warm, thinkin' av Dinah an' all, but I crup out wid the bugle for to look round in case there was a rush; an' the 'Tini was flashin' at the fore-ind av the camp, an' the hill near by was fair flickerin' wid long-range fire. Undher the starlight I behild Love-o'-Women settin' on a rock wid his belt an' helmet off. He shouted wanst or twice, an' thin I heard him say: "They shud ha' got the range long ago. Maybe they'll fire at the flash." Thin he fired agin, an' that dhrew a fresh volley, an' the long slugs that they chew in their teeth came floppin' among the rocks like tree-toads av a hot night. "That's betther," sez Love-o'-Women. "Oh, Lord, how long, how long!" he sez, an' at that he lit a match an' hild ut above his head.

' "Mad," thinks I, "mad as a coot," an' I tuk wan stip forward, an' the nixt I knew was the sole av my boot flappin' like a cavalry gydon an' the funny-bone av my toes tinglin'. 'Twas a clane-cut shot—a slug—that niver touched sock or hide, but set me barefut on the rocks. At that I tuk Love-o'-Women by the scruff an' threw him undher a bowlder, an' whin I sat down I heard the bullets patterin' on that same good stone.

' "Ye may dhraw your own wickud fire," I sez, shakin' him, "but I'm not goin' to be kilt too."

' "Ye've come too soon," he sez. "Ye've come too soon. In another minut' they cudn't ha' missed me. Mother av God," he sez, "fwhy did ye not lave me be? Now 'tis all to do again," an' he hides his face in his hands.

' "So that's ut," I sez, shakin' him agin. "That's the manin' av your disobeyin' ordhers."

' "I dare not kill mesilf," he sez, rockin' to and fro. "My own hand wud not let me die, an' there's not a bullet this month past wud touch me. I'm to die slow," he sez. "I'm to die slow. But I'm in Hell now," he sez, shriekin' like a woman. "I'm in Hell now!"

' "God be good to us all," I sez, for I saw his face. "Will ye tell a man the throuble? If 'tis not murther, maybe we'll mend it yet."

'At that he laughed. "D'you remimber fwhat I said in the Tyrone barricks about comin' to ye for ghostly consolation? I have not forgot," he sez. "That came back, an' the rest av my time is on

me now, Terence. I've fought ut off for months an' months, but
the liquor will not bite any more. Terence," he sez. "I can't get
dhrunk!"

'Thin I knew he spoke the truth about bein' in Hell, for whin
liquor does not take hoult the sowl av a man is rotten in him. But
me bein' such as I was, fwhat cud I say to him?

' "Di'monds an' pearls," he begins agin. "Di'monds an' pearls
I have thrown away wid both hands—an' fwhat have I left? Oh,
fwhat have I left?"

'He was shakin' an' tremblin' up against my shouldher, an' the
slugs were singin' overhead, an' I was wondherin' whether my
little bhoy wud have sinse enough to kape his men quiet through
all this firin'.

' "So long as I did not think," sez Love-o'-Women, "so long I
did not see—I wud not see, but I can now, fwhat I've lost. The
time an' the place," he sez, "an' the very words I said whin ut
pleased me to go off alone to Hell. But thin, even thin," he sez,
wrigglin' tremenjus, "I wud not ha' been happy. There was too
much behind av me. How cud I ha' believed her sworn oath—me
that have bruk mine agin an' agin for the sport av seein' thim cry?
An' there are the others," he sez. "Oh, fwhat will I do—fwhat will
I do?" He rocked back an' forward agin, an' I think he was cryin'
like anny av his women.

'The full half av fwhat he said was Brigade Ordhers to me, but
from the rest an' the remnint I suspicioned somethin' av his
throuble. 'Twas the judgemint av God had grup the heel av him,
as I tould him 'twud in the Tyrone barricks. The slugs was singin'
over our rock more an' more, an' I sez for to divart him: "Let bad
alone," I sez. "They'll be thryin' to rush the camp in a minut'."

'I had no more than said that whin a Paythan man crep' up on
his belly wid his knife betune his teeth, not twinty yards from us.
Love-o'-Women jumped up an' fetched a yell, an' the man saw
him an' ran at him (he'd left his rifle undher the rock) wid the
knife. Love-o'-Women niver turned a hair, but by the Living
Power, for I saw ut, a stone twisted undher the Paythan man's
feet an' he came down full sprawl, an' his knife wint tinklin' acrost
the rocks! "I tould you I was Cain," sez Love-o'-Women. "Fwhat's
the use av killin' him? He's an honust man—by compare."

'I was not dishputin' about the morils av Paythans that tide,
so I dhropped Love-o'-Women's butt acrost the man's face, an'
"Hurry into camp," I sez, "for this may be the first av a rush."

'There was no rush afther all, though we waited undher arms to

give thim a chanst. The Paythan man must ha' come alone for the
mischief, an' afther a while Love-o'-Women wint back to his tint
wid that quare lurchin' sind-off in his walk that I cud niver
undherstand. Begad, I pitied him, an' the more bekaze he made me
think for the rest av the night av the day whin I was confirmed
Corp'ril, not actin' Leftinant, an' my thoughts was not good to me.

'Ye can undherstand that afther that night we came to talkin'
a dale together, an' bit by bit ut came out fwhat I'd suspicioned.
The whole av his carr'in's on an' divilmints had come back on him
hard, as liquor comes back whin you've been on the dhrink for a
wake. All he'd said an' all he'd done, an' only he cud tell how much
that was, come back, an' there was niver a minut's peace in his
sowl. 'Twas the Horrors widout any cause to see, an' yet, an' yet—
fwhat am I talkin' av? He'd ha' taken the Horrors wid thankful-
ness. Beyon' the repentince av the man, an' that was beyon' the
natur' av man—awful, awful, to behould!—there was more that
was worse than any repentince. Av the scores an' scores that he
called over in his mind (an' they were dhrivin' him mad), there was,
mark you, wan woman av all, an' she was not his wife, that cut
him to the quick av his marrow. 'Twas there, he said, that he'd
thrown away di'monds an' pearls past count, an' thin he'd begin
again like a blind *byle* in an oil-mill, walkin' round and round, to
considher (him that was beyond all touch av bein' happy this side
Hell!) how happy he wud ha' been wid *her*. The more he consid-
hered, the more he'd consate himself that he'd lost mighty happiness; an' thin he wud work ut all backwards, an' cry that he niver
cud ha' been happy anyways.

'Time an' time an' agin in camp, on p'rade, ay, an' in action,
I've seen that man shut his eyes an' duck his head as ye wud
duck to the flicker av a bay'nit. For 'twas thin, he tould me, that
the thought av all he'd missed came an' stud forninst him like red-
hot irons. For fwhat he'd done wid the others he was sorry, but
he did not care; but this wan woman that I've tould av, by the
Hilts av God, she made him pay for all the others twice over!
Niver did I know that a man cud enjure such tormint widout his
heart crackin' in his ribs, an' I have been'—Terence turned the
pipe-stem slowly between his teeth—'I have been in some black
cells. All I iver suffered, tho', was not to be talked av alongside av
him . . . an' fwhat cud I do? Paternosters was no more than peas
on plates for his sorrows.

'Evenshually we finished our prom'nade acrost the hills, and,
thanks to me for the same, there was no casualties an' no glory.

The campaign was comin' to an ind, an' all the rig'mints was being dhrawn together for to be sint back home. Love-o'-Women was mighty sorry bekaze he had no work to do, an' all his time to think in. I've heard that man talkin' to his belt-plate an' his side-arms while he was soldierin' thim, all to prevint himself from thinkin'; an' ivry time he got up afther he had been settin' down or wint on from the halt, he'd start wid that kick an' traverse that I tould you av—his legs sprawlin' all ways to wanst. He wud niver go see the docthor, tho' I tould him to be wise. He'd curse me up an' down for my advice; but I knew he was no more a man to be reckoned wid than the little bhoy was a Commandin' Orf'cer; so I let his tongue run if ut aised him.

'Wan day—'twas on the way back—I was walkin' round camp wid him, an' he stopped an' struck ground wid his right fut three or four times doubtful. "Fwhat is ut?" I sez. "Is that ground?" sez he; an' while I was thinkin' his mind was goin', up comes the docthor, who'd been anatomizin' a dead bullock. Love-o'-Women starts to go on quick, an' lands me a kick on the knee while his legs was fallin' into marchin' ordher.

' "Hould on there," sez the docthor; an' Love-o'-Women's face, that was lined like a gridiron, turns red as brick.

' " 'Tention," says the docthor; an' Love-o'-Women stud so. "Now shut your eyes," sez the docthor. "No, ye must not hould by your comrade."

' " 'Tis all up," sez Love-o'-Women, thrying to smile. "I'd fall, docthor, an' you know ut."

' "Fall?" I sez. "Fall at attention wid your eyes shut! Fwhat do you mane?"

' "The docthor knows," he sez. "I've hild up as long as I can, but, begad, I'd glad 'tis all done. But I will die slow," he sez, "I will die very slow."

'I cud see by the docthor's face that he was mortial sorry for the man, an' he ordhered him to hospital. We wint back together, an' I was dumb-struck. Love-o'-Women was cripplin' an' crumblin' at ivry stip. He walked wid a hand on my shouldher all slued sideways, an' his right leg swingin' like a lame camel. Me not knowin' more than the dead fwhat ailed him, 'twas just as though the docthor's word had done ut all—as if Love-o'-Women had but been waitin' for the word to let go.

'In hospital he sez somethin' to the docthor that I cud not catch.

' "Holy Shmoke!" sez the docthor, "an' who are you to be givin' names to your diseases? 'Tis agin' all the reg'lations."

' "I'll not be a privit much longer," sez Love-o'-Women in his gentleman's voice, an' the docthor jumped.

' "Thrate me as a study, Docthor Lowndes," he sez; an' that was the first time I'd iver heard a docthor called by name.

' "Good-bye, Terence," sez Love-o'-Women. " 'Tis a dead man I am widout the pleasure av dyin'. You'll come an' set wid me sometimes for the peace av my sowl."

'Now, I had been minded for to ask Crook to take me back to the Ould Rig'mint; the fightin' was over, an' I was wore out wid the ways av the bhoys in the Tyrone; but I shifted my will, an' hild on, and wint to set wid Love-o'-Women in the hospital. As I have said, sorr, the man bruk all to little pieces undher my hand. How long he had hild up an' forced himself fit to march I cannot tell, but in hospital but two days later he was such as I hardly knew. I shuk hands wid him, an' his grip was fair strong, but his hands wint all ways to wanst, an' he cud not button his tunic.

' "I'll take long an' long to die yet," he sez, "for the wages av sin they're like interest in the Rig'mintal savin's-bank—sure, but a damned long time bein' paid."

'The docthor sez to me, quiet one day, "Has Tighe there anythin' on his mind?" he sez. "He's burnin' himself out."

' "How shud I know, sorr?" I sez, as innocint as putty.

' "They call him Love-o'-Women in the Tyrone, do they not?" he sez. "I was a fool to ask. Be wid him all you can. He's houldin' on to your strength."

' "But fwhat ails him, docthor?" I sez.

' "They call ut Locomotus Attacks-us," he sez, "bekaze," sez he, "ut attacks us like a locomotive, if ye know fwhat that manes. An' ut comes," sez he, lookin' at me, "ut comes from bein' called Love-o'-Women."

' "You're jokin', docthor," I sez.

' "Jokin'!" sez he. "If iver you feel that you've got a felt sole in your boot instid av a Governmint bull's-wool, come to me," he sez, "an I'll show you whether 'tis a joke."

'You wud not belave ut, sorr, but that, an' seein' Love-o'-Women overtuk widout warnin', put the cowld fear av Attacks-us on me so strong that for a week an' more I was kickin' my toes against stones an' stumps for the pleasure av feelin' thim hurt.

'An' Love-o'-Women lay in the cot (he might have gone down wid the wounded before an' before, but he asked to stay wid me), and fwhat there was in his mind had full swing at him night an' day an' ivry hour av the day an' the night; an' he shrivelled like beef-rations in a hot sun, an' his eyes was like owl's eyes, an' his hands was mut'nous.

'They was gettin' the rig'mints away wan by wan, the campaign bein' inded, but as ushuil they was behavin' as if niver a rig'mint had been moved before in the mem'ry av man. Now, fwhy is that, sorr? There's fightin', in an' out, nine months av the twelve somewhere in the Arrmy. There has been—for years an' years an' years; an' I wud ha' thought they'd begin to get the hang av providin' for throops. But no! Ivry time 'tis like a girls' school meetin' a big red bull whin they're goin' to church; an' "Mother av God," sez the Commissariat an' the Railways an' the Barrick-masters, "fwhat will we do now?" The ordhers came to us av the Tyrone an' the Ould Rig'mint an' half-a-dozen more to go down, an' there the ordhers stopped dumb. We wint down, by the special grace av God —down the Khyber anyways. There was sick wid us, an' I'm thinkin' that some av thim was jolted to death in the *doolies*, but they was anxious to be kilt so if they cud get to Peshawur alive the sooner. I walked by Love-o'-Women—there was no marchin', an' Love-o'-Women was not in a stew to get on. "If I'd only ha' died up there," sez he through the *dooli*-curtains, an' thin he'd twist up his eyes an' duck his head for the thoughts that come an' raked him.

'Dinah was in Depôt at Pindi, but I wint circumspectuous, for well I knew 'tis just at the rump-ind av all things that his luck turns on a man. By token I had seen a dhriver of a batthery goin' by at a trot singin' "Home, swate home" at the top av his shout, an' takin' no heed to his bridle-hand—I had seen that man dhrop under the gun in the middle of a word, and come out by the limber like—like a frog on a pavestone. No. I wud *not* hurry, though, God knows, my heart was all in Pindi. Love-o'-Women saw fwhat was in my mind, an' "Go on, Terence," he sez, "I know fwhat's waitin' for you." "I will not," I sez. " 'Twill kape a little yet."

'Ye know the turn of the pass forninst Jumrood and the nine-mile road on the flat to Peshawur? All Peshawur was along that road day an' night waitin' for frinds—men, women, childher, and bands. Some av the throops was camped round Jumrood, an' some wint on to Peshawur to get away down to their cantonmints. We came through in the early mornin', havin' been awake the night through, and we dhruv sheer into the middle av the mess. Mother av Glory, will I iver forget that comin' back? The light was not fair lifted, an' the first we heard was "For 'tis my delight av a shiny night," frum a band that thought we was the second four comp'nies av the

Lincolnshire. At that we was forced to sind them a yell to say who we was, an' thin up wint "The Wearin' av the Green." It made me crawl all up my backbone, not havin' taken my brequist. Then right smash into our rear came fwhat was left av the Jock Elliotts—wid four pipers an' not half a kilt among thim, playin' for the dear life, an' swingin' their rumps like buck-rabbits, an' a native rig'mint shriekin' blue murther. Ye niver heard the like! There was men cryin' like women that did—an' faith, I do not blame thim! Fwhat bruk me down was the Lancers' Band—shinin' an' spick like angils, wid the ould dhrum-horse at the head an' the silver kettle-dhrums an' all an' all, waitin' for their men that was behind us. They shtruck up the Cavalry Canter; an' begad, those poor ghosts that had not a sound fut in a throop they answered to ut; the men rockin' in their saddles. We thried to cheer thim as they wint by, but ut came out like a big gruntin' cough, so there must have been many that was feelin' like me. Oh, but I'm forgettin'! The Fly-by-Nights was waitin' for their second battalion, an' whin ut came out, there was the Colonel's horse led at the head—saddle-empty. The men fair worshipped him, an' he'd died at Ali Musjid on the road down. They waited till the remnint av the battalion was up, an' thin—clane against ordhers, for who wanted *that* chune that day?—they wint back to Peshawur slow-time an' tearin' the bowils out av ivry man that heard, wid "The Dead March." Right acrost our line they wint, an' ye know their uniforms are as black as the Sweeps, crawlin' past like the dead, an' the other bands damnin' them to let be.

'Little they cared. The carpse was wid thim, an' they'd ha' taken ut so through a Coronation. Our ordhers was to go into Peshawur, an' we wint hotfut past the Fly-by-Nights, not singin', to lave that chune behind us. That was how we tuk the road av the other corps.

' 'Twas ringin' in my ears still whin I felt in the bones av me that Dinah was comin', an' I heard a shout, an' thin I saw a horse an' a tattoo latherin' down the road, hell-to-shplit, undher women. I knew—I knew! Wan was the Tyrone Colonel's wife—ould Beeker's lady—her grey hair flyin' an' her fat round carkiss rowlin' in the saddle, an' the other was Dinah, that shud ha' been at Pindi. The Colonel's lady, she charged the head av our column like a stone wall, an' she all but knocked Beeker off his horse, throwin' her arrums round his neck an' blubberin', "Me bhoy! me bhoy!" an' Dinah wheeled left an' came down our flank, an' I let a yell that had suffered inside av me for months an'—Dinah came. Will I iver forget that while I live! She'd come on pass from Pindi, an' the

Colonel's lady had lint her the tattoo. They'd been huggin' an' cryin' in each other's arms all the long night.

'So she walked along wid her hand in mine, askin' forty questions to wanst, an' beggin' me on the Virgin to maké oath that there was not a bullet consaled in me, unbeknownst somewhere, an' thin I remimbered Love-o'-Women. He was watchin' us, an' his face was like the face av a divil that has been cooked too long. I did not wish Dinah to see ut, for whin a woman's runnin' over wid happiness she's like to be touched, for harm afterwards, by the laste little thing in life. So I dhrew the curtain, an' Love-o'-Women lay back an' groaned.

'Whin we marched into Peshawur Dinah wint to barricks to wait for me, an', me feelin' so rich that tide, I wint on to take Love-o'-Women to hospital. It was the last I cud do, an' to save him the dust an' the smother I turned the *dooli*-men down a road well clear av the rest av the throops, an' we wint along, me talkin' through the curtains. Av a sudden I heard him say:

' "Let me look. For the mercy av Hiven, let me look!" I had been so tuk up wid gettin' him out av the dust an' thinkin' av Dinah that I had not kept my eyes about me. There was a woman ridin' a little behind av us; an', talkin' ut over wid Dinah afterwards, that same woman must ha' rid out far on the Jumrood road. Dinah said that she had been hoverin' like a kite on the left flank av the columns.

'I halted the *dooli* to set the curtains, an' she rode by, walkin' pace, an' Love-o'-Women's eyes wint afther her as if he wud fair haul her down from the saddle.

' "Follow there," was all he sez, but I niver heard a man speak in that voice before or since; an' I knew by those two wan words an' the look in his face that she was Di'monds-an'-Pearls that he'd talked av in his disthresses.

'We followed till she turned into the gate av a little house that stud near the Edwardes Gate. There was two gurls in the veranda, an' they ran in whin they saw us. Faith, at long eye-range it did not take me a wink to see fwhat kind av house ut was. The throops bein' there an' all, there was three or four such; but afterwards the Polis bade thim go. At the veranda Love-o'-Women sez, catchin' his breath, "Stop here," an' thin, an' thin, wid a grunt that must ha' tore the heart up from his stummick, he swung himself out av the *dooli*, an', my troth, he stud up on his feet wid the sweat pourin' down his face! If Mackie was to walk in here now I'd be less tuk back than I was thin. Where he'd dhrawn his power from,

God knows—or the Divil—but 'twas a dead man walkin' in the sun, wid the face av a dead man an' the breath av a dead man, hild up by the Power, an' the legs an' the arms av the carpse obeyin' ordhers.

'The woman stud in the veranda. She'd been a beauty, too, though her eyes was sunk in her head, an' she looked Love-o'-Women up an' down terrible. "An'," she sez, kickin' back the tail av her habit—"An'," she sez, "fwhat are you doin' *here*, married man?"

'Love-o'-Women said nothin', but a little froth came to his lips, an' he wiped ut off wid his hand an' looked at her an' the paint on her, an' looked, an' looked, an' looked.

' "An' yet," she sez, wid a laugh—(Did you hear Raines's wife laugh whin Mackie died? Ye did not? Well for you.)—"An' yet," she sez, "who but you have betther right?" sez she. "You taught me the road. You showed me the way," she sez. "Ay, look," she sez, "for 'tis your work; you that tould me—d'you remimber it?—that a woman who was false to wan man cud be false to two. I have been that," she sez, "that an' more, for you always said I was a quick learner, Ellis. Look well," she sez, "for it is me that you called your wife in the sight av God long since." An' she laughed.

'Love-o'-Women stud still in the sun widout answerin'. Thin he groaned an' coughed to wanst, an' I thought 'twas the death-rattle, but he niver tuk his eyes off her face, not for a blink. Ye cud ha' put her eyelashes through the flies av an E.P. tint, they were that long.

' "Fwhat do you do here?" she sez, word by word, "that have taken away my joy in my man this five years gone—that have broken my rest an' killed my body an' damned my soul for the sake av seein' how 'twas done. Did your expayrience aftherwards bring you acrost any woman that give you more than I did? Wud I not ha' died for you, an' wid you, Ellis? Ye know that, man! If iver your lyin' sowl saw truth in uts life ye know that."

'An' Love-o'-Women lifted up his head and said, "I knew," an' that was all. While she was spakin' the Power hild him up p'radeset in the sun, an' the sweat dhripped undher his helmet. 'Twas more an' more throuble for him to talk, an' his mouth was runnin' twistways.

' "Fwhat do you do *here*?" she sez, an' her voice wint up. 'Twas like bells tollin' before. "Time was whin you were quick enough wid your words—you that talked me down to Hell. Are ye dumb now?" An' Love-o'-Women got his tongue, an' sez simple, like a little child, "May I come in?" he sez.

' "The house is opin day an' night," she sez, wid a laugh; an' Love-o'-Women ducked his head an' hild up his hand as tho' he was gyardin'. The Power was on him still—ut hild him up still, for, by my sowl, as I'll niver save ut, he walked up the veranda steps that had been a livin' carpse in hospital for a month!

' "An' now?" she sez, lookin' at him; an' the red paint stud lone on the white av her face like a bull's-eye on a target.

'He lifted up his eyes, slow an' very slow, an' he looked at her long an' very long, an' he tuk his spache betune his teeth wid a wrench that shuk him.

' "I'm dyin', Aigypt—dyin'," he sez. Ay, those were his words, for I rimimber the name he called her. He was turnin' the death-colour, but his eyes niver rowled. They were set—set on her. Widout word or warnin' she opened her arrums full stretch, an' "Here!" she sez. (Oh, fwhat a golden mericle av a voice ut was!) "Die here!" she sez; an' Love-o'-Women dhropped forward, an' she hild him up; for she was a fine big woman.

'I had no time to turn, bekaze that minut' I heard the sowl quit him—tore out in the death-rattle—an' she laid him back in a long chair, an' she sez to me, "Misther soldier," she sez, "will ye not wait an' talk to wan av the gurls? This sun's too much for him."

'Well I knew there was no sun he'd iver see, but I cud not spake, so I wint away wid the empty *dooli* to find the docthor. He'd been breakfastin' an' lunchin' iver since we'd come in, an' he was full as a tick.

' "Faith, ye've got dhrunk mighty soon," he sez, whin I'd tould him, "to see that man walk. Barrin' a puff or two av life, he was a carpse before we left Jumrood. I've a great mind," he sez, "to confine you."

' "There's a dale av liquor runnin' about, docthor," I sez, solemn as a hard-boiled egg. "Maybe 'tis so; but will ye not come an' see the carpse at the house?"

' " 'Tis dishgraceful," he sez, "that I wud be expected to go to a place like that. Was she a pretty woman?" he sez, an' at that he set off double-quick.

'I cud see that the two was in the veranda where I'd left thim, an' I knew by the hang av her head an' the noise av the crows fwhat had happened. 'Twas the first an' the last time that I'd iver known woman to use the pistol. They fear the shot as a rule, but Di'monds-an'-Pearls she did not—she did not.

'The docthor touched the long black hair av her head ('twas all loose upon Love-o'-Women's tunic), an' that cleared the liquor out av him. He stud considherin' a long time, his hands in his pockets, an' at last he sez to me, "Here's a double death from naturil causes, most naturil causes; an' in the present state av affairs the Rig'mint will be thankful for wan grave the less to dig. *Issiwasti*," he sez. "*Issiwasti*, Privit Mulvaney, these two will be buried together in the Civil Cemet'ry at my expinse; an' may the good God," he sez, "make ut so much for me whin my time comes. Go you to your wife," he sez. "Go an' be happy. I'll see to this all."

'I left him still considherin'. They was buried in the Civil Cemet'ry together, wid a Church av England service. There was too many buryin's thin to ask questions, an' the docthor—he ran away wid Major—Major Van Dyce's lady that year—he saw to ut all. Fwhat the right an' the wrong av Love-o'-Women an' Di'-monds-an'-Pearls was I niver knew, an' I will niver know; but I've tould ut as I came across ut—here an' there in little pieces. *So*, being fwhat I am, an' knowin' fwhat I knew, that's fwhy I say in this shootin'-case here, Mackie that's dead an' in Hell is the lucky man. There are times, sorr, whin 'tis betther for the man to die than to live, an' by consequince forty million times betther for the woman.'

*

'H'up there!' said Ortheris. 'It's time to go.'

The witnesses and guard formed up in the thick white dust of the parched twilight and swung off, marching easy and whistling. Down the road to the green by the church I could hear Ortheris, the black Book-lie still uncleansed on his lips, setting, with a fine sense of the fitness of things, the shrill quickstep that runs—

> '*Oh, do not despise the advice of the wise,*
> *Learn wisdom from those that are older,*
> *And don't try for things that are out of your reach—*
> *An' that's what the Girl told the Soldier!*
> *Soldier! Soldier!*
> *Oh, that's what the Girl told the Soldier!*

Many Inventions, 1893

The Devil and the Deep Sea

*'All supplies very bad and dear, and there are no facilities
for even the smallest repairs.'*
Sailing Directions

HER NATIONALITY was British, but you will not find her
house-flag in the list of our Mercantile Marine. She was a nine-
hundred-ton, iron, schooner-rigged, screw cargo-boat, differing ex-
ternally in no way from any other tramp of the sea. But it is with
steamers as it is with men. There are those who will for a consideration sail extremely close to the wind; and, in the present state of a
fallen world, such people and such steamers have their use. From
the hour that the *Aglaia* first entered the Clyde—new, shiny, and
innocent, with a quart of cheap champagne trickling down her cutwater—Fate and her owner, who was also her captain, decreed that
she should deal with embarrassed crowned heads, fleeing Presidents,
financiers of over-extended ability, women to whom change of air
was imperative, and the lesser law-breaking Powers. Her career led
her sometimes into the Admiralty Courts, where the sworn statements of her skipper filled his brethren with envy. The mariner
cannot tell or act a lie in the face of the sea, or mislead a tempest;
but, as lawyers have discovered, he makes up for chances withheld
when he returns to shore, an affidavit in either hand.

The *Aglaia* figured with distinction in the great *Mackinaw*
salvage case. It was her first slip from virtue, and she learned how
to change her name, but not her heart, and to run across the sea.
As the *Guiding Light* she was very badly wanted in a South
American port for the little matter of entering harbour at full speed,
colliding with a coal-hulk and the State's only man-of-war, just as
that man-of-war was going to coal. She put to sea without explanations, though three forts fired at her for half an hour. As the *Julia
M'Gregor* she had been concerned in picking up from a raft certain
gentlemen who should have stayed in Nouméa, but who preferred
making themselves vastly unpleasant to authority in quite another
quarter of the world; and as the *Shah-in-Shah* she had been overtaken on the high seas, indecently full of munitions of war, by the
cruiser of an agitated Power at issue with its neighbour. That time
she was very nearly sunk, and her riddled hull gave eminent lawyers
of two countries great profit. After a season she reappeared as the

Martin Hunt, painted a dull slate colour, with a pure saffron funnel, and boats of sparrow's-egg blue, engaging in the Odessa trade till she was invited (and the invitation could not well be disregarded) to keep away from Black Sea ports altogether.

She had ridden through many waves of depression. Freights might drop out of sight, Seamen's Unions throw spanners and nuts at certificated masters, or stevedores combine till cargo perished on the dock-head; but the boat of many names came and went, busy, alert, and inconspicuous always. Her skipper made no complaint of hard times, and port officers observed that her crew signed and signed again with the regularity of Atlantic liner boatswains. Her name she changed as occasion called; her well-paid crew never; and a large percentage of the profits of her voyages was spent with an open hand on her engine-room. She never troubled the underwriters, and very seldom stopped to talk with a signal-station; for her business was urgent and private.

But an end came to her tradings, and she perished in this manner. Deep peace brooded over Europe, Asia, Africa, America, Australasia, and Polynesia. The Powers dealt together more or less honestly; banks paid their depositors to the hour; diamonds of price came safely to the hands of their owners; republics rested content with their dictators; diplomats found no one whose presence in the least incommoded them; monarchs lived openly with their lawfully wedded wives. It was as though the whole earth had put on its best Sunday bib and tucker; and business was very bad for the *Martin Hunt.* The great, virtuous calm engulfed her, slate sides, yellow funnel, and all, but cast up in another hemisphere the steam-whaler *Haliotis,* black and rusty, with a manure-coloured funnel, a litter of dingy white boats, and an enormous stove, or furnace, for boiling blubber on her forward well-deck. There could be no doubt that her trip was successful, for she lay at several ports not too well known, and the smoke of her trying-out insulted the beaches.

Anon she departed, at the speed of the average London four-wheeler, and entered a semi-inland sea, warm, still, and blue, which is, perhaps, the most strictly preserved water in the world. There she stayed for a certain time, and the great stars of those mild skies beheld her playing puss-in-the-corner among islands where whales are never found. All that time she smelt abominably, and the smell, though fishy, was not whalesome. One evening calamity descended upon her from the island of Pygang-Watai, and she fled, while her crew jeered at a fat black-and-brown gunboat puffing far behind. They knew to the last revolution the capacity of every boat, on those seas, that they were anxious to avoid. A British ship with a good conscience does not, as a rule, flee from the man of-war of a foreign Power, and it is also considered a breach of etiquette to stop and search British ships at sea. These things the skipper of the *Haliotis* did not pause to prove, but held on at an inspiriting eleven knots till nightfall. One thing only he overlooked.

The Power that kept an expensive steam-patrol moving up and down those waters (they had dodged the two regular ships of the station with an ease that bred contempt) had newly brought up a third and a fourteen-knot boat with a clean bottom to help the work; and that was why the *Haliotis*, driving hard from the east to the west, found herself at daylight in such a position that she could not help seeing an arrangement of four flags, a mile and a half behind, which read: 'Heave to, or take the consequences!'

She had her choice, and she took it, and the end came when, presuming on her lighter draught, she tried to draw away northward over a friendly shoal. The shell that arrived by way of the Chief Engineer's cabin was some five inches in diameter, with a practice, not a bursting, charge. It had been intended to cross her bows, and that was why it knocked the framed portrait of the Chief Engineer's wife—and she was a very pretty girl—on to the floor, splintered his wash-stand, crossed the alleyway into the engine-room, and striking on a grating, dropped directly in front of the forward engine, where it burst, neatly fracturing both the bolts that held the connecting-rod to the forward crank.

What follows is worth consideration. The forward engine had no more work to do. Its released piston-rod, therefore, drove up fiercely, with nothing to check it, and started most of the nuts of the cylinder-cover. It came down again, the full weight of the steam behind it, and the foot of the disconnected connecting-rod, useless as the leg of a man with a sprained ankle, flung out to the right and struck the starboard, or right-hand, cast-iron supporting-column of the forward engine, cracking it clean through about six inches above the base, and wedging the upper portion outwards three inches towards the ship's side. There the connecting-rod jammed. Meantime, the after-engine, being as yet unembarrassed, went on with its work, and in so doing brought round at its next revolution the crank of the forward engine, which smote the already jammed connecting-rod, bending it and therewith the piston-rod cross-head—the big cross-piece that slides up and down so smoothly.

The cross-head jammed sideways in the guides, and, in addition

to putting further pressure on the already broken starboard supporting-column, cracked the port or left-hand supporting-column
in two or three places. There being nothing more that could be
made to move, the engines brought up, all standing, with a hiccup
that seemed to lift the *Haliotis* a foot out of the water; and the
engine-room staff, opening every steam outlet that they could find
in the confusion, arrived on deck somewhat scalded, but calm.
There was a sound below of things happening—a rushing, clicking,
purring, grunting, rattling noise that did not last for more than a
minute. It was the machinery adjusting itself, on the spur of the
moment, to an hundred altered conditions. Mr Wardrop, one foot
on the upper grating, inclined his ear sideways and groaned. You
cannot stop engines working at twelve knots in three seconds without disorganizing them. The *Haliotis* slid forward in a cloud of
steam, shrieking like a wounded horse. There was nothing more to
do. The five-inch shell with a reduced charge had settled the situation. And when you are full, all three holds, of strictly preserved
pearls; when you have cleaned out the Tanna Bank, the Sea-Horse
Bank, and four other banks from one end to the other of the Aman-
ala Sea—when you have ripped out the very heart of a rich Government monopoly so that five years will not repair your wrong-doings
—you must smile and take what is in store. But the skipper reflected, as a launch put out from the man-of-war, that he had been
bombarded on the high seas, with the British flag—several of them
—picturesquely disposed above him, and tried to find comfort in
the thought.

'Where,' said the stolid naval lieutenant hoisting himself aboard,
'where are those dam' pearls?'

They were there beyond evasion. No affidavit could do away
with the fearful smell of decayed oysters, the diving-dresses, and
the shell-littered hatches. They were there to the value of seventy
thousand pounds, more or less; and every pound poached.

The man-of-war was annoyed; for she had used up many tons of
coal, she had strained her tubes, and, worse than all, her officers and
crew had been hurried. Everyone on the *Haliotis* was arrested and
rearrested several times, as each officer came aboard; then they
were told by what they esteemed to be the equivalent of a midship-
man that they were to consider themselves prisoners, and finally
were put under arrest.

'It's not the least good,' said the skipper suavely. 'You'd much
better send us a tow——'

'Be still—you are arrest!' was the reply.

'Where the devil do you expect we are going to escape to? We're helpless. You've got to tow us into somewhere, and explain why you fired on us. Mr Wardrop, we're helpless, aren't we?'

'Ruined from end to end,' said the man of machinery. 'If she rolls, the forward cylinder will come down and go through her bottom. Both columns are clean cut through. There's nothing to hold anything up.'

The council of war clanked off to see if Mr Wardrop's words were true. He warned them that it was as much as a man's life was worth to enter the engine-room, and they contented themselves with a distant inspection through the thinning steam. The *Haliotis* lifted to the long, easy swell, and the starboard supporting-column ground a trifle, as a man grits his teeth under the knife. The forward cylinder was depending on that unknown force men call the pertinacity of materials, which now and then balances that other heart-breaking power, the perversity of inanimate things.

'You see!' said Mr Wardrop, hurrying them away. 'The engines aren't worth their price as old iron.'

'We tow,' was the answer. 'Afterwards we shall confiscate.'

The man-of-war was short-handed, and did not see the necessity for putting a prize-crew aboard the *Haliotis*. So she sent one sub-lieutenant, whom the skipper kept very drunk, for he did not wish to make the tow too easy, and moreover, he had an inconspicuous little rope hanging from the stern of his ship.

Then they began to tow at an average speed of four knots. The *Haliotis* was very hard to move, and the gunnery-lieutenant, who had fired the five-inch shell, had leisure to think upon consequences. Mr Wardrop was the busy man. He borrowed all the crew to shore up the cylinders, with spars and blocks, from the bottom and sides of the ship. It was a day's risky work; but anything was better than drowning at the end of a tow-rope; and if the forward cylinder had fallen, it would have made its way to the sea-bed, and taken the *Haliotis* after.

'Where are we going to, and how long will they tow us?' he asked of the skipper.

'God knows! and this prize-lieutenant's drunk. What do you think you can do?'

'There's just the bare chance,' Mr Wardrop whispered, though no one was within hearing—'there's just the bare chance o' repairin' her, if a man knew how. They've twisted the very guts out of her, bringing her up with that jerk; but I'm saying that, with time and patience, there's just the chance of making steam yet. *We* could do it.'

The skipper's eye brightened. 'Do you mean,' he began, 'that she is any good?'

'Oh no,' said Mr Wardrop. 'She'll need three thousand pounds in repairs, at the lowest, if she's to take the sea again, an' that apart from any injury to her structure. She's like a man fallen down five pair o' stairs. We can't tell for months what has happened; but we know she'll never be good again without a new inside. Ye should see the condenser-tubes an' the steam connections to the donkey, for two things only. I'm not afraid of them repairin' her. I'm afraid of them stealin' things.'

'They've fired on us. They'll have to explain that.'

'Our reputation's not good enough to ask for explanations. Let's take what we have and be thankful. Ye would not have consuls rememberin' the *Guidin' Light*, an' the *Shah-in-Shah*, an' the *Aglaia* at this most alarmin' crisis. We've been no better than pirates these ten years. Under Providence we're no worse than thieves now. We've much to be thankful for—if we e'er get back to her.'

'Make it your own way, then,' said the skipper, 'if there's the least chance——'

'I'll leave none,' said Mr Wardrop—'none that they'll dare to take. Keep her heavy on the tow, for we need time.'

The skipper never interfered with the affairs of the engine-room, and Mr Wardrop—an artist in his profession—turned to and composed a work terrible and forbidding. His background was the dark-grained sides of the engine-room; his material the metals of power and strength, helped out with spars, baulks, and ropes. The man-of-war towed sullenly and viciously. The *Haliotis* behind her hummed like a hive before swarming. With extra and totally unneeded spars her crew blocked up the space round the forward engine till it resembled a statue in its scaffolding, and the butts of the shores interfered with every view that a dispassionate eye might wish to take. And that the dispassionate mind might be swiftly shaken out of its calm, the well-sunk bolts of the shores were wrapped round untidily with loose ends of ropes, giving a studied effect of most dangerous insecurity. Next, Mr Wardrop took up a collection from the after engine, which, as you will remember, had not been affected in the general wreck. The cylinder escape-valve he abolished with a flogging-hammer. It is difficult in far-off ports to come by such valves, unless, like Mr Wardrop, you keep duplicates in store. At the same time men took off the nuts of two of the great holding-down bolts that serve to keep the engines in place on their solid

bed. An engine violently arrested in mid-career may easily jerk off
the nut of a holding-down bolt, and this accident looked very
natural.

Passing along the tunnel, he removed several shaft coupling-
bolts and nuts, scattering other and ancient pieces of iron under
foot. Cylinder-bolts he cut off to the number of six from the after
engine cylinder, so that it might match its neighbour, and stuffed
the bilge- and feed-pumps with cotton-waste. Then he made a neat
bundle of the various odds and ends that he had gathered from the
engines—little things like nuts and valve-spindles, all carefully
tallowed—and retired with them under the floor of the engine-
room, where he sighed, being fat, as he passed from manhole to
manhole of the double bottom, and in a fairly dry submarine compartment hid them. Any engineer, particularly in an unfriendly
port, has a right to keep his spare stores where he chooses; and
the foot of one of the cylinder shores blocked all entrance into the
regular store-room, even if that had not been already closed with
steel wedges. In conclusion, he disconnected the after engine, laid
piston and connecting-rod, carefully tallowed, where it would be
most inconvenient to the casual visitor, took out three of the eight
collars of the thrust-block, hid them where only he could find them
again, filled the boilers by hand, wedged the sliding doors of the
coal-bunkers, and rested from his labours. The engine-room was a
cemetery, and it did not need the contents of an ash-lift through the
skylight to make it any worse.

He invited the skipper to look at the completed work.

'Saw ye ever such a forsaken wreck as that?' said he proudly. 'It
almost frights *me* to go under those shores. Now, what d'you think
they'll do to us?'

'Wait till we see,' said the skipper. 'It'll be bad enough when it
comes.'

He was not wrong. The pleasant days of towing ended all too
soon, though the *Haliotis* trailed behind her a heavily weighted jib
stayed out into the shape of a pocket; and Mr Wardrop was no
longer an artist of imagination, but one of seven-and-twenty
prisoners in a prison full of insects. The man-of-war had towed
them to the nearest port, not to the headquarters of the colony, and
when Mr Wardrop saw the dismal little harbour, with its ragged
line of Chinese junks, its one crazy tug, and the boat-building shed
that, under the charge of a philosophical Malay, represented a
dockyard, he sighed and shook his head.

'I did well,' he said. 'This is the habitation o' wreckers an' thieves.

We're at the uttermost ends of the earth. Think you they'll ever know in England?'

"Doesn't look like it,' said the skipper.

They were marched ashore with what they stood up in, under a generous escort, and were judged according to the customs of the country, which, though excellent, are a little out of date. There were the pearls; there were the poachers; and there sat a small but hot Governor. He consulted for a while, and then things began to move with speed, for he did not wish to keep a hungry crew at large on the beach, and the man-of-war had gone up the coast. With a wave of his hand—a stroke of the pen was not necessary—he consigned them to the *blakgang-tana*, the back country, and the hand of the Law removed them from his sight and the knowledge of men. They were marched into the palms, and the back country swallowed them up—all the crew of the *Haliotis*.

Deep peace continued to brood over Europe, Asia, Africa, America, Australasia, and Polynesia.

*

It was the firing that did it. They should have kept their counsel; but when a few thousand foreigners are bursting with joy over the fact that a ship under the British flag has been fired at on the high seas, news travels quickly; and when it came out that the pearl-stealing crew had not been allowed access to their consul (there was no consul within a few hundred miles of that lonely port) even the friendliest of Powers has a right to ask questions. The great heart of the British public was beating furiously on account of the performances of a notorious race-horse, and had not a throb to waste on distant accidents; but somewhere deep in the hull of the ship of State there is machinery which more or less accurately takes charge of foreign affairs. That machinery began to revolve, and who so shocked and surprised as the Power that had captured the *Haliotis*? It explained that colonial Governors and far-away men-of-war were difficult to control, and promised that it would most certainly make an example both of the Governor and the vessel. As for the crew, reported to be pressed into military service in tropical climes, it would produce them as soon as possible, and it would apologize, if necessary. Now, no apologies were needed. When one nation apologizes to another, millions of amateurs who have no earthly concern with the difficulty hurl themselves into the strife and embarrass the trained specialist. It was requested that the crew be found, if they were still alive—they had been eight months be-

yond knowledge—and it was promised that all would be forgotten.

The little Governor of the little port was pleased with himself.
Seven-and-twenty white men made a very compact force to throw
away on a war that had neither beginning nor end—a jungle-and-
stockade fight that flickered and smouldered through the wet, hot
years in the hills a hundred miles away, and was the heritage of
every wearied official. He had, he thought, deserved well of his
country; and if only someone would buy the unhappy *Haliotis*,
moored in the harbour below his veranda, his cup would be full. He
looked at the neatly silvered lamps that he had taken from her
cabins, and thought of much that might be turned to account. But
his countrymen in that moist climate had no spirit. They would
peep into the silent engine-room, and shake their heads. Even the
men-of-war would not tow her farther up the coast, where the
Governor believed that she could be repaired. She was a bad bar-
gain; but her cabin carpets were undeniably beautiful, and his wife
approved of her mirrors.

Three hours later cables were bursting round him like shells, for,
though he knew it not, he was being offered as a sacrifice by the
nether to the upper millstone, and his superiors had no regard for
his feelings. He had, said the cables, grossly exceeded his power, and
failed to report on events. He would, therefore—at this he cast
himself back in his hammock—produce the crew of the *Haliotis*.
He would send for them, and, if that failed, he would put his dignity
on a pony and fetch them himself. He had no conceivable right to
make pearl-poachers serve in any war. He would be held responsible.

Next morning the cables wished to know whether he had found
the crew of the *Haliotis*. They were to be found, freed, and fed—he
was to feed them—till such time as they could be sent to the nearest
English port in a man-of-war. If you abuse a man long enough in
great words flashed over the sea-beds, things happen. The Governor
sent inland swiftly for his prisoners, who were also soldiers; and
never was a militia regiment more anxious to reduce its strength.
No power short of death could make these mad men wear the uniform of their service. They would not fight, except with their
fellows, and it was for that reason the regiment had not gone to war,
but stayed in a stockade, reasoning with the new troops. The
autumn campaign had been a fiasco, but here were the Englishmen.
All the regiment marched back to guard them, and the hairy
enemy, armed with blow-pipes, rejoiced in the forest. Five of the

crew had died, but there lined up on the Governor's veranda two-and-twenty men marked about the legs with the scars of leech-bites. A few of them wore fringes that had once been trousers; the others used loin-cloths of gay patterns; and they existed beauti-fully but simply in the Governor's veranda; and when he came out they sang at him. When you have lost seventy thousand pounds' worth of pearls, your pay, your ship, and all your clothes, and have lived in bondage for eight months beyond the faintest pretences of civilization, you know what true independence means, for you become the happiest of created things—natural man.

The Governor told the crew that they were evil, and they asked for food. When he saw how they ate, and when he remembered that none of the pearl patrol-boats were expected for two months, he sighed. But the crew of the *Haliotis* lay down in the veranda, and said that they were pensioners of the Governor's bounty. A grey-bearded man, fat and bald-headed, his one garment a green-and-yellow loin-cloth, saw the *Haliotis* in the harbour, and bellowed with joy. The men crowded to the veranda-rail, kicking aside the long cane chairs. They pointed, gesticulated, and argued freely, without shame. The militia regiment sat down in the Governor's garden. The Governor retired to his hammock—it was as easy to be killed lying as standing—and his women squeaked from the shuttered rooms.

'She sold?' said the grey-bearded man, pointing to the *Haliotis*. He was Mr Wardrop.

'No good,' said the Governor, shaking his head. 'No one come buy.'

'He's taken my lamps, though,' said the skipper. He wore one leg of a pair of trousers, and his eye wandered along the veranda. The Governor quailed. There were cuddy camp-stools and the skipper's writing-table in plain sight.

'They've cleaned her out, o' course,' said Mr Wardrop. 'They would. We'll go aboard an' take an inventory. See!' He waved his hands over the harbour. 'We—live—there—now. Sorry?'

The Governor smiled a smile of relief.

'He's glad of that,' said one of the crew reflectively. 'I don't wonder.'

They flocked down to the harbour-front, the militia regiment clattering behind, and embarked themselves in what they found—it happened to be the Governor's boat. Then they disappeared over the bulwarks of the *Haliotis*, and the Governor prayed that they might find occupation inside.

Mr Wardrop's first bound took him to the engine-room; and when the others were patting the well-remembered decks, they heard him giving God thanks that things were as he had left them. The wrecked engines stood over his head untouched; no inexpert hand had meddled with his shores; the steel wedges of the store-room were rusted home; and, best of all, the hundred and sixty tons of good Australian coal in the bunkers had not diminished.

'I don't understand it,' said Mr Wardrop. 'Any Malay knows the use o' copper. They ought to have cut away the pipes. And with Chinese junks coming here, too. It's a special interposition o' Providence.'

'You think so,' said the skipper, from above. 'There's only been one thief here, and he's cleaned her out of all *my* things, any-how.'

Here the skipper spoke less than the truth, for under the planking of his cabin, only to be reached by a chisel, lay a little money which never drew any interest—his sheet-anchor to windward. It was all in clean sovereigns that pass current the world over, and might have amounted to more than a hundred pounds.

'He's left me alone. Let's thank God,' repeated Mr Wardrop.

'He's taken everything else; look!'

The *Haliotis*, except as to her engine-room, had been systematic-ally and scientifically gutted from one end to the other, and there was strong evidence that an unclean guard had camped in the skipper's cabin to regulate that plunder. She lacked glass, plate, crockery, cutlery, mattresses, cuddy carpets and chairs, all boats, and her copper ventilators. These things had been removed, with her sails and as much of the wire rigging as would not imperil the safety of the masts.

'He must have sold those,' said the skipper. 'The other things are in his house, I suppose.'

Every fitting that could be prised or screwed out was gone. Port, starboard, and masthead lights; teak gratings; sliding sashes of the deck-house; the captain's chest of drawers, with charts and chart-table; photographs, brackets, and looking-glasses; cabin doors; rubber cuddy-mats; hatch irons; half the funnel-stays; cork fenders; carpenter's grindstone and tool-chest; holy-stones, swabs, squeegees; all cabin and pantry lamps; galley fittings *en bloc*; flags and flag-locker; clocks, chronometers; the forward compass and the ship's bell and belfry, were among the missing.

There were great scarred marks on the deck-planking, over which the cargo-derricks had been hauled. One must have fallen by the way, for the bulwark-rails were smashed and bent and the side-plates bruised.

'It's the Governor,' said the skipper. 'He's been selling her on the instalment plan.'

'Let's go up with spanners and shovels, and kill 'em all,' shouted the crew. 'Let's drown him, and keep the women!'

'Then we'll be shot by that black-and-tan regiment—*our* regiment. What's the trouble ashore? They've camped our regiment on the beach.'

'We're cut off, that's all. Go and see what they want,' said Mr Wardrop. 'You've the trousers.'

In his simple way the Governor was a strategist. He did not desire that the crew of the *Haliotis* should come ashore again, either singly or in detachments, and he proposed to turn their steamer into a convict-hulk. They would wait—he explained this from the quay to the skipper in the barge—and they would continue to wait till the man-of-war came along, exactly where they were. If one of them set foot ashore, the entire regiment would open fire, and he would not scruple to use the two cannon of the town. Meantime food would be sent daily in a boat under an armed escort. The skipper, bare to the waist, and rowing, could only grind his teeth; and the Governor improved the occasion, and revenged himself for the bitter words in the cables, by telling what he thought of the morals and manners of the crew. The barge returned to the *Haliotis* in silence, and the skipper climbed aboard, white on the cheek-bones and blue about the nostrils.

'I knew it,' said Mr Wardrop; 'and they won't give us good food, either. We shall have bananas morning, noon, and night, an' a man can't work on fruit. *We* know that.'

Then the skipper cursed Mr Wardrop for importing frivolous side-issues into the conversation; and the crew cursed one another, and the *Haliotis*, the voyage, and all that they knew or could bring to mind. They sat down in silence on the empty decks, and their eyes burned in their heads. The green harbour water chuckled at them overside. They looked at the palm-fringed hills inland, at the white houses above the harbour road, at the single tier of native craft by the quay, at the stolid soldiery sitting round the two cannon, and, last of all, at the blue bar of the horizon. Mr Wardrop was buried in thought, and scratched imaginary lines with his untrimmed fingernails on the planking.

'I make no promise,' he said at last, 'for I can't say what may or may not have happened to them. But here's the ship, and here's us.'

There was a little scornful laughter at this, and Mr Wardrop knitted his brows. He recalled that in the days when he wore trousers he had been Chief Engineer of the *Haliotis*.

'Harland, Mackesy, Noble, Hay, Naughton, Fink, O'Hara, Trumbull.'

'Here, sir!' The instinct of obedience waked to answer the roll-call of the engine-room.

'Below!'

They rose and went.

'Captain, I'll trouble you for the rest of the men as I want them. We'll get my stores out, and clear away the shores we don't need, and then we'll patch her up. *My* men will remember that they're in the *Haliotis*—under me.'

He went into the engine-room, and the others stared. They were used to the accidents of the sea, but this was beyond their experience. None who had seen the engine-room believed that anything short of new engines from end to end could stir the *Haliotis* from her moorings.

The engine-room stores were unearthed, and Mr Wardrop's face, red with the filth of the bilges and the exertion of travelling on his stomach, lit with joy. The spare gear of the *Haliotis* had been unusually complete, and two-and-twenty men, armed with screw-jacks, differential blocks, tackle, vices, and a forge or so, can look Kismet between the eyes without winking. The crew were ordered to replace the holding-down and shaft-bearing bolts, and return the collars of the thrust-block. When they had finished, Mr Wardrop delivered a lecture on repairing compound engines without the aid of the shops, and the men sat about on the cold machinery. The cross-head jammed in the guides leered at them drunkenly, but offered no help. They ran their fingers hopelessly into the cracks of the starboard supporting-column, and picked at the ends of the ropes round the shores, while Mr Wardrop's voice rose and fell echoing, till the quick tropic night closed down over the engine-room skylight.

Next morning the work of reconstruction began.

It has been explained that the foot of the connecting-rod was forced against the foot of the starboard supporting-column, which it had cracked through and driven outward towards the ship's skin. To all appearance the job was more than hopeless, for rod and column seemed to have been welded into one. But herein Providence smiled on them for one moment to hearten them through the weary weeks ahead. The Second Engineer—more reckless than resourceful—struck at random with a cold chisel into the cast-iron of the column, and a greasy, grey flake of metal flew from under the imprisoned foot of the connecting-rod, while the rod itself fell away slowly, and brought up with a thunderous clang somewhere in the dark of the crank-pit. The guide-plates above were still jammed fast in the guides, but the first blow had been struck. They spent the rest of the day grooming the cargo-winch, which stood immediately forward of the engine-room hatch. Its tarpaulin, of course, had been stolen, and eight warm months had not improved the working parts. Further, the last dying hiccup of the *Haliotis* seemed—or it might have been the Malay from the boat-house—to have lifted the thing bodily from its bolts, and set it down inaccurately as regarded its steam connections.

'If we only had one single cargo-derrick!' Mr Wardrop sighed. 'We can take the cylinder-cover off by hand, if we sweat; but to get the rod out o' the piston's not possible unless we use steam. Well, there'll be steam the morn, if there's nothing else. She'll fizzle!'

Next morning men from the shore saw the *Haliotis* through a cloud, for it was as though the decks smoked. Her crew were chasing steam through the shaken and leaky pipes to its work in the forward donkey-engine; and where oakum failed to plug a crack, they stripped off their loin-cloths for lapping, and swore, half-boiled and mother-naked. The donkey-engine worked—at a price—the price of constant attention and furious stoking—worked long enough to allow a wire rope (it was made up of a funnel and a foremast stay) to be led into the engine-room and made fast on the cylinder-cover of the forward engine. That rose easily enough, and was hauled through the skylight and on to the deck, many hands assisting the doubtful steam. Then came the tug-of-war, for it was necessary to get to the piston and the jammed piston-rod. They removed two of the piston junk-ring studs, screwed in two strong iron eye-bolts by way of handles, doubled the wire rope, and set half-a-dozen men to smite with an extemporized battering-ram at the end of the piston-rod, where it peered through the piston, while the donkey-engine hauled upwards on the piston itself. After four hours of this killing work the piston-rod suddenly slipped, and the piston rose with a jerk, knocking one or two men over into the engine-room. But when Mr Wardrop declared that the piston had not split, they cheered, and thought nothing of their wounds; and the donkey-engine was hastily stopped; its boiler being no thing to tamper with.

And day by day their supplies reached them by boat. The skipper humbled himself once more before the Governor, and as a concession had leave to get drinking-water from the Malay boat-builder on the quay. It was not good drinking-water, but the Malay was anxious to supply anything in his power, if he were paid for it.

Now, when the jaws of the forward engine stood, as it were, stripped and empty, they began to wedge up the shores of the cylinder itself. That work alone filled the better part of three days —warm and sticky days, when the hands slipped and sweat ran into the eyes. When the last wedge was hammered home there was no longer an ounce of weight on the supporting-columns; and Mr Wardrop rummaged the ship for boiler-plate three-quarters of an inch thick, where he could find it. There was not much available, but what there was was more than beaten gold to him. In one desperate forenoon the entire crew, naked and lean, haled back, more or less to place, the starboard supporting-column, which, as you remember, was cracked clean through. Mr Wardrop found them asleep where they had finished the work, and gave them a day's rest, smiling upon them as a father while he drew chalk-marks about the cracks. They woke to new and more trying labour; for over each one of those cracks a plate of three-quarter-inch boiler-iron was to be worked hot, the rivet-holes being drilled by hand. All that time they were fed on fruits, chiefly bananas, with some sago.

Those were the days when the men swooned over the ratchet-drill and the hand-forge, and where they fell they had leave to lie unless their bodies were in the way of their fellows' feet. And so, patch upon patch, and a patch over all, the starboard supporting-column was clouted; but when they thought all was secure, Mr Wardrop decreed that the noble patchwork would never support working engines: at the best, it could only hold the guide-bars approximately true. The dead weight of the cylinders must be borne by vertical struts; and, therefore, a gang would repair to the bows, and take out, with files, the big bow-anchor davits, each of which was some three inches in diameter. They threw hot coals at Wardrop, and threatened to kill him, those who did not weep (they were ready to weep on the least provocation); but he hit them with iron bars heated at the end, and they limped forward, and the davits came with them when they returned. They slept sixteen hours on the strength of it, and in three days two struts were in place, bolted from the foot of the starboard supporting-column to the under side of the cylinder. There remained now the port, or condenser-column, which, though not so badly cracked as its fellow, had also been strengthened in four places with boiler-plate patches, but needed struts. They took away the main stanchions of the bridge for that work, and, crazy with toil, did not see till all was in place that the rounded bars of iron must be flattened from top to bottom to allow the air-pump levers to clear them. It was Wardrop's oversight, and he wept bitterly before the men as he gave the order to unbolt the struts and flatten them with hammer and the flame. Now the broken engine was underpinned firmly, and they took away the wooden shores from under the cylinders, and gave them to the robbed bridge, thanking God for even half a day's work on gentle, kindly wood instead of the iron that had entered into their souls. Eight months in the back country among the leeches, at a temperature of 85° moist, is very bad for the nerves.

They had kept the hardest work to the last, as boys save Latin prose, and, worn though they were, Mr Wardrop did not dare to give them rest. The piston-rod and connecting-rod were to be straightened, and this was a job for a regular dockyard with every appliance. They fell to it, cheered by a little chalk-showing of work done and time consumed which Mr Wardrop wrote up on the engine-room bulkhead. Fifteen days had gone—fifteen days of killing labour—and there was hope before them.

It is curious that no man knows how the rods were straightened. The crew of the *Haliotis* remember that week very dimly, as a fever patient remembers the delirium of a long night. There were fires everywhere, they say; the whole ship was one consuming furnace, and the hammers were never still. Now, there could have not been more than one fire at the most, for Mr Wardrop distinctly recalls that no straightening was done except under his own eye. They remember, too, that, for many years, voices gave orders which they obeyed with their bodies, but their minds were abroad on all the seas. It seems to them that they stood through days and nights slowly sliding a bar backwards and forwards through a white glow that was part of the ship. They remember an intolerable noise in their burning heads from the walls of the stoke-hole, and they remember being savagely beaten by men whose eyes seemed asleep. When their shift was over they would draw straight lines in the air, anxiously and repeatedly, and would question one another in their sleep, crying, 'Is she straight?'

At last—they do not remember whether this was by day or by night—Mr Wardrop began to dance clumsily, and wept the while; and they too danced and wept, and went to sleep twitching all over; and when they woke, men said that the rods were straightened, and

no one did any work for two days, but lay on the decks and ate fruit. Mr Wardrop would go below from time to time, and pat the two rods where they lay, and they heard him singing hymns.

Then his trouble of mind went from him, and at the end of the third day's idleness he made a drawing in chalk upon the deck, with letters of the alphabet at the angles. He pointed out that, though the piston-rod was more or less straight, the piston-rod cross-head —the thing that had been jammed sideways in the guides—had been badly strained, and had cracked the lower end of the piston-rod. He was going to forge and shrink a wrought-iron collar on the neck of the piston-rod where it joined the cross-head, and from the collar he would bolt a Y-shaped piece of iron whose lower arms should be bolted into the cross-head. If anything more were needed, they could use up the last of the boiler-plate.

So the forges were lit again, and men burned their bodies, but hardly felt the pain. The finished connection was not beautiful, but it seemed strong enough—at least, as strong as the rest of the machinery; and with that job their labours came to an end. All that remained was to connect up the engines, and to get food and water. The skipper and four men dealt with the Malay boat-builder—by night chiefly; it was no time to haggle over the price of sago and dried fish. The others stayed aboard and replaced piston, piston-rod, cylinder-cover, cross-head, and bolts, with the aid of the faithful donkey-engine. The cylinder-cover was hardly steam-proof, and the eye of science might have seen in the connecting-rod a flexure something like that of a Christmas-tree candle which has melted and been straightened by hand over a stove, but, as Mr Wardrop said, 'She didn't hit anything.'

As soon as the last bolt was in place, men tumbled over one another in their anxiety to get to the hand turning-gear, the wheel and the worm, by which some engines can be moved when there is no steam aboard. They nearly wrenched off the wheel, but it was evident to the blindest eye that the engines stirred. They did not revolve in their orbits with any enthusiasm, as good machines should; indeed, they groaned not a little; but they moved over and came to rest in a way which proved that they still recognized man's hand. Then Mr Wardrop sent his slaves into the darker bowels of the engine-room and the stoke-hole, and followed them with a flare-lamp. The boilers were sound, but would take no harm from a little scaling and cleaning. Mr Wardrop would not have anyone over-zealous, for he feared what the next stroke of the tool might show. 'The less we know about her now,' said he, 'the better for us all, I'm thinkin'. Ye'll understand me when I say that this is no sense regular engineerin'.'

As his raiment, when he spoke, was his grey beard and uncut hair, they believed him. They did not ask too much of what they met, but polished and tallowed and scraped it to a false brilliancy.

'A lick of paint would make me easier in my mind,' said Mr Wardrop, plaintively. 'I know half the condenser-tubes are started; and the propeller-shaftin's God knows how far out of the true, and we'll need a new air-pump, an' the main-steam leaks like a sieve, and there's worse each way I look; but—paint's like clothes to a man, an' ours is near all gone.'

The skipper unearthed some stale ropy paint of the loathsome green that they used for the galleys of sailing-ships, and Mr Wardrop spread it abroad lavishly to give the engines self-respect.

His own was returning day by day, for he wore his loin-cloth continuously; but the crew, having worked under orders, did not feel as he did. The completed work satisfied Mr Wardrop. He would at the last have made shift to run to Singapore, and gone home, without vengeance taken, to show his engines to his brethren in the craft; but the others and the captain forbade him. They had not yet recovered their self-respect.

'It would be safer to make what ye might call a trial trip, but beggars mustn't be choosers; an' if the engines will go over to the hand gear, the probability—I'm only saying it's a probability—the chance is that they'll hold up when we put steam on her.'

'How long will you take to get steam?' said the skipper.

'God knows! Four hours—a day—half a week. If I can raise sixty pounds I'll not complain.'

'Be sure of her first. We can't afford to go out half a mile, and break down.'

'My soul and body, man, we're one continuous breakdown, fore an' aft! We might fetch Singapore, though.'

'We'll break down at Pygang-Watai, where we can do good,' was the answer, in a voice that did not allow argument. 'She's *my* boat, and—I've had eight months to think in.'

No man saw the *Haliotis* depart, though many heard her. She left at two in the morning, having cut her moorings, and it was none of her crew's pleasure that the engines should strike up a thundering half-seas-over chanty that echoed among the hills. Mr Wardrop wiped away a tear as he listened to the new song.

'She's gibberin'—she's just gibberin',' he whimpered. 'Yon's the voice of a maniac.'

And if engines have any soul, as their masters believe, he was quite right. There were outcries and clamours, sobs and bursts of chattering laughter, silences where the trained ear yearned for the clear note, and torturing reduplications where there should have been one deep voice. Down the screw-shaft ran murmurs and warnings, while a heart-diseased flutter without told that the propeller needed re-keying.

'How does she make it?' said the skipper.

'She moves, but—but she's breakin' my heart. The sooner we're at Pygang-Watai, the better. She's mad, and we're waking the town.'

'Is she at all near safe?'

'What do *I* care how safe she is! She's mad. Hear that, now! To be sure, nothing's hittin' anything, an' the bearin's are fairly cool, but—can ye not hear?'

'If she goes,' said the skipper, 'I don't care a curse. And she's *my* boat, too.'

She went, trailing a fathom of weed behind her. From a slow two knots she crawled up to a triumphant four. Anything beyond that made the struts quiver dangerously, and filled the engine-room with steam. Morning showed her out of sight of land, and there was a visible ripple under her bows; but she complained bitterly in her bowels, and, as though the noise had called it, there shot along across the purple sea a swift, dark proa, hawk-like and curious, which presently ranged alongside and wished to know if the *Haliotis* were helpless. Ships, even the steamers of the white men, had been known to break down in those waters, and the honest Malay and Javanese traders would sometimes aid them in their own peculiar way. But this ship was not full of lady passengers and well-dressed officers. Men, white, naked, and savage, swarmed down her sides— some with red-hot iron bars and others with large hammers, threw themselves upon those innocent inquiring strangers, and, before any man could say what had happened, were in full possession of the proa, while the lawful owners bobbed in the water overside. Half an hour later the proa's cargo of sago and tripang, as well as a doubtful-minded compass, was in the *Haliotis*. The two huge triangular mat sails, with their seventy-foot yards, had followed the cargo, and were being fitted to the stripped masts of the steamer.

They rose, they swelled, they filled, and the empty steamer visibly laid over as the wind took them. They gave her nearly three knots, and what better could men ask? But if she had been forlorn before, this new purchase made her horrible to see. Imagine a respectable charwoman in the tights of a ballet-dancer rolling drunk along the streets, and you will come to some faint notion of the appearance of that nine-hundred-ton, well-decked, once schooner-rigged cargo-boat as she staggered under her new help, shouting and raving across the deep. With steam and sail that marvellous voyage continued; and the bright-eyed crew looked over the rail, desolate, unkempt, unshorn, shamelessly clothed—beyond the decencies.

At the end of the third week she sighted the island of Pygang-Watai, whose harbour is the turning-point of a pearling sea-patrol. Here the gunboats stay for a week ere they retrace their line. There is no village at Pygang-Watai, only a stream of water, some palms, and a harbour safe to rest in till the first violence of the south-east monsoon has blown itself out. They opened up the low coral beach, with its mound of whitewashed coal ready for supply, the deserted huts for the sailors, and the flagless flagstaff.

Next day there was no *Haliotis*—only a little proa rocking in the warm rain at the mouth of the harbour, whose crew watched with hungry eyes the smoke of a gunboat on the horizon.

Months afterwards there were a few lines in an English newspaper to the effect that some gunboat of some foreign Power had broken her back at the mouth of some far-away harbour by running at full speed into a sunken wreck.

The Day's Work, 1898 *

* *Graphic*, 1895.

·007

A LOCOMOTIVE IS, next to a marine engine, the most sensitive thing man ever made; and No. ·007, besides being sensitive, was new. The red paint was hardly dry on his spotless bumper-bar, his headlight shone like a fireman's helmet, and his cab might have been a hardwood-finish parlour. They had run him into the round-house after his trial—he had said good-bye to his best friend in the shops, the overhead travelling-crane—the big world was just out-side; and the other locos were taking stock of him. He looked at the semicircle of bold, unwinking headlights, heard the low purr and mutter of the steam mounting in the gauges—scornful hisses of con-tempt as a slack valve lifted a little—and would have given a month's oil for leave to crawl through his own driving-wheels into the brick ash-pit beneath him. ·007 was an eight-wheeled 'American' loco, slightly different from others of his type, and as he stood he was worth ten thousand dollars on the Company's books. But if you had bought him at his own valuation, after half an hour's waiting in the darkish, echoing round-house, you would have saved exactly nine thousand nine hundred and ninety-nine dollars and ninety-eight cents.

A heavy Mogul freight, with a short cow-catcher and a fire-box that came down within three inches of the rail, began the impolite game, speaking to a Pittsburgh Consolidation, who was visiting.

'Where did this thing blow in from?' he asked, with a dreamy puff of light steam.

'It's all I can do to keep track of our own makes,' was the answer, 'without lookin' after *your* back-numbers. Guess it's something Peter Cooper left over when he died.'

·007 quivered; his steam was getting up, but he held his tongue. Even a hand-car knows what sort of locomotive it was that Peter Cooper experimented upon in the far-away 'Thirties. It carried its coal and water in two apple-barrels, and was not much bigger than a bicycle.

Then up and spoke a small, newish switching-engine, with a little step in front of his bumper-timber, and his wheels so close together that he looked like a broncho getting ready to buck.

'Something's wrong with the road when a Pennsylvania gravel-pusher tells us anything about our stock, *I* think. That kid's all right. Eustis designed him, and Eustis designed me. Ain't that good enough?'

·007 could have carried the switching-loco round the yard in his tender, but he felt grateful for even this little word of consolation.

'We don't use hand-cars on the Pennsylvania,' said the Consolidation. 'That—er—peanut-stand's old enough and ugly enough to speak for himself.'

'He hasn't bin spoken to yet. He's bin spoken *at*. Hain't ye any manners on the Pennsylvania?' said the switching-loco.

'You ought to be in the yard, Pony,' said the Mogul severely. 'We're all long-haulers here.'

'That's what you think,' the little fellow replied. 'You'll know more 'fore the night's out. I've bin down to Track 17, and the freight there—oh, Christmas!'

'I've trouble enough in my own division,' said a lean, light suburban loco with very shiny brake-shoes. 'My commuters wouldn't rest till they got a parlour-car. They've hitched her back of all, and she hauls worse'n a snow-plough. I'll snap her off some day sure, and then they'll blame everyone except their fool selves. They'll be askin' me to haul a vestibuled next!'

'They made you in New Jersey, didn't they?' said Pony. 'Thought so. Commuters and truck-wagons ain't any sweet haulin', but I tell *you* they're a heap better'n cuttin' out refrigerator-cars or oil-tanks. Why, I've hauled——'

'Haul! You?' said the Mogul contemptuously. 'It's all you can do to bunt a cold-storage car up the yard. Now, I'—he paused a little to let the words sink in—'I handle the Flying Freight—e-leven cars worth just anything you please to mention. On the stroke of eleven I pull out; and I'm timed for thirty-five the hour. Costly—perishable—fragile—immediate—that's me! Suburban traffic's only but one degree better than switching. Express freight's what pays.'

'Well, I ain't given to blowing, as a rule——' began the Pittsburgh Consolidation.

'No? You was sent in here because you grunted on the grade, Pony interrupted.

'Where I grunt, you'd lie down, Pony; but, as I was saying, I don't blow much. Notwithstandin', *if* you want to see freight that *is* freight moved lively, you should see me warbling through the Alleghanies with thirty-seven ore-cars behind me, and my brakemen fightin' tramps so's they can't attend to my tooter. *I* have to

do all the holdin' back then, and, though I say it, I've never had a
load get away from me yet. *No*, sir. Haulin's one thing, but judgement and discretion's another. You want judgement in my business.'

'Ah! But—but are you not paralysed by a sense of your overwhelming responsibilities?' said a curious husky voice from a
corner.

'Who's that?' ·007 whispered to the Jersey commuter.

'Compound—experiment—N. G. She's bin switchin' in the B. &
A. yards for six months, when she wasn't in the shops. She's
economical (*I* call it mean) in her coal, but she takes it out in
repairs. Ahem! I presume you found Boston somewhat isolated,
madam, after your New York season?'

'I am never so well occupied as when I am alone.' The Compound
seemed to be talking from half-way up her smoke-stack.

'Sure,' said the irreverent Pony, under his breath. 'They don't
hanker after her any in the yard.'

'But, with my constitution and temperament—my work lies in
Boston—I find your *outrecuidance*——'

'Outer which?' said the Mogul freight. 'Simple cylinders are good
enough for me.'

'Perhaps I should have said *faroucherie*,' hissed the Compound.

'I don't hold with any make of papier-mâché wheel,' the Mogul
insisted.

The Compound sighed pityingly, and said no more.

'Git 'em all shapes in this world, don't ye?' said Pony. 'That's
Mass'chusetts all over. They half start, an' then they stick on a
dead-centre, an' blame it all on other folk's ways o' treatin' them.
Talkin' o' Boston, Comanche told me, last night, he had a hot-box
just beyond the Newtons, Friday. That was why, *he* says, the
Accommodation was held up. Made out no end of a tale, Comanche
did.'

'If I'd heard that in the shops, with my boiler out for repairs, I'd
know 'twas one o' Comanche's lies,' the New Jersey commuter
snapped. 'Hot-box! Him! What happened was they'd put an extra
car on, and he just lay down on the grade and squealed. They had
to send 127 to help him through. Made it out a hot-box, did he?
Time before that he said he was ditched! Looked me square in the
headlight and told me that as cool as—as a water-tank in a cold
wave. Hot-box! You ask 127 about Comanche's hot-box. Why,
Comanche he was side-tracked, and 127 (*he* was just about as mad
as they make 'em on account o' being called out at ten o'clock at

night) took hold and whirled her into Boston in seventeen minutes. Hot-box! Hot fraud! That's what Comanche is.'

Then ·007 put both drivers and his pilot into it, as the saying is, for he asked what sort of thing a hot-box might be.

'Paint my bell sky-blue!' said Pony, the switcher. 'Make me a surface-railroad loco with a hardwood skirtin'-board round my wheels! Break me up and cast me into five-cent sidewalk-fakirs' mechanical toys! Here's an eight-wheel-coupled "American" don't know what a hot-box is! Never heard of an emergency-stop either, did ye? Don't know what ye carry jack-screws for? You're too innocent to be left alone with your own tender. Oh, you—you flat-car!'

There was a roar of escaping steam before anyone could answer, and ·007 nearly blistered his paint off with pure mortification.

'A hot-box,' began the Compound, picking and choosing the words as though they were coal, 'a hot-box is the penalty exacted from inexperience by haste. Ahem!'

'Hot-box!' said the Jersey Suburban. 'It's the price you pay for going on the tear. It's years since I've had one. It's a disease that don't attack short-haulers, as a rule.'

'We never have hot-boxes on the Pennsylvania,' said the Consolidation. 'They get 'em in New York—same as nervous prostration.'

'Ah, go home on a ferry-boat,' said the Mogul. 'You'd think because you use worse grades than our road 'ud allow, you're a kind of Alleghany angel. Now I'll tell you what you . . . Here's my folk. Well, I can't stop. See you later, perhaps.'

He rolled forward majestically to the turn-table, and swung like a man-of-war in a tideway, till he picked up his track. 'But as for you, you pea-green swivellin' coffee-pot' (this to ·007), 'you go out and learn something before you associate with those who've made more mileage in a week than you'll roll up in a year. Costly—perishable—fragile—immediate—that's me! S'long.'

'Split my tubes if that's actin' polite to a new member o' the Brotherhood,' said Pony. 'There wasn't any call to trample on ye like that. But manners was left out when Moguls was made. Keep up your fire, kid, an' burn your own smoke. Guess we'll all be wanted in a minute.'

Men were talking rather excitedly in the round-house. One man, in a dingy jersey, said that he hadn't any locomotives to waste on the yard. Another man, with a piece of crumpled paper in his hand, said that the yard-master said that he was to say that, if the other man said anything, he (the other man) was to shut his head. Then the other man waved his arms, and wanted to know if he was expected to keep locomotives in his hip-pocket. Then a man in a black Prince Albert coat, without a collar, came up dripping, for it was a hot August night, and said that what *he* said went; and between the three of them the locomotives began to go, too—first the Compound, then the Consolidation, then ·007.

Now, deep down in his fire-box, ·007 had cherished a hope that as soon as his trial was done, he would be led forth with songs and shoutings, and attached to a green-and-chocolate vestibuled flyer, under charge of a bold and noble engineer, who would pat him on his back, and weep over him, and call him his Arab steed. (The boys in the shops where he was built used to read wonderful stories of railroad life, and ·007 expected things to happen as he had heard.) But there did not seem to be many vestibuled flyers in the roaring, rumbling, electric-lighted yards, and his engineer only said:

'Now, what sort of a fool-sort of an injector has Eustis loaded on to this rig this time?' And he put the lever over with an angry snap, crying: 'Am I supposed to switch with this thing, hey?'

The collarless man mopped his head, and replied that, in the present state of the yard and freight and a few other things, the engineer would switch and keep on switching till the cows came home. ·007 pushed out gingerly, his heart in his headlight, so nervous that the clang of his own bell almost made him jump the track. Lanterns waved, or danced up and down, before and behind him; and on every side, six tracks deep, sliding backward and forward, with clashings of couplers and squeals of hand-brakes, were cars—more cars than ·007 had dreamed of. There were oil-cars, and hay-cars, and stock-cars full of lowing beasts, and ore-cars, and potato-cars with stovepipe-ends sticking out in the middle; cold-storage and refrigerator cars dripping ice-water on the tracks; ventilated fruit- and milk-cars; flat-cars with truck-wagons full of market-stuff; flat-cars loaded with reapers and binders, all red and green and gilt under the sizzling electric lights; flat-cars piled high with strong-scented hides, pleasant hemlock-plank, or bundles of shingles; flat-cars creaking to the weight of thirty-ton castings, angle-irons, and rivet-boxes for some new bridge; and hundreds and hundreds and hundreds of box-cars loaded, locked, and chalked. Men—hot and angry—crawled among and between and under the thousand wheels; men took flying jumps through his cab, when he halted for a moment; men sat on his pilot as he went forward, and on his tender as he returned; and regiments of men ran along the tops of the box-cars beside him, screwing down brakes, waving their arms, and shouting curious things.

He was pushed forward a foot at a time, whirled backwards, his rear drivers clinking and clanking, a quarter of a mile; jerked into a switch (yard-switches are *very* stubby and unaccommodating), bunted into a Red D, or Merchants' Transport car, and, with no hint or knowledge of the weight behind him, started up anew. When his load was fairly on the move, three or four cars would be cut off, and ·007 would bound forward, only to be held hiccupping on his brake. Then he would wait a few minutes, watching the whirled lanterns, deafened with the clang of the bells, giddy with the vision of the sliding cars, his brake-pump panting forty to the minute, his front coupler lying sideways on his cow-catcher, like a tired dog's tongue in his mouth, and the whole of him covered with half-burnt coal-dust.

' 'Tain't so easy switching with a straight-backed tender,' said his little friend of the round-house, bustling by at a trot. 'But you're comin' on pretty fair. Ever seen a flyin' switch? No? Then watch me.'

Pony was in charge of a dozen heavy flat-cars. Suddenly he shot away from them with a sharp '*Whutt!*' A switch opened in the shadows ahead; he turned up it like a rabbit, it snapped behind him, and the long line of twelve-foot-high lumber jolted on into the arms of a full-sized road-loco, who acknowledged receipt with a dry howl.

'My man's reckoned the smartest in the yard at that trick,' he said, returning. 'Gives me cold shivers when another fool tries it, though. That's where my short wheel-base comes in. Like as not you'd have your tender scraped off if *you* tried it.'

·007 had no ambitions that way, and said so.

'No? Of course this ain't your regular business, but say, don't you think it's interestin'? Have you seen the yard-master? Well, he's the greatest man on earth, an' don't you forget it. When are we through? Why, kid, it's always like this, day *an*' night—Sundays and week-days. See that thirty-car freight slidin' in, four, no, five, tracks off? She's all mixed freight, sent here to be sorted out into straight trains. That's why we're cuttin' out the cars one by one.' He gave a vigorous push to a west-bound car as he spoke, and started back with a little snort of surprise, for the car was an old friend—an M. T. K. box-car.

'Jack my drivers, but it's Homeless Kate! Why, Katie, ain't there *no* gettin' you back to your friends? There's forty chasers out for you from your road, if there's one. Who's holdin' you now?'

'Wish I knew,' whimpered Homeless Kate. 'I belong in Topeka, but I've bin to Cedar Rapids; I've bin to Winnipeg; I've bin to Newport Noos; I've bin all down the old Atlanta and West Point; an' I've bin to Buffalo. Maybe I'll fetch up at Haverstraw. I've only bin out ten months, but I'm homesick—I'm just achin' homesick.'

'Try Chicago, Katie,' said the switching-loco; and the battered old car lumbered down the track, jolting: 'I want to be in Kansas when the sunflowers bloom.'

'Yard's full o' Homeless Kates an' Wanderin' Willies,' he explained to ·007. 'I knew an old Fitchburg flat-car out seventeen months; an' one of ours was gone fifteen 'fore ever we got track of her. Dunno quite how our men fix it. Swap around, I guess. Anyway, I've done *my* duty. She's on her way to Kansas, via Chicago; but I'll lay my next boilerful she'll be held there to wait consignee's convenience, and sent back to us with wheat in the fall.'

Just then the Pittsburgh Consolidation passed, at the head of a dozen cars.

'I'm goin' home,' he said proudly.

'Can't get all them twelve on to the flat. Break 'em in half, Dutchy!' cried Pony. But it was ·007 who was backed down to the last six cars, and he nearly blew up with surprise when he found himself pushing them on to a huge ferry-boat. He had never seen deep water before, and shivered as the flat drew away and left his bogies within six inches of the black, shiny tide.

After this he was hurried to the freight-house, where he saw the yard-master, a smallish, white-faced man in shirt, trousers, and slippers, looking down upon a sea of trucks, a mob of bawling truckmen, and squadrons of backing, turning, sweating, spark-striking horses.

'That's shippers' carts loadin' on to the receivin' trucks,' said the small engine reverently. 'But *he* don't care. He lets 'em cuss. He's Czar—King—Boss! He says "Please," and then they kneel down an' pray. There's three or four strings o' today's freight to be pulled before he can attend to *them*. When he waves his hand that way, things happen.'

A string of loaded cars slid out down the track, and a string of empties took their place. Bales, crates, boxes, jars, carboys, frails, cases, and packages, flew into them from the freight-house as though the cars had been magnets and they iron filings.

'Ki-yah!' shrieked little Pony. 'Ain't it great?'

A purple-faced truckman shouldered his way to the yard-master, and shook his fist under his nose. The yard-master never looked up from his bundle of freight-receipts. He crooked his forefinger slightly, and a tall young man in a red shirt, lounging carelessly beside him, hit the truckman under the left ear, so that he dropped, quivering and clucking, on a hay-bale.

'Eleven, seven, ninety-seven, L. Y. S.; fourteen ought ought three; nineteen thirteen; one one four; seventeen ought twenty-one M. B.; *and* the ten west-bound. All straight except the last two. Cut 'em off at the junction. An' *that's* all right. Pull that string.' The yard-master, with mild blue eyes, looked out over the howling truckmen at the waters in the moonlight beyond, and hummed:

> 'All *things bright and beautiful,*
> *All creatures great and small,*
> All *things wise and wonderful,*
> *The Lawd Gawd made them all!'*

·007 moved the cars out and delivered them to the regular road-engine. He had never felt quite so limp in his life.

'Curious, ain't it?' said Pony, puffing, on the next track. 'You an' me, if we got that man under our bumpers, we'd work him into red waste and not know what we'd done; but—up there—with the steam hummin' in his boiler that awful quiet way . . .'

'*I* know,' said ·007. 'Makes me feel as if I'd dropped my fire an' was getting cold. He *is* the greatest man 'top of earth.'

They were at the far north end of the yard now, under a switch-tower, looking down on the four-track way of the main traffic. The Boston Compound was to haul ·007's string to some far-away northern junction over an indifferent road-bed, and she mourned aloud for the ninety-six-pound rails of the B. & A.

'You're young; you're young,' she coughed. 'You don't realize your responsibilities.'

'Yes, he does,' said Pony sharply; 'but he don't lie down under 'em.' Then, with a side-spurt of steam, exactly like a tough spitting: 'There ain't more than fifteen thousand dollars' worth o' freight behind her anyway, and she carries on as if 'twere a hundred thousand—same as the Mogul's. Excuse me, madam, but you've the track. . . . She's stuck on a dead-centre again—bein' specially designed not to.'

The Compound crawled across the tracks on a long slant, groaning horribly at each switch, and moving like a cow in a snow-drift. There was a little pause along the yard after her tail-lights had disappeared; switches locked crisply, and everyone seemed to be waiting.

'Now I'll show you something worth,' said Pony. 'When the
Purple Emperor ain't on time, it's about time to amend the Constitution. The first stroke of twelve is——'

'Boom!' went the clock in the big yard-tower, and far away ·007
heard a full vibrating '*Yah! Yah! Yah!*' A headlight twinkled on
the horizon like a star, grew an overpowering blaze, and whooped
up the humming track to the roaring music of a happy giant's
song:

> '*With a michnai—ghignai—shtingal! Yah! Yah! Yah!*
> *Ein—zwei—drei, Mutter! Yah! Yah! Yah!*
> *She climb upon der shteeple,*
> *Und she frighten all der people,*
> *Singin' michnai—ghignai—shtingal! Yah! Yah!*'

The last defiant 'Yah! Yah!' was delivered a mile and a half beyond
the passenger-depôt; but ·007 had caught one glimpse of the superb
six-wheel-coupled racing-locomotive, who hauled the pride and
glory of the road—the gilt-edged Purple Emperor, the millionaires'
south-bound express, laying the miles over his shoulder as a man
peels shavings from a soft board. The rest was a blur of maroon
enamel, a bar of white light from the electrics in the cars, and a
flicker of nickel-plated hand-rail on the rear platform.

'Ooh!' said ·007.

'Seventy-five miles an hour these five miles. Baths, I've heard;
barber's shop; ticker; and a library and the rest to match. Yes, sir;
seventy-five an hour! But he'll talk to you in the round-house just
as democratic as I would. And I—cuss my wheel-base!—I'd kick
clean off the track at half his gait. He's the Master of our Lodge.
Cleans up at our house. I'll introduce you some day. He's worth
knowin'! There ain't many can sing that song, either.'

·007 was too full of emotions to answer. He did not hear a raging
of telephone-bells in the switch-tower, nor the man, as he leaned
out and called to ·007's engineer: 'Got any steam?'

' 'Nough to run her a hundred mile out o' this, if I could,' said the
engineer, who belonged to the open road and hated switching.

'Then git! The Flying Freight's ditched forty mile out, with fifty
rod o' track ploughed up. No. No one's hurt, but both tracks are
blocked. Lucky the wreckin'-car an' derrick are this end of the
yard. Crew'll be along in a minute. Hurry! You've the track.'

'Well, I could jest kick my little sawed-off self,' said Pony, as
·007 was backed, with a bang, on to a grim and grimy car like a
caboose, but full of tools—a flat-car and a derrick behind it. 'Some

folks are one thing, an' some are another; but *you*'re in luck, kid.
They push a wrecking-car. Now, don't get rattled. Your wheel-base
will keep you on the track, and there ain't any curves worth men-
tionin'. Oh, say! Comanche told me there's one section o' saw-edged
track that's liable to jounce ye a little. Fifteen an' a half out, *after*
the grade at Jackson's crossin'. You'll know it by a farmhouse an' a
windmill and five maples in the dooryard. Windmill's west o' the
maples. An' there's an eighty-foot iron bridge in the middle o' that
section with no guard-rails. See you later. Luck!'

Before he knew well what had happened, ·007 was flying up the
track into the dumb dark world. Then fears of the night beset him.
He remembered all he had ever heard of landslides, rain-piled
boulders, blown trees, and strayed cattle; all that the Boston
Compound had ever said of responsibility; and a great deal more
that came out of his own head. With a very quavering voice he
whistled for his first grade crossing (an event in the life of a locomotive), and his nerves were in no way restored by the sight of a
frantic horse and a white-faced man in a buggy less than a yard
from his right shoulder. Then he was sure he would jump the track;
felt his flanges mounting the rail at every curve; knew that his first
grade would make him lie down even as Comanche had done at the
Newtons. He swept down the grade to Jackson's crossing, saw the
windmill west of the maples, felt the badly-laid rails spring under
him, and sweated big drops all over his boiler. At each jarring bump
he believed an axle had smashed; and he took the eighty-foot bridge
without the guard-rail as a hunted cat takes the top of a fence.
Then a wet leaf stuck against the glass of his headlight and threw a
flying shadow on the track, so that he thought it was some little
dancing animal that would feel soft if he ran over it; and anything
soft underfoot frightens a locomotive as it does an elephant. But the
men behind seemed quite calm. The wrecking-crew were climbing
carelessly from the caboose to the tender—even jesting with the
engineer, for he heard a shuffling of feet among the coal, and the
snatch of a song, something like this:

> 'Oh, the Empire State must learn to wait,
> And the Cannon-ball go hang,
> When the West-bound's ditched, and the tool-car's hitched,
> And it's 'way for the Breakdown Gang (*Ta-rara!*).
> 'Way for the Breakdown Gang!'

'Say! Eustis knew what he was doin' when he designed this rig.
She's a hummer. New, too.'

'Snff! Phew! She *is* new. That ain't paint. That's——'

A burning pain shot through ·007's right rear driver—a crippling, stinging pain.

'This,' said ·007, as he flew, 'is a hot-box. Now I know what it means. I shall go to pieces, I guess. My first road-run too!'

'Het a bit, ain't she?' the fireman ventured to suggest to the engineer.

'She'll hold for all we want of her. We're there. Guess you chaps back had better climb into your car,' said the engineer, his hand on the brake-lever. 'I've seen men snapped off——'

But the crew fled laughing. They had no wish to be jerked on to the track. The engineer half turned his wrist, and ·007 found his drivers pinned firm.

'Now it's come!' said ·007, as he yelled aloud, and slid like a sleigh. For the moment he fancied that he would jerk bodily from off his underpinnings.

'That must be the emergency-stop Pony guyed me about,' he gasped, as soon as he could think. 'Hot-box—emergency-stop. They both hurt. But *now* I can talk back in the round-house.'

He was halted, all hissing hot, a few feet in the rear of what doctors would call a compound-comminuted car. His engineer was kneeling down among his drivers, but he did not call ·007 his 'Arab steed,' nor cry over him, as the engineers did in the newspapers. He just bad-worded ·007, and pulled yards of charred cotton-waste from about the axles, and hoped he might some day catch the idiot who had packed it. Nobody else attended to him, for Evans, the Mogul's engineer, a little cut about the head, but very angry, was exhibiting, by lantern-light, the mangled corpse of a slim blue pig.

''Tweren't even a decent-sized hog,' he said. ''Twere a shote.'

'Dangerousest beasts they are,' said one of the crew. 'Get under the pilot an' sort o' twiddle ye off the track, don't they?'

'Don't they?' roared Evans, who was a red-headed Welshman. 'You talk as if I was ditched by a hog every fool-day o' the week. *I* ain't friends with all the cussed half-fed shotes in the State o' New York. No, indeed! Yes, this is him—an' look what he's done!'

It was not a bad night's work for one stray piglet. The Flying Freight seemed to have flown in every direction, for the Mogul had mounted the rails and run diagonally a few hundred feet from right to left, taking with him such cars as cared to follow. Some did not. They broke their couplers and lay down, while rear cars frolicked over them. In that game, they had ploughed up and removed and twisted a good deal of the left-hand track. The Mogul himself had waddled into a corn-field, and there he knelt—fantastic wreaths of green twisted round his crank-pins; his pilot covered with solid clods of field, on which corn nodded drunkenly; his fire put out with dirt (Evans had done that as soon as he recovered his senses); and his broken headlight half full of half-burnt moths. His tender had thrown coal all over him, and he looked like a disreputable buffalo who had tried to wallow in a general store. For there lay, scattered over the landscape, from the burst cars, typewriters, sewing-machines, bicycles in crates, a consignment of silver-plated imported harness, French dresses and gloves, a dozen finely moulded hardwood mantels, a fifteen-foot naphtha launch, with a solid brass bedstead crumpled around her bows, a case of telescopes and microscopes, two coffins, a case of very best candies, some gilt-edged dairy produce, butter and eggs in an omelette, a broken box of expensive toys, and a few hundred other luxuries. A camp of tramps hurried up from nowhere, and generously volunteered to help the crew. So the brakemen, armed with coupler-pins, walked up and down on one side, and the freight-conductor and the fireman patrolled the other with their hands in their hip-pockets. A long-bearded man came out of a house beyond the corn-field, and told Evans that if the accident had happened a little later in the year, all his corn would have been burned, and accused Evans of care-lessness. Then he ran away, for Evans was at his heels shrieking, ' ''Twas his hog done it—his hog done it! Let me kill him! Let me kill him!' Then the wrecking-crew laughed; and the farmer put his head out of a window and said that Evans was no gentleman.

But ·007 was very sober. He had never seen a wreck before, and it frightened him. The crew still laughed, but they worked at the same time; and ·007 forgot horror in amazement at the way they handled the Mogul freight. They dug round him with spades; they put ties in front of his wheels, and jack-screws under him; they embraced him with the derrick-chain and tickled him with crow-bars; while ·007 was hitched on to wrecked cars and backed away till the knot broke or the cars rolled clear of the track. By dawn thirty or forty men were at work, replacing and ramming down the ties, gauging the rails and spiking them. By daylight all cars who could move had gone on in charge of another loco; the track was free for traffic; and ·007 had hauled the old Mogul over a small pave-ment of ties, inch by inch, till his flanges bit the rail once more, and he settled down with a clank. But his spirit was broken, and his nerve was gone.

' 'Tweren't even a hog,' he repeated dolefully. ' 'Twere a shote; and you—*you* of all of 'em—had to help me on.'

'But how in the whole long road did it happen?' asked ·007, sizzling with curiosity.

'Happen! It didn't happen! It just come! I sailed right on top of him around that last curve—thought he was a skunk. Yes; he was all as little as that. He hadn't more'n squealed once 'fore I felt my bogies lift (he'd rolled right under the pilot), an' I couldn't catch the track again to save me. Swivelled clean off, I was. Then I felt him sling himself along, all greasy, under my left leadin' driver, and, oh, Boilers! that mounted the rail. I heard my flanges zippin' along the ties, an' the next I knew I was playin' "Sally, Sally Waters" in the corn, my tender shuckin' coal through my cab, an' old man Evans lyin' still an' bleedin' in front o' me. Shook? There ain't a stay or a bolt or a rivet in me that ain't sprung to glory somewhere.'

'Umm!' said ·007. 'What d'you reckon you weigh?'

'Without these lumps o' dirt I'm all of a hundred thousand pound.'

'And the shote?'

'Eighty. Call him a hundred pounds at the outside. He's worth about four'n a half dollars. Ain't it awful? Ain't it enough to give you nervous prostration? Ain't it paralysin'? Why, I come just around that curve——' and the Mogul told the tale again, for he was very badly shaken.

'Well, it's all in the day's run, I guess,' said ·007 soothingly; 'an' —an' a corn-field's pretty soft fallin'.'

'If it had bin a sixty-foot bridge, an' I could ha' slid off into deep water, an' blown up an' killed both men, same as others have done, I wouldn't ha' cared; but to be ditched by a shote—an' you to help me out—in a corn-field—an' an old hayseed in his nightgown cussin' me like as if I was a sick truck-horse! . . . Oh, it's awful! Don't call me Mogul! I'm a sewin'-machine. They'll guy my sand-box off in the yard.'

And ·007, his hot-box cooled and his experience vastly enlarged, hauled the Mogul freight slowly to the round-house.

'Hello, old man! Bin out all night, hain't ye?' said the irrepressible Pony, who had just come off duty. 'Well, I must say you look it. Costly—perishable—fragile—immediate—that's you! Go to the shops, take them vine-leaves out o' your hair, an' git 'em to play the hose on you.'

'Leave him alone, Pony,' said ·007 severely, as he was swung on the turn-table, 'or I'll——'

'Didn't know the old granger was any special friend o' yours, kid. He wasn't over civil to you last time I saw him.'

'I know it; but I've seen a wreck since then, and it has about scared the paint off me. I ain't going to guy anyone as long as I steam—not when they're new to the business an' anxious to learn. And I'm not goin' to guy the old Mogul either, though I did find him wreathed around with roastin'-ears. 'Twas a little bit of a shote—not a hog—just a shote, Pony—no bigger'n a lump of anthracite—I saw it—that made all the mess. Anybody can be ditched, I guess.'

'Found that out already, have you? Well, that's a good beginnin'.' It was the Purple Emperor, with his high, tight, plate-glass cab and green velvet cushion, waiting to be cleaned for his next day's fly.

'Let me make you two gen'lemen acquainted,' said Pony. 'This is our Purple Emperor, kid, whom you were admirin' and, I may say, envyin' last night. This is a new brother, Worshipful Sir, with most of his mileage ahead of him, but, so far as a serving-brother can, I'll answer for him.'

'Happy to meet you,' said the Purple Emperor, with a glance round the crowded round-house. 'I guess there are enough of us here to form a full meetin'. Ahem! By virtue of the authority vested in me as Head of the Road, I hereby declare and pronounce No. ·007 a full and accepted Brother of the Amalgamated Brotherhood of Locomotives, and as such entitled to all shop, switch, track, tank, and round-house privileges throughout my jurisdiction, in the Degree of Superior Flier, it bein' well known and credibly reported to me that our Brother has covered forty-one miles in thirty-nine minutes and a half on an errand of mercy to the afflicted. At a convenient time, I myself will communicate to you the Song and Signal of this Degree whereby you may be recognized in the darkest night. Take your stall, newly entered Brother among Locomotives!'

*

Now, in the darkest night, even as the Purple Emperor said, if you will stand on the bridge across the freight-yard, looking down upon the four-track way, at 2.30 A.M., neither before nor after, when the White Moth, that takes the overflow from the Purple Emperor, tears south with her seven vestibuled cream-white cars, you will hear, as the yard-clock makes the half-hour, a far-away sound like the bass of a violoncello, and then, a hundred feet to each word:

'*With a michnai—ghignai—shtingal! Yah! Yah! Yah!*
Ein—zwei—drei, Mutter! Yah! Yah! Yah!
 She climb upon der shteeple,
 Und she frighten all der people,
Singin' michnai—ghignai—shtingal! Yah! Yah! '

That is ·007 covering his one hundred and fifty-six miles in two hundred and twenty-one minutes.

The Day's Work, 1898 *

---

* *Scribner's Magazine,* 1897.

The Maltese Cat

THEY HAD GOOD REASON to be proud, and better reason to be afraid, all twelve of them; for, though they had fought their way, game by game, up the teams entered for the polo tournament, they were meeting the Archangels that afternoon in the final match; and the Archangels' men were playing with half-a-dozen ponies apiece. As the game was divided into six quarters of eight minutes each, that meant a fresh pony after every halt. The Skidars' team, even supposing there were no accidents, could only supply one pony for every other change; and two to one is heavy odds. Again, as Shiraz, the grey Syrian, pointed out, they were meeting the pink and pick of the polo-ponies of Upper India; ponies that had cost from a thousand rupees each, while they themselves were a cheap lot gathered, often from country carts, by their masters who belonged to a poor but honest native infantry regiment.

'Money means pace and weight,' said Shiraz, rubbing his black silk nose dolefully along his neat-fitting boot, 'and by the maxims of the game as I know it——'

'Ah, but we aren't playing the maxims,' said the Maltese Cat. 'We're playing the game, and we've the great advantage of knowing the game. Just think a stride, Shiraz. We've pulled up from bottom to second place in two weeks against all those fellows on the ground here; and that's because we play with our heads as well as with our feet.'

'It makes me feel undersized and unhappy all the same,' said Kittiwynk, a mouse-coloured mare with a red browband and the cleanest pair of legs that ever an aged pony owned. 'They've twice our size, these others.'

Kittiwynk looked at the gathering and sighed. The hard, dusty Umballa polo-ground was lined with thousands of soldiers, black and white, not counting hundreds and hundreds of carriages, and drags, and dog-carts, and ladies with brilliant-coloured parasols, and officers in uniform and out of it, and crowds of natives behind them; and orderlies on camels who had halted to watch the game, instead of carrying letters up and down the Station, and native horse-dealers running about on thin-eared Baluchi mares, looking for a chance to sell a few first-class polo-ponies. Then there were the

ponies of thirty teams that had entered for the Upper India Free-for-All Cup—nearly every pony of worth and dignity from Mhow to Peshawur, from Allahabad to Multan; prize ponies, Arabs, Syrian, Barb, countrybred, Deccanee, Waziri, and Kabul ponies of every colour and shape and temper that you could imagine. Some of them were in mat-roofed stables close to the polo-ground, but most were under saddle while their masters, who had been defeated in the earlier games, trotted in and out and told each other exactly how the game should have been played.

It was a glorious sight, and the come-and-go of the little quick hoofs, and the incessant salutations of ponies that had met before on other polo-grounds or racecourses, were enough to drive a four-footed thing wild.

But the Skidars' team were careful not to know their neighbours, though half the ponies on the ground were anxious to scrape acquaintance with the little fellows that had come from the North, and, so far, had swept the board.

'Let's see,' said a soft, golden-coloured Arab, who had been playing very badly the day before, to the Maltese Cat, 'didn't we meet in Abdul Rahman's stable in Bombay four seasons ago? I won the Paikpattan Cup next season, you may remember.'

'Not me,' said the Maltese Cat politely. 'I was at Malta then, pulling a vegetable cart. I don't race. I play the game.'

'O-oh!' said the Arab, cocking his tail and swaggering off.

'Keep yourselves to yourselves,' said the Maltese Cat to his companions. 'We don't want to rub noses with all those goose-rumped half-breeds of Upper India. When we've won this Cup they'll give their shoes to know us.'

'*We* shan't win the Cup,' said Shiraz. 'How do you feel?'

'Stale as last night's feed after a musk-rat has run over it,' said Polaris, a rather heavy-shouldered grey, and the rest of the team agreed with him.

'The sooner you forget that the better,' said the Maltese Cat cheerfully. 'They've finished tiffin in the big tent. We shall be wanted now. If your saddles are not comfy, kick. If your bits aren't easy, rear, and let the *saises* know whether your boots are tight.'

Each pony had his *sais*, his groom, who lived and ate and slept with the pony, and had betted a great deal more than he could afford on the result of the game. There was no chance of anything going wrong, and, to make sure, each *sais* was shampooing the legs of his pony to the last minute. Behind the *saises* sat as many of the Skidars' regiment as had leave to attend the match—about half the native officers, and a hundred or two dark, black-bearded men with the regimental pipers nervously fingering the big beribboned bagpipes. The Skidars were what they call a Pioneer regiment; and the bagpipes made the national music of half the men. The native officers held bundles of polo-sticks, long cane-handled mallets, and as the grand-stand filled after lunch they arranged themselves by ones and twos at different points round the ground, so that if a stick were broken the player would not have far to ride for a new one. An impatient British cavalry band struck up 'If you want to know the time, ask a p'leeceman!' and the two umpires in light dust-coats danced out on two little excited ponies. The four players of the Archangels' team followed, and the sight of their beautiful mounts made Shiraz groan again.

'Wait till we know,' said the Maltese Cat. 'Two of 'em are playing in blinkers, and that means they can't see to get out of the way of their own side, or they *may* shy at the umpires' ponies. They've *all* got white web reins that are sure to stretch or slip!'

'And,' said Kittiwynk, dancing to take the stiffness out of her, 'they carry their whips in their hands instead of on their wrists. Hah!'

'True enough. No man can manage his stick and his reins and his whip that way,' said the Maltese Cat. 'I've fallen over every square yard of the Malta ground, and *I* ought to know.' He quivered his little flea-bitten withers just to show how satisfied he felt; but his heart was not so light. Ever since he had drifted into India on a troopship, taken, with an old rifle, as part payment for a racing debt, the Maltese Cat had played and preached polo to the Skidars' team on the Skidars' stony polo-ground. Now a polo-pony is like a poet. If he is born with a love for the game he can be made. The Maltese Cat knew that bamboos grew solely in order that polo-balls might be turned from their roots, that grain was given to ponies to keep them in hard condition, and that ponies were shod to prevent them slipping on a turn. But, besides all these things, he knew every trick and device of the finest game of the world, and for two seasons he had been teaching the others all he knew or guessed.

'Remember,' he said for the hundredth time as the riders came up, 'we *must* play together, and you *must* play with your heads. Whatever happens, follow the ball. Who goes out first?'

Kittiwynk, Shiraz, Polaris, and a short high little bay fellow with tremendous hocks and no withers worth speaking of (he was called Corks) were being girthed up, and the soldiers in the background stared with all their eyes.

'I want you men to keep quiet,' said Lutyens, the captain of the team, 'and especially *not* to blow your pipes.'

'Not if we win, Captain Sahib?' asked a piper.

'If we win, you can do what you please,' said Lutyens with a smile, as he slipped the loop of his stick over his wrist, and wheeled to canter to his place. The Archangels' ponies were a little bit above themselves on account of the many-coloured crowd so close to the ground. Their riders were excellent players, but they were a team of crack players instead of a crack team; and that made all the difference in the world. They honestly meant to play together, but it is very hard for four men, each the best of the team he is picked from, to remember that in polo no brilliancy of hitting or riding makes up for playing alone. Their captain shouted his orders to them by name, and it is a curious thing that if you call his name aloud in public after an Englishman you make him hot and fretty. Lutyens said nothing to his men because it had all been said before. He pulled up Shiraz, for he was playing 'back,' to guard the goal. Powell on Polaris was half-back, and Macnamara and Hughes on Corks and Kittiwynk were forwards. The tough bamboo-root ball was put into the middle of the ground one hundred and fifty yards from the ends, and Hughes crossed sticks, heads-up, with the captain of the Archangels, who saw fit to play forward, and that is a place from which you cannot easily control the team. The little click as the cane-shafts met was heard all over the ground, and then Hughes made some sort of quick wrist-stroke that just dribbled the ball a few yards. Kittiwynk knew that stroke of old, and followed as a cat follows a mouse. While the captain of the Archangels was wrenching his pony round Hughes struck with all his strength, and next instant Kittiwynk was away, Corks following close behind her, their little feet pattering like rain-drops on glass.

'Pull out to the left,' said Kittiwynk between her teeth, 'it's coming our way, Corks!'

The back and half-back of the Archangels were tearing down on her just as she was within reach of the ball. Hughes leaned forward with a loose rein, and cut it away to the left almost under Kittiwynk's feet, and it hopped and skipped off to Corks, who saw that, if he were not quick, it would run beyond the boundaries. That long bouncing drive gave the Archangels time to wheel and send three men across the ground to head off Corks. Kittiwynk stayed where she was, for she knew the game. Corks was on the ball half a fraction of a second before the others came up, and Macnamara, with a back-handed stroke, sent it back across the ground to Hughes, who saw the way clear to the Archangels' goal, and smacked the ball in before anyone quite knew what had happened.

'That's luck,' said Corks, as they changed ends. 'A goal in three minutes for three hits and no riding to speak of.'

'Don't know,' said Polaris. 'We've made 'em angry too soon. Shouldn't wonder if they try to rush us off our feet next time.'

'Keep the ball hanging then,' said Shiraz. 'That wears out every pony that isn't used to it.'

Next time there was no easy galloping across the ground. All the Archangels closed up as one man, but there they stayed, for Corks, Kittiwynk, and Polaris were somewhere on the top of the ball, marking time among the rattling sticks, while Shiraz circled about outside, waiting for a chance.

'*We* can do this all day,' said Polaris, ramming his quarters into the side of another pony. 'Where do you think you're shoving to?'

'I'll—I'll be driven in an *ekka* if I know,' was the gasping reply, 'and I'd give a week's feed to get my blinkers off. I can't see anything.'

'The dust *is* rather bad. Whew! That was one for my off hock. Where's the ball, Corks?'

'Under my tail. Anyhow a man's looking for it there. This is beautiful. They can't use their sticks, and it's driving 'em wild. Give old Blinkers a push and he'll go over!'

'Here, don't touch me! I can't see. I'll—I'll back out, I think,' said the pony in blinkers, who knew that if you can't see all round your head you cannot prop yourself against a shock.

Corks was watching the ball where it lay in the dust close to his near fore, with Macnamara's shortened stick tap-tapping it from time to time. Kittiwynk was edging her way out of the scrimmage, whisking her stump of a tail with nervous excitement.

'Ho! They've got it,' she snorted. 'Let me out!' and she galloped like a rifle-bullet just behind a tall lanky pony of the Archangels, whose rider was swinging up his stick for a stroke.

'Not today, thank you,' said Hughes, as the blow slid off his raised stick, and Kittiwynk laid her shoulder to the tall pony's quarters, and shoved him aside just as Lutyens on Shiraz sent the ball where it had come from, and the tall pony went skating and slipping away to the left. Kittiwynk, seeing that Polaris had joined Corks in the chase for the ball up the ground, dropped into Polaris's place, and then time was called.

The Skidars' ponies wasted no time in kicking or fuming. They knew each minute's rest meant so much gain, and trotted off to the rails and their *saises*, who began to scrape and blanket and rub them at once.

'Whew!' said Corks, stiffening up to get all the tickle out of the big vulcanite scraper. 'If we were playing pony for pony we'd bend those Archangels double in half an hour. But they'll bring out fresh ones and fresh ones, and fresh ones after that—you see.'

'Who cares?' said Polaris. 'We've drawn first blood. Is my hock swelling?'

'Looks puffy,' said Corks. 'You must have got rather a wipe. Don't let it stiffen. You'll be wanted again in half an hour.'

'What's the game like?' said the Maltese Cat.

'Ground's like your shoe, except where they've put too much water on it,' said Kittiwynk. 'Then it's slippery. Don't play in the centre. There's a bog there. I don't know how their next four are going to behave, but we kept the ball hanging and made 'em lather for nothing. Who goes next? Two Arabs and a couple of country-breds! That's bad. What a comfort it is to wash your mouth out!'

Kitty was talking with the neck of a leather-covered soda-water bottle between her teeth and trying to look over her withers at the same time. This gave her a very coquettish air.

'What's bad?' said Grey Dawn, giving to the girth and admiring his well-set shoulders.

'You Arabs can't gallop fast enough to keep yourselves warm— that's what Kitty means,' said Polaris, limping to show that his hock needed attention. 'Are you playing "back," Grey Dawn?'

'Looks like it,' said Grey Dawn, as Lutyens swung himself up. Powell mounted the Rabbit, a plain bay countrybred much like Corks, but with mulish ears. Macnamara took Faiz Ullah, a handy short-backed little red Arab with a long tail, and Hughes mounted Benami, an old and sullen brown beast, who stood over in front more than a polo-pony should.

'Benami looks like business,' said Shiraz. 'How's your temper, Ben?' The old campaigner hobbled off without answering, and the Maltese Cat looked at the new Archangel ponies prancing about on the ground. They were four beautiful blacks, and they saddled big enough and strong enough to eat the Skidars' team and gallop away with the meal inside them.

'Blinkers again,' said the Maltese Cat. 'Good enough!'

'They're chargers—cavalry chargers!' said Kittiwynk indignantly. '*They*'ll never see thirteen-three again.'

'They've all been fairly measured and they've all got their certificates,' said the Maltese Cat, 'or they wouldn't be here. We must take things as they come along, and keep our eyes on the ball.'

The game began, but this time the Skidars were penned to their own end of the ground, and the watching ponies did not approve of that.

'Faiz Ullah is shirking, as usual,' said Polaris, with a scornful grunt.

'Faiz Ullah is eating whip,' said Corks. They could hear the leather-thonged polo-quirt lacing the little fellow's well-rounded barrel. Then the Rabbit's shrill neigh came across the ground. 'I can't do all the work,' he cried.

'Play the game, don't talk,' the Maltese Cat whickered; and all the ponies wriggled with excitement, and the soldiers and the grooms gripped the railings and shouted. A black pony with blinkers had singled out old Benami, and was interfering with him in every possible way. They could see Benami shaking his head up and down and flapping his underlip.

'There'll be a fall in a minute,' said Polaris. 'Benami is getting stuffy.'

The game flickered up and down between goal-post and goal-post, and the black ponies were getting more confident as they felt they had the legs of the others. The ball was hit out of a little scrimmage, and Benami and the Rabbit followed it; Faiz Ullah only too glad to be quiet for an instant.

The blinkered black pony came up like a hawk, with two of his own side behind him, and Benami's eye glittered as he raced. The question was which pony should make way for the other; each rider was perfectly willing to risk a fall in a good cause. The black who had been driven nearly crazy by his blinkers trusted to his weight and his temper; but Benami knew how to apply his weight and how to keep his temper. They met, and there was a cloud of dust. The black was lying on his side with all the breath knocked out of his body. The Rabbit was a hundred yards up the ground with the ball, and Benami was sitting down. He had slid nearly ten yards, but he had had his revenge, and sat cracking his nostrils till the black pony rose.

'That's what you get for interfering. Do you want any more?' said Benami, and he plunged into the game. Nothing was done, because Faiz Ullah would not gallop, though Macnamara beat him whenever he could spare a second. The fall of the black pony had impressed his companions tremendously, and so the Archangels could not profit by Faiz Ullah's bad behaviour.

But as the Maltese Cat said, when time was called and the four came back blowing and dripping, Faiz Ullah ought to have been kicked all round Umballa. If he did not behave better next time, the Maltese Cat promised to pull out his Arab tail by the root and eat it.

There was no time to talk, for the third four were ordered out.

The third quarter of a game is generally the hottest, for each side thinks that the others must be pumped; and most of the winning play in a game is made about that time.

Lutyens took over the Maltese Cat with a pat and a hug, for Lutyens valued him more than anything else in the world. Powell had Shikast, a little grey rat with no pedigree and no manners outside polo; Macnamara mounted Bamboo, the largest of the team, and Hughes took Who's Who, *alias* The Animal. He was supposed to have Australian blood in his veins, but he looked like a clothes-horse, and you could whack him on the legs with an iron crowbar without hurting him.

They went out to meet the very flower of the Archangels' team, and when Who's Who saw their elegantly booted legs and their beautiful satiny skins he grinned a grin through his light, well-worn bridle.

'My word!' said Who's Who. 'We must give 'em a little football. These gentlemen need a rubbing-down.'

'No biting,' said the Maltese Cat warningly, for once or twice in his career Who's Who had been known to forget himself in that way.

'Who said anything about biting? I'm not playing tiddlywinks. I'm playing the game.'

The Archangels came down like a wolf on the fold, for they were tired of football and they wanted polo. They got it and much more. Just after the game began, Lutyens hit a ball that was coming towards him rapidly, and it rose in the air, as a ball sometimes will, with the whirr of a frightened partridge. Shikast heard, but could not see it for the minute, though he looked everywhere and up into the air as the Maltese Cat had taught him. When he saw it ahead and overhead, he went forward with Powell as fast as he could put foot to ground. It was then that Powell, a quiet and level-headed man as a rule, became inspired and played a stroke which sometimes comes off successfully on a quiet afternoon of long practice. He took his stick in both hands, and standing up in his stirrups, swiped at the ball in the air, Manipur fashion. There was one second of paralysed astonishment, and then all four sides of the ground went up in a yell of applause and delight as the ball flew true (you could see the

amazed Archangels ducking in their saddles to get out of the line
of flight, and looking at it with open mouths), and the regimental
pipes of the Skidars squealed from the railings as long as the pipers
had breath.

Shikast heard the stroke; but he heard the head of the stick fly
off at the same time. Nine hundred and ninety-nine ponies out of a
thousand would have gone tearing on after the ball with a useless
player pulling at their heads, but Powell knew him, and he knew
Powell; and the instant he felt Powell's right leg shift a trifle on the
saddle-flap he headed for the boundary, where a native officer was
frantically waving a new stick. Before the shouts had ended
Powell was armed again.

Once before in his life the Maltese Cat had heard that very same
stroke played off his own back, and had profited by the confusion it
made. This time he acted on experience, and leaving Bamboo to
guard the goal in case of accidents, came through the others like a
flash, head and tail low, Lutyens standing up to ease him—swept
on and on before the other side knew what was the matter, and
nearly pitched on his head between the Archangels' goal-posts as
Lutyens tipped the ball in after a straight scurry of a hundred and
fifty yards. If there was one thing more than another upon which
the Maltese Cat prided himself it was on this quick, streaking kind
of run half across the ground. He did not believe in taking balls
round the field unless you were clearly over-matched. After this
they gave the Archangels five minutes' football, and an expensive
fast pony hates football because it rumples his temper.

Who's Who showed himself even better than Polaris in this game.
He did not permit any wriggling away, but bored joyfully into the
scrimmage as if he had his nose in a feed-box, and were looking for
something nice. Little Shikast jumped on the ball the minute it got
clear, and every time an Archangel pony followed it he found
Shikast standing over it asking what was the matter.

'If we can live through this quarter,' said the Maltese Cat, 'I
shan't care. Don't take it out of yourselves. Let *them* do the lather-
ing.'

So the ponies, as their riders explained afterwards, 'shut up.'
The Archangels kept them tied fast in front of their goal, but it cost
the Archangels' ponies all that was left of their tempers; and ponies
began to kick, and men began to repeat compliments, and they
chopped at the legs of Who's Who, and he set his teeth and stayed
where he was, and the dust stood up like a tree over the scrimmage
till that hot quarter ended.

They found the ponies very excited and confident when they went to their *saises*; and the Maltese Cat had to warn them that the worst of the game was coming.

'Now *we* are all going in for the second time,' said he, 'and *they* are trotting out fresh ponies. You'll think you can gallop, but you'll find you can't; and then you'll be sorry.'

'But two goals to nothing is a halter-long lead,' said Kittiwynk, prancing.

'How long does it take to get a goal?' the Maltese Cat answered. 'For Pity's sake, don't run away with the notion that the game is half-won just because we happen to be in luck now. They'll ride you into the grand-stand if they can. You mustn't give 'em a chance. Follow the ball.'

'Football, as usual?' said Polaris. 'My hock's half as big as a nose-bag.'

'Don't let them have a look at the ball if you can help it. Now leave me alone. I must get all the rest I can before the last quarter.'

He hung down his head and let all his muscles go slack; Shikast, Bamboo, and Who's Who copying his example.

'Better not watch the game,' he said. 'We aren't playing, and we shall only take it out of ourselves if we grow anxious. Look at the ground and pretend it's fly-time.'

They did their best, but it was hard advice to follow. The hoofs were drumming and the sticks were rattling all up and down the ground, and yells of applause from the English troops told that the Archangels were pressing the Skidars hard. The native soldiers behind the ponies groaned and grunted, and said things in under-tones, and presently they heard a long-drawn shout and a clatter of hurrahs!

'One to the Archangels,' said Shikast, without raising his head. 'Time's nearly up. Oh, my sire and—dam!'

'Faiz Ullah,' said the Maltese Cat, 'if you don't play to the last nail in your shoes this time, I'll kick you on the ground before all the other ponies.'

'I'll do my best when my time comes,' said the little Arab sturdily.

The *saises* looked at each other gravely as they rubbed their ponies' legs. This was the first time when long purses began to tell, and everybody knew it. Kittiwynk and the others came back with the sweat dripping over their hoofs and their tails telling sad stories.

'They're better than we are,' said Shiraz. 'I knew how it would be.'

'Shut your big head,' said the Maltese Cat; 'we've one goal to the good yet.'

'Yes, but it's two Arabs and two countrybreds to play now,' said Corks. 'Faiz Ullah, remember!' He spoke in a biting voice.

As Lutyens mounted Grey Dawn he looked at his men, and they did not look pretty. They were covered with dust and sweat in streaks. Their yellow boots were almost black, their wrists were red and lumpy, and their eyes seemed two inches deep in their heads, but the expression in their eyes was satisfactory.

'Did you take anything at tiffin?' said Lutyens, and the team shook their heads. They were too dry to talk.

'All right. The Archangels did. They are worse pumped than we are.'

'They've got the better ponies,' said Powell. 'I shan't be sorry when this business is over.'

That fifth quarter was a sad one in every way. Faiz Ullah played like a little red demon; and the Rabbit seemed to be everywhere at once, and Benami rode straight at anything and everything that came in his way, while the umpires on their ponies wheeled like gulls outside the shifting game. But the Archangels had the better mounts—they had kept their racers till late in the game—and never allowed the Skidars to play football. They hit the ball up and down the width of the ground till Benami and the rest were outpaced. Then they went forward, and time and again Lutyens and Grey Dawn were just, and only just, able to send the ball away with a long splitting backhander. Grey Dawn forgot that he was an Arab; and turned from grey to blue as he galloped. Indeed, he forgot too well, for he did not keep his eyes on the ground as an Arab should, but stuck out his nose and scuttled for the dear honour of the game. They had watered the ground once or twice between the quarters, and a careless waterman had emptied the last of his skinful all in one place near the Skidars' goal. It was close to the end of play, and for the tenth time Grey Dawn was bolting after a ball when his near hind foot slipped on the greasy mud and he rolled over and over, pitching Lutyens just clear of the goal-post; and the triumphant Archangels made their goal. Then time was called—two goals all; but Lutyens had to be helped up, and Grey Dawn rose with his near hind leg strained somewhere.

'What's the damage?' said Powell, his arm round Lutyens.

'Collar-bone, of course,' said Lutyens between his teeth. It was the third time he had broken it in two years, and it hurt him.

Powell and the others whistled. 'Game's up,' said Hughes.

'Hold on. We've five good minutes yet, and it isn't my right hand,' said Lutyens. 'We'll stick it out.'

'I say,' said the captain of the Archangels, trotting up. 'Are you hurt, Lutyens? We'll wait if you care to put in a substitute. I wish —I mean—the fact is, you fellows deserve this game if any team does. Wish we could give you a man or some of our ponies—or something.'

'You're awfully good, but we'll play it to a finish, I think.'

The captain of the Archangels stared for a little. 'That's not half bad,' he said, and went back to his own side, while Lutyens borrowed a scarf from one of his native officers and made a sling of it. Then an Archangel galloped up with a big bath-sponge and advised Lutyens to put it under his arm-pit to ease his shoulder, and between them they tied up his left arm scientifically, and one of the native officers leaped forward with four long glasses that fizzed and bubbled.

The team looked at Lutyens piteously, and he nodded. It was the last quarter, and nothing would matter after that. They drank out the dark golden drink, and wiped their moustaches, and things looked more hopeful.

The Maltese Cat had pushed his nose into the front of Lutyens' shirt, and was trying to say how sorry he was.

'He knows,' said Lutyens proudly. 'The little beggar knows. I've played him without a bridle before now—for fun.'

'It's no fun now,' said Powell. 'But we haven't a decent substitute.'

'No,' said Lutyens. 'It's the last quarter, and we've got to make our goal and win. I'll trust the Cat.'

'If you fall this time you'll suffer a little,' said Macnamara.

'I'll trust the Cat,' said Lutyens.

'You hear that?' said the Maltese Cat proudly to the others. 'It's worth while playing polo for ten years to have that said of you. Now then, my sons, come along. We'll kick up a little bit, just to show the Archangels *this* team haven't suffered.'

And, sure enough, as they went on to the ground the Maltese Cat, after satisfying himself that Lutyens was home in the saddle, kicked out three or four times, and Lutyens laughed. The reins were caught up anyhow in the tips of his strapped fingers, and he never pretended to rely on them. He knew the Cat would answer to the least pressure of the leg, and by way of showing off—for his shoulder hurt him very much—he bent the little fellow in a close figure-of-eight in and out between the goal-posts. There was a roar from the native officers and men, who dearly loved a piece of *dugabashi* [horse-trick work], as they called it, and the pipes very quietly and scornfully droned out the first bars of a common bazar-tune called 'Freshly Fresh and Newly New,' just as a warning to the other regiments that the Skidars were fit. All the natives laughed.

'And now,' said the Cat, as they took their place, 'remember that this is the last quarter, and follow the ball!'

'Don't need to be told,' said Who's Who.

'Let me go on. All those people on all four sides will begin to crowd in—just as they did at Malta. You'll hear people calling out, and moving forward and being pushed back, and that is going to make the Archangel ponies very unhappy. But if a ball is struck to the boundary, you go after it, and let the people get out of your way. I hopped over the pole of a four-in-hand once, and picked a game out of the dust by it. Back me up when I run, and follow the ball.'

There was a sort of an all-round sound of sympathy and wonder as the last quarter opened, and then there began exactly what the Maltese Cat had foreseen. People crowded in close to the boundaries, and the Archangels' ponies kept looking sideways at the narrowing space. If you know how a man feels to be cramped at tennis—not because he wants to run out of the court, but because he likes to know that he can at a pinch—you will guess how ponies must feel when they are playing in a box of human beings.

'I'll bend some of those men if I can get away,' said Who's Who, as he rocketed behind the ball; and Bamboo nodded without speaking. They were playing the last ounce in them, and the Maltese Cat had left the goal undefended to join them. Lutyens gave him every order that he could to bring him back, but this was the first time in his career that the little wise grey had ever played polo on his own responsibility, and he was going to make the most of it.

'What are you doing here?' said Hughes, as the Cat crossed in front of him and rode off an Archangel.

'The Cat's in charge—mind the goal!' shouted Lutyens, and bowing forward hit the ball full, and followed on, forcing the Archangels towards their own goal.

'No football,' said the Cat. 'Keep the ball by the boundaries and cramp 'em. Play open order and drive 'em to the boundaries.'

Across and across the ground in big diagonals flew the ball, and whenever it came to a flying rush and a stroke close to the boundaries the Archangel ponies moved stiffly. They did not care to go headlong at a wall of men and carriages, though if the ground had been open they could have turned on a sixpence.

'Wriggle her up the sides,' said the Cat. 'Keep her close to the crowd. They hate the carriages. Shikast, keep her up this side.'

Shikast with Powell lay left and right behind the uneasy scuffle of an open scrimmage, and every time the ball was hit away Shikast galloped on it at such an angle that Powell was forced to hit it towards the boundary; and when the crowd had been driven away from that side, Lutyens would send the ball over to the other, and Shikast would slide desperately after it till his friends came down to help. It was billiards, and no football, this time—billiards in a corner pocket; and the cues were not well chalked.

'If they get us out in the middle of the ground they'll walk away from us. Dribble her along the sides,' cried the Cat.

So they dribbled all along the boundary, where a pony could not come on their right-hand side; and the Archangels were furious, and the umpires had to neglect the game to shout at the people to get back, and several blundering mounted policemen tried to restore order, all close to the scrimmage, and the nerves of the Archangels' ponies stretched and broke like cobwebs.

Five or six times an Archangel hit the ball up into the middle of the ground, and each time the watchful Shikast gave Powell his chance to send it back, and after each return, when the dust had settled, men could see that the Skidars had gained a few yards.

Every now and again there were shouts of ' 'Side! Off side!' from the spectators; but the teams were too busy to care, and the umpires had all they could do to keep their maddened ponies clear of the scuffle.

At last Lutyens missed a short easy stroke, and the Skidars had to fly back helter-skelter to protect their own goal, Shikast leading. Powell stopped the ball with a backhander when it was not fifty yards from the goal-posts, and Shikast spun round with a wrench that nearly hoisted Powell out of his saddle.

'Now's our last chance,' said the Cat, wheeling like a cockchafer on a pin. 'We've got to ride it out. Come along.'

Lutyens felt the little chap take a deep breath, and, as it were, crouch under his rider. The ball was hopping towards the right-hand boundary, an Archangel riding for it with both spurs and a whip; but neither spur nor whip would make his pony stretch himself as he neared the crowd. The Maltese Cat glided under his very nose, picking up his hind legs sharp, for there was not a foot to spare between his quarters and the other pony's bit. It was as neat an exhibition as fancy figure-skating. Lutyens hit with all the strength he had left, but the stick slipped a little in his hand, and the ball

flew off to the left instead of keeping close to the boundary. Who's
Who was far across the ground, thinking hard as he galloped. He
repeated, stride for stride, the Cat's manoeuvres with another
Archangel pony, nipping the ball away from under his bridle, and
clearing his opponent by half a fraction of an inch, for Who's Who
was clumsy behind. Then he drove away towards the right as the
Maltese Cat came up from the left; and Bamboo held a middle
course exactly between them. The three were making a sort of
Government-broad-arrow-shaped attack; and there was only the
Archangels' back to guard the goal; but immediately behind them
were three Archangels racing all they knew, and mixed up with
them was Powell, sending Shikast along on what he felt was their
last hope. It takes a very good man to stand up to the rush of seven
crazy ponies in the last quarter of a Cup game, when men are riding
with their necks for sale, and the ponies are delirious. The Archangels' back missed his stroke, and pulled aside just in time to let
the rush go by. Bamboo and Who's Who shortened stride to give
the Maltese Cat room, and Lutyens got the goal with a clean smooth,
smacking stroke that was heard all over the field. But there was no
stopping the ponies. They poured through the goal-posts in one
mixed mob, winners and losers together, for the pace had been
terrific. The Maltese Cat knew by experience what would happen,
and to save Lutyens, turned to the right with one last effort that
strained a back-sinew beyond hope of repair. As he did so he heard
the right-hand goal-post crack as a pony cannoned into it—crack,
splinter, and fall like a mast. It had been sawed three parts through
in case of accidents, but it upset the pony nevertheless, and he
blundered into another, who blundered into the left-hand post, and
then there was confusion and dust and wood. Bamboo was lying on
the ground, seeing stars; an Archangel pony rolled beside him,
breathless and angry; Shikast had sat down dog-fashion to avoid
falling over the others, and was sliding along on his little bob-tail in
a cloud of dust; and Powell was sitting on the ground, hammering
with his stick and trying to cheer. All the others were shouting at
the top of what was left of their voices, and the men who had been
spilt were shouting too. As soon as the people saw no one was hurt,
ten thousand native and English shouted and clapped and yelled,
and before anyone could stop them the pipers of the Skidars broke
on to the ground with all the native officers and men behind them,
and marched up and down, playing a wild northern tune called
'Zakhme Bagān,' and through the insolent blaring of the pipes and
the high-pitched native yells you could hear the Archangels' band

hammering 'For they are all jolly good fellows,' and then reproach-
fully to the losing team, 'Ooh, Kafoozalum! Kafoozalum! Kafoozalum!'

Besides all these things and many more, there was a Commander-
in-Chief, and an Inspector-General of Cavalry, and the principal
Veterinary Officer in all India, standing on the top of a regimental
coach, yelling like schoolboys; and Brigadiers and Colonels and
Commissioners, and hundreds of pretty ladies joined the chorus. But
the Maltese Cat stood with his head down, wondering how many
legs were left to him; and Lutyens watched the men and ponies pick
themselves out of the wreck of the two goal-posts, and he patted
the Cat very tenderly.

'I say,' said the captain of the Archangels, spitting a pebble out
of his mouth, 'will you take three thousand for that pony—as he
stands?'

'No, thank you. I've an idea he's saved my life,' said Lutyens,
getting off and lying down at full length. Both teams were on the
ground too, waving their boots in the air, and coughing and drawing deep breaths, as the *saises* ran up to take away the ponies, and
an officious water-carrier sprinkled the players with dirty water till
they sat up.

'My Aunt!' said Powell, rubbing his back and looking at the
stumps of the goal-posts. 'That was a game!'

They played it over again, every stroke of it, that night at the
big dinner, when the Free-for-All Cup was filled and passed down
the table, and emptied and filled again, and everybody made most
eloquent speeches. About two in the morning, when there might
have been some singing, a wise little, plain little, grey little head
looked in through the open door.

'Hurrah! Bring him in,' said the Archangels; and his *sais*, who
was very happy indeed, patted the Maltese Cat on the flank, and he
limped in to the blaze of light and the glittering uniforms, looking
for Lutyens. He was used to Messes, and officers' bedrooms, and
places where ponies are not usually encouraged, and in his youth
had jumped on and off a Mess-table for a bet. So he behaved himself very politely, and ate bread dipped in salt, and was petted all
round the table, moving gingerly; and they drank his health, because he had done more to win the Cup than any man or horse on
the ground.

That was glory and honour enough for the rest of his days, and
the Maltese Cat did not complain much when his veterinary surgeon said that he would be no good for polo any more. When

Lutyens married, his wife did not allow him to play, so he was
forced to be an umpire; and his pony on these occasions was a flea-
bitten grey with a neat polo-tail, lame all round, but desperately
quick on his feet, and, as everybody knew, Past Pluperfect
Prestissimo Player of the Game.

The Day's Work, 1898*

* *Pall Mall Gazette*, 1895.

The Elephant's Child

IN THE HIGH AND FAR-OFF TIMES the Elephant, O Best Beloved, had no trunk. He had only a blackish, bulgy nose, as big as a boot, that he could wriggle about from side to side; but he couldn't pick up things with it. But there was one Elephant—a new Elephant—an Elephant's Child—who was full of 'satiable curtiosity, and that means he asked ever so many questions. *And* he lived in Africa, and he filled all Africa with his 'satiable curtiosities. He asked his tall aunt, the Ostrich, why her tail-feathers grew just so, and his tall aunt the Ostrich spanked him with her hard, hard claw. He asked his tall uncle, the Giraffe, what made his skin spotty, and his tall uncle, the Giraffe, spanked him with his hard, hard hoof. And still he was full of 'satiable curtiosity! He asked his broad aunt, the Hippopotamus, why her eyes were red, and his broad aunt, the Hippopotamus, spanked him with her broad, broad hoof; and he asked his hairy uncle, the Baboon, why melons tasted just so, and his hairy uncle, the Baboon, spanked him with his hairy, hairy paw. And *still* he was full of 'satiable curtiosity! He asked questions about everything that he saw, or heard, or felt, or smelt, or touched, and all his uncles and his aunts spanked him. And still he was full of 'satiable curtiosity!

One fine morning in the middle of the Precession of the Equinoxes this 'satiable Elephant's Child asked a new fine question that he had never asked before. He asked, 'What does the Crocodile have for dinner?' Then everybody said, 'Hush!' in a loud and dretful tone, and they spanked him immediately and directly, without stopping, for a long time.

By and by, when that was finished, he came upon Kolokolo Bird sitting in the middle of a wait-a-bit thorn-bush, and he said, 'My Father has spanked me, and my mother has spanked me; all my aunts and uncles have spanked me for my 'satiable curtiosity; and *still* I want to know what the Crocodile has for dinner!'

Then Kolokolo Bird said, with a mournful cry, 'Go to the banks of the great grey-green, greasy Limpopo River, all set about with fever-trees, and find out.'

That very next morning, when there was nothing left of the Equinoxes, because the Precession had preceded according to precedent, this 'satiable Elephant's Child took a hundred pounds of bananas (the little short red kind), and a hundred pounds of sugarcane (the long purple kind), and seventeen melons (the greencrackly kind), and said to all his dear families, 'Good-bye. I am going to the great grey-green, greasy Limpopo River, all set about with fever-trees, to find out what the Crocodile has for dinner.' And they all spanked him once more for luck, though he asked them most politely to stop.

Then he went away, a little warm, but not at all astonished, eating melons, and throwing the rind about, because he could not pick it up.

He went from Graham's Town to Kimberley, and from Kimberley to Khama's Country, and from Khama's Country he went east by north, eating melons all the time, till at last he came to the banks of the great grey-green, greasy Limpopo River, all set about with fever-trees, precisely as Kolokolo Bird had said.

Now you must know and understand, O Best Beloved, that till that very week, and day, and hour, and minute, this 'satiable Elephant's Child had never seen a Crocodile, and did not know what one was like. It was all his 'satiable curtiosity.

The first thing that he found was a Bi-Coloured-Python-Rock-Snake curled round a rock.

''Scuse me,' said the Elephant's Child most politely, 'but have you seen such a thing as a Crocodile in these promiscuous parts?'

'*Have* I seen a Crocodile?' said the Bi-Coloured-Python-Rock-Snake, in a voice of dretful scorn. 'What will you ask me next?'

''Scuse me,' said the Elephant's Child, 'but could you kindly tell me what he has for dinner?'

Then the Bi-Coloured-Python-Rock-Snake uncoiled himself very quickly from the rock, and spanked the Elephant's Child with his scalesome, flailsome tail.

'That is odd,' said the Elephant's Child, 'because my father and my mother, and my uncle and my aunt, not to mention my other aunt, the Hippopotamus, and my other uncle, the Baboon, have all spanked me for my 'satiable curtiosity—and I suppose this is the same thing.'

So he said good-bye very politely to the Bi-Coloured-Python-Rock-Snake, and helped to coil him up on the rock again, and went on, a little warm, but not at all astonished, eating melons, and throwing the rind about, because he could not pick it up, till he trod on what he thought was a log of wood at the very edge of the great grey-green, greasy Limpopo River, all set about with fever-trees.

But it was really the Crocodile, O Best Beloved, and the Crocodile winked one eye—like this!

' 'Scuse me,' said the Elephant's Child most politely, 'but do you happen to have seen a Crocodile in these promiscuous parts?'

Then the Crocodile winked the other eye, and lifted half his tail out of the mud; and the Elephant's Child stepped back most politely, because he did not wish to be spanked again.

'Come hither, Little One,' said the Crocodile. 'Why do you ask such things?'

' 'Scuse me,' said the Elephant's Child most politely, 'but my father has spanked me, my mother has spanked me, not to mention my tall aunt, the Ostrich, and my tall uncle, the Giraffe, who can kick ever so hard, as well as my broad aunt, the Hippopotamus, and my hairy uncle, the Baboon, *and* including the Bi-Coloured-Python-Rock-Snake, with the scalesome, flailsome tail, just up the bank, who spanks harder than any of them; and *so*, if it's quite all the same to you, I don't want to be spanked any more.'

'Come hither, Little One,' said the Crocodile, 'for I am the Crocodile,' and he wept crocodile-tears to show it was quite true.

Then the Elephant's Child grew all breathless, and panted, and kneeled down on the bank and said, 'You are the very person I have been looking for all these long days. Will you please tell me what you have for dinner?'

'Come hither, Little One,' said the Crocodile, 'and I'll whisper.'

Then the Elephant's Child put his head down close to the Crocodile's musky, tusky mouth, and the Crocodile caught him by his little nose, which up to that very week, day, hour, and minute, had been no bigger than a boot, though much more useful.

'I think,' said the Crocodile—and he said it between his teeth, like this—'I think today I will begin with Elephant's Child!'

At this, O Best Beloved, the Elephant's Child was much annoyed, and he said, speaking through his nose, like this, 'Led go! You are hurtig be!'

Then the Bi-Coloured-Python-Rock-Snake scuffled down from the bank and said, 'My young friend, if you do not now, immediately and instantly, pull as hard as ever you can, it is my opinion that your acquaintance in the large-pattern leather ulster' (and by this he meant the Crocodile) 'will jerk you into yonder limpid stream before you can say Jack Robinson.'

This is the way Bi-Coloured-Python-Rock-Snakes always talk.

Then the Elephant's Child sat back on his little haunches, and pulled, and pulled, and pulled, and his nose began to stretch. And the Crocodile floundered into the water, making it all creamy with great sweeps of his tail, and *he* pulled, and pulled, and pulled.

And the Elephant's Child's nose kept on stretching; and the Elephant's Child spread all his little four legs and pulled, and pulled, and pulled, and his nose kept on stretching; and the Crocodile threshed his tail like an oar, and *he* pulled, and pulled, and pulled, and at each pull the Elephant's Child's nose grew longer and longer —and it hurt him hijjus!

Then the Elephant's Child felt his legs slipping, and he said through his nose, which was now nearly five feet long, 'This is too butch for be!'

Then the Bi-Coloured-Python-Rock-Snake came down from the bank, and knotted himself in the double-clove-hitch round the Elephant's Child's hind-legs, and said, 'Rash and inexperienced traveller, we will now seriously devote ourselves to a little high tension, because if we do not, it is my impression that yonder self-propelling man-of-war with the armour-plated upper deck' (and by this, O Best Beloved, he meant the Crocodile) 'will permanently vitiate your future career.'

That is the way all Bi-Coloured-Python-Rock-Snakes always talk.

So he pulled, and the Elephant's Child pulled, and the Crocodile pulled; but the Elephant's Child and the Bi-Coloured-Python-Rock-Snake pulled hardest; and at last the Crocodile let go of the Elephant's Child's nose with a plop that you could hear all up and down the Limpopo.

Then the Elephant's Child sat down most hard and sudden; but first he was careful to say 'Thank you' to the Bi-Coloured-Python-Rock-Snake; and next he was kind to his poor pulled nose, and wrapped it all up in cool banana leaves, and hung it in the great grey-green, greasy Limpopo to cool.

'What are you doing that for?' said the Bi-Coloured-Python-Rock-Snake.

' 'Scuse me,' said the Elephant's Child, 'but my nose is badly out of shape, and I am waiting for it to shrink.'

'Then you will have to wait a long time,' said the Bi-Coloured-Python-Rock-Snake. 'Some people do not know what is good for them.'

The Elephant's Child sat there for three days waiting for his nose to shrink. But it never grew any shorter, and, besides, it made him squint. For, O Best Beloved, you will see and understand that the Crocodile had pulled it out into a really truly trunk same as all Elephants have today.

At the end of the third day a fly came and stung him on the shoulder, and before he knew what he was doing he lifted up his trunk and hit that fly dead with the end of it.

' 'Vantage number one!' said the Bi-Coloured-Python-Rock-Snake. 'You couldn't have done that with a mere-smear nose. Try and eat a little now.'

Before he thought what he was doing the Elephant's Child put out his trunk and plucked a large bundle of grass, dusted it clean against his fore-legs, and stuffed it into his own mouth.

' 'Vantage number two!' said the Bi-Coloured-Python-Rock-Snake. 'You couldn't have done that with a mere-smear nose. Don't you think the sun is very hot here?'

'It is,' said the Elephant's Child, and before he thought what he was doing he schlooped up a schloop of mud from the banks of the great grey-green, greasy Limpopo, and slapped it on his head, where it made a cool schloopy-sloshy mud-cap all trickly behind his ears.

' 'Vantage number three!' said the Bi-Coloured-Python-Rock-Snake. 'You couldn't have done that with a mere-smear nose. Now how do you feel about being spanked again?'

' 'Scuse me,' said the Elephant's Child, 'but I should not like it at all.'

'How would you like to spank somebody?' said the Bi-Coloured-Python-Rock-Snake.

'I should like it very much indeed,' said the Elephant's Child.

'Well,' said the Bi-Coloured-Python-Rock-Snake, 'you will find that new nose of yours very useful to spank people with.'

'Thank you,' said the Elephant's Child. 'I'll remember that; and now I think I'll go home to all my dear families and try.'

So the Elephant's Child went home across Africa frisking and whisking his trunk. When he wanted fruit to eat he pulled fruit down from a tree, instead of waiting for it to fall as he used to do. When he wanted grass he plucked grass up from the ground, instead of going on his knees as he used to do. When the flies bit him he broke off the branch of a tree and used it as a fly-whisk; and he made himself a new, cool, slushy-squshy mud-cap whenever the sun was hot. When he felt lonely walking through Africa he sang to himself down his trunk, and the noise was louder than several brass bands. He went specially out of his way to find a broad Hippopotamus (she was no relation of his), and he spanked her very hard, to make sure that the Bi-Coloured-Python-Rock-Snake had spoken the truth about his new trunk. The rest of the time he picked up the melon-rinds that he had dropped on his way to the Limpopo—for he was a Tidy Pachyderm.

One dark evening he came back to all his dear families, and he coiled up his trunk and said, 'How do you do?' They were very glad to see him, and immediately said, 'Come here and be spanked for your 'satiable curiosity.'

'Pooh!' said the Elephant's Child. 'I don't think you peoples know anything about spanking; but *I* do, and I'll show you.'

Then he uncurled his trunk and knocked two of his dear brothers head over heels.

'O Bananas!' said they, 'where did you learn that trick, and what have you done to your nose?'

'I got a new one from the Crocodile on the banks of the great grey-green, greasy Limpopo River,' said the Elephant's Child. 'I asked him what he had for dinner, and he gave me this to keep.'

'It looks very ugly,' said his hairy uncle, the Baboon.

'It does,' said the Elephant's Child. 'But it's very useful,' and he picked up his hairy uncle, the Baboon, by one hairy leg, and hove him into a hornets' nest.

Then that bad Elephant's Child spanked all his dear families for a long time, till they were very warm and greatly astonished. He pulled out his tall Ostrich aunt's tail-feathers; and he caught his tall uncle, the Giraffe, by the hind leg, and dragged him through a thorn-bush; and he shouted at his broad aunt, the Hippopotamus, and blew bubbles into her ear when she was sleeping in the water after meals; but he never let anyone touch Kolokolo Bird.

At last things grew so exciting that his dear families went off one by one in a hurry to the banks of the great grey-green, greasy Limpopo River, all set about with fever-trees, to borrow new noses from the Crocodile. When they came back nobody spanked anybody any more; and ever since that day, O Best Beloved, all the Elephants you will ever see, besides all those that you won't, have trunks precisely like the trunk of the 'satiable Elephant's Child.

Just So Stories, 1902 *

* *Ladies Home Journal*, 1900.

The House Surgeon

O N AN EVENING after Easter Day, I sat at a table in a home-
ward-bound steamer's smoking-room, where half-a-dozen of us
told ghost stories. As our party broke up, a man, playing Patience
in the next alcove, said to me: 'I didn't quite catch the end of that
last story about the Curse on the family's first-born.'

'It turned out to be drains,' I explained. 'As soon as new ones
were put into the house the Curse was lifted, I believe. I never
knew the people myself.'

'Ah! I've had *my* drains up twice; I'm on gravel too.'

'You don't mean to say you've a ghost in your house? Why didn't
you join our party?'

'Any more orders, gentlemen, before the bar closes?' the steward
interrupted.

'Sit down again and have one with me,' said the Patience player.
'No, it isn't a ghost. Our trouble is more depression than anything
else.'

'How interesting! Then it's nothing anyone can see?'

'It's—it's nothing worse than a little depression. And the odd
part is that there hasn't been a death in the house since it was built
—in 1863. The lawyer said so. That decided me—my good lady,
rather—and he made me pay an extra thousand for it.'

'How curious. Unusual, too!' I said.

'Yes, ain't it? It was built for three sisters—Moultrie was the
name—three old maids. They all lived together; the eldest owned
it. I bought it from her lawyer a few years ago, and if I've spent a
pound on the place first and last, I must have spent five thousand. Electric light, new servants' wing, garden—all that sort of
thing. A man and his family ought to be happy after so much
expense, ain't it?' He looked at me through the bottom of his
glass.

'Does it affect your family much?'

'My good lady—she's a Greek by the way—and myself are
middle-aged. We can bear up against depression; but it's hard on
my little girl. I say little; but she's twenty. We send her visiting to
escape it. She almost lived at hotels and hydros last year, but that
isn't pleasant for her. She used to be a canary—a perfect canary—

always singing. You ought to hear her. She doesn't sing now. That sort of thing's unwholesome for the young, ain't it?'

'Can't you get rid of the place?' I suggested.

'Not except at a sacrifice, and we are fond of it. Just suits us three. We'd love it if we were allowed.'

'What do you mean by not being allowed?'

'I mean because of the depression. It spoils everything.'

'What's it like exactly?'

'I couldn't very well explain. It must be seen to be appreciated, as the auctioneers say. Now, I was much impressed by the story you were telling just now.'

'It wasn't true,' I said.

'My tale is true. If you would do me the pleasure to come down and spend a night at my little place, you'd learn more than you would if I talked till morning. Very likely 'twouldn't touch your good self at all. You might be—immune, ain't it? On the other hand, if this influenza-influence *does* happen to affect you, why, I think it will be an experience.'

While he talked he gave me his card, and I read his name was L. Maxwell M'Leod, Esq., of Holmescroft. A City address was tucked away in a corner.

'My business,' he added, 'used to be furs. If you are interested in furs—I've given thirty years of my life to 'em.'

'You're very kind,' I murmured.

'Far from it, I assure you. I can meet you next Saturday afternoon anywhere in London you choose to name, and I'll be only too happy to motor you down. It ought to be a delightful run at this time of year—the rhododendrons will be out. I mean it. You don't know how truly I mean it. Very probably—it won't affect you at all. And—I think I may say I have the finest collection of narwhal tusks in the world. All the best skins and horns have to go through London, and L. Maxwell M'Leod, he knows where they come from, and where they go to. That's his business.'

For the rest of the voyage up-Channel Mr M'Leod talked to me of the assembling, preparation, and sale of the rarer furs; and told me things about the manufacture of fur-lined coats which quite shocked me. Somehow or other, when we landed on Wednesday, I found myself pledged to spend that week-end with him at Holmescroft.

On Saturday he met me with a well-groomed motor, and ran me out in an hour and a half to an exclusive residential district of dust-less roads and elegantly designed country villas, each standing in from three to five acres of perfectly appointed land. He told me land was selling at eight hundred pounds the acre, and the new golf links, whose Queen Anne pavilion we passed, had cost nearly twenty-four thousand pounds to create.

Holmescroft was a large, two-storied, low, creeper-covered residence. A veranda at the south side gave on to a garden and two tennis courts, separated by a tasteful iron fence from a most park-like meadow of five or six acres, where two Jersey cows grazed. Tea was ready in the shade of a promising copper beech, and I could see groups on the lawn of young men and maidens appropriately clothed, playing lawn tennis in the sunshine.

'A pretty scene, ain't it?' said Mr M'Leod. 'My good lady's sitting under the tree, and that's my little girl in pink on the far court. But I'll take you to your room, and you can see 'em all later.'

He led me through a wide parquet-floored hall furnished in pale lemon, with huge cloisonné vases, an ebonized and gold grand piano, and banks of pot flowers in Benares brass bowls, up a pale oak staircase to a spacious landing, where there was a green velvet settee trimmed with silver. The blinds were down, and the light lay in parallel lines on the floors.

He showed me my room, saying cheerfully: 'You may be a little tired. One often is without knowing it after a run through traffic. Don't come down till you feel quite restored. We shall all be in the garden.'

My room was rather close, and smelt of perfumed soap. I threw up the window at once, but it opened so close to the floor and worked so clumsily that I came within an ace of pitching out, where I should certainly have ruined a rather lopsided laburnum below. As I set about washing off the journey's dust, I began to feel a little tired. But, I reflected, I had not come down here in this weather and among these new surroundings to be depressed, so I began to whistle.

And it was just then that I was aware of a little grey shadow, as it might have been a snowflake seen against the light, floating at an immense distance in the background of my brain. It annoyed me, and I shook my head to get rid of it. Then my brain telegraphed that it was the forerunner of a swift-striding gloom which there was yet time to escape if I would force my thoughts away from it, as a man leaping for life forces his body forward and away from the fall of a wall. But the gloom overtook me before I could take in the meaning of the message. I moved towards the bed, every nerve already aching with the foreknowledge of the pain that was to be dealt it, and sat down, while my amazed and angry soul dropped, gulf by gulf, into that Horror of great darkness which is spoken of in the Bible, and which, as auctioneers say, must be experienced to be appreciated.

Despair upon despair, misery upon misery, fear after fear, each causing their distinct and separate woe, packed in upon me for an unrecorded length of time, until at last they blurred together, and I heard a click in my brain like the click in the ear when one descends in a diving-bell, and I knew that the pressures were equalized within and without, and that, for the moment, the worst was at an end. But I knew also that at any moment the darkness might come down anew; and while I dwelt on this speculation precisely as a man torments a raging tooth with his tongue, it ebbed away into the little grey shadow on the brain of its first coming, and once more I heard my brain, which knew what would recur, telegraph to every quarter for help, release, or diversion.

The door opened, and M'Leod reappeared. I thanked him politely, saying I was charmed with my room, anxious to meet Mrs M'Leod, much refreshed with my wash, and so on and so forth. Beyond a little stickiness at the corners of my mouth, it seemed to me that I was managing my words admirably, the while that I myself cowered at the bottom of unclimbable pits. M'Leod laid his hand on my shoulder, and said: 'You've got it now already, ain't it?'

'Yes,' I answered, 'it's making me sick!'

'It will pass off when you come outside. I give you my word it will pass off. Come!'

I shambled out behind him, and wiped my forehead in the hall.

'You mustn't mind,' he said. 'I expect the run tired you. My good lady is sitting there under the copper beech.'

She was a fat woman in an apricot-coloured gown, with a heavily powdered face, against which her black long-lashed eyes showed like currants in dough. I was introduced to many fine ladies and gentlemen of those parts. Magnificently appointed landaus and covered motors swept in and out of the drive, and the air was gay with the merry outcries of the tennis-players.

As twilight drew on they all went away, and I was left alone with Mr and Mrs M'Leod, while tall men-servants and maidservants took away the tennis and tea things. Miss M'Leod had walked a little down the drive with a light-haired young man, who apparently knew everything about every South American railway

stock. He had told me at tea that these were the days of financial
specialization.

'I think it went off beautifully, my dear,' said Mr M'Leod to his
wife; and to me: 'You feel all right now, ain't it? Of course you do.'

Mrs M'Leod surged across the gravel. Her husband skipped
nimbly before her into the south veranda, turned a switch, and all
Holmescroft was flooded with light.

'You can do that from your room also,' he said as they went in.
'There is something in money, ain't it?'

Miss M'Leod came up behind me in the dusk. 'We have not yet
been introduced,' she said, 'but I suppose you are staying the
night?'

'Your father was kind enough to ask me,' I replied.

She nodded. 'Yes, *I* know; and you know too, don't you? I saw
your face when you came to shake hands with mamma. You felt the
depression very soon? It is simply frightful in that bedroom sometimes. What do you think it is—bewitchment? In Greece, where I
was a little girl, it might have been; but not in England, do you
think? Or *do* you?'

'I don't know what to think,' I replied. 'I never felt anything like
it. Does it happen often?'

'Yes, sometimes. It comes and goes.'

'Pleasant!' I said, as we walked up and down the gravel at the
lawn edge. 'What has been your experience of it?'

'That is difficult to say, but—sometimes that—that depression is
like as it were'—she gesticulated in most un-English fashion—'a
light. Yes, like a light turned into a room—only a light of blackness,
do you understand?—into a happy room. For sometimes we are so
happy, all we three—so *very* happy. Then this blackness, it is
turned on us just like—ah, I know what I mean now—like the
head-lamp of a motor, and we are eclip-sed. And there is another
thing——'

The dressing-gong roared, and we entered the over-lighted hall.
My dressing was a brisk athletic performance, varied with outbursts
of song—careful attention paid to articulation and expression. But
nothing happened. As I hurried downstairs, I thanked Heaven that
nothing had happened.

Dinner was served breakfast-fashion; the dishes were placed on
the sideboard over heaters, and we helped ourselves.

'We always do this when we are alone, so we talk better,' said
Mr M'Leod.

'And we are always alone,' said the daughter.

'Cheer up, Thea. It will all come right,' he insisted

'No, papa.' She shook her dark head. 'Nothing is right while *it* comes.'

'It is nothing that we ourselves have ever done in our lives—that I will swear to you,' said Mrs M'Leod suddenly. 'And we have changed our servants several times. So we know it is not *them*.'

'Never mind. Let us enjoy ourselves while we can,' said Mr M'Leod, opening the champagne.

But we did not enjoy ourselves. The talk failed. There were long silences.

'I beg your pardon,' I said, for I thought someone at my elbow was about to speak.

'Ah! That is the other thing!' said Miss M'Leod. Her mother groaned.

We were silent again, and, in a few seconds it must have been, a live grief beyond words—not ghostly dread or horror, but aching, helpless grief—overwhelmed us, each, I felt, according to his or her nature, and held steady like the beam of a burning-glass. Behind that pain I was conscious there was a desire on somebody's part to explain something on which some tremendously important issue hung.

Meantime I rolled bread pills and remembered my sins; M'Leod considered his own reflection in a spoon; his wife seemed to be praying, and the girl fidgeted desperately with hands and feet till the darkness passed on—as though the malignant rays of a burning-glass had been shifted from us.

'There,' said Miss M'Leod, half rising. 'Now you see what makes a happy home. Oh, sell it—sell it, father mine, and let us go away!'

'But I've spent thousands on it. You shall go to Harrogate next week, Thea dear.'

'I'm only just back from hotels. I am *so* tired of packing.'

'Cheer up, Thea. It is over. You know it does not often come here twice in the same night. I think we shall dare now to be comfortable.'

He lifted a dish-cover, and helped his wife and daughter. His face was lined and fallen like an old man's after a debauch, but his hand did not shake, and his voice was clear. As he worked to restore us by speech and action, he reminded me of a grey-muzzled collie herding demoralized sheep.

After dinner we sat round the dining-room fire—the drawing-room might have been under the Shadow for aught we knew—talking with the intimacy of gipsies by the wayside, or of wounded

comparing notes after a skirmish. By eleven o'clock the three between them had given me every name and detail they could recall
that in any way bore on the house, and what they knew of its
history.

We went to bed in a fortifying blaze of electric light. My one fear
was that the blasting gust of depression would return—the surest
way, of course, to bring it. I lay awake till dawn, breathing quickly
and sweating lightly, beneath what De Quincey inadequately
describes as 'the oppression of inexpiable guilt.' Now as soon as the
lovely day was broken, I fell into the most terrible of all dreams—
that joyous one in which all past evil has not only been wiped out of
our lives, but has never been committed; and in the very bliss of
our assured innocence, before our loves shriek and change countenance, we wake to the day we have earned.

It was a coolish morning, but we preferred to breakfast in the
south veranda. The forenoon we spent in the garden, pretending to
play games that come out of boxes, such as croquet and clock-golf.
But most of the time we drew together and talked. The young man
who knew all about South American railways took Miss M'Leod for
a walk in the afternoon, and at five M'Leod thoughtfully whirled us
all up to dine in town.

'Now, don't say you will tell the Psychological Society, and that
you will come again,' said Miss M'Leod, as we parted. 'Because I
know you will not.'

'You should not say that,' said her mother. 'You should say,
"Good-bye, Mr Perseus. Come again." '

'Not him!' the girl cried. 'He has seen the Medusa's head!'

Looking at myself in the restaurant's mirrors, it seemed to me
that I had not much benefited by my week-end. Next morning I
wrote out all my Holmescroft notes at fullest length, in the hope
that by so doing I could put it all behind me. But the experience
worked on my mind, as they say certain imperfectly understood
rays work on the body.

I am less calculated to make a Sherlock Holmes than any man I
know, for I lack both method and patience, yet the idea of following up the trouble to its source fascinated me. I had no theory to go
on, except a vague idea that I had come between two poles of a dis-
charge, and had taken a shock meant for someone else. This was
followed by a feeling of intense irritation. I waited cautiously on
myself, expecting to be overtaken by horror of the supernatural,
but my self persisted in being humanly indignant, exactly as though
it had been the victim of a practical joke. It was in great pains and

upheavals—that I felt in every fibre—but its dominant idea, to put it coarsely, was to get back a bit of its own. By this I knew that I might go forward if I could find the way.

After a few days it occurred to me to go to the office of Mr J. M. M. Baxter—the solicitor who had sold Holmescroft to M'Leod. I explained I had some notion of buying the place. Would he act for me in the matter?

Mr Baxter, a large, greyish, throaty-voiced man, showed no enthusiasm. 'I sold it to Mr M'Leod,' he said. 'It 'ud scarcely do for me to start on the running-down tack now. But I can recommend——'

'I know he's asking an awful price,' I interrupted, 'and atop of it he wants an extra thousand for what he calls your clean bill of health.'

Mr Baxter sat up in his chair. I had all his attention.

'Your guarantee with the house. Don't you remember it?'

'Yes, yes. That no death had taken place in the house since it was built. I remember perfectly.'

He did not gulp as untrained men do when they lie, but his jaws moved stickily, and his eyes, turning towards the deed-boxes on the wall, dulled. I counted seconds, one, two, three—one, two, three—up to ten. A man, I knew, can live through ages of mental depression in that time.

'I remember perfectly.' His mouth opened a little as though it had tasted old bitterness.

'Of course *that* sort of thing doesn't appeal to me,' I went on. '*I* don't expect to buy a house free from death.'

'Certainly not. No one does. But it was Mr M'Leod's fancy—his wife's rather, I believe; and since we could meet it—it was my duty to my clients—at whatever cost to my own feelings—to make him pay.'

'That's really why I came to you. I understood from him you knew the place well.'

'Oh yes. Always did. It originally belonged to some connections of mine.'

'The Misses Moultrie, I suppose. How interesting! They must have loved the place before the country round about was built up.'

'They were very fond of it indeed.'

'I don't wonder. So restful and sunny. I don't see how they could have brought themselves to part with it.'

Now it is one of the most constant peculiarities of the English that in polite conversation—and I had striven to be polite—no one ever does or sells anything for mere money's sake.

'Miss Agnes—the youngest—fell ill' (he spaced his words a little), 'and, as they were very much attached to each other, that broke up the home.'

'Naturally. I fancied it must have been something of that kind. One doesn't associate the Staffordshire Moultries' (my Demon of Irresponsibility at that instant created 'em) 'with—with being hard up.'

'I don't know whether we're related to them,' he answered importantly. 'We may be, for our branch of the family comes from the Midlands.'

I give this talk at length, because I am so proud of my first attempt at detective work. When I left him, twenty minutes later, with instructions to move against the owner of Holmescroft with a view to purchase, I was more bewildered than any Doctor Watson at the opening of a story.

Why should a middle-aged solicitor turn plover's-egg colour and drop his jaw when reminded of so innocent and festal a matter as that no death had ever occurred in a house that he had sold? If I knew my English vocabulary at all, the tone in which he said the youngest sister 'fell ill' meant that she had gone out of her mind. That might explain his change of countenance, and it was just possible that her demented influence still hung about Holmescroft. But the rest was beyond me.

I was relieved when I reached M'Leod's City office, and could tell him what I had done—not what I thought.

M'Leod was quite willing to enter into the game of the pretended purchase, but did not see how it would help if I knew Baxter.

'He's the only living soul I can get at who was connected with Holmescroft,' I said.

'Ah! Living soul is good,' said M'Leod. 'At any rate our little girl will be pleased that you are still interested in us. Won't you come down some day this week?'

'How is it there now?' I asked.

He screwed up his face. 'Simply frightful!' he said. 'Thea is at Droitwich.'

'I should like it immensely, but I must cultivate Baxter for the present. You'll be sure and keep him busy your end, won't you?'

He looked at me with quiet contempt. 'Do not be afraid. I shall be a good Jew. I shall be my own solicitor.'

Before a fortnight was over, Baxter admitted ruefully that

M'Leod was better than most firms in the business. We buyers were coy, argumentative, shocked at the price of Holmescroft, inquisitive, and cold by turns, but Mr M'Leod the seller easily met and surpassed us; and Mr Baxter entered every letter, telegram, and consultation at the proper rates in a cinematograph-film of a bill. At the end of a month he said it looked as though M'Leod, thanks to him, were really going to listen to reason. I was some pounds out of pocket, but I had learned something of Mr Baxter on the human side. I deserved it. Never in my life have I worked to conciliate, amuse, and flatter a human being as I worked over my solicitor.

It appeared that he golfed. Therefore, I was an enthusiastic beginner, anxious to learn. Twice I invaded his office with a bag (M'Leod lent it) full of the spelicans needed in this detestable game, and a vocabulary to match. The third time the ice broke, and Mr Baxter took me to his links, quite ten miles off, where in a maze of tramway-lines, railroads, and nursery-maids, we skelped our divoted way round nine holes like barges plunging through head seas. He played vilely and had never expected to meet anyone worse; but as he realized my form, I think he began to like me, for he took me in hand by the two hours together. After a fortnight he could give me no more than a stroke a hole, and when, with this allowance, I once managed to beat him by one, he was honestly glad, and assured me that I should be a golfer if I stuck to it. I was sticking to it for my own ends, but now and again my conscience pricked me; for the man was a nice man. Between games he supplied me with odd pieces of evidence, such as that he had known the Moultries all his life, being their cousin, and that Miss Mary, the eldest, was an unforgiving woman who would never let bygones be. I naturally wondered what she might have against him; and somehow connected him unfavourably with mad Agnes.

'People ought to forgive and forget,' he volunteered one day between rounds. 'Specially where, in the nature of things, they can't be sure of their deductions. Don't you think so?'

'It all depends on the nature of the evidence on which one forms one's judgement,' I answered.

'Nonsense!' he cried. 'I'm lawyer enough to know that there's nothing in the world so misleading as circumstantial evidence. Never was.'

'Why? Have you ever seen men hanged on it?'

'Hanged? People have been supposed to be eternally lost on it.' His face turned grey again. 'I don't know how it is with you, but my consolation is that God must know. He *must*! Things that seem on the face of 'em like murder, or say suicide, may appear different to God. Heh?'

'That's what the murderer and the suicide can always hope—I suppose.'

'I have expressed myself clumsily as usual. The facts as God knows 'em—may *be* different—even after the most clinching evidence. I've always said that—both as a lawyer and a man, but some people won't—I don't want to judge 'em—we'll say they can't—believe it; whereas *I* say there's always a working chance— a certainty—that the worst hasn't happened.' He stopped and cleared his throat. 'Now, let's come on! This time next week I shall be taking my holiday.'

'What links?' I asked carelessly, while twins in a perambulator got out of our line of fire.

'A potty little nine-hole affair at a Hydro in the Midlands. My cousins stay there. Always will. Not but what the fourth and the seventh holes take some doing. You could manage it, though,' he said encouragingly. 'You're doing much better. It's only your approach-shots that are weak.'

'You're right. I can't approach for nuts! I shall go to pieces while you're away—with no one to coach me,' I said mournfully.

'I haven't taught you anything,' he said, delighted with the compliment.

'I owe all I've learned to you, anyhow. When will you come back?'

'Look here,' he began. 'I don't know your engagements, but I've no one to play with at Burry Mills. Never have. Why couldn't you take a few days off and join me there? I warn you it will be rather dull. It's a throat and gout place—baths, massage, electricity, and so forth. But the fourth and the seventh holes really take some doing.'

'I'm for the game,' I answered valiantly, Heaven well knowing that I hated every stroke and word of it.

'That's the proper spirit. As their lawyer I must ask you not to say anything to my cousins about Holmescroft. It upsets 'em. Always did. But speaking as man to man, it would be very pleasant for me if you could see your way to——'

I saw it as soon as decency permitted, and thanked him sincerely. According to my now well-developed theory he had certainly mis-appropriated his aged cousins' monies under power of attorney, and had probably driven poor Agnes Moultrie out of her wits, but I wished that he was not so gentle, and good-tempered, and innocent-eyed.

Before I joined him at Burry Mills Hydro, I spent a night at Holmescroft. Miss M'Leod had returned from her Hydro, and first we made very merry on the open lawn in the sunshine over the manners and customs of the English resorting to such places. She knew dozens of Hydros, and warned me how to behave in them, while Mr and Mrs M'Leod stood aside and adored her.

'Ah! That's the way she always comes back to us,' he said. 'Pity it wears off so soon, ain't it? You ought to hear her sing "With mirth, thou pretty bird." '

We had the house to face through the evening, and there we neither laughed nor sang. The gloom fell on us as we entered, and did not shift till ten o'clock, when we crawled out, as it were, from beneath it.

'It has been bad this summer,' said Mrs M'Leod in a whisper after we realized that we were freed. 'Sometimes I think the house will get up and cry out—it is so bad.'

'How?'

'Have you forgotten what comes after the depression?'

So then we waited about the small fire, and the dead air in the room presently filled and pressed down upon us with the sensation (but words are useless here) as though some dumb and bound power were striving against gag and bond to deliver its soul of an articulate word. It passed in a few minutes, and I fell to thinking about Mr Baxter's conscience and Agnes Moultrie, gone mad in the well-lit bedroom that waited me. These reflections secured me a night during which I rediscovered how, from purely mental causes, a man can be physically sick. But the sickness was bliss compared with my dreams when the birds waked. On my departure, M'Leod gave me a beautiful narwhal's horn much as a nurse gives a child sweets for being brave at a dentist's.

'There's no duplicate of it in the world,' he said, 'else it would have come to old Max M'Leod,' and he tucked it into the motor. Miss M'Leod on the far side of the car whispered, 'Have you found out anything, Mr Perseus?'

I shook my head.

'Then I shall be chained to my rock all my life,' she went on. 'Only don't tell papa.'

I supposed she was thinking of the young gentleman who specialized in South American rails, for I noticed a ring on the third finger of her left hand.

I went straight from that house to Burry Mills Hydro, keen for the first time in my life on playing golf, which is guaranteed to occupy the mind. Baxter had taken me a room communicating with his own, and after lunch introduced me to a tall, horse-headed elderly lady of decided manners, whom a white-haired maid pushed along in a bath-chair through the park-like grounds of the Hydro. She was Miss Mary Moultrie, and she coughed and cleared her throat just like Baxter. She suffered—she told me it was the Moultrie caste-mark—from some obscure form of chronic bronchitis, complicated with spasm of the glottis; and, in a dead flat voice, with a sunken eye that looked and saw not, told me what washes, gargles, pastilles, and inhalations she had proved most beneficial. From her I was passed on to her younger sister, Miss Elizabeth, a small and withered thing with twitching lips, victim, she told me, to very much the same sort of throat, but secretly devoted to another set of medicines. When she went away with Baxter and the bath-chair, I fell across a Major of the Indian Army with gout in his glassy eyes, and a stomach which he had taken all round the Continent. He laid everything before me; and him I escaped only to be confided in by a matron with a tendency to follicular tonsilitis and eczema. Baxter waited hand and foot on his cousins till five o'clock, trying, as I saw, to atone for his treatment of the dead sister. Miss Mary ordered him about like a dog.

'I warned you it would be dull,' he said when we met in the smoking-room.

'It's tremendously interesting,' I said. 'But how about a look round the links?'

'Unluckily damp always affects my eldest cousin. I've got to buy her a new bronchitis-kettle. Arthurs broke her old one yesterday.'

We slipped out to the chemist's shop in the town, and he bought a large glittering tin thing whose workings he explained.

'I'm used to this sort of work. I come up here pretty often,' he said. 'I've the family throat too.'

'You're a good man,' I said. 'A very good man.'

He turned towards me in the evening light among the beeches, and his face was changed to what it might have been a generation before.

'You see,' he said huskily, 'there was the youngest—Agnes. Before she fell ill, you know. But she didn't like leaving her sisters. Never would.' He hurried on with his odd-shaped load and left me among the ruins of my black theories. The man with that face had done Agnes Moultrie no wrong.

*

We never played our game. I was waked between two and three in the morning from my hygienic bed by Baxter in an ulster over orange-and-white pyjamas, which I should never have suspected from his character.

'My cousin has had some sort of a seizure,' he said. 'Will you come? I don't want to wake the doctor. Don't want to make a scandal. Quick!'

So I came quickly, and, led by the white-haired Arthurs in a jacket and petticoat, entered a double-bedded room reeking with steam and Friar's Balsam. The electrics were all on. Miss Mary—I knew her by her height—was at the open window, wrestling with Miss Elizabeth,who gripped her round the knees. Her hand was at her throat, which was streaked with blood.

'She's done it. She's done it too!' Miss Elizabeth panted. 'Hold her! Help me!'

'Oh, I say! Women don't cut their throats,' Baxter whispered.

'My God! Has she cut her throat?' the maid cried, and with no warning rolled over in a faint. Baxter pushed her under the wash-basins, and leaped to hold the gaunt woman who crowed and whistled as she struggled towards the window. He took her by the shoulder, and she struck out wildly.

'All right! She's only cut her hand,' he said. 'Wet towel—quick!'

While I got that he pushed her backward. Her strength seemed almost as great as his. I swabbed at her throat when I could, and found no mark; then helped him to control her a little. Miss Elizabeth leaped back to bed, wailing like a child.

'Tie up her hand somehow,' said Baxter. 'Don't let it drip about the place. She'—he stepped on broken glass in his slippers—'she must have smashed a pane.'

Miss Mary lurched towards the open window again, dropped on her knees, her head on the sill, and lay quiet, surrendering the cut hand to me.

'What did she do?' Baxter turned towards Miss Elizabeth in the far bed.

'She was going to throw herself out of the window,' was the answer. 'I stopped her, and sent Arthurs for you. Oh, we can never hold up our heads again!'

Miss Mary writhed and fought for breath. Baxter found a shawl which he threw over her shoulders.

'Nonsense!' said he. 'That isn't like Mary'; but his face worked when he said it.

'You wouldn't believe about Aggie, John. Perhaps you will now!'

said Miss Elizabeth. 'I *saw* her do it, and she's cut her throat too!'

'She hasn't,' I said. 'It's only her hand.'

Miss Mary suddenly broke from us with an indescribable grunt, flew, rather than ran, to her sister's bed, and there shook her as one furious schoolgirl would shake another.

'No such thing,' she croaked. 'How dare you think so, you wicked little fool?'

'Get into bed, Mary,' said Baxter. 'You'll catch a chill.'

She obeyed, but sat up with the grey shawl round her lean shoulders, glaring at her sister. 'I'm better now,' she crowed. 'Arthurs let me sit out too long. Where's Arthurs? The kettle.'

'Never mind Arthurs,' said Baxter. '*You* get the kettle.' I hastened to bring it from the side-table. 'Now, Mary, as God sees you, tell me what you've done.'

His lips were dry, and he could not moisten them with his tongue.

Miss Mary applied herself to the mouth of the kettle, and between indraws of steam said: 'The spasm came on just now, while I was asleep. I was nearly choking to death. So I went to the window. I've done it often before, without waking anyone. Bessie's such an old maid about draughts! I tell you I was choking to death. I couldn't manage the catch, and I nearly fell out. That window opens too low. I cut my hand trying to save myself. Who has tied it up in this filthy handkerchief? I wish you had had my throat, Bessie. I never was nearer dying!' She scowled on us all impartially, while her sister sobbed.

From the bottom of the bed we heard a quivering voice: 'Is she dead? Have they took her away? Oh, I never could bear the sight o' blood!'

'Arthurs,' said Miss Mary, 'you are an hireling. Go away!'

It is my belief that Arthurs crawled out on all fours, but I was busy picking up broken glass from the carpet.

Then Baxter, seated by the side of the bed, began to cross-examine in a voice I scarcely recognized. No one could for an instant have doubted the genuine rage of Miss Mary against her sister, her cousin, or her maid; and that the doctor should have been called in —for she did me the honour of calling me doctor—was the last drop. She was choking with her throat; had rushed to the window for air; had nearly pitched out, and in catching at the window-bars had cut her hand. Over and over she made this clear to the intent Baxter. Then she turned on her sister and tongue-lashed her savagely.

'You mustn't blame me,' Miss Bessie faltered at last. 'You know
what we think of night and day.'

'I'm coming to that,' said Baxter. 'Listen to me. What *you* did,
Mary, misled four people into thinking you—you meant to do away
with yourself.'

'Isn't one suicide in the family enough? Oh, God, help and pity
us! You *couldn't* have believed that!' she cried.

'The evidence was complete. Now, don't you think'—Baxter's
finger wagged under her nose—'*can't* you think that poor Aggie did
the same thing at Holmescroft when she fell out of the window?'

'She had the same throat,' said Miss Elizabeth. 'Exactly the
same symptoms. Don't you remember, Mary?'

'Which was her bedroom?' I asked of Baxter in an undertone.

'Over the south veranda, looking on to the tennis lawn.'

'I nearly fell out of that very window when I was at Holmescroft
—opening it to get some air. The sill doesn't come much above your
knees,' I said.

'You hear that, Mary? Mary, do you hear what this gentleman
says? Won't you believe that what nearly happened to you must
have happened to poor Aggie that night? For God's sake—for her
sake—Mary, *won't* you believe?'

There was a long silence while the steam-kettle puffed.

'If I could have proof—if I could have proof,' said she, and broke
into most horrible tears.

Baxter motioned to me, and I crept away to my room, and lay
awake till morning, thinking more specially of the dumb Thing at
Holmescroft which wished to explain itself. I hated Miss Mary as
perfectly as though I had known her for twenty years, but I felt
that, alive or dead, I should not like her to condemn me.

Yet at mid-day, when I saw Miss Mary in her bath-chair,
Arthurs behind and Baxter and Miss Elizabeth on either side, in the
park-like grounds of the Hydro, I found it difficult to arrange my
words.

'Now that you know all about it,' said Baxter aside, after the
first strangeness of our meeting was over, 'it's only fair to tell you
that my poor cousin did not die *in* Holmescroft at all. She was dead
when they found her under the window in the morning. Just dead.'

'Under that laburnum outside the window?' I asked, for I suddenly remembered the crooked evil thing.

'Exactly. She broke the tree in falling. But no death has ever
taken place *in* the house, so far as we were concerned. You can
make yourself quite easy on that point. Mr M'Leod's extra thousand

for what you called the "clean bill of health" was something towards my cousins' estate when we sold. It was my duty as their lawyer to get it for them—at any cost to my own feelings.'

I know better than to argue when the English talk about their duty. So I agreed with my solicitor.

'Their sister's death must have been a great blow to your cousins,' I went on. The bath-chair was behind me.

'Unspeakable,' Baxter whispered. 'They brooded on it day and night. No wonder. If their theory of poor Aggie making away with herself was correct, she was eternally lost!'

'Do you believe that she made away with herself?'

'No, thank God! Never have! And after what happened to Mary last night, I see perfectly what happened to poor Aggie. She had the family throat too. By the way, Mary thinks you are a doctor. Otherwise she wouldn't like your having been in her room.'

'Very good. Is she convinced now about her sister's death?'

'She'd give anything to be able to believe it, but she's a hard woman, and brooding along certain lines makes one groovy. I have sometimes been afraid for her reason—on the religious side, don't you know. Elizabeth doesn't matter. Brain of a hen. Always had.'

Here Arthurs summoned me to the bath-chair, and the ravaged face, beneath its knitted Shetland wool hood, of Miss Mary Moultrie.

'I need not remind you, I hope, of the seal of secrecy—absolute secrecy—in your profession,' she began. 'Thanks to my cousin's and my sister's stupidity, you have found out——' She blew her nose.

'Please don't excite her, sir,' said Arthurs at the back.

'But, my dear Miss Moultrie, I only know what I've seen, of course, but it seems to me that what you thought was a tragedy in your sister's case, turns out, on your own evidence, so to speak, to have been an accident—a dreadfully sad one—but absolutely an accident.'

'Do you believe that too?' she cried. 'Or are you only saying it to comfort me?'

'I believe it from the bottom of my heart. Come down to Holmescroft for an hour—for half an hour—and satisfy yourself.'

'Of what? You don't understand. I see the house every day—every night. I am always there in spirit—waking or sleeping. I couldn't face it in reality.'

'But you must,' I said. 'If you go there in the spirit the greater need for you to go there in the flesh. Go to your sister's room once more, and see the window—I nearly fell out of it myself. It's—it's awfully low and dangerous. That would convince you,' I pleaded.

'Yet Aggie had slept in that room for years,' she interrupted.

'You've slept in your room here for a long time, haven't you? But you nearly fell out of the window when you were choking.'

'That is true. That is one thing true,' she nodded. 'And I might have been killed as—perhaps—Aggie was killed.'

'In that case your own sister and cousin and maid would have said you had committed suicide, Miss Moultrie. Come down to Holmescroft, and go over the place just once.'

'You are lying,' she said quite quietly. 'You don't want me to come down to see a window. It is something else. I warn you we are Evangelicals. We don't believe in prayers for the dead. "As the tree falls——"'

'Yes. I daresay. But you persist in thinking that your sister committed suicide——'

'No! No! I have always prayed that I might have misjudged her.'

Arthurs at the bath-chair spoke up: 'Oh, Miss Mary! you *would* 'ave it from the first that poor Miss Aggie 'ad made away with herself; an', of course, Miss Bessie took the notion from y ou Only Master—Mister John stood out, and—and I'd 'ave taken my Bible oath *you* was making away with yourself last night.'

Miss Mary leaned towards me, one finger on my sleeve.

'If going to Holmescroft kills me,' she said, 'you will have the murder of a fellow-creature on your conscience for all eternity.'

'I'll risk it,' I answered. Remembering what torment the mere reflection of her torments had cast on Holmescroft, and remembering, above all, the dumb Thing that filled the house with its desire to speak, I felt that there might be worse things.

Baxter was amazed at the proposed visit, but at a nod from that terrible woman went off to make arrangements. Then I sent a telegram to M'Leod bidding him and his vacate Holmescroft for that afternoon. Miss Mary should be alone with her dead, as I had been alone.

I expected untold trouble in transporting her, but to do her justice, her promise given for the journey, she underwent it without murmur, spasm, or unnecessary word. Miss Bessie, pressed in a corner by the window, wept behind her veil, and from time to time tried to take hold of her sister's hand. Baxter wrapped himself in his newly-found happiness as selfishly as a bridegroom, for he sat still and smiled.

'So long as I know that Aggie didn't make away with herself,' he explained, 'I tell you frankly I don't care what happened. She's as hard as a rock—Mary. Always was. *She* won't die.'

We led her out on to the platform like a blind woman, and so got her into the fly. The half-hour crawl to Holmescroft was the most racking experience of the day. M'Leod had obeyed my instructions. There was no one visible in the house or the gardens; and the front door stood open.

Miss Mary rose from beside her sister, stepped forth first, and entered the hall.

'Come, Bessie,' she cried.

'I daren't. Oh, I daren't.'

'Come!' Her voice had altered. I felt Baxter start. 'There's nothing to be afraid of.'

'Good heavens!' said Baxter. 'She's running up the stairs. We'd better follow.'

'Let's wait below. She's going to the room.'

We heard the door of the bedroom I knew open and shut, and we waited in the lemon-coloured hall, heavy with the scent of flowers.

'I've never been into it since it was sold,' Baxter sighed. 'What a lovely restful place it is! Poor Aggie used to arrange the flowers.'

'Restful?' I began, but stopped of a sudden, for I felt all over my bruised soul that Baxter was speaking truth. It was a light, spacious, airy house, full of the sense of well-being and peace—above all things, of peace. I ventured into the dining-room where the thoughtful M'Leods had left a small fire. There was no terror there present or lurking; and in the drawing-room, which for good reasons we had never cared to enter, the sun and the peace and the scent of the flowers worked together as is fit in an inhabited house. When I returned to the hall, Baxter was sweetly asleep on a couch, looking most unlike a middle-aged solicitor who had spent a broken night with an exacting cousin.

There was ample time for me to review it all—to felicitate myself upon my magnificent acumen (barring some errors about Baxter as a thief and possibly a murderer), before the door above opened, and Baxter, evidently a light sleeper, sprang awake.

'I've had a heavenly little nap,' he said, rubbing his eyes with the backs of his hands like a child. 'Good Lord! That's not *their* step!'

But it was. I had never before been privileged to see the Shadow turned backward on the dial—the years ripped bodily off poor human shoulders—old sunken eyes filled and alight—harsh lips moistened and human.

'John,' Miss Mary called, 'I know now. Aggie didn't do it!' and 'She didn't do it!' echoed Miss Bessie, and giggled.

'I did not think it wrong to say a prayer,' Miss Mary continued. 'Not for her soul, but for our peace. Then I was convinced.'

'Then we got conviction,' the younger sister piped.

'We've misjudged poor Aggie, John. But I feel she knows now. Wherever she is, she knows that we know she is guiltless.'

'Yes, she knows. I felt it too,' said Miss Elizabeth.

'I never doubted,' said John Baxter, whose face was beautiful at that hour. 'Not from the first. Never have!'

'You never offered me proof, John. Now, thank God, it will not be the same any more. I can think henceforward of Aggie without sorrow.' She tripped, absolutely tripped, across the hall. 'What ideas these Jews have of arranging furniture!' She spied me behind a big cloisonné vase.

'I've seen the window,' she said remotely. 'You took a great risk in advising me to undertake such a journey. However, as it turns out . . . I forgive you, and I pray you may never know what mental anguish means! Bessie! Look at this peculiar piano! Do you suppose, Doctor, these people would offer one tea? I miss mine.'

'I will go and see,' I said, and explored M'Leod's new-built servants' wing. It was in the servants' hall that I unearthed the M'Leod family bursting with anxiety.

'Tea for three, quick,' I said. 'If you ask me any questions now, I shall have a fit!' So Mrs M'Leod got it, and I was butler, amid murmured apologies from Baxter, still smiling and self-absorbed, and the cold disapproval of Miss Mary, who thought the pattern of the china vulgar. However, she ate well, and even asked me whether I would not like a cup of tea for myself.

They went away in the twilight—the twilight that I had once feared. They were going to an hotel in London to rest after the fatigues of the day, and as their fly turned down the drive, I capered on the doorstep, with the all-darkened house behind me.

Then I heard the uncertain feet of the M'Leods, and bade them not to turn on the lights, but to feel—to feel what I had done; for the Shadow was gone, with the dumb desire in the air. They drew short, but afterwards deeper, breaths, like bathers entering chill water, separated one from the other, moved about the hall, tiptoed upstairs, raced down, and then Miss M'Leod, and I believe her mother, though she denies this, embraced me. I know M'Leod did.

It was a disgraceful evening. To say we rioted through the house is to put it mildly. We played a sort of Blind Man's Buff along the darkest passages, in the unlighted drawing-room, and the little dining-room, calling cheerily to each other after each exploration that here, and here, and here, the trouble had removed itself. We came up to *the* bedroom—mine for the night again—and sat, the women on the bed, and we men on chairs, drinking in blessed draughts of peace and comfort and cleanliness of soul, while I told them my tale in full, and received fresh praise, thanks, and blessing.

When the servants, returned from their day's outing, gave us a supper of cold fried fish, M'Leod had sense enough to open no wine. We had been practically drunk, since nightfall, and grew incoherent on water and milk.

'I like that Baxter,' said M'Leod. 'He's a sharp man. The death wasn't *in* the house, but he ran it pretty close, ain't it?'

'And the joke of it is that he supposes I want to buy the place from you,' I said. 'Are you selling?'

'Not for twice what I paid for it—now,' said M'Leod. 'I'll keep you in furs all your life; but not our Holmescroft.'

'No—never our Holmescroft,' said Miss M'Leod. 'We'll ask *him* here on Tuesday, mamma.' They squeezed each other's hands.

'Now tell me,' said Mrs M'Leod—'that tall one I saw out of the scullery window—did *she* tell you she was always here in the spirit? I hate her. She made all this trouble. It was *not* her house after she had sold it. What do you think?'

'I suppose,' I answered, 'she brooded over what she believed was her sister's suicide night and day—she confessed she did—and her thoughts being concentrated on this place, they felt like a—like a burning-glass.'

'Burning-glass is good,' said M'Leod.

'I said it was like a light of blackness turned on us,' cried the girl, twiddling her ring. 'That must have been when the tall one thought worst about her sister and the house.'

'Ah, the poor Aggie!' said Mrs M'Leod. 'The poor Aggie, trying to tell everyone it was not so! No wonder we felt Something wished to say Something. Thea, Max, do you remember that night——'

'We need not remember any more,' M'Leod interrupted. 'It is not our trouble. They have told each other now.'

'Do you think, then,' said Miss M'Leod, 'that those two, the living ones, were actually told something—upstairs—in your—in the room?'

'I can't say. At any rate they were made happy, and they ate a big tea afterwards. As your father says, it is not our trouble any longer—thank God!'

'Amen!' said M'Leod. 'Now, Thea, let us have some music after all these months. "With mirth, thou pretty bird," ain't it? You ought to hear that.'

And in the half-lighted hall, Thea sang an old English song that I had never heard before:

> With mirth, thou pretty bird, rejoice
>   Thy Maker's praise enhancèd;
> Lift up thy shrill and pleasant voice,
>   Thy God is high advancèd!
> Thy Food before He did provide,
> And gives it in a fitting side,
>   Wherewith be thou sufficèd!
> Why shouldst thou now unpleasant be,
>   Thy wrath against God venting,
> That He a little bird made thee,
>   Thy silly head tormenting,
> Because He made thee not a man?
> Oh, Peace! He hath well thought thereon,
>   Therewith be thou sufficèd!

Actions and Reactions, 1909

Regulus

Regulus, a Roman general, defeated the Carthaginians 256 B.C., but was next year defeated and taken prisoner by the Carthaginians, who sent him to Rome with an embassy to ask for peace or an exchange of prisoners. Regulus strongly advised the Roman Senate to make no terms with the enemy. He then returned to Carthage and was put to death.

THE FIFTH FORM had been dragged several times in its collective life, from one end of the school Horace to the other. Those were the years when Army examiners gave thousands of marks for Latin, and it was Mr King's hated business to defeat them.

Hear him, then, on a raw November morning at second lesson.

'Aha!' he began, rubbing his hands. '*Cras ingens iterabimus aequor.* Our portion today is the Fifth Ode of the Third Book, I believe—concerning one Regulus, a gentleman. And how often have we been through it?'

'Twice, sir,' said Malpass, head of the Form.

Mr King shuddered. 'Yes, twice, quite literally,' he said. 'Today, with an eye to your Army *viva-voce* examinations—ugh!—I shall exact somewhat freer and more florid renditions. With feeling and comprehension if that be possible. I except'—here his eye swept the back benches—'our friend and companion Beetle, from whom, now as always, I demand an absolutely literal translation.' The Form laughed subserviently.

'Spare his blushes! Beetle charms us first.'

Beetle stood up, confident in the possession of a guaranteed construe, left behind by M'Turk, who had that day gone into the sick-house with a cold. Yet he was too wary a hand to show confidence.

'*Credidimus,* we—believe—we have believed,' he opened in hesitating slow time, '*tonantem Jovem,* thundering Jove—*regnare,* to reign—*caelo,* in heaven. *Augustus,* Augustus—*habebitur,* will be held or considered—*praesens divus,* a present God—*adjectis Britannis,* the Britons being added—*imperio,* to the Empire—*gravibusque Persis,* with the heavy—er—stern Persians.'

'What?'

'The grave or stern Persians.' Beetle pulled up with the 'Thank-God-I-have-done-my-duty' air of Nelson in the cockpit.

'I am quite aware,' said King, 'that the first stanza is about the extent of your knowledge, but continue, sweet one, continue. *Gravibus*, by the way, is usually translated as "troublesome." '

Beetle drew a long and tortured breath. The second stanza (which carries over to the third) of that Ode is what is technically called a 'stinker.' But M'Turk had done him handsomely.

'*Milesne Crassi*, had—has the soldier of Crassus—*vixit*, lived—*turpis maritus*, a disgraceful husband——'

'You slurred the quantity of the word after *turpis*,' said King. 'Let's hear it.'

Beetle guessed again, and for a wonder hit the correct quantity. 'Er—a disgraceful husband—*conjuge barbara*, with a barbarous spouse.'

'Why do you select *that* disgustful equivalent out of all the dictionary?' King snapped. 'Isn't "wife" good enough for you?'

'Yes, sir. But what do I do about this bracket, sir? Shall I take it now?'

'Confine yourself at present to the soldier of Crassus.'

'Yes, sir. *Et*, and—*consenuit*, has he grown old—*in armis*, in the—er—arms—*hostium socerorum*, of his father-in-law's enemies.'

'Who? How? Which?'

'Arms of his enemies' fathers-in-law, sir.'

'Tha-anks. By the way, what meaning might you attach to *in armis*?'

'Oh, weapons—weapons of war, sir.' There was a virginal note in Beetle's voice as though he had been falsely accused of uttering indecencies. 'Shall I take the bracket now, sir?'

'Since it seems to be troubling you.'

'*Pro Curia*, O for the Senate House—*inversique mores*, and manners upset—upside down.'

'Ve-ry like your translation. Meantime, the soldier of Crassus?'

'*Sub rege Medo*, under a Median King—*Marsus et Apulus*, he being a Marsian and an Apulian.'

'Who? The Median King?'

'No, sir. The soldier of Crassus. *Oblittus* agrees with *milesne Crassi*, sir,' volunteered too hasty Beetle.

'Does it? It doesn't with *me*.'

'*Oh-blight-us*,' Beetle corrected hastily, 'forgetful—*anciliorum*, of the shields, or trophies—*et nominis*, and the—his name—*et togae*, and the toga—*eternaeque Vestae*, and eternal Vesta—*incolumi Jove*, Jove being safe—*et urbe Roma*, and the Roman city.' With an air of hardly restrained zeal—'Shall I go on, sir?'

Mr King winced. 'No, thank you. You have indeed given us a

translation! May I ask if it conveys any meaning whatever to your so-called mind?'

'Oh, I think so, sir.' This with gentle toleration for Horace and all his works.

'We envy you. Sit down.'

Beetle sat down relieved, well knowing that a reef of uncharted genitives stretched ahead of him, on which in spite of M'Turk's sailing-directions he would infallibly have been wrecked.

Rattray, who took up the task, steered neatly through them and came unscathed to port.

'Here we require drama,' said King. 'Regulus himself is speaking now. Who shall represent the provident-minded Regulus? Winton, will you kindly oblige?'

Winton of King's House, a long, heavy, tow-headed Second Fifteen forward, overdue for his First Fifteen colours, and in aspect like an earnest, elderly horse, rose up, and announced, among other things, that he had seen 'signs affixed to Punic deluges.' Half the Form shouted for joy, and the other half for joy that there was something to shout about.

Mr King opened and shut his eyes with great swiftness. '*Signa adfixa delubris*,' he gasped. 'So *delubris* is "deluges," is it? Winton, in all our dealings, have I ever suspected you of a jest?'

'No, sir,' said the rigid and angular Winton, while the Form rocked about him.

'And yet you assert *delubris* means "deluges." Whether I am a fit subject for such a jape is, of course, a matter of opinion, but. . . . Winton, you are normally conscientious. May we assume you looked out *delubris*?'

'No, sir.' Winton was privileged to speak that truth dangerous to all who stand before Kings.

'Made a shot at it then?'

Every line of Winton's body showed he had done nothing of the sort. Indeed, the very idea that 'Pater' Winton (and a boy is not called 'Pater' by companions for his frivolity) would make a shot at anything was beyond belief. But he replied, 'Yes,' and all the while worked with his right heel as though he were heeling a ball at puntabout.

Though none dared to boast of being a favourite with King, the taciturn, three-cornered Winton stood high in his House-master's opinion. It seemed to save him neither rebuke nor punishment, but the two were in some fashion sympathetic.

'Hm!' said King drily. 'I was going to say—*Flagitio additis*

damnum, but I think—I think I see the process. Beetle, the translation of *delubris*, please.'

Beetle raised his head from his shaking arm long enough to
answer: 'Ruins, sir.'

There was an impressive pause while King checked off crimes
on his fingers. Then to Beetle the much-enduring man addressed
winged words:

'Guessing,' said he—'Guessing, Beetle, as usual, from the look of
delubris that it bore some relation to *diluvium* or deluge, you im-
parted the result of your half-baked lucubrations to Winton, who
seems to have been lost enough to have accepted it. Observing,
next, your companion's fall, from the presumed security of your un-
distinguished position in the rear-guard, you took another pot-shot.
The turbid chaos of your mind threw up some memory of the word
"dilapidations" which you have pitifully attempted to disguise
under the synonym of "ruins." '

As this was precisely what Beetle had done he looked hurt but
forgiving. 'We will attend to this later,' said King. 'Go on, Winton,
and retrieve yourself.'

Delubris happened to be the one word which Winton had not
looked out and had asked Beetle for, when they were settling into
their places. He forged ahead with no further trouble. Only when he
rendered *scilicet* as 'forsooth,' King erupted.

'Regulus,' he said, 'was *not* a leader-writer for the penny press,
nor, for that matter, was Horace. Regulus says: "The soldier ran-
somed by gold will come keener for the fight—will he, by—by
Gum!" *That's* the meaning of *scilicet*. It indicates contempt—bitter
contempt. "Forsooth," forsooth! You'll be talking about "speckled
beauties" and "eventually transpire" next. Howell, what do you
make of that doubled *Vidi ego—ego vidi*? It wasn't put in to fill up
the metre, you know.'

'Isn't it intensive, sir?' said Howell, afflicted by a genuine interest
in what he read. 'Regulus was a bit in earnest about Rome making
no terms with Carthage—and he wanted to let the Romans understand it, didn't he, sir?'

'Less than your usual grace, but the fact. Regulus *was* in earnest.
He was also engaged at the same time in cutting his own throat with
every word he uttered. He knew Carthage, which (your examiners
won't ask you this, so you needn't take notes) was a sort of God-
forsaken nigger Manchester. Regulus was not thinking about his
own life. He was telling Rome the truth. He was playing for his side.
Those lines from the eighteenth to the fortieth ought to be written

in blood. Yet there are things in human garments which will tell you
that Horace was a *flâneur*—a man about town. Avoid such beings.
Horace knew a very great deal. *He* knew! *Erit ille fortis*—"will he be
brave who once to faithless foes has knelt?" And again (stop pawing
with your hooves, Thornton!) *hic unde vitam sumeret inscius.* That
means roughly—but I perceive I am ahead of my translators. Begin
at *hic unde*, Vernon, and let us see if you have the spirit of Regulus.'

Now no one expected fireworks from gentle Paddy Vernon, sub-
prefect of Hartopp's House, but, as must often be the case with
growing boys, his mind was in abeyance for the time being, and he
said, all in a rush, on behalf of Regulus: '*O magna Carthago probrosis
altior Italiae ruinis,* O Carthage, thou wilt stand forth higher than
the ruins of Italy.'

Even Beetle, most lenient of critics, was interested at this point,
though he did not join the half-groan of reprobation from the wiser
heads of the Form.

'*Please* don't mind me,' said King, and Vernon very kindly did
not. He ploughed on thus: 'He (Regulus) is related to have removed
from himself the kiss of the shameful wife and of his small children
as less by the head, and, being stern, to have placed his virile visage
on the ground.'

Since King loved 'virile' about as much as he did 'spouse' or 'forsooth' the Form looked up hopefully. But Jove thundered not.

'Until,' Vernon continued, 'he should have confirmed the sliding
fathers as being the author of counsel never given under an alias.'

He stopped, conscious of stillness round him like the dread calm of
the typhoon's centre. King's opening voice was sweeter than honey.

'I am painfully aware by bitter experience that I cannot give you
any idea of the passion, the power, the—the essential guts of the lines
which you have so foully outraged in our presence. But——' the
note changed, 'so far as in me lies, I will strive to bring home to you,
Vernon, the fact that there exist in Latin a few pitiful rules of grammar, of syntax, nay, even of declension, which were not created for
your incult sport—your Boetian diversion. You will, therefore, Vernon, write out and bring to me tomorrow a word-for-word English–
Latin translation of the Ode, together with a full list of all adjectives—an adjective is not a verb, Vernon, as the Lower Third will
tell you—all adjectives, their number, case, and gender. Even now
I haven't begun to deal with you faithfully.'

'I—I'm very sorry, sir,' Vernon stammered.

'You mistake the symptoms, Vernon. You are possibly discom-
fited by the imposition, but sorrow postulates some sort of mind,

intellect, *nous.* Your rendering of *probrosis* alone stamps you as lower than the beasts of the field. Will someone take the taste out of our mouths? And—talking of tastes——' He coughed. There was a distinct flavour of chlorine gas in the air. Up went an eyebrow, though King knew perfectly well what it meant.

'Mr Hartopp's Sti—Science class next door,' said Malpass.

'Oh yes. I had forgotten. Our newly established Modern Side, of course. Perowne, open the windows; and Winton, go on once more from *interque maerentes.*'

'And hastened away,' said Winton, 'surrounded by his mourning friends, into—into illustrious banishment. But I got that out of Conington, sir,' he added in one conscientious breath.

'I am aware. The master generally knows his ass's crib, though I acquit *you* of any intention that way. Can you suggest anything for *egregius exul*? Only "egregious exile"? I fear "egregious" is a good word ruined. No! You can't in this case improve on Conington. Now then for *atqui sciebat quae sibi barbarus tortor pararet.* The whole force of it lies in the *atqui.*'

'Although he knew,' Winton suggested.

'Stronger than that, I think.'

'He who knew well,' Malpass interpolated.

'Ye-es. "Well though he knew." I don't like Conington's "well-witting." It's Wardour Street.'

'Well though he knew what the savage torturer was—was getting ready for him,' said Winton.

'Ye-es. Had in store for him.'

'Yet he brushed aside his kinsmen and the people delaying his return.'

'Ye-es; but then how do you render *obstantes*?'

'If it's a free translation mightn't *obstantes* and *morantem* come to about the same thing, sir?'

'Nothing comes to "about the same thing" with Horace, Winton. As I have said, Horace was not a journalist. No, I take it that his kinsmen bodily withstood his departure, whereas the crowd—*populumque*—the democracy stood about futilely pitying him and getting in the way. Now for that noblest of endings—*quam si clientum,*' and King ran off into the quotation:

> *'As though, some tedious business o'er*
> *Of clients' court, his journey lay*
> *Towards Venafrum's grassy floor*
> *Or Sparta-built Tarentum's bay.*

All right, Winton. Beetle, when you've quite finished dodging the fresh air yonder, give me the meaning of *tendens*—and turn down your collar.'

'Me, sir? *Tendens*, sir? Oh! Stretching away in the direction of, sir.'

'Idiot! Regulus was not a feature of the landscape. He was a man, self-doomed to death by torture. *Atqui sciebat*—knowing it—having it—having achieved it for his country's sake—can't you hear that *atqui* cut like a knife?—he moved off with some dignity. That is why Horace out of the whole golden Latin tongue chose the one word *tendens*—which is utterly untranslatable.'

The gross injustice of being asked to translate it converted Beetle into a young Christian martyr, till King buried his nose in his handkerchief again.

'I think they've broken another gas-bottle next door, sir,' said Howell. 'They're always doing it.' The Form coughed as more chlorine came in.

'Well, I suppose we must be patient with the Modern Side,' said King. 'But it is almost insupportable for this Side. Vernon, what are you grinning at?'

Vernon's mind had returned to him glowing and inspired. He chuckled as he underlined his Horace.

'It appears to amuse you,' said King. 'Let us participate. What is it?'

'The last two lines of the Tenth Ode, in this Book, sir,' was Vernon's amazing reply.

'What? Oh, I see. *Non hoc semper erit liminis aut aquae caelestis patiens latus.*'* King's mouth twitched to hide a grin. 'Was that done with intention?'

'I—I thought it fitted, sir.'

'It does. It's distinctly happy. What put it into your thick head, Paddy?'

'I don't know, sir, except we did the Ode last term.'

'And you remembered? The same head that minted *probrosis* as a verb! Vernon, you are an enigma. No! This Side will *not* always be patient of unheavenly gases and waters. I will make representations to our so-called Moderns. Meantime (who shall say I am not just?) I remit you your accrued pains and penalties in regard to *probrosim, probrosis, probrosit*, and other enormities. I oughtn't to do it, but this Side is occasionally human. By no means bad, Paddy.'

* 'This side will not always be patient of rain and waiting on the threshold.'

'Thank you, sir,' said Vernon, wondering how inspiration had visited him.

Then King, with a few brisk remarks about Science, headed them back to Regulus, of whom and of Horace and Rome and evil-minded commercial Carthage and of the democracy eternally futile, he explained, in all ages and climes, he spoke for ten minutes; passing thence to the next Ode—*Delicta majorum*—where he fetched up, full-voiced, upon—'*Dis te minorem quod geris imperas*' (Thou rulest because thou bearest thyself as lower than the Gods)—making it a text for a discourse on manners, morals, and respect for authority as distinct from bottled gases, which lasted till the bell rang. Then Beetle, concertinaing his books, observed to Winton, 'When King's really on tap he's an interestin' dog. Hartopp's chlorine uncorked him.'

'Yes; but why did you tell me *delubris* was "deluges," you silly ass?' said Winton.

'Well, that uncorked him too. Look out, you hoof-handed old owl!' Winton had cleared for action as the Form poured out like puppies at play and was scragging Beetle. Stalky from behind collared Winton low. The three fell in confusion.

'*Dis te minorem quod geris imperas*,' quoth Stalky, ruffling Winton's lint-white locks. 'Mustn't jape with Number Five study. Don't be too virtuous. Don't brood over it. 'Twon't count against you in your future caree-ah. Cheer up, Pater.'

'Pull him off my—er—essential guts, will you?' said Beetle from beneath. 'He's squashin' 'em.'

They dispersed to their studies.

*

No one, the owner least of all, can explain what is in a growing boy's mind. It might have been the blind ferment of adolescence; Stalky's random remarks about virtue might have stirred him; like his betters he might have sought popularity by way of clowning; or, as the Head asserted years later, the only known jest of his serious life might have worked on him, as a sober-sided man's one love colours and dislocates all his after days. But, at the next lesson, mechanical drawing with Mr Lidgett, who as drawing-master had very limited powers of punishment, Winton fell suddenly from grace and let loose a live mouse in the form-room. The whole Form, shrieking and leaping high, threw at it all the plaster cones, pyramids, and fruit in high relief—not to mention ink-pots—that they could lay hands on. Mr Lidgett reported at once to the Head; Winton owned up to his crime, which, venial in the Upper Third, pardonable at a price in the Lower Fourth, was, of course, rank ruffianism on the part of a Fifth Form boy; and so, by graduated stages, he arrived at the Head's study just before lunch, penitent, perturbed, annoyed with himself, and—as the Head said to King in the corridor after the meal—more human than he had known him in seven years.

'You see,' the Head drawled on, 'Winton's only fault is a certain costive and unaccommodating virtue. So this comes very happily.'

'I've never noticed any sign of it,' said King. Winton was in King's House, and though King as pro-consul might, and did, infernally oppress his own Province, once a black-and-yellow cap was in trouble at the hands of the Imperial authority King fought for him to the very last steps of Caesar's throne.

'Well, you yourself admitted just now that a mouse was beneath the occasion,' the Head answered.

'It was.' Mr King did not love Mr Lidgett. 'It should have been a rat. But—but—I hate to plead it—it's the lad's first offence.'

'Could you have damned him more completely, King?'

'Hm. What is the penalty?' said King, in retreat, but keeping up a rear-guard action.

'Only my usual few lines of Virgil to be shown up by tea-time.'

The Head's eyes turned slightly to that end of the corridor where Mullins, Head of Games ('Pot,' 'old Pot,' or 'Potiphar' Mullins), was pinning up the usual Wednesday notice—'Big, Middle, and Little Side Football—A to K, L to Z, 3 to 4.45 P.M.

You cannot write out the Head's usual few (which means five hundred) Latin lines and play football for one hour and three-quarters between the hours of 1.30 and 5 P.M. Winton had evidently no intention of trying to do so, for he hung about the corridor with a set face and an uneasy foot. Yet it was law in the school, compared with which that of the Medes and Persians was no more than a non-committal resolution, that any boy, outside the First Fifteen, who missed his football for any reason whatever, and had not a written excuse, duly signed by competent authority, to explain his absence, would receive not less than three strokes with a ground-ash from the Head of Games, generally a youth between seventeen and eighteen years, rarely under eleven stone (Pot was nearer thirteen), and always in hard condition.

King knew without inquiry that the Head had given Winton no such excuse.

'But he is practically a member of the First Fifteen. He has played for it all this term,' said King. 'I believe his Cap should have arrived last week.'

'His Cap has not been given him. Officially, therefore, he is naught. I rely on old Pot.'

'But Mullins is Winton's study-mate,' King persisted.

Pot Mullins and Pater Winton were cousins and rather close friends.

'That will make no difference to Mullins—or Winton, if I know 'em,' said the Head.

'But—but,' King played his last card desperately, 'I was going to recommend Winton for extra sub-prefect in my House, now Carton has gone.'

'Certainly,' said the Head. 'Why not? He will be excellent by tea-time, I hope.'

At that moment they saw Mr Lidgett, tripping down the corridor, waylaid by Winton.

'It's about that mouse business at mechanical drawing,' Winton opened, swinging across his path.

'Yes, yes, highly disgraceful,' Mr Lidgett panted.

'I know it was,' said Winton. 'It—it was a cad's trick because——'

'Because you knew I couldn't give you more than fifty lines,' said Mr Lidgett.

'Well, anyhow, I've come to apologize for it.'

'Certainly,' said Mr Lidgett, and added, for he was a kindly man, 'I think that shows quite right feeling. I'll tell the Head at once I'm satisfied.'

'No—no!' The boy's still unmended voice jumped from the growl to the squeak. 'I didn't mean *that*! I—I did it on principle. Please don't—er—do anything of the kind.'

Mr Lidgett looked him up and down and, being an artist, understood.

'Thank you, Winton,' he said. 'This shall be between ourselves.'

'You heard?' said King, indecent pride in his voice.

'Of course. You thought he was going to get Lidgett to beg him off the impot.'

King denied this with so much warmth that the Head laughed and King moved away in a huff.

'By the way,' said the Head, 'I've told Winton to do his lines in your form-room—not in his study.'

'Thanks,' said King over his shoulder, for the Head's orders had saved Winton and Mullins, who was doing extra Army work in the study, from an embarrassing afternoon together.

An hour later, King wandered into his still form-room as though by accident. Winton was hard at work.

'Aha!' said King, rubbing his hands. 'This does not look like games, Winton. Don't let me arrest your facile pen. Whence this sudden love for Virgil?'

'Impot from the Head, sir, for that mouse business this morning.'

'Rumours thereof have reached us. That was a lapse on your part into Lower Thirdery which I don't quite understand.'

The 'tump-tump' of the puntabouts before the sides settled to games came through the open window. Winton, like his House-master, loved fresh air. Then they heard Paddy Vernon, sub-prefect on duty, calling the roll in the field and marking defaulters. Winton wrote steadily. King curled himself up on a desk, hands round knees. One would have said that the man was gloating over the boy's misfortune, but the boy understood.

'*Dis te minorem quod geris imperas*,' King quoted presently. 'It is necessary to bear oneself as lower than the local gods—even than drawing-masters who are precluded from effective retaliation. I *do* wish you'd tried that mouse game with me, Pater.'

Winton grinned; then sobered. 'It was a cad's trick, sir, to play on Mr Lidgett.' He peered forward at the page he was copying.

'Well, "the sin *I* impute to each frustrate ghost"——' King stopped himself. 'Why do you goggle like an owl? Hand me the Mantuan and I'll dictate. No matter. Any rich Virgilian measures will serve. I may peradventure recall a few.' He began:

> '*Tu regere imperio populos Romane memento;*
> *Hae tibi erunt artes pacisque imponere morem,*
> *Parcere subjectis et debellare superbos.*

There you have it all, Winton. Write that out twice and yet once again.'

For the next forty minutes, with never a glance at the book, King paid out the glorious hexameters (and King could read Latin as though it were alive), Winton hauling them in and coiling them away behind him as trimmers in a telegraph-ship's hold coil away deep-sea cable. King broke from the Aeneid to the Georgics and back again, pausing now and then to translate some specially loved line or to dwell on the treble-shot texture of the ancient fabric. He did not allude to the coming interview with Mullins except at the last, when he said, 'I think at this juncture, Pater, I need not ask you for the precise significance of *atqui sciebat quae sibi barbarus tortor pararet.*'

The ungrateful Winton flushed angrily, and King loafed out to take five o'clock call-over, after which he invited little Hartopp to tea and a talk on chlorine gas. Hartopp accepted the challenge like a bantam, and the two went up to King's study about the same time as Winton returned to the form-room beneath it to finish his lines.

Then half-a-dozen of the Second Fifteen who should have been washing strolled in to condole with Pater Winton, whose misfortune and its consequences were common talk. No one was more sincere than the long, red-headed, knotty-knuckled Paddy Vernon, but, being a careless animal, he joggled Winton's desk.

'Curse you for a silly ass!' said Winton. 'Don't do that.'

No one is expected to be polite while under punishment, so Vernon, sinking his sub-prefectship, replied peacefully enough:

'Well, don't be wrathy, Pater.'

'I'm not,' said Winton. 'Get out! This ain't your House form-room.'

'Form-room don't belong to you. Why don't you go to your own study?' Vernon replied.

'Because Mullins is there waitin' for the victim,' said Stalky delicately, and they all laughed. 'You ought to have shaken that mouse out of your trouser-leg, Pater. That's the way *I* did in my youth. Pater's revertin' to his second childhood. Never mind, Pater, we all respect you and your future caree-ah.'

Winton, still writhing, growled. Vernon, leaning on the desk, somehow shook it again. Then he laughed.

'What are you grinning at?' Winton asked.

'I was only thinkin' of *you* being sent up to take a lickin' from Pot. I swear I don't think it's fair. You've never shirked a game in your life, and you're as good as in the First Fifteen already. Your Cap ought to have been delivered last week, oughtn't it?'

It was law in the school that no man could by any means enjoy the privileges and immunities of the First Fifteen till the black velvet cap with the gold tassel, made by dilatory Exeter outfitters, had been actually set on his head. Ages ago, a large-built and unruly Second Fifteen had attempted to change this law, but the prefects of that age were still larger, and the lively experiment had never been repeated.

'Will you,' said Winton very slowly, 'kindly mind your own damned business, you cursed, clumsy, fat-headed fool?'

The form-room was as silent as the empty field in the darkness outside. Vernon shifted his feet uneasily.

'Well, *I* shouldn't like to take a lickin' from Pot,' he said.

'Wouldn't you?' Winton asked, as he paged the sheets of lines with hands that shook.

'No, I shouldn't,' said Vernon, his freckles growing more distinct on the bridge of his white nose.

'Well, I'm going to take it'—Winton moved clear of the desk as he spoke. 'But *you're* going to take a lickin' from me first.' Before anyone realized it, he had flung himself neighing against Vernon. No decencies were observed on either side, and the rest looked on amazed. The two met confusedly, Vernon trying to do what he could with his longer reach; Winton, insensible to blows, only concerned to drive his enemy into a corner and batter him to pulp. This he managed over against the fireplace, where Vernon dropped half-stunned. 'Now I'm going to give you your lickin',' said Winton. 'Lie there till I get a ground-ash and I'll cut you to pieces. If you move, I'll chuck you out of the window.' He wound his hands into the boy's collar and waistband, and had actually heaved him half off the ground before the others with one accord dropped on his head, shoulders, and legs. He fought them crazily in an awful hissing silence. Stalky's sensitive nose was rubbed along the floor; Beetle received a jolt in the wind that sent him whistling and crowing against the wall; Perowne's forehead was cut, and Malpass came out with an eye that explained itself like a dying rainbow through a whole week.

'Mad! Quite mad!' said Stalky, and for the third time wriggled back to Winton's throat. The door opened and King came in, Hartopp's little figure just behind him. The mound on the floor panted and heaved but did not rise, for Winton still squirmed vengefully. 'Only a little play, sir,' said Perowne. 'Only hit my head against a form.' This was quite true.

'Oh,' said King. '*Dimovit obstantes propinquos.* You, I presume, are the *populus* delaying Winton's return to—Mullins, eh?'

'No, sir,' said Stalky behind his claret-coloured handkerchief. 'We're the *maerentes amicos.*'

'Not bad! You see, some of it sticks after all,' King chuckled to Hartopp, and the two masters left without further inquiries.

The boys sat still on the now passive Winton.

'Well,' said Stalky at last, 'of all the putrid he-asses, Pater, you are *the*——'

'I'm sorry. I'm awfully sorry,' Winton began, and they let him rise. He held out his hand to the bruised and bewildered Vernon. 'Sorry, Paddy. I—I must have lost my temper. I—I don't know what's the matter with me.'

'Fat lot of good that'll do my face at tea,' Vernon grunted. 'Why couldn't you say there was something wrong with you instead of lamming out like a lunatic? Is my lip puffy?'

'Just a trifle. Look at my beak! Well, we got all these pretty marks at footer—owin' to the zeal with which we played the game,' said Stalky, dusting himself. 'But d'you think you're fit to be let loose again, Pater? Sure you don't want to kill another sub-prefect? I wish *I* was Pot. I'd cut your sprightly young soul out.'

'I s'pose I ought to go to Pot now,' said Winton.

'And let all the other asses see you lookin' like this! Not much. We'll all come up to Number Five study and wash off in hot water. Beetle, you aren't damaged. Go along and light the gas-stove.'

'There's a tin of cocoa in my study somewhere,' Perowne shouted after him. 'Rootle round till you find it, and take it up.'

Separately, by different roads, Vernon's jersey pulled half over his head, the boys repaired to Number Five study. Little Hartopp and King, I am sorry to say, leaned over the banisters of King's landing and watched.

'Ve-ry human,' said little Hartopp. 'Your virtuous Winton, having got himself into trouble, takes it out of my poor old Paddy. I wonder what precise lie Paddy will tell about his face.'

'But surely you aren't going to embarrass him by asking?' said King.

'*Your* boy won,' said Hartopp.

'To go back to what we were discussing,' said King quickly, 'do you pretend that your modern system of inculcating unrelated facts about chlorine, for instance, all of which may be proved fallacies by the time the boys grow up, can have any real bearing on education —even the low type of it that examiners expect?'

'I maintain nothing. But is it any worse than your Chinese re-iteration of uncomprehended syllables in a dead tongue?'

'Dead, forsooth!' King fairly danced. 'The only living tongue on earth! Chinese! On my word, Hartopp!'

'And at the end of seven years—how often have I said it?' Hartopp went on—'seven years of two hundred and twenty days of six hours each, your victims go away with nothing, absolutely nothing, except, perhaps, if they've been very attentive, a dozen—no, I'll grant you twenty—one score of totally unrelated Latin tags which any child of twelve could have absorbed in two terms.'

'But—but can't you realize that if our system brings later—at any rate—at a pinch—a simple understanding—grammar and Latinity apart—a mere glimpse of the significance (foul word!) of, we'll say, one Ode of Horace, one twenty lines of Virgil, we've got what we poor devils of ushers are striving after?'

'And what might that be?' said Hartopp.

'Balance, proportion, perspective—life. Your scientific man is the unrelated animal—the beast without background. Haven't you ever realized *that* in your atmosphere of stinks?'

'Meantime you make them lose life for the sake of living, eh?'

'Blind again, Hartopp! I told you about Paddy's quotation this morning. (But he made *probrosis* a verb, he did!) You yourself heard young Corkran's reference to *maerentes amicos*. It sticks among the barbarians.'

'Absolutely and essentially Chinese,' said little Hartopp, who, alone of the Common-room, refused to be outfaced by King. 'But I don't yet understand how Paddy came to be licked by Winton. Paddy's supposed to be something of a boxer.'

'Beware of vinegar made from honey,' King replied. 'Pater, like some other people, is patient and long-suffering, but he has his limits. The Head is oppressing him damnably, too. As I pointed out, the boy has practically been in the First Fifteen since term began.'

'But, my dear fellow, I've known you give a boy an impot and refuse him leave off games, again and again.'

'Ah, but that was when there was real need to get at some oaf who couldn't be sensitized in any other way. Now, in our esteemed Head's action I see nothing but——'

The conversation from this point does not concern us.

Meantime Winton, very penitent and especially polite towards Vernon, was being cheered with cocoa in Number Five study. They had some difficulty in stemming the flood of his apologies. He himself pointed out to Vernon that he had attacked a sub-prefect for no reason whatever, and, therefore, deserved official punishment.

'I can't think what was the matter with me today,' he mourned. 'Ever since that blasted mouse business——'

'Well, then, don't think,' said Stalky. 'Or do you want Paddy to make a row about it before all the Coll.?'

Here Vernon was understood to say that he would see Winton and all the Coll. somewhere else.

'And if you imagine Perowne and Malpass and me are goin' to give evidence at a prefects' meetin' just to soothe your beastly conscience, you jolly well err,' said Beetle. 'I know what you did.'

'What?' croaked Pater, out of the valley of his humiliation.

'You went Berserk. I've read all about it in *Hypatia*.'

'What's "going Berserk"?' Winton asked.

'Never you mind,' was the reply. 'Now, don't you feel awfully weak and seedy?'

'I *am* rather tired,' said Winton, sighing.

'That's what you ought to be. You've gone Berserk and pretty soon you'll go to sleep. But you'll probably be liable to fits of it all your life,' Beetle concluded. 'Shouldn't wonder if you murdered someone some day.'

'Shut up—you and your Berserks!' said Stalky. 'Go to Mullins now and get it over, Pater.'

'I call it filthy unjust of the Head,' said Vernon. 'Anyhow, you've given me my lickin', old man. I hope Pot'll give you yours.'

'I'm awfully sorry—awfully sorry,' was Winton's last word.

It was the custom in that consulship to deal with games' defaulters between five o'clock call-over and tea. Mullins, who was old enough to pity, did not believe in letting boys wait through the night till the chill of the next morning for their punishments. He was finishing off the last of the small fry and their excuses when Winton arrived.

'But, please, Mullins'—this was Babcock tertius, a dear little twelve-year-old mother's darling—'I had an awful hack on the knee. I've been to the Matron about it and she gave me some iodine. I've been rubbing it in all day. I thought that would be an excuse off.'

'Let's have a look at it,' said the impassive Mullins. 'That's a shin-bruise—about a week old. Touch your toes. I'll give you the iodine.'

Babcock yelled loudly as he had many times before. The face of Jevons, aged eleven, a new boy that dark wet term, low in the House, low in the Lower School, and lowest of all in his homesick little mind, turned white at the horror of the sight. They could hear his working lips part stickily as Babcock wailed his way out of hearing.

'Hullo, Jevons! What brings you here?' said Mullins.

'Pl-ease, sir, I went for a walk with Babcock tertius.'

'Did you? Then I bet you went to the tuck-shop—and you paid, didn't you?'

A nod. Jevons was too terrified to speak.

'Of course, and I bet Babcock told you that old Pot 'ud let you off because it was the first time.'

Another nod with a ghost of a smile in it.

'All right.' Mullins picked Jevons up before he could guess what was coming, laid him on the table with one hand, with the other gave him three emphatic spanks, then held him high in air.

'Now you tell Babcock tertius that he's got you a licking from me, and see you jolly well pay it back to him. And when you're Head of Games don't you let any one shirk his footer without a written excuse. Where d'you play in your game?'

'Forward, sir.'

'You can do better than that. I've seen you run like a young buck-rabbit. Ask Dickson from me to try you as three-quarter next game, will you? Cut along.'

Jevons left, warm for the first time that day, enormously set up n his own esteem, and very hot against the deceitful Babcock.

Mullins turned to Winton. 'Your name's on the list, Pater.' Winton nodded.

'I know it. The Head landed me with an impot for that mouse business at mechanical drawing. No excuse.'

'He meant it then?' Mullins jerked his head delicately towards the ground-ash on the table. 'I heard something about it.'

Winton nodded. 'A rotten thing to do,' he said. 'Can't think what I was doing ever to do it. It counts against a fellow so; and there's some more too——'

'All right, Pater. Just stand clear of our photo-bracket, will you?'

The little formality over, there was a pause. Winton swung round, yawned in Pot's astonished face, and staggered towards the window-seat.

'What's the matter with you, Dick? Ill?'

'No. Perfectly all right, thanks. Only—only a little sleepy.' Winton stretched himself out, and then and there fell deeply and placidly asleep.

'It isn't a faint,' said the experienced Mullins, 'or his pulse wouldn't act. 'Tisn't a fit or he'd snort and twitch. It can't be sun-stroke, this term, and he hasn't been over-training for anything.' He opened Winton's collar, packed a cushion under his head, threw a rug over him and sat down to listen to the regular breathing. Before long Stalky arrived, on pretence of borrowing a book. He looked at the window-seat.

'Noticed anything wrong with Winton lately?' said Mullins.

'Notice anything wrong with my beak?' Stalky replied. 'Pater went Berserk after call-over, and fell on a lot of us for jestin' with him about his impot. You ought to see Malpass's eye.'

'You mean that Pater fought?' said Mullins.

'Like a devil. Then he nearly went to sleep in our study just now.
I expect he'll be all right when he wakes up. Rummy business! Conscientious old bargee. You ought to have heard his apologies.'

'But Pater can't fight one little bit,' Mullins repeated.

' 'Twasn't fightin'. He just tried to murder everyone.' Stalky described the affair, and when he left Mullins went off to take counsel
with the Head, who, out of a cloud of blue smoke, told him that all
would yet be well.

'Winton,' said he, 'is a little stiff in his moral joints. He'll get over
that. If he asks you whether today's doings will count against him
in his——'

'But you know it's important to him, sir. His people aren't—very
well off,' said Mullins.

'That's why I'm taking all this trouble. You must reassure him,
Pot. I have overcrowded him with new experiences. Oh, by the way,
has his Cap come?'

'It came at dinner, sir.' Mullins laughed.

Sure enough, when he waked at tea-time, Winton proposed to
take Mullins all through every one of his day's lapses from grace,
and 'Do you think it will count against me?' said he.

'Don't you fuss so much about yourself and your silly career,'
said Mullins. 'You're all right. And oh—here's your First Cap at
last. Shove it up on the bracket and come on to tea.'

They met King on their way, stepping statelily and rubbing his
hands. 'I have applied,' said he, 'for the services of an additional
sub-prefect in Carton's unlamented absence. Your name, Winton,
seems to have found favour with the powers that be, and—and all
things considered—I am disposed to give my support to the
nomination. You are therefore a quasi-lictor.'

'Then it didn't count against me,' Winton gasped as soon as they
were out of hearing.

A Head of Games can jest with a sub-prefect publicly.

'You utter ass!' said Mullins, and caught him by the back of his
stiff neck and ran him down to the hall, where the sub-prefects, who
sit below the salt, made him welcome with the economical bloater-
paste of mid-term.

*

King and little Hartopp were sparring in the Reverend John
Gillett's study at 10 P.M.—classical *versus* modern as usual.

'Character—proportion—background,' snarled King. 'That is
the essence of the Humanities.'

'Analects of Confucius,' little Hartopp answered.

'Time,' said the Reverend John behind the soda-water. 'You men oppress me. Hartopp, what did you say to Paddy in your dormitories tonight? Even *you* couldn't have overlooked his face.'

'But I did,' said Hartopp calmly. 'I wasn't even humorous about it, as some clerics might have been. I went straight through and said naught.'

'Poor Paddy! Now, for my part,' said King, 'and you know I am not lavish in my praises, I consider Winton a first-class type; absolutely first-class.'

'Ha-ardly,' said the Reverend John. 'First-class of the second class, I admit. The very best type of second class, but'—he shook his head—'it should have been a rat. Pater'll never be anything more than a Colonel of Engineers.'

'What do you base that verdict on?' said King stiffly.

'He came to me after prayers—with all his conscience.'

'Poor old Pater. Was it the mouse?' said little Hartopp.

'That, and what he called his uncontrollable temper, and his responsibilities as sub-prefect.'

'And you?'

'If we had had what is vulgarly called a pi-jaw he'd have had hysterics. So I recommended a dose of Epsom salts. He'll take it, too—conscientiously. Don't eat me, King. Perhaps he'll be a K.C.B.'

Ten o'clock struck and the Army Class boys in the further studies coming to their Houses after an hour's extra work passed along the gravel path below. Someone was chanting, to the tune of 'White sand and grey sand,' *Dis te minorem quod geris imperas.* He stopped outside Mullins' study. They heard Mullins' window slide up and then Stalky's voice:

'Ah! Good-evenin', Mullins, my *barbarus tortor.* We're the waits. We have come to inquire after the local Berserk. Is he doin' as well as can be expected in his new caree-ah?'

'Better than you will, in a sec, Stalky,' Mullins grunted.

'Glad of that. We thought he'd like to know that Paddy has been carried to the sick-house in ravin' delirium. They think it's concussion of the brain.'

'Why, he was all right at prayers,' Winton began earnestly, and they heard a laugh in the background as Mullins slammed down the window.

' 'Night, Regulus,' Stalky sang out, and the light footsteps went on.

'You see. It sticks. A little of it sticks among the barbarians,' said King.

'Amen,' said the Reverend John. 'Go to bed.'

A Diversity of Creatures, 1917*

*Dated 1908 in the text.

'My Son's Wife'

H E HAD SUFFERED from the disease of the century since his early youth, and before he was thirty he was heavily marked with it. He and a few friends had rearranged Heaven very comfortably, but the reorganization of Earth, which they called Society, was even greater fun. It demanded Work in the shape of many taxi-rides daily; hours of brilliant talk with brilliant talkers; some sparkling correspondence; a few silences (but on the understanding that their own turn should come soon) while other people expounded philosophies; and a fair number of picture-galleries, tea-fights, concerts, theatres, music-halls, and cinema shows; the whole trimmed with love-making to women whose hair smelt of cigarette-smoke. Such strong days sent Frankwell Midmore back to his flat assured that he and his friends had helped the World a step nearer the Truth, the Dawn, and the New Order.

His temperament, he said, led him more towards concrete data than abstract ideas. People who investigate detail are apt to be tired at the day's end. The same temperament, or it may have been a woman, made him early attach himself to the Immoderate Left of his Cause in the capacity of an experimenter in Social Relations. And since the Immoderate Left contains plenty of women anxious to help earnest inquirers with large independent incomes to arrive at evaluations of essentials, Frankwell Midmore's lot was far from contemptible.

At that hour Fate chose to play with him. A widowed aunt, widely separated by nature, and more widely by marriage, from all that Midmore's mother had ever been or desired to be, died and left him possessions. Mrs Midmore, having that summer embraced a creed which denied the existence of death, naturally could not stoop to burial; but Midmore had to leave London for the dank country at a season when Social Regeneration works best through long, cushioned conferences, two by two, after tea. There he faced the bracing ritual of the British funeral, and was wept at across a raw grave by an elderly coffin-shaped female with a long nose who called him 'Master Frankie'; and there he was congratulated behind an echoing top-hat by a man he mistook for a mute, who turned out to

be his aunt's lawyer. He wrote his mother next day, after a bright
account of the funeral:

'So far as I can understand, she has left me between four and five
hundred a year. It all comes from Ther Land, as they call it down
here. The unspeakable attorney, Sperrit, and a green-eyed daughter,
who hums to herself as she tramps but is silent on all subjects
except "huntin'," insisted on taking me to see it. Ther Land is
brown and green in alternate slabs like chocolate and pistachio
cakes, speckled with occasional peasants who do not utter. In case
it should not be wet enough there is a wet brook in the middle of it.
Ther House is by the brook. I shall look into it later. If there should
be any little memento of Jenny that you care for, let me know.
Didn't you tell me that mid-Victorian furniture is coming into the
market again? Jenny's old maid—it is called Rhoda Dolbie—tells
me that Jenny promised it thirty pounds a year. The will does not.
Hence, I suppose, the tears at the funeral. But that is close on ten
per cent of the income. I fancy Jenny has destroyed all her private
papers and records of her *vie intime*, if, indeed, life be possible in
such a place. The Sperrit man told me that if I had means of my
own I might come and live on Ther Land. I didn't tell him how
much I would pay not to! I cannot think it right that any human
being should exercise mastery over others in the merciless fashion
our tom-fool social system permits; so, as it is all mine, I intend to
sell it whenever the unholy Sperrit can find a purchaser.'

And he went to Mr Sperrit with the idea next day, just before
returning to Town.

'Quite so,' said the lawyer. 'I see your point, of course. But the
house itself is rather old-fashioned—hardly the type purchasers
demand nowadays. There's no park, of course, and the bulk of the
land is let to a life-tenant, a Mr Sidney. As long as he pays his rent,
he can't be turned out, and even if he didn't'—Mr Sperrit's face
relaxed a shade—'you might have a difficulty.'

'The property brings in four hundred a year, I understand,' said
Midmore.

'Well, hardly—ha-ardly. Deducting land and income tax, tithes,
fire insurance, cost of collection, and repairs of course, it returned
two hundred and eighty-four pounds last year. The repairs are rather
a large item—owing to the brook. I call it Liris—out of Horace,
you know.'

Midmore looked at his watch impatiently.

'I suppose you can find somebody to buy it?' he repeated.

'We will do our best, of course, if those are your instructions.

Then, that is all except'—here Midmore half rose, but Mr Sperrit's little grey eyes held his large brown ones firmly—'except about Rhoda Dolbie, Mrs Werf's maid. I may tell you that we did not draw up your aunt's last will. She grew secretive towards the last— elderly people often do—and had it done in London. I expect her memory failed her, or she mislaid her notes. She used to put them in her spectacle-case. . . . My motor only takes eight minutes to get to the station, Mr Midmore . . . but, as I was saying, whenever she made her will with *us*, Mrs Werf always left Rhoda thirty pounds per annum. Charlie, the wills!' A clerk with a baldish head and a long nose dealt documents on to the table like cards, and breathed heavily behind Midmore. 'It's in no sense a legal obligation, of course,' said Mr Sperrit. 'Ah, that one is dated January the 11th, eighteen eighty-nine.'

Midmore looked at his watch again and found himself saying with no good grace: 'Well, I suppose she'd better have it—for the present at any rate.'

He escaped with an uneasy feeling that two hundred and fifty-four pounds a year was not exactly four hundred, and that Charlie's long nose annoyed him. Then he returned, first-class, to his own affairs.

Of the two, perhaps three, experiments in Social Relations which he had then in hand, one interested him acutely. It had run for some months and promised most variegated and interesting developments, on which he dwelt luxuriously all the way to town. When he reached his flat he was not well prepared for a twelve-page letter explaining, in the diction of the Immoderate Left which rubricates its I's and illuminates its T's, that the lady had realized greater attractions in another Soul. She re-stated, rather than pleaded, the gospel of the Immoderate Left as her justification, and ended in an impassioned demand for her right to express herself in and on her own life, through which, she pointed out, she could pass but once. She added that if, later, she should discover Midmore was 'essentially complementary to her needs,' she would tell him so. That Midmore had himself written much the same sort of epistle— barring the hint of return—to a woman of whom his needs for self-expression had caused him to weary three years before, did not assist him in the least. He expressed himself to the gas-fire in terms essential but not complimentary. Then he reflected on the detached criticism of his best friends and her best friends, male and female, with whom he and she and others had talked so openly while their gay adventure was in flower. He recalled, too—this must have been about midnight—her analysis from every angle, remote and most intimate, of the mate to whom she had been adjudged under the base convention which is styled marriage. Later, at that bad hour when the cattle wake for a little, he remembered her in other aspects and went down into the hell appointed; desolate, desiring, with no God to call upon. About eleven o'clock next morning Eliphaz the Temanite, Bildad the Shuhite, and Zophar the Naamathite called upon him, 'for they had made appointment together' to see how he took it; but the janitor told them that Job had gone—into the country, he believed.

Midmore's relief when he found his story was not written across his aching temples for Mr Sperrit to read—the defeated lover, like the successful one, believes all earth privy to his soul—was put down by Mr Sperrit to quite different causes. He led him into a morning-room. The rest of the house seemed to be full of people, singing to a loud piano idiotic songs about cows, and the hall smelt of damp cloaks.

'It's our evening to take the winter cantata,' Mr Sperrit explained. 'It's "High Tide on the Coast of Lincolnshire." I hoped you'd come back. There are scores of little things to settle. As for the house, of course, it stands ready for you at any time. I couldn't get Rhoda out of it—nor could Charlie for that matter. She's the sister, isn't she, of the nurse who brought you down here when you were four, she says, to recover from measles?'

'Is she? Was I?' said Midmore through the bad tastes in his mouth. 'D'you suppose I could stay there the night?'

Thirty joyous young voices shouted appeal to someone to leave their 'pipes of parsley 'ollow—'ollow—'ollow!' Mr Sperrit had to raise his voice above the din.

'Well, if I asked you to stay *here*, I should never hear the last of it from Rhoda. She's a little cracked, of course, but the soul of devotion and capable of anything. *Ne sit ancillae,* you know.'

'Thank you. Then I'll go. I'll walk.' He stumbled out dazed and sick into the winter twilight, and sought the square house by the brook.

It was not a dignified entry, because when the door was unchained and Rhoda exclaimed, he took two valiant steps into the hall and then fainted—as men sometimes will after twenty-two hours of strong emotion and little food.

'I'm sorry,' he said when he could speak. He was lying at the foot of the stairs, his head on Rhoda's lap.

'Your 'ome is your castle, sir,' was the reply in his hair. 'I smelt it wasn't drink. You lay on the sofa till I get your supper.'

She settled him in a drawing-room hung with yellow silk, heavy with the smell of dead leaves and oil lamp. Something murmured soothingly in the background and overcame the noises in his head. He thought he heard horses' feet on wet gravel and a voice singing about ships and flocks and grass. It passed close to the shuttered bay-window.

> *'But each will mourn his own, she saith,*
> *And sweeter woman ne'er drew breath*
> *Than my son's wife, Elizabeth . . .*
> *Cusha—cusha—cusha—calling.'*

The hoofs broke into a canter as Rhoda entered with the tray. 'And then I'll put you to bed,' she said. 'Sidney's coming in the morning.' Midmore asked no questions. He dragged his poor bruised soul to bed and would have pitied it all over again, but the food and warm sherry and water drugged him to instant sleep.

Rhoda's voice wakened him, asking whether he would have ' 'ip, foot, or sitz,' which he understood were the baths of the establishment. 'Suppose you try all three,' she suggested. 'They're all yours, you know, sir.'

He would have renewed his sorrows with the daylight, but her words struck him pleasantly. Everything his eyes opened upon was his very own to keep for ever. The carved four-post Chippendale bed, obviously worth hundreds; the wavy walnut William and Mary chairs—he had seen worse ones labelled twenty guineas apiece; the oval medallion mirror; the delicate eighteenth-century wire fireguard; the heavy brocaded curtains, were his—all his. So, too, a great garden full of birds that faced him when he shaved; a mulberry-tree, a sun-dial, and a dull, steel-coloured brook that murmured level with the edge of a lawn a hundred yards away. Peculiarly and privately his own was the smell of sausages and coffee that he sniffed at the head of the wide square landing, all set round with mysterious doors and Bartolozzi prints. He spent two hours after breakfast in exploring his new possessions. His heart leaped up at such things as sewing-machines, a rubber-tyred bath-chair in a tiled passage, a malachite-headed Malacca cane, boxes and boxes of unopened stationery, seal-rings, bunches of keys, and at the bottom of a steel-net reticule a little leather purse with seven pounds ten shillings in gold and eleven shillings in silver.

'You used to play with that when my sister brought you down

here after your measles,' said Rhoda, as he slipped the money into
his pocket. 'Now, this was your pore dear auntie's business-room.'
She opened a low door. 'Oh, I forgot about Mr Sidney! There he is.'
An enormous old man with rheumy red eyes that blinked under
downy white eyebrows sat in an Empire chair, his cap in his hands.
Rhoda withdrew sniffing. The man looked Midmore over in silence,
then jerked a thumb towards the door. 'I reckon she told you who
I be,' he began. 'I'm the only farmer you've got. Nothin' goes off
my place 'thout it walks on its own feet. What about my pig-
pound?'

'Well, what about it?' said Midmore.

'That's just what I be come about. The County Councils are
getting more particular. Did ye know there was swine fever at
Pashell's? There *be*. It'll 'ave to be in brick.'

'Yes,' said Midmore politely.

'I've bin at your aunt that was, plenty times about it. I don't say
she wasn't a just woman, but she didn't read the lease same way I
did. I be used to bein' put upon, but there's no doing any longer
'thout that pig-pound.'

'When would you like it?' Midmore asked. It seemed the easiest
road to take.

'Any time or other suits me, I reckon. He ain't thrivin' where he
is, an' I paid eighteen shillin' for him.' He crossed his hands on his
stick and gave no further sign of life.

'Is that all?' Midmore stammered.

'All now—excep' '—he glanced fretfully at the table beside him
—'excep' my usuals. Where's that Rhoda?'

Midmore rang the bell. Rhoda came in with a bottle and a glass.
The old man helped himself to four stiff fingers, rose in one piece,
and stumped out. At the door he cried ferociously: 'Don't suppose
it's any odds to you whether I be drowned or not, but them flood-
gates want a wheel and winch, they do. I be too old for liftin' 'em
with the bar—my time o' life.'

'Good riddance if 'e *was* drowned,' said Rhoda. 'But don't you
mind him. He's only amusin' himself. You pore dear auntie used to
give 'im 'is usuals—'tisn't the whisky *you* drink—an' send 'im
about 'is business.'

'I see. Now, is a pig-pound the same thing as a pig-sty?'

Rhoda nodded. ' 'E needs one, too, but 'e ain't entitled to it. You
look at 'is lease—third drawer on the left in that Bombay cab'net—
an' next time 'e comes you ask 'im to read it. That'll choke 'im off,
because 'e can't!'

There was nothing in Midmore's past to teach him the message and significance of a hand-written lease of the late 'eighties, but Rhoda interpreted.

'It don't mean anything reely,' was her cheerful conclusion, 'excep' you mustn't get rid of him anyhow, an' 'e can do what 'e likes always. Lucky for us 'e *do* farm; and if it wasn't for 'is woman——'

'Oh, there's a Mrs Sidney, is there?'

'Lor, *no*! The Sidneys don't marry. They keep. That's his fourth since—to my knowledge. He was a takin' man from the first.'

'Any families?'

'They'd be grown up by now if there was, wouldn't they? But you can't spend all your days considerin' 'is interests. That's what gave your pore aunt 'er indigestion. 'Ave you seen your gun-room?'

Midmore held strong views on the immorality of taking life for pleasure. But there was no denying that the late Colonel Werf's seventy-guinea breechloaders were good at their filthy job. He loaded one, took it out, and pointed—merely pointed—it at a cock-pheasant which rose out of a shrubbery behind the kitchen, and the flaming bird came down in a long slant on the lawn, stone dead. Rhoda from the scullery said it was a lovely shot, and told him lunch was ready.

He spent the afternoon gun in one hand, a map in the other, beating the bounds of his lands. They lay altogether in a shallow, uninteresting valley, flanked with woods and bisected by a brook. Up stream was his own house; down stream, less than half a mile, a low red farm-house squatted in an old orchard, beside what looked like small lock-gates on the Thames. There was no doubt as to ownership. Mr Sidney saw him while yet far off, and bellowed at him about pig-pounds and flood-gates. These last were two great sliding shutters of weedy oak across the brook, which were prised up inch by inch with a crowbar along a notched strip of iron, and when Sidney opened them they at once let out half the water. Midmore watched it shrink between its aldered banks like some conjuring trick. This, too, was his very own.

'I see,' he said. 'How interesting! Now, what's that bell for?' he went on, pointing to an old ship's bell in a rude belfry at the end of an outhouse. 'Was that a chapel once?' The red-eyed giant seemed to have difficulty in expressing himself for the moment and blinked savagely.

'Yes,' he said at last. 'My chapel. When you 'ear that bell ring you'll 'ear something. Nobody but me 'ud put up with it—but I reckon it don't make any odds to you.' He slammed the gates down again, and the brook rose behind them with a suck and a grunt.

Midmore moved off, conscious that he might be safer with Rhoda to hold his conversational hand. As he passed the front of the farmhouse a smooth fat woman, with neatly parted grey hair under a widow's cap, curtsied to him deferentially through the window. By every teaching of the Immoderate Left she had a perfect right to express herself in any way she pleased, but the curtsey revolted him. And on his way home he was hailed from behind a hedge by a manifest idiot with no roof to his mouth, who hallooed and danced round him.

'What did that beast want?' he demanded of Rhoda at tea.

'Jimmy? He only wanted to know if you 'ad any telegrams to send. 'E'll go anywhere so long as 'tisn't across running water. That gives 'im 'is seizures. Even talkin' about it for fun, like, makes 'im shake.'

'But why isn't he where he can be properly looked after?'

'What 'arm's 'e doing? 'E's a love-child, but 'is family can pay for 'im. If 'e was locked up 'e'd die all at once, like a wild rabbit. Won't you, please, look at the drive, sir?'

Midmore looked in the fading light. The neat gravel was pitted with large roundish holes, and there was a punch or two of the same sort on the lawn.

'That's the 'unt comin' 'ome,' Rhoda explained. 'Your pore dear auntie always let 'em use our drive for a short cut after the Colonel died. The Colonel wouldn't so much, because he preserved; but your auntie was always an 'orsewoman till 'er sciatica.'

'Isn't there someone who can rake it over or—or something?' said Midmore vaguely.

'Oh yes. You'll never see it in the morning, but—you was out when they came 'ome an' Mister Fisher—he's the Master—told me to tell you with 'is compliments that if you wasn't preservin' and cared to 'old to the old understandin', 'is gravel-pit is at your service same as before. 'E thought, perhaps, you mightn't know, and it 'ad slipped my mind to tell you. It's good gravel, Mister Fisher's, and it binds beautiful on the drive. We 'ave to draw it, o' course, from the pit, but——'

Midmore looked at her helplessly.

'Rhoda,' said he, 'what am I supposed to do?'

'Oh, let 'em come through,' she replied. 'You never know. You may want to 'unt yourself some day.'

That evening it rained and his misery returned on him, the worse

for having been diverted. At last he was driven to paw over a few
score books in a panelled room called the library, and realized with
horror what the late Colonel Werf's mind must have been in its
prime. The volumes smelt of a dead world as strongly as they did of
mildew. He opened and thrust them back, one after another, till
crude coloured illustrations of men on horses held his eye. He began
at random and read a little, moved into the drawing-room with the
volume, and settled down by the fire still reading. It was a foul
world into which he peeped for the first time—a heavy-eating,
hard-drinking hell of horse-copers, swindlers, matchmaking
mothers, economically dependent virgins selling themselves blush-
ingly for cash and lands, Jews, tradesmen, and an ill-considered
spawn of Dickens-and-horsedung characters (I give Midmore's own
criticism), but he read on, fascinated, and behold, from the pages
leaped, as it were, the brother to the red-eyed man of the brook,
bellowing at a landlord (here Midmore realized that *he* was that
very animal) for new barns; and another man who, like himself
again, objected to hoof-marks on gravel. Outrageous as thought
and conception were, the stuff seemed to have the rudiments of
observation. He dug out other volumes by the same author, till
Rhoda came in with a silver candlestick.

'Rhoda,' said he, 'did you ever hear about a character called
James Pigg—and Batsey?'

'Why, o' course,' said she. 'The Colonel used to come into the
kitchen in 'is dressin'-gown an' read us all those Jorrockses.'

'Oh, Lord!' said Midmore, and went to bed with a book called
Handley Cross under his arm, and a lonelier Columbus into a
stranger world the wet-ringed moon never looked upon.

*

Here we omit much. But Midmore never denied that for the
epicure in sensation the urgent needs of an ancient house, as
interpreted by Rhoda pointing to daylight through attic-tiles held
in place by moss, gives an edge to the pleasure of Social Research
elsewhere. Equally he found that the reaction following prolonged
research loses much of its grey terror if one knows one can at will
bathe the soul in the society of plumbers (all the water-pipes had
chronic appendicitis), village idiots (Jimmy had taken Midmore
under his weak wing and camped daily at the drive-gates), and a
giant with red eyelids whose every action is an unpredictable outrage.

Towards spring Midmore filled his house with a few friends of the

Immoderate Left. It happened to be the day when, all things and
Rhoda working together, a cartload of bricks, another of sand, and
some bags of lime had been dispatched to build Sidney his almost
daily demanded pig-pound. Midmore took his friends across the flat
fields with some idea of showing them Sidney as a type of 'the
peasantry.' They hit the minute when Sidney, hoarse with rage,
was ordering bricklayer, mate, carts and all off his premises. The
visitors disposed themselves to listen.

'You never give me no notice about changin' the pig,' Sidney
shouted. The pig—at least eighteen inches long—reared on end in
the old sty and smiled at the company.

'But, my good man——' Midmore opened.

'I ain't! For aught you know I be a dam' sight worse than you be.
You can't come and be'ave arbit'ry with me. You *are* be'avin'
arbit'ry! All you men go clean away an' don't set foot on my land
till I bid ye.'

'But you asked'—Midmore felt his voice jump up—'to have the
pig-pound built.'

'S'pose I did. That's no reason you shouldn't send me notice to
change the pig. Comin' down on me like this 'thout warnin'! That
pig's got to be got into the cowshed an' all.'

'Then open the door and let him run in,' said Midmore.

'Don't you be'ave arbit'ry with *me*! Take all your dam' men
'ome off my land. I won't be treated arbit'ry.'

The carts moved off without a word, and Sidney went into the
house and slammed the door.

'Now, I hold that is enormously significant,' said a visitor. 'Here
you have the logical outcome of centuries of feudal oppression—the
frenzy of fear.' The company looked at Midmore with grave pain.

'But he *did* worry my life out about his pig-sty,' was all Midmore
found to say.

Others took up the parable and proved to him if he only held true
to the gospels of the Immoderate Left the earth would soon be
covered with 'jolly little' pig-sties, built in the intervals of morris-
dancing by 'the peasant' himself.

Midmore felt grateful when the door opened again and Mr Sidney
invited them all to retire to the road which, he pointed out, was
public. As they turned the corner of the house, a smooth-faced
woman in a widow's cap curtsied to each of them through the
window.

Instantly they drew pictures of that woman's lot, deprived of all
vehicle for self-expression—'the set grey life and apathetic end,'

one quoted—and they discussed the tremendous significance of village theatricals. Even a month ago Midmore would have told them all that he knew and Rhoda had dropped about Sidney's forms of self-expression. Now, for some strange reason, he was content to let the talk run on from village to metropolitan and world drama.

Rhoda advised him after the visitors left that 'if he wanted to do that again' he had better go up to Town.

'But we only sat on cushions on the floor,' said her master.

'They're too old for romps,' she retorted, 'an' it's only the beginning of things. I've seen what *I*'ve seen. Besides, they talked and laughed in the passage going to their baths—such as took 'em.'

'Don't be a fool, Rhoda,' said Midmore. No man—unless he has loved her—will casually dismiss a woman on whose lap he has laid his head.

'Very good,' she snorted, 'but that cuts both ways. An' now, you go down to Sidney's this evenin' and put him where he ought to be. He was in his right about you givin' 'im notice about changin' the pig, but he 'adn't any right to turn it up before your company. No manners, no pig-pound. He'll understand.'

Midmore did his best to make him. He found himself reviling the old man in speech and with a joy quite new in all his experience. He wound up—it was a plagiarism from a plumber—by telling Mr Sidney that he looked like a turkey-cock, had the morals of a parish bull, and need never hope for a new pig-pound as long as he or Midmore lived.

'Very good,' said the giant. 'I reckon you thought you 'ad something against me, and now you've come down an' told it me like man to man. Quite right. I don't bear malice. Now, you send along those bricks an' sand, an' I'll make a do to build the pig-pound myself. If you look at my lease you'll find out you're bound to provide me materials for the repairs. Only—I thought there'd be no 'arm in my askin' you to do it throughout, like.'

Midmore fairly gasped. 'Then, why the devil did you turn my carts back when—when I sent them up here to do it throughout for you?'

Mr Sidney sat down on the flood-gates, his eyebrows knitted in thought.

'I'll tell you,' he said slowly. ' 'Twas too dam' like cheatin' a suckin' baby. My woman, she said so too.'

For a few seconds the teachings of the Immoderate Left, whose humour is all their own, wrestled with those of Mother Earth, who has her own humours. Then Midmore laughed till he could scarcely stand. In due time Mr Sidney laughed too—crowing and wheezing crescendo till it broke from him in roars. They shook hands, and Midmore went home grateful that he had held his tongue among his companions.

When he reached his house he met three or four men and women on horseback, very muddy indeed, coming down the drive. Feeling hungry himself, he asked them if they were hungry. They said they were, and he bade them enter. Jimmy took their horses, who seemed to know him. Rhoda took their battered hats, led the women upstairs for hairpins, and presently fed them all with tea-cakes, poached eggs, anchovy toast, and drinks from a coromandel-wood liqueur-case which Midmore had never known that he possessed.

'And I *will* say,' said Miss Connie Sperrit, her spurred foot on the fender and a smoking muffin in her whip-hand, 'Rhoda does one top-hole. She always did since I was eight.'

'Seven, Miss, was when you began to 'unt,' said Rhoda, setting down more buttered toast.

'And so,' the M.F.H. was saying to Midmore, 'when he got to your brute Sidney's land, we had to whip 'em off. It's a regular Alsatia for 'em. They know it. Why'—he dropped his voice—'I don't want to say anything against Sidney as your tenant, of course, but I do believe the old scoundrel's perfectly capable of putting down poison.'

'Sidney's capable of anything,' said Midmore with immense feeling; but once again he held his tongue. They were a queer community; yet when they had stamped and jingled out to their horses again, the house felt hugely big and disconcerting.

This may be reckoned the conscious beginning of his double life. It ran in odd channels that summer—a riding-school, for instance, near Hayes Common and a shooting-ground near Wormwood Scrubs. A man who has been saddle-galled or shoulder-bruised for half the day is not at his London best of evenings; and when the bills for his amusements come in he curtails his expenses in other directions. So a cloud settled on Midmore's name. His London world talked of a hardening of heart and a tightening of purse-strings which signified disloyalty to the Cause. One man, a confidant of the old expressive days, attacked him robustiously and demanded account of his soul's progress. It was not furnished, for Midmore was calculating how much it would cost to repave stables so dilapidated that even the village idiot apologized for putting visitors' horses into them. The man went away, and served up what he had

heard of the pig-pound episode as a little newspaper sketch, calculated to annoy. Midmore read it with an eye as practical as a
woman's, and since most of his experiences had been among women,
at once sought out a woman to whom he might tell his sorrow at the
disloyalty of his own familiar friend. She was so sympathetic that
he went on to confide how his bruised heart—she knew all about it
—had found so-lace, with a long O, in another quarter which he
indicated rather carefully in case it might be betrayed to other
loyal friends. As his hints pointed directly towards facile Hamp-
stead, and as his urgent business was the purchase of a horse from a
dealer, Beckenham way, he felt he had done good work. Later,
when his friend, the scribe, talked to him alluringly of 'secret
gardens' and those so-laces to which every man who follows the
Wider Morality is entitled, Midmore lent him a five-pound note
which he had got back on the price of a ninety-guinea bay gelding.
So true it is, as he read in one of the late Colonel Werf's books, that
'the young man of the present day would sooner lie under an
imputation against his morals than against his knowledge of horse-
flesh.'

Midmore desired more than he desired anything else at that
moment to ride and, above all, to jump on a ninety-guinea bay
gelding with black points and a slovenly habit of hitting his fences.
He did not wish many people except Mr Sidney, who very kindly
lent his soft meadow behind the flood-gates, to be privy to the
matter, which he rightly foresaw would take him to the autumn.
So he told such friends as hinted at country week-end visits that he
had practically let his newly inherited house. The rent, he said, was
an object to him, for he had lately lost large sums through ill-
considered benevolences. He would name no names, but they could
guess. And they guessed loyally all round the circle of his acquaintance as they spread the news that explained so much.

There remained only one couple of his once intimate associates to
pacify. They were deeply sympathetic and utterly loyal, of course,
but as curious as any of the apes whose diet they had adopted. Midmore met them in a suburban train, coming up to town, not twenty
minutes after he had come off two hours' advanced tuition (one
guinea an hour) over hurdles in a hall. He had, of course, changed
his kit, but his too heavy bridle-hand shook a little among the
newspapers. On the inspiration of the moment, which is your
natural liar's best hold, he told them that he was condemned to a
rest-cure. He would lie in semi-darkness drinking milk, for weeks
and weeks, cut off even from letters. He was astonished and

delighted at the ease with which the usual lie confounds the unusual intellect. They swallowed it as swiftly as they recommended him to live on nuts and fruit; but he saw in the woman's eyes the exact reason she would set forth for his retirement. After all, she had as much right to express herself as he purposed to take for himself; and Midmore believed strongly in the fullest equality of the sexes.

That retirement made one small ripple in the strenuous world. The lady who had written the twelve-page letter ten months before sent him another of eight pages, analysing all the motives that were leading her back to him—should she come?—now that he was ill and alone. Much might yet be retrieved, she said, out of the waste of jarring lives and piteous misunderstandings. It needed only a hand.

But Midmore needed two, next morning very early, for a devil's diversion, among wet coppices, called 'cubbing.'

'You haven't a bad seat,' said Miss Sperrit through the morning mists. 'But you're worrying him.'

'He pulls so,' Midmore grunted.

'Let him alone, then. Look out for the branches,' she shouted, as they whirled up a splashy ride. Cubs were plentiful. Most of the hounds attached themselves to a straight-necked youngster of education who scuttled out of the woods into the open fields below.

'Hold on!' someone shouted. 'Turn 'em, Midmore. That's your brute Sidney's land. It's all wire.'

'Oh, Connie, stop!' Mrs Sperrit shrieked as her daughter charged at a boundary-hedge.

'Wire be damned! I had it all out a fortnight ago. Come on!' This was Midmore, buffeting into it a little lower down.

'*I* knew that!' Connie cried over her shoulder, and she flitted across the open pasture, humming to herself.

'Oh, of course! If some people have private information, they can afford to thrust.' This was a snuff-coloured habit into which Miss Sperrit had cannoned down the ride.

'What! Midmore got Sidney to heel! *You* never did that, Sperrit.' This was Mr Fisher, M.F.H., enlarging the breach Midmore had made.

'No, confound him!' said the father testily. 'Go on, sir! *Injecto ter pulvere*—you've kicked half the ditch into my eye already.'

They killed that cub a little short of the haven his mother had told him to make for—the two-acre Alsatia of a gorse-patch to which the M.F.H. had been denied access for the last fifteen seasons.

He expressed his gratitude before all the field and Mr Sidney, at Mr Sidney's farm-house door.

'And if there should be any poultry claims——' he went on.

'There won't be,' said Midmore. 'It's too like cheating a sucking child, isn't it, Mr Sidney?'

'You've got me!' was all the reply. 'I be used to bein' put upon, but you've got me, Mus' Midmore.'

Midmore pointed to a new brick pig-pound built in strict disregard of the terms of the life-tenant's lease. The gesture told the tale to the few who did not know, and they shouted.

Such pagan delights as these were followed by pagan sloth of evenings when men and women elsewhere are at their brightest. But Midmore preferred to lie out on a yellow silk couch, reading works of debasing vulgarity; or, by invitation, to dine with the Sperrits and savages of their kidney. These did not expect flights of fancy or phrasing. They lied, except about horses, grudgingly and of necessity, not for art's sake; and, men and women alike, they expressed themselves along their chosen lines with the serene indifference of the larger animals. Then Midmore would go home and identify them, one by one, out of the natural-history books by the late Mr Surtees, on the table beside the sofa. At first they looked upon him coolly, but when the tale of the removed wire and the recaptured gorse had gone the rounds, they accepted him as a person willing to play their games. True, a faction suspended judgement for a while, because they shot, and hoped that Midmore would serve the glorious Mammon of pheasant-raising rather than the unkempt god of fox-hunting. But after he had shown his choice, they did not ask by what intellectual process he had arrived at it. He hunted three, sometimes four, times a week, which necessitated not only one bay gelding (£94:10s.), but a mannerly white-stockinged chestnut (£114), and a black mare, rather long in the back but with a mouth of silk (£150), who so evidently preferred to carry a lady that it would have been cruel to have baulked her. Besides, with that handling she could be sold at a profit. And besides, the hunt was a quiet, intimate, kindly little hunt, not anxious for strangers, of good report in the *Field*, the servant of one M.F.H., given to hospitality, riding well its own horses, and, with the exception of Midmore, not novices. But as Miss Sperrit observed, after the M.F.H. had said some things to him at a gate: 'It *is* a pity you don't know as much as your horse; but you will in time. It takes years and yee-ars. I've been at it for fifteen and I'm only just learning. But you've made a decent kick-off.'

So he kicked off in wind and wet and mud, wondering quite sincerely why the bubbling ditches and sucking pastures held him from day to day, or what so-lace he could find on off days in chasing grooms and bricklayers round outhouses.

To make sure he uprooted himself one week-end of heavy midwinter rain, and re-entered his lost world in the character of Galahad fresh from a rest-cure. They all agreed, with an eye over his shoulder for the next comer, that he was a different man; but when they asked him for the symptoms of nervous strain, and led him all through their own, he realized he had lost much of his old skill in lying. His three months' absence, too, had put him hopelessly behind the London field. The movements, the allusions, the slang of the game had changed. The couples had rearranged themselves or were re-crystallizing in fresh triangles, whereby he put his foot in it badly. Only one great soul (he who had written the account of the pig-pound episode) stood untouched by the vast flux of time, and Midmore lent him another fiver for his integrity. A woman took him, in the wet afternoon, to a pronouncement of the Oneness of Impulse in Humanity, which struck him as a polysyllabic *résumé* of Mr Sidney's domestic arrangements, plus a clarion-call to 'shock civilization into common sense.'

'And you'll come to tea with me tomorrow?' she asked, after lunch, nibbling cashew nuts from a saucer. Midmore replied that there were great arrears of work to overtake when a man had been put away for so long.

'But you've come back like a giant refreshed. . . . I hope that Daphne'—this was the lady of the twelve- and the eight-page letter—'will be with us too. She has misunderstood herself, like so many of us,' the woman murmured, 'but I think eventually . . .' She flung out her thin little hands. 'However, these are things that each lonely soul must adjust for itself.'

'Indeed, yes,' said Midmore with a deep sigh. The old tricks were sprouting in the old atmosphere like mushrooms in a dung-pit. He passed into an abrupt reverie, shook his head, as though stung by tumultuous memories, and departed without any ceremony of farewell to—catch a mid-afternoon express where a man meets associates who talk horse, and weather as it affects the horse, all the way down. What worried him most was that he had missed a day with the hounds.

He met Rhoda's keen old eyes without flinching; and the drawing-room looked very comfortable that wet evening at tea. After all, his visit to Town had not been wholly a failure. He had burned

quite a bushel of letters at his flat. A flat—here he reached mechanically towards the worn volumes near the sofa—a flat was a consuming animal. As for Daphne . . . he opened at random on the words:
'His lordship then did as desired and disclosed a *tableau* of con-
siderable strength and variety.' Midmore reflected: 'And I used to
think . . . But she wasn't . . . We were all babblers and skirters
together . . . I didn't babble much—thank goodness—but I
skirted.' He turned the pages backward for more *Sortes Surteesianae*,
and read: 'When at length they rose to go to bed it struck each man
as he followed his neighbours upstairs, that the man before him
walked very crookedly.' He laughed aloud at the fire.

'What about tomorrow?' Rhoda asked, entering with garments
over her shoulder. 'It's never stopped raining since you left. You'll
be plastered out of sight an' all in five minutes. You'd better wear
your next best, 'adn't you? I'm afraid they've shrank. 'Adn't you
best try 'em on?'

'Here?' said Midmore.

'Suit yourself. I bathed you when you wasn't larger than a leg o'
lamb,' said the ex-ladies'-maid.

'Rhoda, one of these days I shall get a valet, and a married
butler.'

'There's many a true word spoke in jest. But nobody's huntin'
tomorrow.'

'Why? Have they cancelled the meet?'

'They say it only means slipping and over-reaching in the mud,
and they all 'ad enough of that today. Charlie told me so just
now.'

'Oh!' It seemed that the word of Mr Sperrit's confidential clerk
had weight.

'Charlie came down to help Mr Sidney lift his gates,' Rhoda continued.

'The flood-gates? They are perfectly easy to handle now. I've put
in a wheel and a winch.'

'When the brook's really up they must be took clean out on
account of the rubbish blockin' 'em. That's why Charlie came down.'

Midmore grunted impatiently. 'Everybody has talked to me
about that brook ever since I came here. It's never done anything
yet.'

'This 'as been a dry summer. If you care to look now, sir, I'll get
you a lantern.'

She paddled out with him into a large wet night. Half-way down
the lawn her light was reflected on shallow brown water, pricked

through with grass blades at the edges. Beyond that light, the brook was strangling and kicking among hedges and tree-trunks.

'What on earth will happen to the big rose-bed?' was Midmore's first word.

'It generally 'as to be restocked after a flood. Ah!' She raised her lantern. 'There's two garden-seats knockin' against the sun-dial. Now, that won't do the roses any good.'

'This is too absurd. There ought to be some decently thought-out system—for—for dealing with this sort of thing.' He peered into the rushing gloom. There seemed to be no end to the moisture and the racket. In Town he had noticed nothing.

'It can't be 'elped,' said Rhoda. 'It's just what it does do once in just so often. We'd better go back.'

All earth under foot was sliding in a thousand liquid noises towards the hoarse brook. Somebody wailed from the house: ' 'Fraid o' the water! Come 'ere! 'Fraid o' the water!'

'That's Jimmy. Wet always takes 'im that way,' she explained. The idiot charged into them, shaking with terror.

'Brave Jimmy! How brave of Jimmy! Come into the hall. What Jimmy got now?' she crooned. It was a sodden note which ran: 'Dear Rhoda—Mr Lotten, with whom I rode this afternoon, told me that if this wet keeps up, he's afraid the fish-pond he built last year, where Coxen's old mill-dam was, will go, as the dam did once before, he says. If it does it's bound to come down the brook. It may be all right, but perhaps you had better look out. C. S.'

'If Coxen's dam goes, that means . . . I'll 'ave the drawing-room carpet up at once to be on the safe side. The claw-'ammer is in the libery.'

'Wait a minute. Sidney's gates are out, you said?'

'Both. He'll need it if Coxen's pond goes. . . . I've seen it once.'

'I'll just slip down and have a look at Sidney. Light the lantern again, please, Rhoda.'

'You won't get *him* to stir. He's been there since he was born. But *she* don't know anything. I'll fetch your waterproof and some top-boots.'

' 'Fraid o' the water! 'Fraid o' the water!' Jimmy sobbed, pressed against a corner of the hall, his hands to his eyes.

'All right, Jimmy. Jimmy can help play with the carpet,' Rhoda answered, as Midmore went forth into the darkness and the roarings all round. He had never seen such an utterly unregulated state of affairs. There was another lantern reflected on the streaming drive.

'Hi! Rhoda! Did you get my note? I came down to make sure. I thought, afterwards, Jimmy might funk the water!'

'It's me—Miss Sperrit,' Midmore cried. 'Yes, we got it, thanks.'

'You're back, then. Oh, good! . . . Is it bad down with you?'

'I'm going to Sidney's to have a look.'

'You won't get *him* out. Lucky I met Bob Lotten. I told him he hadn't any business impounding water for his idiotic trout without rebuilding the dam.'

'How far up is it? I've only been there once.'

'Not more than four miles as the water will come. He says he's opened all the sluices.'

She had turned and fallen into step beside him, her hooded head bowed against the thinning rain. As usual she was humming to herself.

'Why on earth did you come out in this weather?' Midmore asked.

'It was worse when you were in Town. The rain's taking off now. If it wasn't for that pond, I wouldn't worry so much. There's Sidney's bell. Come on!' She broke into a run. A cracked bell was jangling feebly down the valley.

'Keep on the road!' Midmore shouted. The ditches were snorting bank-full on either side, and towards the brook-side the fields were afloat and beginning to move in the darkness.

'Catch me going off it! There's his light burning all right.' She halted undistressed at a little rise. 'But the flood's in the orchard. Look!' She swung her lantern to show a front rank of old apple-trees reflected in still, outlying waters beyond the half-drowned hedge. They could hear above the thud-thud of the gorged flood-gates, shrieks in two keys as monotonous as a steam-organ.

'The high one's the pig.' Miss Sperrit laughed.

'All right! I'll get *her* out. You stay where you are, and I'll see you home afterwards.'

'But the water's only just over the road,' she objected.

'Never mind. Don't you move. Promise?'

'All right. You take my stick, then, and feel for holes in case anything's washed out anywhere. This *is* a lark!'

Midmore took it, and stepped into the water that moved sluggishly as yet across the farm road which ran to Sidney's front door and the raised and metalled public road. It was half-way up to his knees when he knocked. As he looked back Miss Sperrit's lantern seemed to float in mid-ocean.

'You can't come in or the water 'll come with you. I've bunged up all the cracks,' Mr Sidney shouted from within. 'Who be ye?'

'Take me out! Take me out!' the woman shrieked, and the pig from his sty behind the house urgently seconded the motion.

'I'm Midmore! Coxen's old mill-dam is likely to go, they say. Come out!'

'I told 'em it would when they made a fish-pond of it. 'Twasn't ever puddled proper. But it's a middlin' wide valley. She's got room to spread. . . . Keep still, or I'll take and duck you in the cellar! . . . You go 'ome, Mus' Midmore, an' take the law o' Mus' Lotten soon's you've changed your socks.'

'Confound you, aren't you coming out?'

'To catch my death o' cold? I'm all right where I be. I've seen it before. But you can take *her*. She's no sort o' use or sense. . . . Climb out through the window! Didn't I tell you I'd plugged the door-cracks, you fool's daughter?' The parlour window opened, and the woman flung herself into Midmore's arms, nearly knocking him down. Mr Sidney leaned out of the window, pipe in mouth.

'Take her 'ome,' he said, and added oracularly:

> *Two women in one house,*
> *Two cats an' one mouse,*
> *Two dogs an' one bone—*
> *Which I will leave alone.*

I've seen it before.' Then he shut and fastened the window.

'A trap! A trap! You had ought to have brought a trap for me! I'll be drowned in this wet,' the woman cried.

'Hold up! You can't be any wetter than you are. Come along!' Midmore did not at all like the feel of the water over his boot-tops.

'Hooray! Come along!' Miss Sperrit's lantern, not fifty yards away, waved cheerily.

The woman threshed towards it like a panic-stricken goose, fell on her knees, was jerked up again by Midmore, and pushed on till she collapsed at Miss Sperrit's feet.

'But you *won't* get bronchitis if you go straight to Mr Midmore's house,' said the unsympathetic maiden.

'O Gawd! O Gawd! I wish our 'eavenly Father 'ud forgive me my sins an' call me 'ome,' the woman sobbed. 'But I won't go to '*er* 'ouse! I won't.'

'All right, then. Stay here. Now, if we run,' Miss Sperrit whispered to Midmore, 'she'll follow us. Not too fast.'

They set off at a considerate trot, and the woman lumbered behind them, bellowing, till they met a third lantern—Rhoda holding Jimmy's hand. She had got the carpet up, she said, and was escorting Jimmy past the water that he dreaded.

'That's all right,' Miss Sperrit pronounced. 'Take Mrs Sidney back with you, Rhoda, and put her to bed. I'll take Jimmy with me. You aren't afraid of the water now, are you, Jimmy?'

'Not afraid of anything now.' Jimmy reached for her hand. 'But get away from the water quick.'

'I'm coming with you,' Midmore interrupted.

'You most certainly are not. You're drenched. She threw you twice. Go home and change. You may have to be out again all night. It's only half-past seven now. I'm perfectly safe.' She flung herself lightly over a stile, and hurried uphill by the footpath, out of reach of all but the boasts of the flood below.

Rhoda, dead-silent, herded Mrs Sidney to the house.

'You'll find your things laid out on the bed,' she said to Midmore as he came up. 'I'll attend to—to this. *She*'s got nothing to cry for.'

Midmore raced into dry kit, and hurried uphill to be rewarded by the sight of the lantern just turning into the Sperrits' gate. He came back by way of Sidney's farm, where he saw the light twinkling across three acres of shining water, for the rain had ceased and the clouds were stripping overhead, though the brook was noisier than ever. Now there was only that doubtful mill-pond to look after—that and his swirling world abandoned to himself alone.

'We shall have to sit up for it,' said Rhoda after dinner. And as the drawing-room commanded the best view of the rising flood, they watched it from there for a long time, while all the clocks of the house bore them company.

' 'Tisn't the water, it's the mud on the skirting-board after it goes down that I mind,' Rhoda whispered. 'The last time Coxen's dam broke, I remember it came up to the second—no, third—step o' Mr Sidney's stairs.'

'What did Sidney do about it?'

'He made a notch on the step. 'E said it was a record. Just like 'im.'

'It's up to the drive now,' said Midmore after another long wait. 'And the rain stopped before eight, you know.'

'Then Coxen's dam 'as broke, and that's the first of the flood-water.' She stared out beside him. The water was rising in sudden pulses—an inch or two at a time, with great sweeps and lagoons and a sudden increase of the brook's proper thunder.

'You can't stand all the time. Take a chair,' Midmore said presently.

Rhoda looked back into the bare room. 'The carpet bein' up *does* make a difference. Thank you, sir, I *will* 'ave a set-down.'

'Right over the drive now,' said Midmore. He opened the window and leaned out. 'Is that wind up the valley, Rhoda?'

'No, that's *it*! But I've 'eard it before.'

There was not so much a roar as the purposeful drive of a tide across a jagged reef, which put down every other sound for twenty minutes. A wide sheet of water hurried up to the little terrace on which the house stood, pushed round either corner, rose again and stretched, as it were, yawning beneath the moonlight, joined other sheets waiting for it in unsuspected hollows, and lay out all in one. A puff of wind followed.

'It's right up to the wall now. I can touch it with my finger.' Midmore bent over the window-sill.

'I can 'ear it in the cellars,' said Rhoda dolefully. 'Well, we've done what we can! I think I'll 'ave a look.' She left the room, and was absent half an hour or more, during which time he saw a full-grown tree hauling itself across the lawn by its naked roots. Then a hurdle knocked against the wall, caught on an iron foot-scraper just outside, and made a square-headed ripple. The cascade through the cellar-windows diminished.

'It's dropping,' Rhoda cried, as she returned. 'It's only tricklin' into my cellars now.'

'Wait a minute. I believe—I believe I can see the scraper on the edge of the drive just showing!'

In another ten minutes the drive itself roughened and became gravel again, tilting all its water towards the shrubbery.

'The pond's gone past,' Rhoda announced. 'We shall only 'ave the common flood to contend with now. You'd better go to bed.'

'I ought to go down and have another look at Sidney before daylight.'

'No need. You can see 'is light burnin' from all the upstairs windows.'

'By the way. I forgot about *her*. Where've you put her?'

'In my bed.' Rhoda's tone was ice. 'I wasn't going to undo a room for *that* stuff.'

'But it—it couldn't be helped,' said Midmore. 'She was half drowned. One mustn't be narrow-minded, Rhoda, even if her position isn't quite—er—regular.'

'Pfff! I wasn't worryin' about that.' She leaned forward to the window. 'There's the edge of the lawn showin' now. It falls as fast

as it rises. Dearie'—the change of tone made Midmore jump—
'didn't you know that I was 'is first? *That*'s what makes it so hard
to bear.' Midmore looked at the long lizard-like back and had no
words.

She went on, still talking through the black window-pane:

'Your pore dear auntie was very kind about it. She said she'd
make all allowances for one, but no more. Never any more. . . .
Then, you didn't know 'oo Charlie was all this time?'

'Your nephew, I always thought.'

'Well, well!' She spoke pityingly. 'Everybody's business being
nobody's business, I suppose no one thought to tell you. But
Charlie made 'is own way for 'imself from the beginnin'! . . . But
her upstairs, she never prodooced anything. Just an 'ousekeeper, as
you might say. Turned over an' went to sleep straight off. She 'ad
the impudence to ask me for 'ot sherry-gruel.'

'Did you give it to her?' said Midmore.

'Me? Your sherry? No!'

The memory of Sidney's outrageous rhyme at the window, and
Charlie's long nose (he thought it looked interested at the time) as
he passed the copies of Mrs Werf's last four wills, overcame Midmore without warning.

'This damp is givin' you a cold,' said Rhoda, rising. 'There you
go again! Sneezin's a sure sign of it. Better go to bed. You can't
do anythin' excep' '—she stood rigid, with crossed arms—'about
me.'

'Well. What about you?' Midmore stuffed the handkerchief into
his pocket.

'Now you know about it, what are you goin' to do—sir?'

She had the answer on her lean cheek before the sentence was
finished.

'Go and see if you can get us something to eat, Rhoda. And
beer.'

'I expec' the larder 'll be in a swim,' she replied, 'but old bottled
stuff don't take any harm from wet.' She returned with a tray, all
in order, and they ate and drank together, and took observations of
the falling flood till dawn opened its bleared eyes on the wreck of
what had been a fair garden. Midmore, cold and annoyed, found
himself humming:

'That flood strewed wrecks upon the grass,
That ebb swept out the flocks to sea.

There isn't a rose left, Rhoda!

> *'An awesome ebb and flow it was*
> *To many more than mine and me.*
> *But each will mourn his . . .*

It'll cost me a hundred.'

'Now we know the worst,' said Rhoda, 'we can go to bed. I'll lay on the kitchen sofa. His light's burnin' still.'

'And *she?*'

'Dirty old cat! You ought to 'ear 'er snore!'

At ten o'clock in the morning, after a maddening hour in his own garden on the edge of the retreating brook, Midmore went off to confront more damage at Sidney's. The first thing that met him was the pig, snowy white, for the water had washed him out of his new sty, calling on high heaven for breakfast. The front door had been forced open, and the flood had registered its own height in a brown dado on the walls. Midmore chased the pig out and called up the stairs.

'I be abed o' course. Which step 'as she rose to?' Sidney cried from above. 'The fourth? Then it's beat all records. Come up.'

'Are you ill?' Midmore asked as he entered the room. The red eyelids blinked cheerfully. Mr Sidney, beneath a sumptuous patchwork quilt, was smoking.

'Nah! I'm only thankin' God I ain't my own landlord. Take that cheer. What's she done?'

'It hasn't gone down enough for me to make sure.'

'Them flood-gates o' yourn 'll be middlin' far down the brook by now; an' your rose-garden 'll have gone after 'em. I saved my chickens, though. You'd better get Mus' Sperrit to take the law o' Lotten an' 'is fish-pond.'

'No, thanks.. I've trouble enough without that.'

'Hev ye?' Mr Sidney grinned. 'How did ye make out with those two women o' mine last night? I lay they fought.'

'You infernal old scoundrel!' Midmore laughed.

'I be—an' then again I bain't,' was the placid answer. 'But, Rhoda, *she* wouldn't ha' left me last night. Fire or flood, she wouldn't.'

'Why didn't you ever marry her?' Midmore asked.

'Waste of good money. She was willin' without.'

There was a step on the gritty mud below, and a voice humming. Midmore rose quickly, saying: 'Well, I suppose you're all right now.'

'I be. I ain't a landlord, nor I ain't young—nor anxious. Oh,

Mus' Midmore! Would it make any odds about her thirty pound comin' regular if I married her? Charlie said maybe 'twould.'

'Did he?' Midmore turned at the door. 'And what did Jimmy say about it?'

'Jimmy?' Mr Sidney chuckled as the joke took him. 'Oh, *he's* none o' mine. He's Charlie's look-out.'

Midmore slammed the door and ran downstairs.

'Well, this is a—sweet—mess,' said Miss Sperrit in shortest skirts and heaviest riding-boots. 'I had to come down and have a look at it. "The old Mayor climbed the belfry tower." Been up all night nursing your family?'

'Nearly that! Isn't it cheerful?' He pointed through the door to the stairs with small twig-drift on the last three treads.

'It's a record, though,' said she, and hummed to herself:

> '*That flood strewed wrecks upon the grass,*
> *That ebb swept out the flocks to sea.*'

'You're always singing that, aren't you?' Midmore said suddenly as she passed into the parlour where slimy chairs had been stranded at all angles.

'Am I? Now I come to think of it I believe I do. They say I always hum when I ride. Have you noticed it?'

'Of course I have. I notice every——'

'Oh,' she went on hurriedly. 'We had it for the village cantata last winter—"The Brides of Enderby." '

'No! "High Tide on the Coast of Lincolnshire." ' For some reason Midmore spoke sharply.

'Just like that.' She pointed to the befouled walls. 'I say. . . . Let's get this furniture a little straight. . . . You know it too?'

'Every word, since you sang it, of course.'`

'When?'

'The first night I ever came down. You rode past the drawing-room window in the dark singing it—"And sweeter woman——" ' '

'I thought the house was empty then. Your aunt always let us use that short cut. Ha-hadn't we better get this out into the passage? It'll all have to come out anyhow. You take the other side.' They began to lift a heavyish table. Their words came jerkily between gasps and their faces were as white as—a newly washed and very hungry pig.

'Look out!' Midmore shouted. His legs were whirled from under him, as the table, grunting madly, careened and knocked the girl out of sight.

The wild boar of Asia could not have cut down a couple more scientifically, but this little pig lacked his ancestor's nerve and fled shrieking over their bodies.

'Are you hurt, darling?' was Midmore's first word, and 'No—I'm only winded—dear,' was Miss Sperrit's, as he lifted her out of her corner, her hat over one eye and her right cheek a smear of mud.

*

They fed him a little later on some chicken-feed that they found in Sidney's quiet barn, a pail of butter-milk out of the dairy, and a quantity of onions from a shelf in the back-kitchen.

'Seed-onions, most likely,' said Connie. 'You'll hear about this.'

'What does it matter? They ought to have been gilded. We must buy him.'

'And keep him as long as he lives,' she agreed. 'But I think I ought to go home now. You see, when I came out I didn't expect . . . Did you?'

'No! Yes. . . . It had to come. . . . But if anyone had told me an hour ago! . . . Sidney's unspeakable parlour—and the mud on the carpet.'

'Oh, I say! Is my cheek clean now?'

'Not quite. Lend me your hanky again a minute, darling. . . . What a purler you came!'

'You can't talk. Remember when your chin hit that table and you said "Blast"! I was just going to laugh.'

'You didn't laugh when I picked you up. You were going "oo-oo-oo" like a little owl.'

'My dear child——'

'Say that again!'

'My dear child. (Do you really like it? I keep it for my best friends.) My *dee-ar* child, I thought I was going to be sick there and then. He knocked every ounce of wind out of me—the angel! But I must really go.'

They set off together, very careful not to join hands or take arms.

'Not across the fields,' said Midmore at the stile. 'Come round by —by your own place.'

She flushed indignantly.

'It will be yours in a little time,' he went on, shaken with his own audacity.

'Not so much of your little times, if you please!' She shied like a colt across the road; then instantly, like a colt, her eyes lit with new curiosity as she came in sight of the drive-gates.

'And not quite so much of your airs and graces, madam,' Midmore returned, 'or I won't let you use our drive as a short cut any more.'

'Oh, I'll be good. I'll be good.' Her voice changed suddenly. 'I swear I'll try to be good, dear. I'm not much of a thing at the best. What made *you* . . .'

'I'm worse—worse! Miles and oceans worse. But what does it matter now?'

They halted beside the gate-pillars.

'I see!' she said, looking up the sodden carriage sweep to the front-door porch where Rhoda was slapping a wet mat to and fro. '*I* see. . . . Now, I really must go home. No! Don't you come. I must speak to Mother first by myself.'

He watched her up the hill till she was out of sight.

A Diversity of Creatures, 1917 *

* Dated 1913 in the text.

A Madonna of the Trenches

Whatever a man of the sons of men
  Shall say to his heart of the lords above,
They have shown man, verily, once and again,
  Marvellous mercies and infinite love.

· · ·

O sweet one love, O my life's delight,
  Dear, though the days have divided us,
Lost beyond hope, taken far out of sight,
  Not twice in the world shall the Gods do thus.
                    Swinburne, LES NOYADES

SEEING HOW MANY unstable ex-soldiers came to the Lodge of Instruction (attached to 'Faith and Works E.C. 5837') in the years after the War, the wonder is there was not more trouble from Brethren whom sudden meetings with old comrades jerked back into their still raw past. But our round, torpedo-bearded local Doctor—Brother Keede, Senior Warden—always stood ready to deal with hysteria before it got out of hand; and when I examined Brethren unknown or imperfectly vouched for on the Masonic side, I passed on to him anything that seemed doubtful. He had had his experience as medical officer of a South London Battalion, during the last two years of the War; and, naturally, often found friends and acquaintances among the visitors.

Brother C. Strangwick, a young, tallish, new-made Brother, hailed from some South London Lodge. His papers and his answers were above suspicion, but his red-rimmed eyes had a puzzled glare that might mean nerves. So I introduced him particularly to Keede, who discovered in him a Headquarters Orderly of his old Battalion, congratulated him on his return to fitness—he had been discharged for some infirmity or other—and plunged at once into Somme memories.

'I hope I did right, Keede,' I said when we were robing before Lodge.

'Oh, quite. He reminded me that I had him under my hands at Sampoux in 'Eighteen, when he went to bits. He was a Runner.'

'Was it shock?' I asked.

'Of sorts—but not what he wanted me to think it was. No, he

wasn't shamming. He had Jumps to the limit—but he played up to mislead me about the reason of 'em. . . . Well, if we could stop patients from lying, medicine would be too easy, I suppose.'

I noticed that, after Lodge-working, Keede gave him a seat a couple of rows in front of us, that he might enjoy a lecture on the Orientation of King Solomon's Temple, which an earnest Brother thought would be a nice interlude between Labour and the high tea that we called our 'Banquet.' Even helped by tobacco it was a dreary performance. About half-way through, Strangwick, who had been fidgeting and twitching for some minutes, rose, drove back his chair grinding across the tessellated floor, and yelped: 'Oh, My Aunt! I can't stand this any longer.' Under cover of a general laugh of assent he brushed past us and stumbled towards the door.

'I thought so!' Keede whispered to me. 'Come along!' We overtook him in the passage, crowing hysterically and wringing his hands. Keede led him into the Tyler's Room, a small office where we stored odds and ends of regalia and furniture, and locked the door.

'I'm—I'm all right,' the boy began piteously.

' 'Course you are.' Keede opened a small cupboard which I had seen called upon before, mixed sal volatile and water in a graduated glass, and, as Strangwick drank, pushed him gently on to an old sofa. 'There,' he went on. 'It's nothing to write home about. I've seen you ten times worse. I expect our talk has brought things back.'

He hooked up a chair behind him with one foot, held the patient's hands in his own, and sat down. The chair creaked.

'Don't!' Strangwick squealed. 'I can't stand it! There's nothing on earth creaks like they do! And—and when it thaws we—we've got to slap 'em back with a spa-ade! Remember those Frenchmen's little boots under the duckboards? . . . What'll I do? What'll I do about it?'

Someone knocked at the door, to know if all were well.

'Oh, quite, thanks!' said Keede over his shoulder. 'But I shall need this room awhile. Draw the curtains, please.'

We heard the rings of the hangings that drape the passage from Lodge to Banquet Room click along their poles, and what sound there had been, of feet and voices, was shut off.

Strangwick, retching impotently, complained of the frozen dead who creak in the frost.

'He's playing up still,' Keede whispered. '*That*'s not his real trouble—any more than 'twas last time.'

'But surely,' I replied, 'men get those things on the brain pretty badly. Remember in October——'

'This chap hasn't, though. I wonder what's really helling him. What are you thinking of?' said Keede peremptorily.

'French End an' Butcher's Row,' Strangwick muttered.

'Yes, there were a few there. But suppose we face Bogey instead of giving him best every time.' Keede turned towards me with a hint in his eye that I was to play up to his leads.

'What was the trouble with French End?' I opened at a venture.

'It was a bit by Sampoux, that we had taken over from the French. They're tough, but you wouldn't call 'em tidy as a nation. They had faced both sides of it with dead to keep the mud back. All those trenches were like gruel in a thaw. Our people had to do the same sort of thing—elsewhere; but Butcher's Row in French End was the—er—show-piece. Luckily, we pinched a salient from Jerry just then, an' straightened things out—so we didn't need to use the Row after November. You remember, Strangwick?'

'My God, yes! When the duckboard-slats were missin' you'd tread on 'em, an' they'd creak.'

'They're bound to. Like leather,' said Keede. 'It gets on one's nerves a bit, but——'

'Nerves? It's real! It's real!' Strangwick gulped.

'But at your time of life, it'll all fall behind you in a year or so. I'll give you another sip of—paregoric, an' we'll face it quietly. Shall we?'

Keede opened his cupboard again and administered a carefully dropped dark dose of something that was not sal volatile. 'This'll settle you in a few minutes,' he explained. 'Lie still, an' don't talk unless you feel like it.'

He faced me, fingering his beard.

'Ye-es. Butcher's Row wasn't pretty,' he volunteered. 'Seeing Strangwick here has brought it all back to me again. Funny thing! We had a Platoon Sergeant of Number Two—what the deuce was his name?—an elderly bird who must have lied like a patriot to get out to the Front at his age; but he was a first-class Non-Com., and the last person, you'd think, to make mistakes. Well, he was due for a fortnight's home leave in January, 'Eighteen. You were at B.H.Q. then, Strangwick, weren't you?'

'Yes. I was Orderly. It was January twenty-first'; Strangwick spoke with a thickish tongue, and his eyes burned. Whatever drug it was, had taken hold.

'About then,' Keede said. 'Well, this Sergeant, instead of coming down from the trenches the regular way an' joinin' Battalion Details after dark, an' takin' that funny little train for Arras, thinks he'll warm himself first. So he gets into a dug-out, in Butcher's Row, that used to be an old French dressing-station, and fugs up between a couple of braziers of pure charcoal! As luck 'ud have it, that was the only dug-out with an inside door opening inwards—some French anti-gas fitting, I expect—and, by what we could make out, the door must have swung to while he was warming. Anyhow, he didn't turn up at the train. There was a search at once. We couldn't afford to waste Platoon Sergeants. We found him in the morning. He'd got his gas all right. A machine-gunner reported him, didn't he, Strangwick?'

'No, sir. Corporal Grant—o' the Trench Mortars.'

'So it was. Yes, Grant—the man with that little wen on his neck. Nothing wrong with your memory, at any rate. What was the Sergeant's name?'

'Godsoe—John Godsoe,' Strangwick answered.

'Yes, that was it. I had to see him next mornin'—frozen stiff between the two braziers—and not a scrap of private papers on him. *That* was the only thing that made me think it mightn't have been—quite an accident.'

Strangwick's relaxing face set, and he threw back at once to the Orderly Room manner.

'I give my evidence—at the time—to you, sir. He passed—overtook me, I should say—comin' down from supports, after I'd warned him for leaf. I thought he was goin' through Parrot Trench as usual; but 'e must 'ave turned off into French End where the old bombed barricade was.'

'Yes. I remember now. You were the last man to see him alive. That was on the twenty-first of January, you say? Now, *when* was it that Dearlove and Billings brought you to me—clean out of your head?' . . . Keede dropped his hand, in the style of magazine detectives, on Strangwick's shoulder. The boy looked at him with cloudy wonder, and muttered: 'I was took to you on the evenin' of the twenty-fourth of January. But you don't think I did him in, do you?'

I could not help smiling at Keede's discomfiture; but he recovered himself. 'Then what the dickens *was* on your mind that evening—before I gave you the hypodermic?'

'The—the things in Butcher's Row. They kept on comin' over me. You've seen me like this before, sir.'

'But I knew that it was a lie. You'd no more got stiffs on the brain then than you have now. You've got something, but you're hiding it.'

' 'Ow do *you* know, Doctor?' Strangwick whimpered.

'D'you remember what you said to me, when Dearlove and Billings were holding you down that evening?'

'About the things in Butcher's Row?'

'Oh, no! You spun me a lot of stuff about corpses creaking; but you let yourself go in the middle of it—when you pushed that telegram at me. What did you mean, f'r instance, by asking what advantage it was for you to fight beasts of officers if the dead didn't rise?'

'Did I say "beasts of officers"?'

'You did. It's out of the Burial Service.'

'I suppose, then, I must have heard it. As a matter of fact, I 'ave.' Strangwick shuddered extravagantly.

'Probably. And there's another thing—that hymn you were shouting till I put you under. It was something about Mercy and Love. Remember it?'

'I'll try,' said the boy obediently, and began to paraphrase, as nearly as possible thus: ' "Whatever a man may say in his heart unto the Lord, yea, verily I say unto you—Gawd hath shown man, again and again, marvellous mercy an'—an' somethin' or other love." ' He screwed up his eyes and shook.

'Now where did you get *that* from?' Keede insisted.

'From Godsoe—on the twenty-first Jan. . . . 'Ow could *I* tell what 'e meant to do?' he burst out in a high, unnatural key—'Any more than I knew *she* was dead.'

'Who was dead?' said Keede.

'Me Auntie Armine.'

'The one the telegram came to you about, at Sampoux, that you wanted me to explain—the one that you were talking of in the passage out here just now when you began: "O Auntie," and changed it to "O Gawd," when I collared you?'

'That's her! I haven't a chance with you, Doctor. *I* didn't know there was anything wrong with those braziers. How could I? We're always usin' 'em. Honest to God, I thought at first go-off he might wish to warm himself before the leaf-train. I—I didn't know Uncle John meant to start—'ouse-keepin'.' He laughed horribly, and then the dry tears came.

Keede waited for them to pass in sobs and hiccoughs before he continued: 'Why? Was Godsoe your uncle?'

'No,' said Strangwick, his head between his hands. 'Only we'd known him ever since we were born. Dad 'ad known him before that. He lived almost next street to us. Him an' Dad an' Ma an'—an' the rest had always been friends. So we called him Uncle—like children do.'

'What sort of man was he?'

'One o' *the* best, sir. Pensioned Sergeant with a little money left him—quite independent—and very superior. They had a sittin'-room full o' Indian curios that him and his wife used to let Sister an' me see when we'd been good.'

'Wasn't he rather old to join up?'

'That made no odds to him. He joined up as Sergeant Instructor at the first go-off, an' when the Battalion was ready he got 'imself sent along. He wangled me into 'is platoon when I went out—early in 'Seventeen. Because Ma wanted it, I suppose.'

'I'd no notion you knew him that well,' was Keede's comment.

'Oh, it made no odds to him. He 'ad no pets in the platoon, but 'e'd write 'ome to Ma about me an' all the doin's. You see'—Strangwick stirred uneasily on the sofa—'we'd known him all our lives—lived in the next street an' all. . . . An' him well over fifty. Oh dear me! *Oh* dear me! What a bloody mix-up things are, when one's as young as me!' he wailed of a sudden.

But Keede held him to the point. 'He wrote to your mother about you?'

'Yes. Ma's eyes had gone bad followin' on air-raids. Blood-vessels broke behind 'em from sittin' in cellars an' bein' sick. She had to 'ave 'er letters read to her by Auntie. Now I think of it, that was the only thing that you might have called anything at all——'

'Was that the aunt that died, and that you got the wire about?' Keede drove on.

'Yes—Auntie Armine—Ma's younger sister, an' she nearer fifty than forty. What a mix-up! An' if I'd been asked any time about it, I'd 'ave sworn there wasn't a single sol'tary item concernin' her that everybody didn't know an' hadn't known all along. No more conceal to her doin's than—than so much shop-front. She'd looked after Sister an' me, when needful—whoopin' cough an' measles—just the same as Ma. We was in an' out of her house like rabbits. You see, Uncle Armine is a cabinet-maker, an' second-'and furniture, an' we liked playin' with the things. She 'ad no children, and when the War came, she said she was glad of it. But she never talked much of her feelin's. She kept herself to herself, you understand.' He stared most earnestly at us to help out our understandings.

'What was she like?' Keede inquired.

'A biggish woman, an' had been 'andsome, I believe, but, bein' used to her, we two didn't notice much—except, per'aps, for one thing. Ma called her 'er proper name, which was Bella; but Sis an' me always called 'er Auntie Armine. See?'

'What for?'

'We thought it sounded more like her—like somethin' movin' slow, in armour.'

'Oh! And she read your letters to your mother, did she?'

'Every time the post came in she'd slip across the road from opposite an' read 'em. An'—an' I'll go bail for it that that was all there was to it for as far back as *I* remember. Was I to swing to-morrow, I'd go bail for *that*! 'Tisn't fair of 'em to 'ave unloaded it all on me, because—because—if the dead *do* rise, why, what in 'ell becomes of me an' all I've believed all me life? I want to know *that*! I—I——'

But Keede would not be put off. 'Did the Sergeant give you away at all in his letters?' he demanded, very quietly.

'There was nothin' to give away—we was too busy—but his letters about me were a great comfort to Ma. I'm no good at writin'. I saved it all up for my leafs. I got me fourteen days every six months an' one over. . . . I was luckier than most, that way.'

'And when you came home, used you to bring 'em news about the Sergeant?' said Keede.

'I expect I must have; but I didn't think much of it at the time. I was took up with me own affairs—naturally. Uncle John always wrote to me once each leaf, tellin' me what was doin' an' what I was li'ble to expect on return, an' Ma 'ud 'ave that read to her. Then o' course I had to slip over to his wife an' pass her the news. An' then there was the young lady that I'd thought of marryin' if I came through. We'd got as far as pricin' things in the windows to-gether.'

'And you didn't marry her—after all?'

Another tremor shook the boy. '*No!*' he cried. ''Fore it ended, I knew what reel things reelly mean! I—I never dreamed such things could be! . . . An' she nearer fifty than forty an' me own Aunt! . . . But there wasn't a sign nor a hint from first to last, so 'ow *could* I tell? Don't you *see* it? All she said to me after me Christmas leaf in 'Eighteen, when I come to say good-bye—all Auntie Armine said to me was: "You'll be seein' Mister Godsoe soon?" "Too soon for my likings," I says. "Well, then, tell 'im from me," she says, "that I expect to be through with my little trouble by the twenty-first of next month, an' I'm dyin' to see him as soon as possible after that date." '

'What sort of trouble was it?' Keede turned professional at once.

'She'd 'ad a bit of a gatherin' in 'er breast, I believe. But she never talked of 'er body much to anyone.'

'*I* see,' said Keede. 'And she said to you?'

Strangwick repeated: ' "Tell Uncle John I hope to be finished of my drawback by the twenty-first, an' I'm dyin' to see 'im as soon as 'e can after that date." An' then she says, laughin': "But you've a head like a sieve. I'll write it down, an' you can give it him when you see 'im." So she wrote it on a bit o' paper an' I kissed 'er good-bye—I was always her favourite, you see—an' I went back to Sampoux. The thing hardly stayed in my mind at all, d'ye see? But the next time I was up in the front line—I was a Runner, d'ye see? —our platoon was in North Bay Trench an' I was up with a message to the Trench Mortar there that Corporal Grant was in charge of. Followin' on receipt of it, he borrowed a couple of men off the platoon, to slue 'er round or somethin'. I give Uncle John Auntie Armine's paper, an' I give Grant a fag, an' we warmed up a bit over a brazier. Then Grant says to me: "I don't like it"; an' he jerks 'is thumb at Uncle John in the bay studyin' Auntie's message. Well, *you* know, sir, you had to speak to Grant about 'is way of prophesyin' things—after Rankine shot himself with the Very light.'

'I did,' said Keede, and he explained to me: 'Grant had the Second Sight—confound him! It upset the men. I was glad when he got pipped. What happened after that, Strangwick?'

'Grant whispers to me: "Look, you damned Englishman. 'E's for it." Uncle John was leanin' up against the bay, an' hummin' that hymn I was tryin' to tell you just now. He looked different all of a sudden—as if 'e'd got shaved. *I* don't know anything of these things, but I cautioned Grant as to his style of speakin', if an officer 'ad 'eard him, an' I went on. Passin' Uncle John in the bay, 'e nods an' smiles, which he didn't often, an' he says, pocketin' the paper: "This suits *me*. I'm for leaf on the twenty-first, too." '

'He said that to you, did he?' said Keede.

'*Pre*cisely the same as passin' the time o' day. O' course I returned the agreeable about hopin' he'd get it, an' in due course I returned to 'Eadquarters. The thing 'ardly stayed in my mind a minute. That was the eleventh January—three days after I'd come back from leaf. You remember, sir, there wasn't anythin' doin' either side round Sampoux the first part o' the month. Jerry was

gettin' ready for his March Push, an' as long as he kept quiet, we
didn't want to poke 'im up.'

'I remember that,' said Keede. 'But what about the Sergeant?'

'I must have met him, on an' off, I expect, goin' up an' down,
through the ensuin' days, but it didn't stay in me mind. Why
needed it? And on the twenty-first Jan., his name was on the leaf-
paper when I went up to warn the leaf-men. I noticed *that*, o' course.
Now that very afternoon Jerry 'ad been tryin' a new trench-
mortar, an' before our 'Eavies could out it, he'd got a stinker into a
bay an' mopped up 'alf-a-dozen. They were bringin' 'em down
when I went up to the supports, an' that blocked Little Parrot,
same as it always did. *You* remember, sir?'

'Rather! And there was that big machine-gun behind the Half-
House waiting for you if you got out,' said Keede.

'I remembered that too. But it was just on dark an' the fog was
comin' off the Canal, so I hopped out of Little Parrot an' cut across
the open to where those four dead Warwicks are heaped up. But the
fog turned me round, an' the next thing I knew I was knee-over in
that old 'alf-trench that runs west o' Little Parrot into French End.
I dropped into it—almost atop o' the machine-gun platform by the
side o' the old sugar-boiler an' the two Zoo-ave skel'tons. That gave
me my bearin's, an' so I went through French End, all up those
missin' duckboards, into Butcher's Row where the *poy-looz* was
laid in six deep each side, an' stuffed under the duckboards. It had
froze tight, an' the drippin's had stopped, an' the creakin's had
begun.'

'Did that really worry you at the time?' Keede asked.

'No,' said the boy with professional scorn. 'If a Runner starts
noticin' such things he'd better chuck. In the middle of the Row,
just before the old dressin'-station you referred to, sir, it come over
me that somethin' ahead on the duckboards was just like Auntie
Armine, waitin' beside the door; an' I thought to meself 'ow truly
comic it would be if she could be dumped where I was then. In 'alf
a second I saw it was only the dark an' some rags o' gas-screen,
'angin' on a bit of board, 'ad played me the trick. So I went on up
to the supports an' warned the leaf-men there, includin' Uncle
John. Then I went up Rake Alley to warn 'em in the front line. I
didn't hurry because I didn't want to get there till Jerry 'ad quieted
down a bit. Well, then a Company Relief dropped in—an' the
officer got the wind up over some lights on the flank, an' tied 'em
into knots, an' I 'ad to hunt up me leaf-men all over the blinkin'
shop. What with one thing an' another, it must 'ave been 'alf-past

eight before I got back to the supports. There I run across Uncle John, scrapin' mud off himself, havin' shaved—quite the dandy. He asked about the Arras train, an' I said, if Jerry was quiet, it might be ten o'clock. "Good!" says 'e. "I'll come with you." So we started back down the old trench that used to run across Halnaker, back of the support dug-outs. *You* know, sir.'

Keede nodded.

'Then Uncle John says something to me about seein' Ma an' the rest of 'em in a few days, an' had I any messages for 'em? Gawd knows what made me do it, but I told 'im to tell Auntie Armine I never expected to see anything like *her* up in our part of the world. And while I told him I laughed. That's the last time I '*ave* laughed. "Oh—you've seen 'er, 'ave you?" says he, quite natural-like. Then I told 'im about the sand-bags an' rags in the dark playin' the trick. "Very likely," says he, brushin' the mud off his puttees. By this time, we'd got to the corner where the old barricade into French End was—before they bombed it down, sir. He turns right an' climbs across it. "No, thanks," says I. "I've been there once this evenin'." But he wasn't attendin' to me. He felt behind the rubbish an' bones just inside the barricade, an' when he straightened up, he had a full brazier in each hand.

' "Come on, Clem," he says, an' he very rarely give me me own name. "You aren't afraid, are you!" he says. "It's just as short, an' if Jerry starts up again he won't waste stuff here. He knows it's abandoned." "Who's afraid now?" I says. "Me for one," says he. "I don't want *my* leaf spoiled at the last minute." Then 'e wheels round an' speaks that bit you said come out o' the Burial Service.'

For some reason Keede repeated it in full, slowly. 'If after the manner of men I have fought with beasts at Ephesus, what advantageth it me, if the dead rise not?'

'That's it,' said Strangwick. 'So we went down French End together—everything froze up an' quiet, except for their creakin's. I remember thinkin'——' His eyes began to flicker.

'Don't think. Tell what happened,' Keede ordered.

'Oh! Beg y' pardon! He went on with his braziers, hummin' his hymn, down Butcher's Row. Just before we got to the old dressin'-station he stops and sets 'em down an' says: "Where did you say she was, Clem? Me eyes ain't as good as they used to be."

' "In 'er bed at 'ome," I says. "Come on down. It's perishin' cold, an' *I*'m not due for leaf."

' "Well, I am," 'e says. "*I* am. . . ." An' then—'give you me word I didn't recognize the voice—he stretches out 'is neck a bit, in a way 'e 'ad, an' he says: "Why, Bella!" 'e says. "Oh, Bella!" 'e says. "Thank Gawd!" 'e says. Just like that! An' then I saw—I tell you I *saw*—Auntie Armine herself standin' by the old dressin'-station door where first I'd thought I'd seen her. He was lookin' at 'er an' she was lookin' at him. I saw it, an' me soul turned over inside me because—because it knocked out everything I'd believed in. I 'ad nothin' to lay 'old of, d'ye see? An' 'e was lookin' at 'er as though he could 'ave et 'er, an' she was lookin' at 'im the same way, out of 'er eyes. Then he says: "Why, Bella," 'e says, "this must be only the second time we've been alone together in all these years." An' I saw 'er half 'old out her arms to 'im in that perishin' cold. An' she nearer fifty than forty an' me own Aunt! You can shop me for a lunatic tomorrow, but I saw it—I *saw* 'er answerin' to his spoken word! . . . Then 'e made a snatch to unsling 'is rifle. Then 'e cuts 'is hand away saying: "No! Don't tempt me, Bella. We've all Eternity ahead of us. An hour or two won't make any odds." Then he picks up the braziers an' goes on to the dug-out door. He's finished with me. He pours petrol on 'em, an' lights it with a match, an' carries 'em inside, flarin'. All that time Auntie Armine stood with 'er arms out—an' a look in 'er face! *I* didn't know such things was or could be! Then he comes out an' says: "Come in, my dear"; an' she stoops an' goes into the dug-out with that look on her face—that look on her face! An' then 'e shuts the door from inside an' starts wedgin' it up. So 'elp me Gawd, I saw an' 'eard all these things with my own eyes an' ears!'

He repeated his oath several times. After a long pause Keede asked him if he recalled what happened next.

'It was a bit of a mix-up, for me, from then on. I must have carried on—they told me I did, but—but I was—I felt a—a long way inside of meself, like—if you've ever had that feelin'. I wasn't rightly on the spot at all. They woke me up sometime next morning, because 'e 'adn't showed up at the train; an' someone had seen him with me. I wasn't 'alf cross-examined by all an' sundry till dinner-time.

'Then, I think, I volunteered for Dearlove, who 'ad a sore toe, for a front-line message. I 'ad to keep movin', you see, because I 'adn't anything to 'old on to. While up there, Grant informed me how 'e'd found Uncle John with the door wedged an' sand-bags stuffed in the cracks. I hadn't waited for that. The knockin' when 'e wedged up was enough for me. Like Dad's coffin.'

'No one told *me* the door had been wedged.' Keede spoke severely.

'No need to black a dead man's name, sir.'

'What made Grant go to Butcher's Row?'

'Because he'd noticed Uncle John had been pinchin' charcoal for a week past an' layin' it up behind the old barricade there. So when the 'unt began, he went that way straight as a string, an' when he saw the door shut, he knew. He told me he picked the sand-bags out of the cracks an' shoved 'is 'and through and shifted the wedges before anyone come along. It looked all right. You said yourself, sir, the door must 'ave blown to.'

'Grant knew what Godsoe meant, then?' Keede snapped.

'Grant knew Godsoe was for it, an' nothin' earthly could 'elp or 'inder. He told me so.'

'And then what did you do?'

'I expect I must 'ave kept on carryin' on, till 'Eadquarters give me that wire from Ma—about Auntie Armine dyin'.'

'When had your aunt died?'

'On the mornin' of the twenty-first. The mornin' of the twenty-first! That tore it, d'ye see? As long as I could think, I had kep' tellin' myself it was like those things you lectured about at Arras when we was billeted in the cellars—the Angels of Mons, and so on. But that wire tore it.'

'Oh! Hallucinations! I remember. And that wire tore it?' said Keede.

'Yes! You see'—he half lifted himself off the sofa—'there wasn't a single gor-dam' thing left abidin' for me to take hold of, 'ere or 'ereaftei. If the dead *do* rise—and I saw 'em—why—why, *anything* can 'appen. Don't you understand?'

He was on his feet now, gesticulating stiffly.

'For I saw 'er,' he repeated. 'I saw 'im an' 'er—she dead since mornin' time, an' he killin' 'imself before my livin' eyes so's to carry on with 'er for all Eternity—an' she 'oldin' out 'er arms for it! I want to know where I'm *at*! Look 'ere, you two—why stand *we* in jeopardy every hour?'

'God knows,' said Keede to himself.

'Hadn't we better ring for someone?' I suggested. 'He'll go off the handle in a second.'

'No, he won't. It's the last kick-up before it takes hold. I know how the stuff works. Hul-lo!'

Strangwick, his hands behind his back and his eyes set, gave tongue in the strained, cracked voice of a boy reciting. 'Not twice in the world shall the Gods do thus,' he cried again and again.

'And I'm damned if it's goin' to be even once for me!' he went on

with sudden insane fury. '*I* don't care whether we '*ave* been pricin'
things in the windows. . . . *Let* 'er sue if she likes! She don't know
what reel things mean. *I* do—I've 'ad occasion to notice 'em. . . .
No, I tell you! I'll 'ave 'em when I want 'em, an' be done with 'em;
but not till I see that look on a face . . . that look. . . . I'm not
takin' any. The reel thing's life an' death. It *begins* at death, d'ye
see? *She* can't understand. . . . Oh, go on an' push off to Hell, you
an' your lawyers. I'm fed up with it—fed up!'

He stopped as abruptly as he had started, and the drawn face
broke back to its natural irresolute lines. Keede, holding both his
hands, led him back to the sofa, where he dropped like a wet towel,
took out some flamboyant robe from a press, and drew it neatly
over him.

'Ye-es. *That*'s the real thing at last,' said Keede. 'Now he's got it
off his mind he'll sleep. By the way, who introduced him?'

'Shall I go and find out?' I suggested.

'Yes; and you might ask him to come here. There's no need for
us to stand to all night.'

So I went to the Banquet, which was in full swing, and was seized
by an elderly, precise Brother from a South London Lodge, who followed me, concerned and apologetic. Keede soon put him at his
ease.

'The boy's had trouble,' our visitor explained. 'I'm most mortified
he should have performed his bad turn here. I thought he'd put it
be'ind him.'

'I expect talking about old days with me brought it all back,
said Keede. 'It does sometimes.'

'Maybe! Maybe! But over and above that, Clem's had post-war
trouble, too.'

'Can't he get a job? He oughtn't to let that weigh on him, at his
time of life,' said Keede cheerily.

''Tisn't that—he's provided for—but'—he coughed confiden-
tially behind his dry hand—'as a matter of fact, Worshipful Sir,
he's—he's implicated for the present in a little breach of promise
action.'

'Ah! That's a different thing,' said Keede.

'Yes. That's his reel trouble. No reason given, you understand.
The young lady in every way suitable, an' she'd make him a good
little wife too, if I'm any judge. But he says she ain't his ideel or
something. No getting at what's in young people's minds these days,
is there?'

'I'm afraid there isn't,' said Keede. 'But he's all right now. He'll sleep. You sit by him, and when he wakes, take him home quietly. ... Oh, we're used to men getting a little upset here. You've nothing to thank us for, Brother—Brother——'

'Armine,' said the old gentleman. 'He's my nephew by marriage.'

'That's all that's wanted!' said Keede.

Brother Armine looked a little puzzled. Keede hastened to explain. 'As I was saying, all he wants now is to be kept quiet till he wakes.'

Debits and Credits, 1926*

**MacLean's Magazine*, 1924.

Dayspring Mishandled

C'est moi, c'est moi, c'est moi!
  Je suis la Mandragore!
La fille des beaux jours qui s'éveille à l'aurore—
  Et qui chante pour toi!

C. Nodier

IN THE DAYS beyond compare and before the Judgements, a
genius called Graydon foresaw that the advance of education
and the standard of living would submerge all mind-marks in one
mudrush of standardized reading-matter, and so created the Fic-
tional Supply Syndicate to meet the demand.

Since a few days' work for him brought them more money than a
week's elsewhere, he drew many young men—some now eminent—
into his employ. He bade them keep their eyes on the Sixpenny
Dream Book, the Army and Navy Stores Catalogue (this for back-
grounds and furniture as they changed), and *The Hearthstone
Friend*, a weekly publication which specialized unrivalledly in the
domestic emotions. Yet, even so, youth would not be denied, and
some of the collaborated love-talk in 'Passion Hath Peril,' and
'Ena's Lost Lovers,' and the account of the murder of the Earl in
'The Wickwire Tragedies'—to name but a few masterpieces now
never mentioned for fear of blackmail—was as good as anything to
which their authors signed their real names in more distinguished
years.

Among the young ravens driven to roost awhile on Graydon's ark
was James Andrew Manallace—a darkish, slow Northerner of the
type that does not ignite, but must be detonated. Given written or
verbal outlines of a plot, he was useless; but, with a half-dozen pictures round which to write his tale, he could astonish.

And he adored that woman who afterwards became the mother
of Vidal Benzaguen,* and who suffered and died because she loved
one unworthy. There was, also, among the company a mannered,
bellied person called Alured Castorley, who talked and wrote about
'Bohemia,' but was always afraid of being 'compromised' by the
weekly suppers at Neminaka's Café in Hestern Square, where the
Syndicate's work was apportioned, and where everyone looked out

* 'The Village that Voted the Earth was Flat.' *A Diversity of Creatures.*

for himself. He, too, for a time, had loved Vidal's mother, in his own way.

Now, one Saturday at Neminaka's, Graydon, who had given Manallace a sheaf of prints—torn from an extinct children's book called *Phillipa's Queen*—on which to improvise, asked for results. Manallace went down into his ulster-pockets, hesitated a moment, and said the stuff had turned into poetry on his hands.

'Bosh!'

'That's what it isn't,' the boy retorted. 'It's rather good.'

'Then it's no use to us.' Graydon laughed. 'Have you brought back the cuts?'

Manallace handed them over. There was a castle in the series; a knight or so in armour; an old lady in a horned head-dress; a young ditto; a very obvious Hebrew; a clerk, with pen and inkhorn, checking wine-barrels on a wharf; and a Crusader. On the back of one of the prints was a note, 'If he doesn't want to go, why can't he be captured and held to ransom?' Graydon asked what it all meant.

'I don't know yet. A comic opera, perhaps,' said Manallace.

Graydon, who seldom wasted time, passed the cuts on to some-one else, and advanced Manallace a couple of sovereigns to carry on with, as usual; at which Castorley was angry and would have said something unpleasant but was suppressed. Half-way through supper, Castorley told the company that a relative had died and left him an independence; and that he now withdrew from 'hackwork' to follow 'Literature.' Generally, the Syndicate rejoiced in a comrade's good fortune, but Castorley had the gift of waking dislike. So the news was received with a vote of thanks, and he went out before the end, and, it was said, proposed to 'Dal Benzaguen's mother, who refused him. He did not come back. Manallace, who had arrived a little exalted, got so drunk before midnight that a man had to stay and see him home. But liquor never touched him above the belt, and when he had slept awhile, he recited to the gas-chandelier the poetry he had made out of the pictures; said that, on second thoughts, he would convert it into comic opera; deplored the Upas-tree influence of Gilbert and Sullivan; sang somewhat to illustrate his point; and—after words, by the way, with a negress in yellow satin—was steered to his rooms.

In the course of a few years, Graydon's foresight and genius were rewarded. The public began to read and reason upon higher planes, and the Syndicate grew rich. Later still, people demanded of their printed matter what they expected in their clothing and furniture. So, precisely as the three-guinea hand-bag is followed in three weeks

by its thirteen-and-sevenpence-ha'penny indistinguishable sister,
they enjoyed perfect synthetic substitutes for Plot, Sentiment, and
Emotion. Graydon died before the Cinema-caption school came in,
but he left his widow twenty-seven thousand pounds.

Manallace made a reputation, and, more important, money for
Vidal's mother after her husband ran away and the first symptoms
of her paralysis showed. His line was the jocundly-sentimental Wardour Street brand of adventure, told in a style that exactly met, but
never exceeded, every expectation.

As he once said when urged to 'write a real book': 'I've got my
label, and I'm not going to chew it off. If you save people thinking,
you can do anything with 'em.' His output apart, he was genuinely
a man of letters. He rented a small cottage in the country and econ-
omized on everything, except the care and charges of Vidal's mother.

Castorley flew higher. When his legacy freed him from 'hackwork,'
he became first a critic—in which calling he loyally scalped all his
old associates as they came up—and then looked for some speciality.
Having found it (Chaucer was the prey), he consolidated his
position before he occupied it, by his careful speech, his cultivated
bearing, and the whispered words of his friends whom he, too, had
saved the trouble of thinking. It followed that, when he published
his first serious articles on Chaucer, all the world which is interested
in Chaucer said: 'This is an authority.' But he was no impostor. He
learned and knew the poet and his age; and in a month-long dog-
fight in an austere literary weekly, met and mangled a recognized
Chaucer expert of the day. He also, 'for old sake's sake,' as he wrote
to a friend, went out of his way to review one of Manallace's books
with an intimacy of unclean deduction (this was before the days of
Freud) which long stood as a record. Some member of the extinct
Syndicate took occasion to ask him if he would—for old sake's sake
—help Vidal's mother to a new treatment. He answered that he had
'known the lady very slightly and the calls on his purse were so
heavy that,' etc. The writer showed the letter to Manallace, who
said he was glad Castorley hadn't interfered. Vidal's mother was
then wholly paralysed. Only her eyes could move, and those always
looked for the husband who had left her. She died thus in Manallace's arms in April of the first year of the War.

During the War he and Castorley worked as some sort of depart-
mental dishwashers in the Office of Co-ordinated Supervisals. Here
Manallace came to know Castorley again. Castorley, having a sweet
tooth, cadged lumps of sugar for his tea from a typist, and when
she took to giving them to a younger man, arranged that she should

be reported for smoking in unauthorized apartments. Manallace possessed himself of every detail of the affair, as compensation for the review of his book. Then there came a night when, waiting for a big air-raid, the two men had talked humanly, and Manallace spoke of Vidal's mother. Castorley said something in reply, and from that hour—as was learned several years later—Manallace's real life-work and interests began.

The War over, Castorley set about to make himself Supreme Pontiff on Chaucer by methods not far removed from the employment of poison-gas. The English Pope was silent, through private griefs, and influenza had carried off the learned Hun who claimed Continental allegiance. Thus Castorley crowed unchallenged from Upsala to Seville, while Manallace went back to his cottage with the photo of Vidal's mother over the mantelpiece. She seemed to have emptied out his life, and left him only fleeting interests in trifles. His private diversions were experiments of uncertain outcome, which, he said, rested him after a day's gadzooking and vitalstapping. I found him, for instance, one week-end, in his toolshed-scullery, boiling a brew of slimy barks which were, if mixed with oak-galls, vitriol, and wine, to become an ink-powder. We boiled it till the Monday, and it turned into an adhesive stronger than birdlime, and entangled us both.

At other times, he would carry me off, once in a few weeks, to sit at Castorley's feet, and hear him talk about Chaucer. Castorley's voice, bad enough in youth, when it could be shouted down, had, with culture and tact, grown almost insupportable. His mannerisms, too, had multiplied and set. He minced and mouthed, postured and chewed his words throughout those terrible evenings; and poisoned not only Chaucer, but every shred of English literature which he used to embellish him. He was shameless, too, as regarded self-advertisement and 'recognition'—weaving elaborate intrigues; forming petty friendships and confederacies, to be dissolved next week in favour of more promising alliances; fawning, snubbing, lecturing, organizing, and lying as unrestingly as a politician, in chase of the Knighthood due not to him (he always called on his Maker to forbid such a thought) but as tribute to Chaucer. Yet, sometimes, he could break from his obsession and prove how a man's work will try to save the soul of him. He would tell us charmingly of copyists of the fifteenth century in England and the Low Countries, who had multiplied the Chaucer MSS., of which there remained—he gave us the exact number—and how each scribe could by him (and, he implied, by him alone) be distinguished from every other by some peculiarity of letter-formation, spacing, or like trick of pen-work;

and how he could fix the dates of their work within five years. Sometimes he would give us an hour of really interesting stuff and then return to his overdue 'recognition.' The changes sickened me, but Manallace defended him, as a master in his own line who had revealed Chaucer to at least one grateful soul.

This, as far as I remember, was the autumn when Manallace holidayed in the Shetlands or the Faroes, and came back with a stone 'quern'—a hand corn-grinder. He said it interested him from the ethnological standpoint. His whim lasted till next harvest, and was followed by a religious spasm which, naturally, translated itself into literature. He showed me a battered and mutilated Vulgate of 1485, patched up the back with bits of legal parchments, which he had bought for thirty-five shillings. Some monk's attempt to rubricate chapter-initials had caught, it seemed, his forlorn fancy, and he dabbled in shells of gold and silver paint for weeks.

That also faded out, and he went to the Continent to get 'local colour' for a love-story about Alva and the Dutch, and the next year I saw practically nothing of him. This released me from seeing much of Castorley, but, at intervals, I would go there to dine with him, when his wife—an unappetizing, ash-coloured woman—made no secret that his friends wearied her almost as much as he did. But at a later meeting, not long after Manallace had finished his Low Countries' novel, I found Castorley charged to bursting-point with triumph and high information hardly withheld. He confided to me that a time was at hand when great matters would be made plain, and 'recognition' would be inevitable. I assumed, naturally, that there was fresh scandal or heresy afoot in Chaucer circles, and kept my curiosity within bounds.

In time, New York cabled that a fragment of a hitherto unknown Canterbury Tale lay safe in the steel-walled vaults of the seven-million-dollar Sunnapia Collection. It was news on an international scale—the New World exultant—the Old deploring the 'burden of British taxation which drove such treasures, etc.,' and the lighter-minded journals disporting themselves according to their publics; for 'our Dan,' as one earnest Sunday editor observed, 'lies closer to the national heart than we wot of.' Common decency made me call on Castorley, who, to my surprise, had not yet descended into the arena. I found him, made young again by joy, deep in just-passed proofs.

Yes, he said, it was all true. He had, of course, been in it from the first. There had been found one hundred and seven new lines of Chaucer tacked on to an abridged end of *The Persone's Tale*, the

whole the work of Abraham Mentzius, better known as Mentzel of
Antwerp (1388–1438/9)—I might remember he had talked about
him—whose distinguishing peculiarities were a certain Byzantine
formation of his *g*'s, the use of a 'sickle-slanted' reed-pen, which cut
into the vellum at certain letters; and, above all, a tendency to spell
English words on Dutch lines, whereof the manuscript carried one
convincing proof. For instance (he wrote it out for me), a girl praying against an undesired marriage says:

> '*Ah! Jesu-Moder, pitie my oe painc.*
> *Daiespringe mishandeelt cometh nat agayne.*'

Would I, please, note the spelling of 'mishandeelt'? Stark Dutch
and Mentzel's besetting sin! But in *his* position one took nothing for
granted. The page had been part of the stiffening of the side of an
old Bible, bought in a parcel by Dredd, the big dealer, because it
had some rubricated chapter-initials, and by Dredd shipped, with a
consignment of similar odds and ends, to the Sunnapia Collection,
where they were making a glass-cased exhibit of the whole history
of illumination and did not care how many books they gutted for
that purpose. There, someone who noticed a crack in the back of the
volume had unearthed it. He went on: 'They didn't know what to
make of the thing at first. But they knew about *me*! They kept quiet
till I'd been consulted. You might have noticed I was out of
England for three months.

'I was over there, of course. It was what is called a "spoil"—a
page Mentzel had spoiled with his Dutch spelling—I expect he had
had the English dictated to him—then had evidently used the vellum for trying out his reeds; and then, I suppose, had put it away.
The "spoil" had been doubled, pasted together, and slipped in as
stiffening to the old book-cover. I had it steamed open, and analysed
the wash. It gave the flour-grains in the paste—coarse, because of
the old millstone—and there were traces of the grit itself. What? Oh,
possibly a handmill of Mentzel's own time. He may have doubled
the spoilt page and used it for part of a pad to steady wood-cuts on.
It may have knocked about his workshop for years. That, indeed,
is practically certain because a beginner from the Low Countries
has tried his reed on a few lines of some monkish hymn—not a bad
lilt tho'—which must have been common form. Oh yes, the page
may have been used in other books before it was used for the Vulgate. That doesn't matter, but *this* does. Listen! I took a wash, for
analysis, from a blot in one corner—that would be after Mentzel had
given up trying to make a possible page of it, and had grown careless

—and I got the actual *ink* of the period! It's a practically eternal stuff compounded on—I've forgotten his name for the minute—the scribe at Bury St Edmunds, of course!—hawthorn bark and wine. Anyhow, on *his* formula. *That* wouldn't interest you either, but, taken with all the other testimony, it clinches the thing. (You'll see it all in my Statement to the Press on Monday.) Overwhelming, isn't it?'

'Overwhelming,' I said, with sincerity. 'Tell me what the tale was about, though. That's more in my line.'

'I know it; but *I* have to be equipped on all sides. The verses are relatively easy for one to pronounce on. The freshness, the fun, the humanity, the fragrance of it all, cries—no, shouts—itself as Dan's work. Why "Daiespringe mishandled" alone stamps it from Dan's mint. Plangent as doom, my dear boy—plangent as doom! It's all in my Statement. Well, substantially, the fragment deals with a girl whose parents wish her to marry an elderly suitor. The mother isn't so keen on it, but the father, an old Knight, is. The girl, of course, is in love with a younger and a poorer man. Common form? Granted. Then the father, who doesn't in the least want to, is ordered off to a Crusade and, by way of passing on the kick, as we used to say during the War, orders the girl to be kept in duresse till his return or her consent to the old suitor. Common form, again? Quite so. That's too much for her mother. She reminds the old Knight of his age and infirmities, and the discomforts of Crusading. Are you sure I'm not boring you?'

'Not at all,' I said, though time had begun to whirl backward through my brain to a red-velvet, pomatum-scented side-room at Neminaka's and Manallace's set face intoning to the gas.

'You'll read it all in my Statement next week. The sum is that the old lady tells him of a certain Knight-adventurer on the French coast, who, for a consideration, waylays Knights who don't relish Crusading and holds them to impossible ransoms till the trooping season is over, or they are returned sick. He keeps a ship in the Channel to pick 'em up and transfers his birds to his castle ashore, where he has a reputation for doing 'em well. As the old lady points out:

> *"And if perchance thou fall into his honde,*
> *By God, how canstow ride to Holilonde?"*

'You see? Modern in essence as Gilbert and Sullivan, but handled as only Dan could! And she reminds him that "Honour and olde bones" parted company long ago. He makes one splendid appeal for the spirit of chivalry:

> *"Lat all men change as Fortune may send,*
> *But Knighthood beareth service to the end,"*

and *then*, of course, he gives in:

> *"For what his woman willeth to be don*
> *Her manne must or wauken Hell anon."*

'Then she hints that the daughter's young lover, who is in the Bordeaux wine-trade, could open negotiations for a kidnapping without compromising him. And *then* that careless brute Mentzel spoils his page and chucks it! But there's enough to show what's going to happen. You'll see it all in my Statement. Was there ever anything in literary finds to hold a candle to it? . . . And they give grocers Knighthoods for selling cheese!'

I went away before he could get into his stride on that course. I wanted to think, and to see Manallace. But I waited till Castorley's Statement came out. He had left himself no loophole. And when, a little later, his (nominally the Sunnapia people's) 'scientific' account of their analyses and tests appeared, criticism ceased, and some journals began to demand 'public recognition.' Manallace wrote me on this subject, and I went down to his cottage, where he at once asked me to sign a Memorial on Castorley's behalf. With luck, he said, we might get him a K.B.E. in the next Honours List. Had I read his Statement?

'I have,' I replied. 'But I want to ask you something first. Do you remember the night you got drunk at Neminaka's, and I stayed behind to look after you?'

'Oh, *that* time,' said he, pondering. 'Wait a minute! I remember Graydon advancing me two quid. He was a generous paymaster. And I remember—now, who the devil rolled me under the sofa—and what for?'

'We all did,' I replied. 'You wanted to read us what you'd written to those Chaucer cuts.'

'I don't remember that. No! I don't remember anything after the sofa episode. . . . *You* always said that you took me home—didn't you?'

'I did, and you told Kentucky Kate outside the old Empire that you had been faithful, Cynara, in your fashion.'

'Did I?' said he. 'My God! Well, I suppose I have.' He stared into the fire. 'What else?'

'Before we left Neminaka's you recited me what you had made of the cuts—the whole tale! So—you see?'

'Ye-es.' He nodded. 'What are you going to do about it?'

'What are *you*?'

'I'm going to help him get his Knighthood—first.'

'Why?'

'I'll tell you what he said about 'Dal's mother—the night there was that air-raid on the offices.'

He told it.

'That's why,' he said. 'Am I justified?'

He seemed to me entirely so.

'But after he gets his Knighthood?' I went on.

'That depends. There are several things I can think of. It interests me.'

'Good Heavens! I've always imagined you a man without interests.'

'So I was. I owe my interests to Castorley. He gave me every one of 'em except the tale itself.'

'How did *that* come?'

'Something in those ghastly cuts touched off something in me—a sort of possession, I suppose. I was in love too. No wonder I got drunk that night. I'd *been* Chaucer for a week! Then I thought the notion might make a comic opera. But Gilbert and Sullivan were too strong.'

'So I remember you told me at the time.'

'I kept it by me, and it made me interested in Chaucer—philologically and so on. I worked on it on those lines for years. There wasn't a flaw in the wording even in 'Fourteen. I hardly had to touch it after.'

'Did you ever tell it to anyone except me?'

'No, only 'Dal's mother—when she could listen to anything—to put her to sleep. But when Castorley said—what he did about her, I thought I might use it. 'Twasn't difficult. *He* taught me. D'you remember my birdlime experiments, and the stuff on our hands? I'd been trying to get that ink for more than a year. Castorley told me where I'd find the formula. And your falling over the quern, too?'

'That accounted for the stone-dust under the microscope?'

'Yes. I grew the wheat in the garden here, and ground it myself. Castorley gave me Mentzel complete. He put me on to an MS. in the British Museum which he said was the finest sample of his work. I copied his "Byzantine *g*'s" for months.'

'And what's a "sickle-slanted" pen?' I asked.

'You nick one edge of your reed till it drags and scratches on the curves of the letters. Castorley told me about Mentzel's spacing and margining. I only had to get the hang of his script.'

'How long did that take you?'

'On and off—some years. I was too ambitious at first—I wanted to give the whole poem. That would have been risky. Then Castorley told me about spoiled pages and I took the hint. I spelt "Daiespringe mishandeelt" Mentzel's way—to make sure of him. It's not a bad couplet in itself. Did you see how he admires the "plangency" of it?'

'Never mind him. Go on!' I said.

He did. Castorley had been his unfailing guide throughout, specifying in minutest detail every trap to be set later for his own feet. The actual vellum was an Antwerp find, and its introduction into the cover of the Vulgate was begun after a long course of amateur bookbinding. At last, he bedded it under pieces of an old deed, and a printed page (1686) of Horace's *Odes*, legitimately used for repairs by different owners in the seventeenth and eighteenth centuries; and at the last moment, to meet Castorley's theory that spoiled pages were used in workshops by beginners, he had written a few Latin words in fifteenth-century script—the Statement gave the exact date—across an open part of the fragment. The thing ran: '*Illa alma Mater ecca, secum afferens me acceptum. Nicolaus Atrib.*' The disposal of the thing was easiest of all. He had merely hung about Dredd's dark bookshop of fifteen rooms, where he was well known, occasionally buying but generally browsing, till, one day, Dredd Senior showed him a case of cheap black-letter stuff, English and Continental—being packed for the Sunnapia people—into which Manallace tucked his contribution, taking care to wrench the back enough to give a lead to an earnest seeker.

'And then?' I demanded.

'After six months or so Castorley sent for me. Sunnapia had found it, and as Dredd had missed it, and there was no money-motive sticking out, they were half convinced it was genuine from the start. But they invited him over. He conferred with their experts, and suggested the scientific tests. *I* put that into his head, before he sailed. That's all. And now, will you sign our Memorial?'

I signed. Before we had finished hawking it round there was a host of influential names to help us, as well as the impetus of all the literary discussion which arose over every detail of the glorious trove. The upshot was a K.B.E.* for Castorley in the next Honours

---

*Officially it was on account of his good work in the Department of Co-ordinated Supervisals, but many true lovers of Literature knew the real reason, and told the papers so.

List; and Lady Castorley, her cards duly printed, called on friends that same afternoon.

Manallace invited me to come with him, a day or so later, to convey our pleasure and satisfaction to them both. We were rewarded by the sight of a man relaxed and ungirt—not to say wallowing naked—on the crest of Success. He assured us that 'The Title' should not make any difference to our future relations, seeing it was in no sense personal, but, as he had often said, a tribute to Chaucer. 'And, after all,' he pointed out, with a glance at the mirror over the mantelpiece, 'Chaucer was the prototype of the "verray parfit, gentil Knyght" of the British Empire so far as that then existed.'

On the way back, Manallace told me he was considering either an unheralded revelation in the baser Press which should bring Castorley's reputation about his own ears some breakfast-time, or a private conversation, when he would make clear to Castorley that he must now back the forgery as long as he lived, under threat of Manallace's betraying it if he flinched.

He favoured the second plan. 'If I pull the string of the shower-bath in the papers,' he said, 'Castorley might go off his verray parfit, gentil nut. I want to keep his intellect.'

'What about your own position? The forgery doesn't matter so much. But if you tell this you'll kill him,' I said.

'I intend that. Oh—my position? I've been dead since—April, 'Fourteen, it was. But there's no hurry. What was it *she* was saying to you just as we left?'

'She told me how much your sympathy and understanding had meant to him. She said she thought that even Sir Alured did not realize the full extent of his obligations to you.'

'She's right, but I don't like her putting it that way.'

'It's only common form—as Castorley's always saying.'

'Not with *her*. She can hear a man think.'

'She never struck me in that light.'

'*You* aren't playing against her.'

'Guilty conscience, Manallace?'

'H'm! I wonder. Mine or hers? I *wish* she hadn't said that. "More even than *he* realizes." I won't call again for a while.'

He kept away till we read that Sir Alured, owing to slight indisposition, had been unable to attend a dinner given in his honour.

Inquiries brought word that it was but natural reaction, after strain, which, for the moment, took the form of nervous dyspepsia, and he would be glad to see Manallace at any time. Manallace reported him as rather pulled and drawn, but full of his new life and position, and proud that his efforts should have martyred him so much. He was going to collect, collate, and expand all his pronouncements and inferences into one authoritative volume.

'I must make an effort of my own,' said Manallace. 'I've collected nearly all his stuff about the Find that has appeared in the papers, and he's promised me everything that's missing. I'm going to help him. It will be a new interest.'

'How will you treat it?' I asked.

'I expect I shall quote his deductions on the evidence, and parallel 'em with my experiments—the ink and the paste and the rest of it. It ought to be rather interesting.'

'But even then there will only be your word. It's hard to catch up with an established lie,' I said. 'Especially when you've started it yourself.'

He laughed. 'I've arranged for *that*—in case anything happens to me. Do you remember the "Monkish Hymn"?'

'Oh yes! There's quite a literature about it already.'

'Well, you write those ten words above each other, and read down the first and second letters of 'em; and see what you get.* My Bank has the formula.'

He wrapped himself lovingly and leisurely round his new task, and Castorley was as good as his word in giving him help. The two practically collaborated, for Manallace suggested that all Castorley's strictly scientific evidence should be in one place, with his deductions and dithyrambs as appendices. He assured him that the public would prefer this arrangement, and, after grave consideration, Castorley agreed.

'That's better,' said Manallace to me. 'Now I shan't have so many hiatuses in my extracts. Dots always give the reader the idea you aren't dealing fairly with your man. I shall merely quote him solid, and rip him up, proof for proof, and date for date, in parallel columns. His book's taking more out of him than I like, though.

> * *Illa*
> *alma*
> *Mater*
> *ecca*
> *secum*
> *afferens*
> *me*
> *acceptum*
> *Nicolaus*
> *Atrib.*

He's been doubled up twice with tummy attacks since I've worked with him. And he's just the sort of flatulent beast who may go down with appendicitis.'

We learned before long that the attacks were due to gall-stones, which would necessitate an operation. Castorley bore the blow very well. He had full confidence in his surgeon, an old friend of theirs; great faith in his own constitution; a strong conviction that nothing would happen to him till the book was finished; and, above all, the 'Will to Live.'

He dwelt on these assets with a voice at times a little out of pitch and eyes brighter than usual beside a slightly-sharpening nose.

I had only met Gleeag, the surgeon, once or twice at Castorley's house, but had always heard him spoken of as a most capable man. He told Castorley that his trouble was the price exacted, in some shape or other, from all who had served their country; and that, measured in units of strain, Castorley had practically been at the Front through those three years he had served in the Office of Co-ordinated Supervisals. However, the thing had been taken betimes, and in a few weeks he would worry no more about it.

'But suppose he dies?' I suggested to Manallace.

'He won't. I've been talking to Gleeag. He says he's all right.'

'Wouldn't Gleeag's talk be common form?'

'I *wish* you hadn't said that. But, surely, Gleeag wouldn't have the face to play with me—or her.'

'Why not? I expect it's been done before.'

But Manallace insisted that, in this case, it would be impossible.

The operation was a success and, some weeks later, Castorley began to recast the arrangement and most of the material of his book. 'Let me have my way,' he said, when Manallace protested. 'They are making too much of a baby of me. I really don't need Gleeag looking in every day now.' But Lady Castorley told us that he required careful watching. His heart had felt the strain, and fret or disappointment of any kind must be avoided. 'Even'—she turned to Manallace—'though you know ever so much better how his book should be arranged than he does himself.'

'But really,' Manallace began, 'I'm very careful not to fuss——'

She shook her finger at him playfully. 'You don't think you do; but, remember, he tells me everything that you tell him, just the same as he told me everything that he used to tell *you*. Oh, I don't mean the things that men talk about. I mean about his Chaucer.'

'I didn't realize that,' said Manallace, weakly.

'I thought you didn't. He never spares me anything; but *I* don't mind,' she replied with a laugh, and went off to Gleeag, who was paying his daily visit. Gleeag said he had no objection to Manallace working with Castorley on the book for a given time—say, twice a week—but supported Lady Castorley's demand that he should not be over-taxed in what she called 'the sacred hours.' The man grew more and more difficult to work with, and the little check he had heretofore set on his self-praise went altogether.

'He says there has never been anything in the History of Letters to compare with it,' Manallace groaned. 'He wants now to inscribe —he never dedicates, you know inscribe it to me, as his "most valued assistant." The devil of it is that *she* backs him up in getting it out soon. Why? How much do you think she knows?'

'Why should she know anything at all?'

'You heard her say he had told her everything that he had told me about Chaucer? (I *wish* she hadn't said that!) If she puts two and two together, she can't help seeing that every one of his notions and theories has been played up to. But then—but then . . . Why is she trying to hurry publication? She talks about *me* fretting him. *She's* at him, all the time, to be quick.'

Castorley must have over-worked, for, after a couple of months, he complained of a stitch in his right side, which Gleeag said was a slight sequel, a little incident of the operation. It threw him back a while, but he returned to his work undefeated.

The book was due in the autumn. Summer was passing, and his publisher urgent, and—he said to me, when after a longish interval I called—Manallace had chosen this time, of all, to take a holiday. He was not pleased with Manallace, once his indefatigable *aide*, but now dilatory, and full of time-wasting objections. Lady Castorley, he said, had noticed it, too.

Meantime, with Lady Castorley's help, he himself was doing the best he could to expedite the book; but Manallace had mislaid (did I think through jealousy?) some essential stuff which had been dictated to him. And Lady Castorley wrote Manallace, who had been delayed by a slight motor accident abroad, that the fret of waiting was prejudicial to her husband's health. Manallace, on his return from the Continent, showed me that letter.

'He has fretted a little, I believe,' I said.

Manallace shuddered. 'If I stay abroad, I'm helping to kill him. If I help him to hurry up the book, I'm expected to kill him. *She* knows,' he said.

'You're mad. You've got this thing on the brain.'

'I have not! Look here! You remember that Gleeag gave me from four to six, twice a week, to work with him. She called them "the sacred hours." You heard her? Well, they *are*! They are Gleeag's and hers. But she's so infernally plain, and I'm such a fool, it took me weeks to find it out.'

'That's their affair,' I answered. 'It doesn't prove she knows anything about the Chaucer.'

'She *does*! He told her everything that he had told me when I was pumping him, all those years. She put two and two together when the thing came out. She saw exactly how I had set my traps. I know it! She's been trying to make me admit it.'

'What did you do?'

'Didn't understand what she was driving at, of course. And then she asked Gleeag, before me, if he didn't think the delay over the book was fretting Sir Alured. He didn't think so. He said getting it out might deprive him of an interest. He had that much decency. *She's* the devil!'

'What do you suppose is her game, then?'

'If Castorley knows he's been had, it'll kill him. She's at me all the time, indirectly, to let it out. I've told you she wants to make it a sort of joke between us. Gleeag's willing to wait. He knows Castorley's a dead man. It slips out when they talk. They say "He was," not "He is." Both of 'em know it. But *she* wants him finished sooner.'

'I don't believe it. What are you going to do?'

'What *can* I? I'm not going to have him killed, though.'

Manlike, he invented compromises whereby Castorley might be lured up by-paths of interest, to delay publication. This was not a success. As autumn advanced Castorley fretted more, and suffered from returns of his distressing colics. At last, Gleeag told him that he thought they might be due to an overlooked gall-stone working down. A second comparatively trivial operation would eliminate the bother once and for all. If Castorley cared for another opinion, Gleeag named a surgeon of eminence. 'And then,' said he, cheerily, 'the two of us can talk you over.' Castorley did not want to be talked over. He was oppressed by pains in his side, which, at first, had yielded to the liver-tonics Gleeag prescribed; but now they stayed —like a toothache—behind everything. He felt most at ease in his bedroom-study, with his proofs round him. If he had more pain than he could stand, he would consider the second operation. Meantime Manallace—'the meticulous Manallace,' he called him—agreed with him in thinking that the Mentzel page-facsimile, done by the Sunnapia Library, was not quite good enough for the great book, and the Sunnapia people were, very decently, having it re-processed. This would hold things back till early spring, which had its advantages, for he could run a fresh eye over all in the interval.

One gathered these things in the course of stray visits as the days shortened. He insisted on Manallace keeping to 'the sacred hours,' and Manallace insisted on my accompanying him when possible. On these occasions he and Castorley would confer apart for half an hour or so, while I listened to an unendurable clock in the drawing-room. Then I would join them and help wear out the rest of the time, while Castorley rambled. His speech, now, was often clouded and uncertain—the result of the 'liver-tonics'; and his face came to look like old vellum.

It was a few days after Christmas—the operation had been postponed till the following Friday—that we called together. She met us with word that Sir Alured had picked up an irritating little winter cough, due to a cold wave, but we were not, therefore, to abridge our visit. We found him in steam perfumed with Friar's Balsam. He waved the old Sunnapia facsimile at us. We agreed that it ought to have been more worthy. He took a dose of his mixture, lay back, and asked us to lock the door. There was, he whispered, something wrong somewhere. He could not lay his finger on it, but it was in the air. He felt he was being played with. He did not like it. There was something wrong all round him. Had we noticed it? Manallace and I severally and slowly denied that we had noticed anything of the sort.

With no longer break than a light fit of coughing, he fell into the hideous, helpless panic of the sick—those worse than captives who lie at the judgement and mercy of the hale for every office and hope. He wanted to go away. Would we help him to pack his Gladstone? Or, if that would attract too much attention in certain quarters, help him to dress and go out? There was an urgent matter to be set right, and now that he had The Title and knew his own mind it would all end happily and he would be well again. *Please* would we let him go out, just to speak to—he named her; he named her by her 'little name' out of the old Neminaka days? Manallace quite agreed, and recommended a pull at the 'liver-tonic' to brace him after so long in the house. He took it, and Manallace suggested that it would be better if, after his walk, he came down to the cottage for a week-end and brought the revise with him. They could then retouch the last chapter. He answered to that drug and to some praise of his work, and presently simpered drowsily. Yes, it *was* good—though he said it who should not. He praised himself awhile till, with a puzzled forehead and shut eyes, he told us that *she* had been saying lately that it was too good—the whole thing, if we understood, was *too* good. He wished us to get the exact shade of her meaning. She had suggested, or rather implied, this doubt. She had said—he would let us draw our own inferences—that the Chaucer find had 'anticipated the wants of humanity.' Johnson, of course. No need to tell *him* that. But what the hell was her implication? Oh, God! Life had always been one long innuendo! *And* she had said that a man could do anything with anyone if he saved him the trouble of thinking. What did she mean by that? *He* had never shirked thought. He had thought sustainedly all his life. It *wasn't* too good, was it? Manallace didn't think it was too good—did he? But this pick-pick-picking at a man's brain and work was too bad, wasn't it? *What* did she mean? Why did she always bring in Manallace, who was only a friend—no scholar, but a lover of the game— Eh?—Manallace could confirm this if he were here, instead of loafing on the Continent just when he was most needed.

'I've come back,' Manallace interrupted, unsteadily. 'I can confirm every word you've said. You've nothing to worry about. It's *your* find—*your* credit—*your* glory and—all the rest of it.'

'Swear you'll tell her so then,' said Castorley. 'She doesn't believe a word I say. She told me she never has since before we were married. Promise!'

Manallace promised, and Castorley added that he had named him his literary executor, the proceeds of the book to go to his wife. 'All profits without deduction,' he gasped. 'Big sales if it's properly handled. *You* don't need money. . . . Graydon'll trust *you* to any extent. It 'ud be a long . . .'

He coughed, and, as he caught breath, his pain broke through all the drugs, and the outcry filled the room. Manallace rose to fetch Gleeag, when a full, high, affected voice, unheard for a generation, accompanied, as it seemed, the clamour of a beast in agony, saying: 'I wish to God someone would stop that old swine howling down there! *I* can't . . . I was going to tell you fellows that it would be a dam' long time before Graydon advanced *me* two quid. . . .'

We escaped together, and found Gleeag waiting, with Lady Castorley, on the landing. He telephoned me, next morning, that Castorley had died of bronchitis, which his weak state made it impossible for him to throw off. 'Perhaps it's just as well,' he added, in reply to the condolences I asked him to convey to the widow. 'We might have come across something we couldn't have coped with.'

Distance from that house made me bold.

'You knew all along, I suppose? What was it, really?'

'Malignant kidney-trouble—generalized at the end. No use worrying him about it. We let him through as easily as possible. Yes! A happy release. . . . What? . . . Oh! Cremation. Friday, at eleven.'

There, then, Manallace and I met. He told me that she had asked him whether the book need now be published; and he had told her this was more than ever necessary, in her interests as well as Castorley's.

'She is going to be known as his widow—for a while, at any rate. Did I perjure myself much with him?'

'Not explicitly,' I answered.

'Well, I have now—with *her*—explicitly,' said he, and took out his black gloves. . . .

As, on the appointed words, the coffin crawled sideways through the noiselessly-closing door-flaps, I saw Lady Castorley's eyes turn towards Gleeag.

Limits and Renewals, 1932*

---

* *MacLean's Magazine,* 1928.